THE ACC[...]

continued . . .

ACCIDENTALLY DEAD

"A laugh-out-loud follow-up to *The Accidental Werewolf*, and it's a winner . . . Ms. Cassidy is an up-and-comer in the world of paranormal romance." —*Fresh Fiction*

"An enjoyable, humorous satire that takes a bite out of the vampire romance subgenre . . . Fans will appreciate the nonstop hilarity." —*Genre Go Round Reviews*

THE ACCIDENTAL HUMAN

"I highly enjoyed every moment of Dakota Cassidy's *The Accidental Human* . . . A paranormal romance with a strong dose of humor." —*Errant Dreams*

"A delightful, at times droll, contemporary tale starring a decidedly human heroine . . . Dakota Cassidy provides a fitting, twisted ending to this amusingly warm urban romantic fantasy." —*Genre Go Round Reviews*

KISS AND HELL

"A fun, lighthearted, paranormal romance that will keep readers entertained. Ms. Cassidy fills the pages of her book with nonstop banter, ghostly activity, and steamy romance." —*Darque Reviews*

"Delaney with her amusing sarcastic asides makes for an entertaining romantic fantasy with a wonderful mystery subplot . . . Readers will relish this lighthearted jocular frolic." —*Genre Go Round Reviews*

"Cassidy has created a hilarious lead in Delaney Markham. Readers will run through all types of emotions while enjoying laugh-out-loud moments, desperate passion, wacky and fun characters, pop-culture references and one intense mystery. The book's charm is apparent from the first page, but the twisted mystery tangled throughout will keep the pages turning."
—*RT Book Reviews*

MORE PRAISE FOR
THE NOVELS OF DAKOTA CASSIDY

"Serious, laugh-out-loud humor with heart, the kind of love story that leaves you rooting for the heroine, sighing for the hero, and looking for your own significant other at the same time."
—Kate Douglas, author of the Wolf Tales books

"Ditzy and daring . . . Pure escapist fun."
—*Romance Reviews Today*

"Dakota Cassidy is going on my must-read list!"
—*Joyfully Reviewed*

"If you're looking for some steamy romance with something that will have you smiling, you have to read [Dakota Cassidy]."
—*The Best Reviews*

THE
ACCIDENTAL
WEREWOLF

DAKOTA CASSIDY

BERKLEY SENSATION, NEW YORK

THE BERKLEY PUBLISHING GROUP
Published by the Penguin Group
Penguin Group (USA) Inc.
375 Hudson Street, New York, New York 10014, USA
Penguin Group (Canada), 90 Eglinton Avenue East, Suite 700, Toronto, Ontario M4P 2Y3, Canada
(a division of Pearson Penguin Canada Inc.)
Penguin Books Ltd., 80 Strand, London WC2R 0RL, England
Penguin Group Ireland, 25 St. Stephen's Green, Dublin 2, Ireland (a division of Penguin Books Ltd.)
Penguin Group (Australia), 250 Camberwell Road, Camberwell, Victoria 3124, Australia
(a division of Pearson Australia Group Pty. Ltd.)
Penguin Books India Pvt. Ltd., 11 Community Centre, Panchsheel Park, New Delhi—110 017, India
Penguin Group (NZ), 67 Apollo Drive, Rosedale, Auckland 0632, New Zealand
(a division of Pearson New Zealand Ltd.)
Penguin Books (South Africa) (Pty.) Ltd., 24 Sturdee Avenue, Rosebank, Johannesburg 2196,
South Africa

Penguin Books Ltd., Registered Offices: 80 Strand, London WC2R 0RL, England

This is a work of fiction. Names, characters, places, and incidents either are the product of the author's imagination or are used fictitiously, and any resemblance to actual persons, living or dead, business establishments, events, or locales is entirely coincidental. The publisher does not have any control over and does not assume any responsibility for author or third-party websites or their content.

THE ACCIDENTAL WEREWOLF

A Berkley Sensation Book / published by arrangement with the author

PRINTING HISTORY
Berkley Sensation trade paperback edition / February 2008
Berkley Sensation mass-market paperback edition / November 2011

ISBN: 978-0-425-24271-1

BERKLEY SENSATION®
Berkley Sensation Books are published by The Berkley Publishing Group,
a division of Penguin Group (USA) Inc.,
375 Hudson Street, New York, New York 10014.
BERKLEY SENSATION® and the "B" design are trademarks of Penguin Group (USA) Inc.

PRINTED IN THE UNITED STATES OF AMERICA

10 9 8 7 6 5 4 3 2 1

To all those who believed, this book is for you. First, my wonderfully warm, funny agent, Deidre Knight, who gets my wackiness and isn't even afraid that she does. The word *fear* just isn't in her color wheel.

To my editor, Cindy Hwang—who really knows how to tip a chick's world on its axis.

To my good friends—friends who pushed me over the edge of the cliff when I was clinging (thanks for that—I think I broke a nail!): Sheri Fogarty, Kate Douglas, Angela Knight, Ann Jacobs, Diane Whiteside, Michelle Hoppe, Isabella Jordon, Jaynie Ritchie, Shelly Laurenston, Nancy Toney, Kira Stone, Renee George, Margaret Riley, Treva Hart, Cassie Walder, Sahara Kelly, Elisa Adams, Maura, Erin, Ter, Vicky Burkland, and Barb D.

The Babes—you chicks and a couple of guys rock the house! Jessica Faust, who taught me more about writing than she'll ever know. My sons, Travis and Cameron—dudes, you're plotters, and you don't even know it. The awesome people who gave me my start four years ago—Linda and Mike at LSB. My mother, Eleanor, who's my right-hand man. And last, but never least—Rob. My knight on a shining dirtbike and the master of a killa title. Finding you was like finding an endless fountain of Starbucks low-fat white chocolate mocha, and I love you like a buttload!

CHAPTER
1

Well, it was official.

Lavender was soooooo not in her color wheel anymore. Not looking like this, anyway.

It clashed with her hair and made her skin look sallow.

Marty Andrews was now an autumn. Thus, fall colors would best suit her new pallor. Greens, gold, and a couple of shades of yellow were presently her complexion's new friends.

But the color lavender?

Not so much.

That was the color she'd once been so suited to. A spring color. Or was it winter?

Spring, winter, spring, winter?

Sweet mother, she couldn't even remember her seasons of color. Where were her color-wheel-of-life skills? Each season had colors it represented. Any woman worth her salt knew that. Didn't they?

She shook her head and fought for a moment of clarity. Lavender was a spring color. It was the color all the newly promoted, first-level Bobbie-Sue Cosmetics reps wore and the color of the suit she'd worn with pride until a week ago.

Jesus, everything was such a blur since that night. She was lucky to remember her own name, let alone her season of color. It had all become a mixed-up myriad of sound, light, and surreal happenings.

It had steadily worsened since *he'd* shown up earlier.

Her eyes darted to the man sitting across from her in her living room. His hard, probing stare made her sink farther into her chair, tucking her legs beneath her.

He was dark, devilish.

Nuts.

"Are you all right, Marty?" His smooth, husky baritone deserved to be showcased on a late-night radio show.

The cloud of confusion she'd been drifting on parted for a moment, and she cocked her head at him. "I don't think I am and, you know, this really isn't a good time for me. I just made the first tier of Bobbie-Sue Cosmetics, and I'm busy. See?" She held up her new suit to show him, recently torn, as a result of the scuffle of that dreadful evening. She'd only had it for a bloody week, and now it was senselessly ruined. She twisted the fabric with hands that shook. "How could this have happened now?"

Of all times.

"Marty, there are things we need to discuss," he pressed with tight words, shifting position and crossing his legs. "Do you think you could try and focus? It's crucial that you do."

Focus. Hmmm. Well, she could try . . . Just not right now. Right now someone needed to hear the pickle she'd been left in, and tag, he was it. "You know what's funny?"

"Ah, no. What's funny?" He was humoring her. That much was clear from his tone.

"Do you know how long I've been working on becoming a lavender? Do you have any clue?"

He shook his dark head, clearly bewildered, while he kept his voice calm and soothing. Though if her wits were sharper, she'd suspect he was coming very close to losing that cool facade, cuz he did have that pinched look around his mouth. "I still don't even know what a, er, lavender is. But I get the feeling I'm going to find out, whether I want to or not."

He was screwing with her chi, and he deserved to know the degree of his chi-screwing. Marty ignored his comment and finally gathered enough steam to spew a weak rant for what she'd lost. "A frickin' year. That's how long. I busted my ass working two jobs, and it might seem meaningless to some, but I did it and not without plenty of doors slammed in my face. Some people make jokes about selling Bobbie-Sue because it's door-to-door sales. I ignored those snide remarks about my dreams of cosmetic greatness. And I was this close." She held her thumb and index fingers together for emphasis. "And now you show up, telling me something like this? It just ruins everything."

"It definitely changes things," he answered dimly, a look of discomfort flitting across his hard features before they returned to their granite scowl.

Changed things? Hell yes, it changed things. Like irrevocably. "I was well on my way to sky blue."

His black eyes flashed more confusion. "Sky blue?"

What didn't this interloper get here? Did she have to explain everything? Spell it out? "Yes! Sky—blue. If I reach the final level at Bobbie-Sue, I get a sky blue convertible. Do you have any idea how important that is to me?" Marty averted her eyes to anywhere he wasn't. She wanted that frickin' sky blue car with a burn in her gut. Damn it, she would have looked so fetching in a sky blue convertible. Well, when she'd been a light blue-eyed, sunshine yellow blonde anyway.

Now sky blue just wouldn't enhance her color aura.

Not after this week.

Ah, the agony of defeat.

"Look, Marty. I'm sorry about the, ah, lavender thing and convertibles and whatever it is you keep harping on so single-mindedly, but you have to listen," he urged through lips clearly compressed due to lack of patience.

Oh, no, she did not either. "This is the color wheel I'm referring to that you just don't seem to care about . . ." Marty offered distractedly, pointing to the chart on the stack of papers in her lap. Frowning, she looked down at the thick ream of documents from the Bobbie-Sue corporate office. The ever-omnipotent palette wheel of colors sat on top of the pile, mocking her.

Clearing her thickening throat, she explained, "Each color represents a rung on the ladder to Bobbie-Sue riches and glory." She wanted this man to know where her life had been headed before he showed up with his wild tales. What he was telling her was something she just couldn't digest.

"It's a very nice color wheel." His voice grew gentle, as if he were trying to appease her.

"Yes, yes it is, and I've only been at this level for a week." Had it only been a week ago that she'd achieved the first step to color greatness?

Cheerist, it felt more like a year.

Her glare met the hunk's on her couch, and she fought another cringe.

She'd been whizzing right along, selling lip gloss by the bazillions, and then, bam!

This.

Her smile grew wistful, thinking of her yearlong climb to success. "I was really good at this cosmetics thing, you know," Marty relayed with a mumble. "I'm good with people."

"Marty, I'm sure you're good at what you do, but we don't have time for this stroll down memory lane. You really have to try and pay attention to what I'm telling you." His reprimand was stern.

She waved a dismissive hand in his direction. Lost in her reverie, she continued to babble as though this man cared about how she'd arrived at where she was now. "Not everyone can do what I did in such a short amount of time. Sadly, some just don't have the kind of dedication I do. Speaking of lack of dedication . . . Oh, no! I forgot Nina and Wanda. How could I forget them? They're my newest recruits."

"Who?"

A sigh escaped her lips, and it screamed exasperation. "Nina Blackman and Wanda Schwartz. They're having problems. Especially Nina . . ." she trailed off, letting her worry carry her away again.

"Nina and Wanda? Are they the two women who were with you that night? Are they your friends?"

"Yes, that's them, but I don't know if they'd call themselves my friends. They think I'm pushy. We met because they answered my Bobbie-Sue ad. They're more like business associates, I guess. I'm their independent sales consultant supervisor." Rolling her tense shoulders, Marty shrugged off a moment of remorse. If you examined her relationship with Nina and Wanda under a microscope, they really were nothing more than business acquaintances. She could've used a friend this past week, making her regret not having cultivated female friendships in favor of her ambition. Nevertheless, she would have some explaining to do to them.

"How can I explain this mess to them? Especially Wanda. She's very fragile right now. Very." Oooooh, God, what would she do about Wanda? If she were any more serene in her sales techniques, she'd be comatose.

The color chart in her lap caught her eye again. She spun the arrow on it with a defeated hand. It landed on lavender. Ugh. This—this was a case of cosmetic cruelty by color wheel faux pas in the first degree.

God. The injustice of it all.

However, there was a bright side. She could buy that cute emerald green dress she'd seen in the display window at Filene's.

Green was *in* her color wheel now.

"Marty! You have to snap out of it. I don't know what the hell you're babbling about, but we—have—to—talk!" the man on her couch finally yelled.

She didn't want to talk to him or anyone else about that night.

So much had changed since then.

Upon reflection, it had all happened so fast, she was still trying to put the pieces of it back together to make sense of it.

Nina and Wanda had accompanied her to the weekly color seminar Bobbie-Sue Cosmetics held. It was designed to keep you pumped up and raring to sell, sell, sell.

They were walking her teacup poodle, Muffin, by her apartment building after the meeting at Bobbie-Sue's corporate headquarters. And well, as was par for the course, Nina was bitching and lagging reluctantly behind them. Marty had been doing her best to stoke Nina and Wanda with motivational nudges and sales stats. She'd tried to encourage them and was failing miserably. Both were rather sullen about the report they'd had to hand in. The one that primarily had zeroes in the box for unit sales.

On this particular night, Marty was growing more agitated than usual by the two of them, and Muffin was being difficult about making potties. Her fluffy, white poodle hated the cold, so she, too, dawdled behind Marty. The shuffle of Wanda's and Nina's despondent feet had left the taste of bad karma in the air, and it clung to her tongue like peanut butter.

"Nina! Wanda! Hurry up, would you?" she'd chastised. "Wasn't it bad enough we were almost late for the 'Coordinate Your Life with Color' seminar? We almost missed it. That would have just been dreadful. Especially if we'd missed hearing Bobbie-Sue speak. She is, after all, the queen of color coordination."

"Oh, yeah. God forbid we should miss the color coordination of one's life, Marty," Nina snorted, stopping in the middle of the sidewalk, her stance defensive, her slender silhouette outlined by the black night. "I don't know how I managed to get to thirty-two without knowing my color aura. Who knew I wasn't living my life to its fullest color potential by coordinating the color of my lipstick with my toilet paper? I don't think I can go on now that I know gold is in my color aura and everything I happen to have is silver. The indignity of it and all, you know?" Nina threw a dramatic hand over her forehead.

Marty's blonde head twitched as did her right eye while she wrapped Muffin's leash tighter around her wrist to keep from slugging Nina. Nina was such a naysayer, but she was holding on to her waning patience like the last set of sheets from a white sale at Macy's. Yet, a touch of her frustration with Nina slipped out anyway. "Why must you be so flippin' negative, Nina?"

Nina, tall and slender, dark and doe-eyed, shrugged her shoulders and rolled her eyes at Marty. "Gee, I can't quite put my finger on it, Marty. Maybe it's because I've sold one shitty lip gloss all goddamned month?"

If Nina could sell her sarcasm-slash-pessimism by the bottle, she'd be rolling in greenbacks.

Marty shook her head and shot for encouraging again. "No, Nina. You sold two. Two. Biiiig difference."

Nina swirled her index finger in the air. "Yeah, whoopee. Do you have any idea what it's like to have to face that bunch of cosmetic Hare Krishnas and declare you sold only two lip glosses? That's not even a unit. Ten is a unit. But wait, you'd know that, wouldn't you? Because you sell hundreds of units."

"It's soooo embarrassing, Marty," Wanda agreed enthusiastically. With a bob of her dark brown head, she stooped to give Muffin a scratch on her ears. Wanda, a recently divorced podiatrist's wife, who'd never worked outside the home, was living off her alimony and fighting to make her way in the world alone. Her way hadn't been much enhanced by her sales quota.

Marty stopped them both by a dark alleyway, planting her hands on her lavender-clad hips, clinging to Muffin's leash. "Look, girls. It takes time is all. You don't think I got to where I am overnight, do you? I worked my ass off."

Wanda giggled and cupped Muffin's face. "Ohh, look. Marty swore, Muff. She's getting pissed. Everyone knows

Bobbie-Sue reps don't use foul language. I think Nina's pushed her too far now."

Nina crossed her slim arms over her small breasts and harrumphed. "Well, your ass is a lavender now, Marty. It's easy for you to preach from where you're standing on the color wheel-of-life game board. Wanda and I don't even have a color yet. We're color queen wannabes. A lighter shade of pale. It sucks."

"Did you fill out your goal sheet, Nina?" Marty asked her testily. "If you can see it, you can be it. Maybe deciding on the level you'd like to achieve at Bobbie-Sue just might give you some much-needed perspective."

Nina's snort filled the chilled night air and blew out of her mouth in a puff of smoke. "I've got perspective all right. I want my old job back. I miss hearing a good case of matrimonial homicide. I was a good stenographer, you know. But I can tell you my perspective sure as hell doesn't include accosting little old ladies with my handy-dandy mascara wand and teaching them about strengthening their auras through mascara fucking application."

Marty's temper flared, and she gasped. "I did not accost a little old lady. I merely suggested and you," she pointed a lavender polished finger at Nina, "are a potty mouth today."

"Damn right I'm a potty mouth. I paid five-hundred bucks for that bullshit color wheel starter kit, and I'm no closer to color orgasm than I was with my last boyfriend. And you did too accost that poor woman. Jesus, Marty! We were in the IHOP, for fuck's sake. Who wants to find out what their season is over pancakes? Not to mention the lesbian you thought might be able to find a man if she'd just wear a little eye shadow."

Marty's lips puckered. "I was only trying to help."

"Help?" Nina shouted with a sharp bark, shoving her hands into her jacket. "She's a lesbian, Marty! Girls! She likes *girls,* and no amount of frosted eye shadow is going to make her want dick."

"Take it easy, Nina." Wanda rose and stepped between

them, her tone edged with worry. "Marty's just trying to help us achieve color success."

Marty's smile was pinched when she looked at them both. "That's exactly right. I want you both to be success-ful. Again, I ask, did you fill out the goal sheet, Nina?"

"Yeah, right after I wiped my ass with it." She cackled a laugh, scaring Muffin into a whimper.

Wanda gasped. "You haven't finished your goal sheet? No wonder you're not making any sales! I filled mine out the day I signed up at Bobbie-Sue, Nina. You have to pay attention to what the video says—if you can see it, you can be it. Seeing your goals is the first visual aide to success!"

Nina made a face and cocked her dark head. "You *are* kidding, right, Wanda? You sold three lip glosses, and one of them was to your mother. She doesn't count." Nina shook her head in obvious disgust and asked, "You actually filled that stupid thing out?"

Wanda's feet shuffled beneath her in obvious embar-rassment, and her dark head hung low between her sloped shoulders. "Sort of . . ."

Thinking back, Marty remembered that she might have stuck her tongue out at Nina's opposition to Wanda's at least trying, but that would have been very unladylike and sooooo not Bobbie-Sue. "Obviously, Wanda's seeing something that you missed by a color-coded country mile."

Nina then cornered Marty, hovering over her and glar-ing at her with those almond-shaped coal eyes. "Well, maybe Wanda's just better at 'being' it than I'll ever be. The only thing I see, Marty, is my credit card balance at its maximum for this starter kit that I couldn't afford and my bank account weighing in at zip. If I don't sell some eye shadow soon, color me doomed. Do they have the color doomed on that stupid, cardboard color wheel chart?"

Marty pursed her lips and narrowed her gaze at Nina. God, they were so frustrating as recruits. Marty had little left up her sleeve to help them make sales. She'd been as perky and bubbly as she could be so far, but Nina had a way of deflating a person's bubble with her pin of pessimism. "You know they don't, and you're not doomed. You're just a slow starter. The same goes for Wanda. We just have to think of a new plan of attack."

Nina's face contorted, and again she'd made Muffin whimper. "Plan of attack? Helllloooo in there, Crayola Color Wheel Queen. I don't have a lot of time left to attack. I have bills to pay, and my cable's going to be shut off if I don't do something soon. I'm not like Wanda here who has alimony to fall back on. Damn it, Marty! I don't know what the frig the problem is with my sales techniques. I've done everything you said, and I sold two stupid lip glosses. I was supposed to be learning from the best."

Her inference that Marty hadn't done her job as a re-cruiter had made Marty bristle.

Wanda placed an insistent hand on Nina's shoulder, drawing her a step back from Marty. "I don't know what I'm doing wrong either, Marty. I hate to agree with Nina, but . . . I mean, I filled out my goal sheet, I attend all the classes. I wear Bobbie-Sue wherever I go because, after all, I am my own best advertisement—"

"Jesus Christ, Wanda," Nina cut her off. "You drank the juice, didn't you? Yum-yum." She rubbed her belly in a circle. "Does it taste just like Kool Aid?"

"What's that supposed to mean?" Wanda yelped.

Nina faced her dead on, eyeballing her with an apparent flash of venom. "It means that you sound just like all the other crazies who sell this shit. It's like some messed-up cult or something. You've been brainwashed is what you've been."

Tears immediately filled Wanda's pretty blue eyes, and she gnawed at her trembling lower lip before responding with a choked cry, "I have not! I don't even like Kool Aid. So there! I'm just trying to figure out life without marriage. I'm trying to find my purpose, and selling cosmetics seemed easy at first. So I did it and I'm not any better at it than you are, but I'm trying, and yelling at Marty because we suck isn't going to help."

Well, this is going swimmingly, Marty remembered thinking. Her two recruits, her only recruits, were at each other's throats, and their fun, festive night out was going down the shitter rapidly. "Okay, stop it right now!" she yelled, facing the two of them with a frown before bending to scoop Muffin up into her arms. "Fighting isn't the answer. If I can do this, you two can do it, too. I was a nobody before Bobbie-Sue. I worked in a mail room, for heaven's sake, but when I found Bobbie-Sue, all of that changed. It took time and determination, but I did it. I've seen lots of others do it, too. There simply isn't any reason you both can't as well."

"Yeah, yeah, yeah," Nina spat, twisting the lavender scarf around her neck, symbolizing her newbie status. "That's easy for you to say. You've got the lavender suit to back up your crass reminder that we're losers, Marty. We have stupid, lavender scarves that blatantly advertise we're newbies, and to make matters worse, lavender isn't even in my color wheel."

Marty's sigh of exasperation echoed against the buildings, and she stroked Muffin's white fur, hoping to slow the rise of her blood pressure. "You know, Nina, I really am growing tired of your negativity. When I brought you on as a recruit, I did so thinking you had the get-up-and-go it takes to sell Bobbie-Sue. I thought we had the same values," she accused. Where she'd ever gotten the idea that a bully like Nina could sell makeup to women left her confuzzled. For a split second, Marty doubted herself. Maybe she really was as rabid as they'd accused her of being, and she just couldn't see the writing on the wall.

"Get up and go this, you two-bit sales ho!" Nina shouted, pulling her hands from the pockets of her jacket and clenching them into fists.

Wanda's hand flew to her mouth and she chided her from between her fingers. "Nina! You cannot call Marty a ho. It's mean and definitely not in the spirit of Bobbie-Sue."

"Okay." Nina loosened her posture, breathing in the

cold night air. "I'm sorry, Marty. I'm just sick of the evan-
gelist-like speeches about the Bobbie-Sue way of life. I'm
also sick to death of the perfectly made-up smiles those
senior cosmetics reps wear. Everyone's so hyped at these
things, chanting the Bobbie-Sue motto and clapping and
shit. I need money, and I need it now. Not two hundred
units down the road. I've looked everywhere for another
job, and in the meantime, I've been sucking sales wind. I
don't know why. I followed all the sales techniques in the
new edition of the Bible known as Bobbie-Sue. I attend all
the meetings, but they kind of freak me out. I mean, it's
makeup, Marty. Not heart valve replacement."

Marty giggled a little and felt immediate remorse for her
anger with Nina. She was in a predicament for sure, and
Bobbie-Sue, if she was honest, could look a little cult-like
to an outsider. In her overzealous, overachieving way,
Marty had tipped her own sales boat overboard. No one
could ever accuse her of not digging in her heels when she
wanted something and she'd wanted the first color on the
tier to Bobbie-Sue worthiness. She didn't plan to stop until
she was a sky blue either. Sky blue was sooo in her color
wheel. "I know sometimes I get a little fanatical, but it's
only because I'd still be in a deadbeat job if not for Bobbie-
Sue, Nina. I really have come a long way, and I know you
guys can, too. Granted, I didn't start without a job. I had
backup, but I was able to quit that job within a year. And
now look. I have a lavender suit." She curtsied, holding out
the lapel of her brand-new jacket.

"You know, Marty? I think I fucking hate the color lavender," Nina quipped.

Marty clung to her rationale and tried once again to
remember that what had brought Nina to Bobbie-Sue was
one part desperation, two parts destitution. Mix together
and you had a dangerous brew of potential new housing in
the way of a cardboard box and curbside service. In other
words, Nina had lost her job due to downsizing and seeing Marty's ad in the paper for cosmetics sales had given
her hope. Marty had tried to cultivate that hope, but it

wasn't working out quite the way she'd planned. "All you need to do is just believe, Nina. You're always making some snarky comment about makeup selling, but if you just believe, you might sell some. However, with your performance and attitude so far . . ."

Nina rolled her eyes again at Marty and flipped her the bird. "My performance? Oh, that's rich, Marty. Just because I don't want to attack every woman who has flaky skin with this Bobbie-Sue bullshit makes me a slacker?"

Wanda, in auto-mode, repeated the third most important commandment from the Bobbie-Sue handbook. "Well, yeah, Nina. You should want everyone to wear Bobbie-Sue makeup. You should care if some poor, lost woman isn't realizing her potential color palettes of life."

Marty watched Nina's eyes flash with anger and prepared for the usual onslaught of now-predictable jokes she resorted to about cosmetics when called on her lack of sales. "It's makeup, Wanda, not a permanent solution for erectile dysfunction we're selling when Marty attacks some poor woman in a buffet line with her samples of eyeliner," she said flatly. "We're not offering them the meaning of life in a jar of cream blush. Not everyone wants to be pretty like you, Princess Marty."

Bingo. Right on cue.

"There it is again," Wanda pointed out before Marty could accuse Nina of being a negative force. "That's your whole problem, Nina. In a nutshell, you just don't believe."

Nina's snort was so loud and raspy, she jolted Muffin who was still nestled in Marty's arms. "Oh, I believed. I believed enough to come to another stupid seminar, didn't I?" Anger, red-hot and spewing like lava, continued to escalate in her tone. "I believed enough to hope that I could earn a modest living selling frosted eye shadow, didn't I? I was willing to believe anything if it meant living above the poverty level, Wanda. I need a job and I spent my last damn dime trying to get one with palettes of life and fucking moisturizer. So back off, Lip Gloss Lady!" she yelled in Marty's face. "I'm sick and tired of you behaving like I just don't want to try, and because I can't talk women into this theory that putting on makeup just to go to the mailbox is critical to breathing that I somehow suck!" Then she returned her attack on Wanda. "And whose fucking side are you on anyway, Wanda?"

That was the very point when Marty decided she'd had enough. Two solid months of Nina's negativity was screwing with her center, and she was eyeball-deep fed up with it. "You, Nina Blackman, are a red today," she offered calmly through clenched teeth. "Very, very angry. So, I'm going to ignore what you just said to me and Wanda, chalk it up to your financial situation, and continue to be a good sponsor by telling you to get your lavender-less ass in gear and help me help you." When she finished, her smile was pinched and fighting a frown.

Upon those words and Nina's aggressive advance on her, things had become a wee bit fuzzy. She remembered hearing Muffin growl and feeling her sharp little nails claw at her arm. Marty's thought was that she was taking a stand against Nina's hostile approach. However, she could distinctly remember the sound of a much deeper growl, coming from behind her in the alleyway.

Muffin had literally hurled herself from Marty's arms by pushing off with her hind legs and landing on the pavement with a frantic click of her paws. Marty had lost her grip on the slender leash, and it dragged behind Muffin, catching on the cement. Her snarl sounded like it had come from a German shepherd instead of a teacup poodle, but she was fiercely devoted to protecting Marty. However, sometimes her devotion was a little OCD.

Muffin thought the umbrella stand in Marty's apartment posed a threat to her beloved owner. Hell, she thought the toilet bowl scrubber in her bathroom did, too.

To say Muffin could be territorial was not a huge hyperbole. She might be small in stature, but in her mind, she had the attitude and build of a Tyrannosaurus rex.

The ensuing moments were fragmented, looking back. Distorted by yipping and snarling, tangled colors of black and white fur, and the momentous event that had eventually led her to where she was now.

Apparently another dog had given Muffin reason to believe Marty was in danger, and she'd taken on the imagined challenge like a WWF champ. Marty's surprise at Muffin's flight to the ground was followed by her scream of shock when she saw the size of the dog that Muffin had decided to duel with.

That much Marty would always remember.

His size.

She, at the time, had assumed he was male, because she couldn't ever remember seeing a dog so bloody big before.

She did remember hearing Nina's surprised exclamation of, "Holy fuck!" Which was part and parcel where Nina was concerned. Her potty mouth wasn't unexpected, and she wasn't far off the mark in her assessment of the beast.

He was ginormous.

A deep black with slashes of blue highlights along his back only the truly raven-haired possessed. His height on all fours reached her waist. Marty remembered that, too, because the sheer magnitude of force with which he'd slammed into her had nearly knocked her off her feet. If not for Nina bracing her, she would have toppled over in her cute lavender heels. As Marty scuffled to grab at Muffin's trailing leash, she'd tripped and fallen on the massive bulk of dog. The crushing blow to her gut left her breathless, and air had wheezed from her throat while she'd struggled to fill her lungs.

Muffin attacked with foam dripping from her mouth, latching onto the long muzzle of the black beast, while Marty'd watched in horror when it tried to shake her off. Unfortunately, Muffin had locked her jaw on the inside of his lip and wouldn't let go for all the Snausages in PetSmart.

Oddly, she could recall that he didn't seem at all aggressive. He was simply trying to detach the small, wildly out-of-control poodle from his chops. His eyes, as black as they were, looked as surprised as Marty's must have that her small dog could create such havoc. Yet, it was Muffin who became more rabid, hanging on in midair and swinging wildly to and fro while only clamping down harder.

She'd captured her prey, and she was going to restrain it and ride it to smack-down glory at all costs.

Muffin's frantic yapping had sounded like shrieks, and her vicious snarling escalated, though muffled by the fact that she held the poor beast in her lion's grip. Marty's trembling hands had fumbled to grab at Muffin, while Nina and Wanda screamed for help, running in circles.

With shaking hands, Marty managed to get a hold of Muffin's muzzle, trying to pry it off the larger dog's. The sudden nip to the meaty part of her hand between her index finger and thumb looked minimal, but felt like it came from Jaws. It seared her flesh with a bolt of electricity that sizzled through her entire body, attacking her senses with flames of fire that licked at her veins.

Nina had somehow found a broken PVC pipe and was thwacking the air with thrusts and jabs that were wildly aimed, missing the dog's body and instead catching Marty's spine.

Marty's screech of pain had resounded, bouncing off the surrounding buildings. "Arghhhhhh!"

"Ohhh, Nina! Watch out. You hit Marty!" Wanda yelled, circling behind the back end of the dog like a defensive linebacker.

From there on out, it was pandemonium. High-pitched squeals and snorting huffs filled the darkened night. Blood dripped from her hand and onto Muffin, which Marty had finally managed to pry off the big dog. She'd clung to her shaking dog's body, while Nina and Wanda stomped their feet and chased off the large animal, which didn't seem in the least angered by her killer teacup poodle.

Actually, he'd seemed rather perplexed, if the last glance he'd given them before taking off like a shot down the dark street was any indication.

Nina and Wanda had fairly dragged Marty to safety, propelling her toward the dark parking garage and over to the elevator.

At some point, Marty had blacked out. What appeared to be a minor bite had taken the piss right out of her. At first she remembered little of that night, but the following week had her discovering enormously frightening changes in her body, the growth of her hair, and more importantly, the change in her coloring. What she'd tried to deny the day after the event had occurred simply could no longer be left without explanation.

So here she was a week later. Sitting across her small living room, clinging to her torn lavender Bobbie-Sue suit, starter kit in her lap, and eyeballing the man whose broad chest Muffin so contentedly curled against.

"Um, so say again?" Marty eyed the man sitting across from her on her pretty leather couch, fighting desperately to stay in the here and now.

"I am the were . . . er, dog that bit you."

Marty heard his words and she couldn't help but think that he was on some kind of drug. Hallucinogenic drugs. Yep, that must be his ticket.

"Marty?"

Looking up, she was immediately sucked into his intense gaze. It called to her with deep, dark twin pools she feared she might get lost in. "What?" her mouth answered without the aid of her brain.

"You need to pay exceptionally close attention to me." He spoke the words slowly, like she was a toddler who needed simple directions given to her in small portions.

"Okay . . ." was what she mustered. It was vague and vacuous, but she was all ears. Well, sorta. The itch in her nose had begun to distract her, and the smell that penetrated her nostrils was driving her bonkers.

"I bit you in the alleyway last week. That was me."

Yeah, she could see that. He had really nice teeth. All pearly white and perfectly straight.

"Do you know what that means, Marty?"

"I'll scar?"

His sigh of exasperation was evident. "I don't know, but that's not what I mean about the bite."

She stroked the material of her suit like it was a comforting blanket and again inhaled. God, whatever he was wearing for cologne was downright sexy. "So what do you mean?"

"It has repercussions."

"Huh?"

"The bite. My biting you has repercussions."

For a moment, Marty saw the forest for the trees. "Oh, you're worried I'll sue. No, I'm not like that. I have good medical insurance. I work for Bobbie-Sue Cosmetics," she stated, her voice hitching with an erratic volume.

"That's not what I mean, either, Marty. Did you hear what I told you before?"

She'd heard, sort of. Before she'd meandered off in her mind to the night this had all happened. Suddenly, this game of round-robin was tweaking her, and she just wanted to be left alone. "Say whatever it is that you came to say and go away. Can't you see I'm busy?"

"Marty, it's critical that you listen carefully. I'm not going to beat around the bush here. I'm just going to say it."

"Then say it!" she yelped.

"I'm not a dog. I'm a werewolf."

Nice. Very nice. "Say again?"

"I'm a werewolf, and now . . . well, because I was the one to bite you, now so are you."

Alrighty then.

A werewolf.

Marty Andrews, Bobbie-Sue Cosmetics's newest sales dynamo, was—via dog bite—a werewolf.

Freaky-deaky Dutch.

CHAPTER
2

"Marty?

"What I'm saying is true. You've seen the changes in your body this past week. That much is clear. I can help you to understand that."

Well, that was mighty generous of him to offer his help, considering he was the supposed perp who did this to her in the first friggin' place. Marty's eyes rose to meet that black, intense gaze once more. Sheesh, his eyes were forceful, drawing her to listen to him against her will. He was a complete dichotomy. He held her small poodle in his arms like she was a fragile newborn, but his very presence was domineering, filling the room with his sheer, raw power. Yet, she couldn't explain why she wasn't at all afraid of him. She should have been leery the moment she opened the door to find a leaner version of the Hulk standing there, but not so much as a single alarm bell had sounded. She'd let him in like he was an old friend and followed behind his lip-smacking butt like that of the hypnotized. He'd scooped Muffin up when she'd scratched at his leg and settled on her couch like he'd always sat there. Muffin had proceeded to fall fast asleep on that big, yummy chest of his with a sigh of pure ecstasy.

She was drifting again. Where were they? Changes in her body. Yes . . . "So can you recommend a good brand of wax? I really think I need some. My legs are just out of control. Bobbie-Sue doesn't have hair depilatory. At least I don't think they do."

"It's more than just the hair on your legs."

Oh, peachy. If she had to start waxing her upper lip at the ripe old age of thirty, she was going to jump from her high-rise. "More?"

He leaned forward, carefully keeping Muffin close to his neck. Muffin stretched her paws out ramrod straight and blew out a soft moan before settling back against his shoulder again. His large, bronzed hand stroked her spine. "A lot more." His hard voice was raspy.

He was starting to come into focus now. The haze that had followed shortly after she'd let him in was lifting, and wouldn't you know, the first thing she clearly saw was what a brick shithouse he was. He really was cuuuute. Very cute, and if he weren't sitting on her couch, telling her he was a— a—what had he said? she just might be game for a little play-time. However, after this hell week of excess body hair, the darkening of her once carefully highlighted, blonde tresses, and a bloody craving for red meat that went against every vegan bone in her body, she was in no mood to have her crank yanked. "I think you have to go home now." Yes. He needed to do that. She was too busy to have her chain pulled today. She had units of moisturizer to organize.

"I can't do that." He didn't say it like he couldn't. He'd said it like he wouldn't.

"Yes, you can. It's easy. Go out the way you came in and leave my dog when you do."

"No. I'm responsible for what's happened to you, Marty. I won't just leave you like this."

It was the "like this" that scared the bejesus out of her. What did "like this" mean? Like hairier than a yeti? "If you mean you can't help with the hairy leg thing, I think I got a grip on it. You can rest assured I'll find an answer to my dilemma. You can leave guilt free."

Now he was growing agitated. She could hear it in his long, drawn-out sigh and the squeaky crunch of him changing positions on her leather couch. She saw it in the tic of his chiseled jaw. Wow, that was super-duper hot. Marty focused on his jaw, strong and set in a hard line of waning patience. He looked like he might snap at any given moment, and if he did, things might be ugly on a number of levels. The air was filled with his forceful aura, consuming the oxygen.

Marty sank farther into her chair and twisted her skirt in her hands.

"If you would just pay attention, I can explain what I mean."

No, no, and no again. She didn't want to know. See no evil, hear no evil. Marty rather liked this protective cocoon she'd spun. It was warm and a lovely shade of ignorant. Whatever the hell was happening to her, she could overlook it if she could just find an entire vat of wax instead of those piddly little jars they sold at the drugstore. Dying her hair wouldn't be a problem. Miss Clairol came in all the colors of the rainbow. She'd also adjust the tones of her makeup to suit her new, darker coloring. There. That was all taken care of. No worries and no more talking to the nut job. No matter how enticing he might be. She mentally brushed her hands together and tried to shut him out.

"Marty?" The husky way he said her name broke into her thoughts. "Do you crave meat? Red meat?"

So? Big freakin' deal. Lots of people liked a rare burger. Ohhh, or better still, what about a nice T-bone, dripping and red with a yummy soft center . . . her stomach growled with a loud snarl. Oh, Jesus. Marty clapped a hand over her mouth as though her internal thoughts might seep out of her mouth and into the air between them. She was a vegan, for crap's sake. "Maybe." Her reply was noncommittal and weak at best.

He nodded sharply, his black head sleek and shiny when it dipped down toward his broad chest. Like the mane of that dog, he had those same blue highlights she remembered from the night of the biting incident. "That's a sign, too."

"Of?"

"Have you been listening to me at all?"

Again, duh. Hell no, she wasn't listening to this whack. Who actually listened to someone who thought they were a—

"A werewolf," he said, seemingly reading her mind. "I'm a werewolf, Marty."

Yeah, that was it. A werewolf.

"And now so are you."

"Because you bit me." She responded with a flat, dead tone. She was hearing the words. They just weren't registering on her Richter scale of sanity. Lifting her hand, Marty could just barely detect the bite that had been so angry and red earlier in the week. She peeked at him through the web of her fingers. "It wasn't a big deal. Really. I used some antibiotic cream, and that cleared it all up. See?" In fact, it had cleared up surprisingly fast.

His face changed, then a small flicker of a shadow flew across it, making it darker, almost remorseful. "Yes, I see, and yes, because I bit you. It wasn't my intention. Killer here"—he pointed to Muffin who thought this odd man was anything but threatening—"had a real grip on the inside of my lip. I was just trying to cut her loose, and you got in the way. She's got some pretty sharp teeth for such a little dog. You should commend her for being so protective of you."

Yeah, bravo. She'd give her precious a standing *O* for best half gainer off a back wall with a full nelson twist, but as a result of Muffin's over-the-top, protective nature, her mistress was now a—a—

Werewolf, her brain whispered sinisterly.

Yeah, one of those.

"She can be kind of crazy sometimes. I don't think she realizes how small she really is," Marty offered apologetically.

His bark of laughter was almost a husky growl. It suited his big, strapping, rippled, cut, sculpted body. God she had to cut that out. Admiring the enemy's physique had to be wrong.

"Obviously."

"You like animals?"

"Sure. Who doesn't?"

Of course he did. It would be discriminating against his own kind if he didn't, wouldn't it? "That's nice," she offered before beginning the retreat back into the place she'd spent so much time in. The place called *confused*, she figured, but couldn't summon up much will to care.

"I'm losing you again, Marty. Try to focus." His words were spoken with a harsh snap. His voice dragged her back from the edge like low tide gently pulling the sand from the shore.

She clawed desperately at the edges of the surreal, dreamlike world she'd visited so often this past week and tried to cling to it. Reality sucked right now. She wanted no part of it, thank you very much.

The shuffle of his leaving her leather couch and crossing the room to stand before her rudely yanked her back. The nearer he came, the more her nose nearly jumped off her face. God, that smell. It clung to her nostrils and wedged its way into all her senses. It was heavy and thick with a musky, outdoor fragrance. Like the sweet smoke of a fireplace.

Plopping Muffin into her lap, he knelt and tipped her chin up, encompassing it with a strong hand. His finger grazed her lower lip and made her jump. "You need to focus. Really focus. I know this week's been a little weird for you, but that's why I'm here."

Weird? Oh, *weird* wasn't even a word applicable to this scenario, and she finally said as much. "Weird? This is beyond weird. This is fucking nuts. You're nuts."

"No. I'm a werewolf."

"Yeah, yeah, and now so am I, right?" She repeated the words he kept saying with biting sarcasm.

"Yep. Now so are you. We have to decide how to handle this, but first we have to get you oriented."

"Orientation? Is there some sort of handbook for being a werewolf? Do you lunar-tics have a handout sheet?"

" 'Lunar-tic.' That's clever, Marty. But again, you're losing focus."

"Oh, sorry. I wouldn't want to lose focus of the fact that some man is in my living room, telling me he bit me and now I'm a werewolf. That would just be rude, huh?" The firm grip he held on her jaw gave way to shivers along her spine. He didn't look like the kind of guy who frigged around when he was trying to make a point. She yanked her face from his grip and narrowed her gaze.

His eyes searched hers. Eyes she could now see were thickly fringed with lashes she thought only Bobbie-Sue's magic mascara wand could achieve. "Let's begin at the beginning. I'm Keegan Flaherty. I bit you last week in an alley when your dog attacked me. My biting you has changed you. Again, I'm sorry. I didn't realize Muffin smelled me until it was too late. I tried to stay hidden while you were talking about colors and life or something with your friends. I was backed into a corner, if you know what I mean."

Marty nodded and inhaled. Lord, his smell was toxic. Keegan Flaherty—an Irish wolf. She'd giggle if it didn't risk the chance of coming out sounding maniacal.

"Anyway, the end result is, you're now a werewolf, too. I can't undo it."

Lifting a dry, unwashed strand of her shoulder-length hair, Marty asked, "So my hair is always going to need the dye job from hell?"

"That I can't answer. Nothing like this has ever happened in the history of our pack."

"Pack?"

"Yes. I come from a pack of werewolves."

He said it like he was saying he came from Piscataway. A pack implied more than one. "There are more of you?"

"Yes." He'd taken on a strange look that Marty actually

noticed but was unable to identify. It made his features softer, if that was possible, easing the tension around his eyes.

"I think this deserves further explanation, don't you?"

"That's what I've been trying to do."

"Then do."

"Do?"

"Explain."

"Are you more coherent now?"

"As coherent as someone can be when another someone tells them they're a werewolf, and they live in a pack, and that now, because she was bitten by said someone, she's a werewolf, too. Surely you see my confusion?"

Muffin sat up on her hind legs and scratched at Keegan's T-shirt-clad chest, begging to be picked up again. Keegan gave her a small smile, revealing deep grooves on either side of his lean cheeks. He placed that big hand on her head again and ruffled her fur, encompassing her small skull. When he looked back at Marty, the smile was replaced with that stoic expression. "You're going to experience more than just hair growth and the craving for red meat. The changes in your body are eventually going to be drastic."

Ohhh, maybe her boobs would get bigger. That'd be a nice swap for being so hairy.

"When the full moon comes, you'll feel the urge to shift."

Okay, probably no boobs. Fine. "Where am I shifting to?"

"You'll shift into your werewolf form."

Oh, okay. She got it. "Like you did last week in the alley?"

"Yes."

"But the moon wasn't full." Oddly, she could remember the moon had been covered by clouds, and it was only a half-moon. Strange the things you remembered when crisis struck.

"I can shift at will. I've been doing this for a long time. You'll need to learn to shift where and when it's appropriate."

"Hoooooooold it right there. When the moon is full I'm going to turn into a dog?"

"A werewolf."

"Whatever. It's semantics, if you ask me. You looked like a dog. That's what I thought you were in the alley." The veil of confusion was lifting with a slow hand. Marty was beginning to see where she stood, and she was sure he'd looked like a dog that night. A big one, but a dog nevertheless. And as if it weren't bad enough that she managed to sit and listen to some man tell her he was the one who bit her, she was playing into this tard's fantasy by telling him he wasn't a werewolf at all. He was a dog. Way to encourage the crazy, Marty.

"I guess if we want to be fundamental then yes, I have many of the senses a dog does and so—"

"Do I," she finished for him. "Well, that's ducky. So what does this mean for me? I bay at the moon? Crave some red meat even though I'm a vegan? I think I can live with that. I don't know about the meat thing, but I'll adjust. Yes, that's what I'll do. Adjust." With that taken care of, Marty began to rise, putting Muffin on the floor and pushing her way past Keegan's crouched form.

He grabbed her arm to thwart her escape. That sizzle he had didn't just extend to his good looks. It was also in his firm hold of her and the way it set her senses on full alert. "Why don't you freshen up, and then we'll talk at length?"

Marty supposed she looked pretty shabby. She couldn't remember when she'd last hit the shower, and her hair was a greasy, limp mess of tangles. Looking down at her nightgown, she realized it was stained from the coffee she'd dribbled down her chin yesterday. Or had that happened Tuesday? Bobbie-Sue would have a chicken if she could see her newest sales rep looking like this.

However, Bobbie-Sue wasn't a werewolf.

Marty Andrews apparently was.

"I don't want to freshen up." She yanked her arm out of his grip.

His nostrils flared. "You might want to reconsider that."

Folding her arms over her chest, Marty made a face at him. "Look, you did what you had to, to absolve yourself of any guilt. Now go away. I can handle whatever being a werewolf means from here. And for right now," she said, looking down at her legs, "I think it means I have to get a new razor. So go away." She cast another stray glance at her legs. "I'm going to be pretty darn busy."

"Marty, this isn't something you can handle alone," he insisted, stepping in front of her. The defined rungs of his abs were accentuated by his dark blue T-shirt. His chest stared her right in the face. Easily, he was at least a foot taller than her five-foot-two.

Her eyes traveled upward, refusing to hit the tropical locales just past his belt buckle. Damn. He had the thickest, most fabulous hair with the kind of volume only a Nine Inch Nails concert had. He kept it longer than she liked on a man. It just grazed his shirt collar, but it suited his razor-sharp cheekbones and deep, dark eyes. Her nose twitched again, and she took a deep breath. The scent of him made her dizzy, and it kept distracting her.

"Marty?"

"How do you know my name, anyway?"

"It was on the business card one of your friends dropped on the night this went down. I went back to the alley and grabbed it. I assumed it was your name on it, seeing as you're the one that's so successful selling, um, lip gloss, is it? And I could sm—"

"Smell me. Yeah, I remember. Okay, it's time you went home now. Before I call the police. I can't spend all day indulging whack-jobs, and I don't need any more explanations about werewolves. Next you'll be telling me you're friends with the Loch Ness Monster. It's all a little Bram Stoker for me, ya know?"

"That's vampires," he retorted.

"Whatever. What's the difference?" She snapped a hand up, palm facing him, and shook her head. "Never mind, don't answer that. I'm fine. Great, in fact. So you can leave with a clear conscience that I'm groovy." Getting behind him, Marty shoved at his broad back and directed him toward her apartment door. He wasn't an easy mark. Not to mention, he had an ass-tastic derriere. But that really was beside the point. It was time she got it together, and there was no better time than the present.

He turned on her with the stealth of a cat, pivoting on his heel and glaring down at her. "Marty, this isn't a good idea." His usual arrogance seeped into his words, while his imposing posture loomed over her. He had this air about him that screamed "bent out of shape," and quite frankly, if he had indeed bitten her, it was a totally uncalled for attitude. She was the bite-ee, not the biter.

"You know, I sense hostility here, and if anyone should be hostile, it's me, Wolfman Jack. I didn't bite you. You bit me. Or at least you think you did. See the difference? Me the victim, you the perpetrator. Now leave. I have things to do." Reaching around him, she popped the heavy lock and opened the door, waving a hand at the opening.

"Fine, have it your way, but eventually you're going to have to come to me and let me help. You'll have no choice. Take my number, Marty. You'll need it in the coming weeks." He rooted in his jeans pocket, shoving a slip of paper into her hand.

How very new millennium. Werewolves have phone numbers. Cell phone numbers by the looks of the reserved-for-cell-phones-only area code she saw scrawled on the scrap of paper. "You wait by the phone. I'll give you a ring-a-ling if I get desperate," she said back, closing the door with a thwack of steel and jamming the deadbolt in place.

Marty leaned forward on the door and let the cool surface graze her hot cheeks.

A werewolf.

Keegan Flaherty was insane.

The dog that had bitten her must have had some disease. Like the black plague or rabies or something. That could explain why she felt the way she did. She'd call the doctor right after she figured out what day it was. They had shots for all sorts of crap. Surely they'd have one for her dog-itis.

She'd call Muffin's vet. He'd have an answer and, hopefully, a cure.

Speaking of Muffin, she lay by the door, scraping her little paw under it and whining with small squeaks. Beckoning yon hunky werewolf to come back, she supposed. Marty frowned down at her. "Muff? Precious? Punkin? This could be called traitorous actions and besides, he's not your type. He's a werewolf," she said on a giggle that was, to her ears, starting to border on hysterical. "I can't even begin to imagine what you two would produce if you mated. That would just be too crazy, don't you think? So stop whining over the crazy guy. And by the way, miss, you know what I want to know? I want to know, if this was really the guy who bit me in the alley, why did you attack him like 'poodles gone wild' when he was in his doggie form, but you didn't have a single problem lying all over him like he was a Snausage when he was on the couch?" Marty shook her head. If this guy was what he said he was, shouldn't Muffin hate him even when he was in his human form?

She snorted. *Human form* . . . That she was even thinking a term as crazy as that was just that. Crazy. Traipsing to her small kitchen, Marty eyed the calendar on her refrigerator and moaned. It was Thursday. It had to be. Her garbage can was empty outside, and she distinctly remembered the strange glances cast her way when she'd carried it down to the front of her apartment in her nightgown.

Thursday was Bobbie-Sue seminar day.

A glance at her wall clock with the cute, pink Hello Kitties on it told her she had little time to work with and a shitload to accomplish.

Christ, she hoped she had fresh razors.

BOBBIE-SUE corporate was packed with people dressed in every color of the rainbow. The crowd was brimming with dialogue, and it was messing with Marty's head. She could hear snippets of conversations with such clarity it made her eyes cross. And her nose was overflowing with the scent of many perfumes. Too many. God, who wore Charlie anymore? Soooo seventies.

Arghhhh, she could jump out of her skin from the overload of sensory perceptions assaulting her.

They'd just finished their sales meeting, and Marty wanted nothing more than to go home to silence. Nina was cranky because, somewhere along the way, Wanda had managed to sell an entire unit of eye shadow. Frosted eye shadow even.

"Loook, Marty. It's Linda Fisher. She just made green. That means she's only a couple of colors away from sky blue," Wanda remarked with a point of her finger, while they made their way through the throng of the brightly clad crowd.

"I heard," she said dryly. "Who hasn't? She's only told the entire face of the planet."

"Well, look who's a cranky pants tonight, miss," Nina commented, striding beside her to make their way to the refreshment table. "Shouldn't you be happy for your fellow Bobbie-Sue-er?"

"I am not cranky, and color me thrilled for Linda Fisher," Marty shot back.

"Are, too. You've been testy all night, and I don't like it. I'm the only one who can be a bitch. So quit trying to be me." Nina grinned a refreshingly crooked smile.

"Nina," Marty spat, stopping to jab a finger into her shoulder. "Don't toy with me tonight. I'm tired, okay?"

Nina's brow furrowed, and her beautiful almond eyes squinted at Marty. "Wow. You're something all right. What's up your ass?"

Wanda interfered, her eyes instantly worried. "Nina, cut it out. Marty looks—looks—um—"

"What? What do I look like, Wanda?" Marty was just begging for a fight she didn't know she was capable of wanting.

Nina lifted a strand of her hair and frowned. "Did you dye your hair? It looks darker. What happened to all those lowlight, highlight things you pay so much for, and how come you have on Poseidon Red lipstick? That's not in your color wheel. I thought you were a Princess Pink?"

"But it looks really good on you, Marty." Wanda came to the rescue with reassurance. "I don't know why though. I didn't think red was a color you could wear unless it had orange in it. I would have thought Hot Tamale Red or Sunset Marguerita was more your color."

Look at who knew their color wheels and product all of a sudden. "Well, you thought wrong, grasshopper. Don't you think I know my own palette?"

Wanda's shoulders slumped again, and she sighed. "Of course you do. It's just a little smudged. C'mere, and I'll fix," she said, licking her thumb and wiping at the corner of Marty's mouth.

Marty waved her off with a dismissive, irritated hand. The slightest of touches made her skin alight with fire.

"Yeah, what gives, Marty, and where were you all week? Wanda tried to call you to tell you she made a pretty good sale, and you didn't answer your cell phone or your house phone either."

"Nothing gives, Nina. I'm just tired. I didn't feel well this week. Remember"—she held up her completely healed hand—"dog bite?" Christ, what was this, the fucking Inquisition?

Immediately, Marty was ashamed at her epithet-riddled thoughts. Who was this person, swearing like a drunken sailor and ready to pounce on anyone who dared try to be nice?

Nina's remark was caustic. "It wasn't that big a deal, and you should be plenty rested after taking an entire week off."

Marty swung to face her, gripping her small, lavender purse. The only lavender thing she had left until her new suit arrived. "For your information, Ni-na. I was bitten by a were—um, a dog last week. I wasn't feeling well. I am allowed to be sick."

"What's a were-dog? Is it a new breed? He looked like a

big German shepherd, if you ask me," Wanda stated with
the innocence only she could possess.

Had she just said that? God, if they heard the tale that
crazy man had told her, they'd call the men in white coats.
"Forget it. I guess I'm still recuperating, that's all."

Wanda peered into Marty's face and pressed the back of
her hand to her flaming cheek. "Did you see a doctor? You
look a little flushed. Maybe the dog was rabid."

Or a werewolf . . . "No, I didn't. I'm fine. Let's go get
some juice and mingle. Potential recruits are everywhere."

"Don't drink the juice, Wanda," Nina cracked in a whisper behind Marty's back. "It'll turn you into Marty."

With the snap of her neck, Marty was all over Nina like
fried on chicken. "Nina Blackman! I've had enough of
your negativity to last me ten lifetimes. Now—shut—up!"
Marty spat with a hiss, then slapped a mortified hand over
her mouth, her eyes wide with horror.

The small crowd they were making their way past
stopped their buzzing conversation momentarily to take
in Marty with a hard stare. They were all probably wondering who dared to utter anything other than nice words
at a Bobbie-Sue meeting. Bobbie-Sue's husband, Donald,
was present, as was their son Terrence. Their stares, especially Mr. Bobbie-Sue's, were astonished. But Marty
found she didn't give a flip. If Jesus and the Apostles had
entered the room, it wouldn't have kept her in check, and
while she realized this wasn't at all like her, she couldn't
seem to stop herself.

Nina's hand on her arm stopped her dead and made her
writhe with discomfort. "What the hell is wrong with you?
Why are you so snappy tonight? It usually takes me at least
another hour to push you over the edge. We're not even
forty-five minutes into this cult gathering, and you're freaking out. What gives?"

"I said I'm tired. That's it. Now let's go mingle before
we make a scene." She zipped past Wanda and Nina, letting
them trail behind her.

When they reached the refreshment table, Linda Fisher

was all aglow about her latest color-making historic climb to the top of Bobbie-Sue-dom's golden ladder. She stood at the head of the table, the cute flip to the ends of her Marlo Thomas hair bobbing with her excited jabber.

Marty scooped some punch from the bowl, filling her cup with the lavender-colored liquid, and fought not to roll her eyes while she halfheartedly listened to Linda gush.

Her nasally voice filled Marty's ears with her latest coup. "Who knew so many women in the secretary pool at Fogerty, Ross, and Carruci were in need of so much help with their auras?" she bragged to the group of women. "That's what did it for me, girls. It's what made me a green, and it can for you, too." Brushing at her new green suit, Linda smiled at her onlookers with confidence. Like she was the new American Idol of Makeup or something.

And hold on one attorney-like second. Had she said Fogerty, Ross, and Carruci? Fogerty, Ross, and Carruci was *her* fucking account. She'd spent four hours with those women, plastering foundation on their faces, lining lips and creating color wheels before she'd gotten the whole lot of them to buy the monthly subscription that included a new test lipstick among other things every month. Marty felt the rising tide of her anger sear her gut. How in the hell had Linda managed to get involved with them?

"Um, Fogerty, Ross, and Carruci, Linda?" Marty spoke up, her mouth a thin line of anger. All eyes turned to her, expectant and waiting.

"Oh, Marty." Linda didn't seem pleased to see her. She cleared her throat and smiled that thin-lipped smile she tried to hide with excess lip liner and too much lipstick. "Yes, that's what I said."

"I heard you, and what I want to know is how did that happen? That's my account, Linda," she accused, slamming her plastic cup of lavender juice down on the table and rolling up the sleeves of her shirt. The juice sloshed out of the cup, but Wanda was right behind her, grabbing at the colored napkins on the table and sopping up the mess.

Linda's smile turned smug. "Well, it *was* your account,

but it seems you missed your follow-up on delivery this month, and I just happened to be in the area."

Yeah, Linda Fisher just *happened* to be somewhere only smart people and potential prisoners hung out. Lucky that, huh? "I was ill this week, Linda, and you're an account stealer!"

The rustle of hushed ooooohhh's went up in the crowd, and each eye turned to see what Linda would say in rebuttal. Marty had thrown down the color gauntlet and they waited with bated breath to witness what she would do.

Linda smoothed a hand over her green skirt and picked invisible lint from it. "I only did what any good Bobbie-Sue representative would do. I ran to the rescue of women who were sorely in need of a rep who was available to them. They liked me so much, they asked for a replacement rep. I was happy to oblige. It happens. It's no big deal."

It was so a big deal. That was a thousand-dollar-a-month account!

The answer was clear.

She was just going to have to kill Linda Fisher.

Marty threaded her way through the gathering crowd and approached Linda with menace in her step. "I bet you were happy to oblige. You sauntered in there just in the nick of time, didn't you? Since when do you visit the downtown financial district? You're still selling house to house. That's account stealing and encroaching on another Bobbie-Sue rep's territory. I'm going to report you to corporate."

"They've been informed." Linda's statement was sly, the pride of an account stolen still gleaming in her eyes.

A tidal wave of fury rolled over Marty, beginning at her toes and pushing along her spine like a steamroller. She saw all sorts of angry colors, but mostly she saw her fist down Linda Fisher's skinny-assed throat. The sudden shift in her mood was odd, she thought briefly just before she stuck her face in Linda's pointed one. "I'll make your life a living hell for this, Linda Fisher. You cheap, account stealing, Bobbie-Sue slut. You couldn't get an account as big as that if you didn't steal it, you scrawny bitch."

Linda's gasp was sharp, and looking back, Marty thought it was because she'd called her a bitch before stomping out of corporate with Nina and Wanda hot on her heels.

However, it was the flash of her teeth that had made Linda gasp.

Her incisors, she would later be told by a stunned, babbling Nina and Wanda.

Her long, sharp, pointy, dripping with a bit of drool incisors.

CHAPTER
3

Keegan stayed a good half block behind Marty and her friends as they exited Bobbie-Sue's corporate offices. The sway of her shapely round ass was enticing when she stomped down the sidewalk to the nearby parking garage like a storm trooper, her friends in tow. The click of her heels on the pavement crashed in his ears with a resounding clackety-clack.

She was clearly cranked about something by the pace of her stride, and Keegan was pretty sure he was responsible for a good portion of that pissed-off.

Probably all of it, he thought with an amused chuckle, then just as quickly put on a somber face. He was supposed to be remorseful about biting an unsuspecting woman, even if it had been an accident. Straightening at that thought, he strode past the tall buildings surrounding downtown Manhattan and focused on what to do next.

Marty waded into the parking garage and threaded her way through the rows of cars, oblivious to his presence. There would come a time when all she could smell was him, but right now, her new, finely tuned olfactory senses were likely on overload.

The snippets of conversation she was having with her friends wafted to his keen ears, and from what little he caught, some shit had gone down at Bobbie-Sue that had turned Marty into a loose-lipped cannon.

From what he could gather, Linda-dumb-bitch-Fisher had stolen something from her, and she'd be dipped in horse puckey if she'd let it go and play kissey-face just because it was politically correct.

Hovering behind a dark SUV, he smothered another chuckle. Controlling her anger was one of the first lessons he'd have to teach Marty. Otherwise, Keegan could envision her in boxing gloves and some cute satin shorts, and that wouldn't be a bad thing in Marty's case. Not the shorts, anyway.

This mess—what had happened—was about as wrong as wrong could get, but it still didn't keep him from admiring the view her backside offered him.

Did that make him a Neanderthal?

If Marty knew what he was thinking, the answer would probably be a decided yes.

Marty Andrews thought he was a raving lunatic. She had every right to believe he was. It was his own fault she believed that. It wasn't every day some strange guy showed up at your door after you'd spent a week dazed and confused by what you thought was a dog bite and told you the explanation for your rapidly changing body and confusion was clear—you were a werewolf. There, feel better?

He'd dropped an atomic bomb on her world, and Keegan had attempted to remember that when gentle persuasion wasn't cutting it with her this afternoon.

He knew time and patience were involved in helping Marty accept this new fate so rudely thrust upon her, but he was short on both.

Christ, he was every kind of asshole for letting his nose lead him around. When he'd smelled her from the alleyway, her fragrance had intoxicated him, drawing him

from the dark corner between the two buildings like a
mosquito to one of those bug zappers. He had to see who
she was. Before he knew it, he was gawking at her like
some horny teenager, and out in the open where her small
dog, Muffin, had smelled him and attacked with ven-
geance.

Damned ankle biter was vicious, too. That cute, little
ball of white, fluffy poodle was a tumbleweed of snarling
terror. She'd nearly torn off his lip before Marty had
dragged her off. Thankfully, he healed rapidly.

Keegan absently rubbed his jaw, now littered with stubble, and considered what to do next. He could just leave her
and let her fend for herself, but he couldn't live with himself if he did that. He'd created this problem. He'd damned
well fix it.

Besides, she'd never survive the shift from human to
were if she didn't have help. Already she was struggling
with the changes in her body, and they were evident if the
photos of her in her apartment were any indication.

Just wait until she turned into a howling-at-the-full-
moon, rare-beef-loving werewolf. She was already retreat-
ing into an abyss of "ignore it, and it'll go away." If Marty
shifted when she was alone, she'd have a conniption. If she
thought her legs were hairy now, the shift would bring a
full-on freak.

Keegan sniffed the chilled night air again to be sure he
hadn't lost track of her, and her scent assailed his senses
with a punch to his gut. Her aroma went deeper than just
her perfume. The tangy, lightly floral smell of her was
overpowering. It sucked him in and wouldn't let him go.
Now that she was one of his kind, her unique fragrance was
making it that much harder for him to concentrate and
tying his innards into a fucking knot.

No one had ever smelled quite that sumptuous to him.

Not even one of his own.

Not even the one that was slated to be his.

Marty was a delicious dichotomy of spicy and sweet,

and Keegan was fighting to shake the temptation to do with her what he wished. What he must.

Whether she liked it or not, and she was definitely not going to like it.

Everything in Marty's life would change.

Forever.

His cell phone vibrated against his chest, and he reached into his jacket, flipping it open to see his brother Sloan's number. "Yeah?" His voice was gruff and brisk.

"Don't get snippy with me, big brother." His little brother's tone was teasing and lighthearted. "This time I'm not the one in trouble. So have you told her?"

The muscle in his jaw worked overtime, and he ran a hand through his thick length of hair. "I'm working on it."

Sloan snorted. "We don't have time for you to fuck around, Keegan. We're cyclical, you know?"

"If I were fucking around, I wouldn't be on the phone with you, and I know how the cycles work, brother. I've got a little time. So give me a break."

"Have I mentioned just how pissed Alana is?"

"Have I mentioned I don't give a shit?" Keegan retorted with a snap.

"Yep, you did, but that doesn't make it easier for the rest of us. She's not exactly happy about giving up her only shot at the family China."

"She never had a shot, and that rose pattern on mom's China wasn't in Alana's color wheel anyway," he joked.

"What?"

Had he just said that? Jesus Christ. How girly. How Marty.

A vision of her from that night in the alleyway flashed before his eyes. Cute and blonde, she had the kind of curves that were soft and sloping. He liked a woman who molded to him with a cushion of rounded flesh. Not some hard body that spent every waking moment trying to find another rung on her abs.

Encased in that lavender suit, with her legs enhanced by

those heels, made for a very sexy package. The gleam of her softly curled, shoulder-length blonde hair had caught his attention under the glow of the streetlamp.

He should never have been listening to her conversation to begin with, but he'd been cornered when Marty and her friends had stopped to talk in the alleyway.

"Keegan?" Sloan's impatience cut in on his thoughts. "What the hell is a color wheel?"

Pressing the heel of his hand to his forehead, Keegan sighed. "Nothing. Forget it. Forget Alana. She'll get over it. Look, this is going to take time. You don't just make something like this happen," he said angrily. How could he possibly tell her something of this magnitude before she'd even adjusted to becoming a werewolf?

"Take her out for a steak, a nice, rare one. Buy her an expensive bottle of wine. Woo her. Whatever it takes." Sloan's suggestion was littered with laughter.

"Did I mention she's a vegan?" Of all the nutritional choices to make and then have something like this happen.

"You're kidding me? Man, bud, when you pick 'em, you pick 'em."

"It was an accident, you little shit," he growled, his teeth clamping together, while his eyes fixed on Marty's car backing out of the parking space. She drove with one hand on the wheel, the other waving wildly, while her mouth moved relentlessly. He figured she'd be safe with her girlfriends. Unless that Nina's mouth got out of hand and Marty flipped a nut over it. Then things might get sticky.

"Well, it was a big one." Sloan seemed to take great pleasure in reminding him. "Now hurry the hell up and fix it before things get out of hand here. Do you know the kind of bullshit I'm putting up with while I hold down your fort?"

Keegan's jaw clamped tighter, spitting a response laced with frustration. "I said I'm on it, okay? Give me a break. Something like this has never happened before in the history of our pack."

"Yeah, I know." He laughed again. "And, incredibly, I had absolutely nothing to do with it. Do you know how cleansing that is? To have you be the one who's caused so much trouble, and not me?"

Yeah, Keegan knew. Sloan wasn't known for his demure take on life. "Look, it's not like I told her she just won the lottery. I turned her into a werewolf, Sloan. Not a millionaire."

His response was to hiss a sigh back, the connection sizzling in Keegan's ears. "Fine, just hurry up. This passel of women is going to send me over the edge," he snapped and hung up.

Keegan flipped his cell phone shut and jammed it back into his jacket pocket. Maybe now Sloan could understand where he was coming from when he'd decided to take the apartment in New York City a few weeks ago. He needed somewhere he could go without the constant pressure of his duties to his pack. Besides, no man on earth could put up with the women in his pack if they didn't have somewhere they could get the hell away to. Even Job would wind up sitting in the fetal position in a corner if he spent an hour with those women.

Being the alpha male of a pack was a heavy burden filled with constantly yakking females, a brother who was more interested in raising hell than he was in being productive, and a demanding business that sucked up all of his energy.

A thought crossed his mind then. Just wait until Marty found out exactly what kind of business his family owned. She'd shit color wheels for a week.

He shrugged his concerns off and focused on the most immediate one while he headed down the rows of parking slots to locate his car. He had to keep a close eye on Marty, and he couldn't do that in Bobbie-Sue's parking garage.

As Keegan climbed into his car, he cocked his head. A strange smell, one that was clear and pungent sent a chill down the length of his back.

Now what the hell was that?

A scent that clearly stood out from the rest of the typical stench in a New York City parking garage nailed his nostrils, making them flare in question.

The odor was that of malevolence, jealousy, anger, simmering frustration, and Keegan scanned the parking lot with his eyes to locate the person it belonged to.

Whoever the owner of all that pissed-off was must have left.

Slamming the door to his car, he let it go. He didn't have time to save the world tonight.

He was too busy trying to save one Marty Andrews.

"I SAID I'm fine, you guys. Let me be, already." Marty brushed between Nina and Wanda while they walked down her apartment building's hallway. Their concern for her was making her bat shit. For the first time since she'd moved to this building, she welcomed the dimly lit corridor. It helped to hide the shame that was surely written all over her face. She felt like she was going to explode and she'd all of a sudden become a potty mouth like Nina.

"You yelled at Linda Fisher, Marty. You even did it in front of Mr. Bobbie-Sue and their son Terrence. I mean, you may as well have done it in front of Bobbie-Sue, for goodness' sake! You almost never yell. I've never seen you like that before, and what happened to your teeth? It was—it was—" Wanda struggled to find the right words.

"Fucked up. It was fucked up, Marty," Nina finished for her with a grimace. "You should have seen your face. Your eyes were all spooky and shiny, and your teeth . . . they got longer or something. Pointy. It was fa-reaky."

Well, then, Linda Fisher shouldn't go around stealing accounts, now should she? She should have kicked her in her scrawny shins right in front of everyone. That'd learn her.

Marty pulled her thoughts up short. Whoa, and whoaaaaa again. What kinds of thoughts were these that consumed her with rage and filled her with an almost inexplicable anger? She was all Mike Tyson–like not only in thought, but in deed.

Running a finger over her teeth, Marty cringed. She'd felt the elongation of them with a distant sort of detachment. At that point, when she'd been staring down the account-whoring, turbo-bitch's face, she wouldn't have much cared if her head spun around and she'd yarked pea soup at warp speed all over her. At least it would have matched Linda's new color ranking. All she could think about was seeing Linda Fisher crumpled in a heap of writhing emerald at her feet. Marty'd tasted her fear, and she'd reveled in it. Then she'd wanted to finish her off.

If not for Wanda and Nina's interference, that might have been exactly what occurred. The very thought that she'd behaved publicly in a very unladylike manner—in front of her fellow Bobbie-Sue reps—made her squirm. Yet, there was a triumphant air to her non-Marty-like behavior, and that was what astonished her the most.

Bubbly, perky Marty Andrews had wanted to rip the bitch's head off and shit down her throat.

Oh, God, what was happening to her? What kind of explanation could she give Wanda and Nina? Marty shrugged her shoulders at them and continued down the hallway, hiding her face with the curtain of her hair. "I don't know what you're talking about. I only know that Linda Fisher stole a very important account from me, and I intend to make sure she hears from corporate about it."

Wanda sympathized with concern-filled eyes. "I can't believe she did that, Marty."

Nina sidled up beside her and said, "Well, I can. There are some serious cutthroat bitches at Bobbie-Sue, and it's about time you realized that, Marty. You see everything through rose-colored glasses."

What she was seeing, standing at her apartment door, was anything but rosy, and wow, would you look at that. Just a couple of weeks ago, she'd been considering going to the ophthalmologist because she was having trouble reading the labels on the back of Bobbie-Sue's cream blusher. Now she could read the name of the grocery store on the label of the flowers the man waiting by her apartment door was holding, from ten doors away.

What, so now she had the eyesight to rival The Bionic Man?

Rubbing her eyes, she only distantly heard Nina and Wanda's chatter as she approached her door and crossed her arms over her chest, letting her purse dangle from her hand. "What are you doing here, Alger?"

His almost too-handsome face broke into a smile. Sleek and polished, Alger was, as always the epitome of *GQ*. It made her want to mess up his perfect hair and wrinkle his flawless suit.

"I'm here to see you, babe." He cocked his slick blond head at her in question, like they'd never broken up three weeks ago, and she was clearly suffering from amnesia.

"Why?"

"Who are you?" Nina asked without preamble, her lean body moving closer to Marty's in a protective huddle, while Wanda shifted nervously from foot to foot to their left.

Alger smiled again. That smile was the one that to the outside world looked innocent, but was thinly veiled by something Marty had never been able to put a finger on. He jammed a hand into his expensive silk trousers and said, "I'm Marty's boyfriend, Alger Brooks. It's a pleasure."

"The one she broke up with three weeks ago?" Wanda asked, with her usual naivety.

Marty moved closer to him, leaning into his taller frame. "Yep," she said to Wanda. Her whisper was firm. Then she turned to Alger. "You're not my boyfriend anymore, Alger."

The smile never left his face when he looked down at her with rather glazed eyes. "That's why I'm here, Marty. I'd like to talk."

Lovely. Of all the times to want to talk. Now—when she was walking a fine line between proper social conduct and let's get ready to rumble—Alger wanted to talk. "Alger," she said, looking up at him with apprehension. "We have nothing to talk about. We're just going in different directions is all. We talked about this. Now, thank you for the flowers." She hovered over them and took a deep whiff. "They're lovely." And they were. She could smell each individual bud with startling clarity. "But I have to go." Hoping that was enough, Marty began to turn away from him, but Alger reached for her arm and held it in a light grip, sending her senses on an all-points bulletin.

"We were good together, Marty. I don't think we should let this go without giving it some serious thought." His hushed words were ever practical, but beneath them was a desperation Marty hadn't heard before.

With a tight smile, Marty searched his light brown eyes. She really didn't have time to do this tonight. Her skin was hot and flushed from the near-homicide of Linda Fisher. She needed a cool shower and a moment to herself.

Squashing her growing irritation, she attempted to appease him. "We had a great time together, Alger, and I'll treasure the good memories, but we want different things. We're at different points in our lives."

Hadn't she explained this when she'd broken up with him? He wanted a family. She wanted to be Bobbie-Sue's newest success story and wait until she was ready for children. He didn't like the long hours she devoted to her work. She didn't like that he lived off his trust fund and dabbled in the stock market, calling that his job. He was free to take time off whenever he wanted. She had to pound the pavement every day to keep her client base up and find new clients in the process.

In essence, Alger wanted to play, and Marty didn't have that kind of time. She couldn't be at his disposal, and they'd argued often about that toward the end of their six-month relationship. She just wasn't ready to make the kind of commitment Alger seemed to want.

"I think you're making a mistake." His response held conviction. His grip on her arm tightened, and his tone lowered, threading with an odd vibration Marty was picking up, but was still unable to put her finger on.

Nina jammed her face between Alger and Marty, giving him a fierce look. Her beautiful face was really kinda scary when she screwed it up and aimed her wrath at him. "Um, I think she said it's over. Take your flowers and scurry on back to your hole," she threatened as only Nina could do. Without prelude and before it was really necessary.

Marty put a hand up to stop Nina from interfering, but Alger was quicker. "I think you should mind your own business," he said dismissively, casting Nina an arrogant, scathing look before seeking Marty's eyes again.

"Hey." Nina poked him in the chest, forcing him to put distance between them and Marty, yet he still held Marty firmly in his grip. "She said she isn't interested. Are you deaf?"

Alger's face, angular and handsome, turned to stone. Cold and unyielding, the smile that had almost reached his eyes faded. It was apparent he wasn't in the mood for Nina's threats. "Who invited you to this conversation?" His high-handed question came off haughty, and Marty knew Nina would react.

"I did." She stuck her face into his, speaking the words between compressed teeth. "Just call me Conversation Crasher. Now let her go and go home. You're starting to look pathetically like a loser." Nina made the shape of an *L* over her forehead with her index finger and thumb.

Alger's face hardened even further, his cheeks now painted with a flushed red. He didn't like to be mocked, and Nina was the queen of a good mocking.

Wanda simply hovered, buzzing like a worried bee around a flower she wanted the pollen from but couldn't decide what bud to begin with first. "I think you should let her go and go home," she reiterated from behind Alger's back, nervous tension tinting her voice.

Alger looked down at Marty in question. "Marty, I need you." The hunger in his voice made her pause.

"I'm sorry, Alger," was all she could manage. The swift rise of her anger was swept away by regret for what she'd once hoped would be something permanent for them. She'd liked Alger. He was fun and good company, but she'd lost interest when he'd become more demanding about her time. Three weeks ago, when she couldn't take time off to skip over to Cabo for a long weekend, he'd whined that all she did was work, and that was the last straw. Minute as the complaint was, it was the collection of complaints in her grievance box that made her decide it was time for them to end this. Alger was spoiled, in that he didn't have to support himself. Marty did. She couldn't pack a thong and run off to Cabo when she had rent to pay.

"I think you're making a stupid choice." His voice was tight with accusation. Alger was used to getting what he wanted, and right now he obviously wanted her.

"Hey, numb-nuts!" Nina moved in closer, eyeing Alger and shoving Marty out of the way. "Did you just call her stupid? You'd better back the fuck off and go home before you piss me off." She plucked the flowers out of his hand and dumped them on the floor, crushing them with a satisfied twist of her heel.

Hoo boy. It was on now.

Alger wouldn't take an insult like that with a grain of salt.

"Nina! Let's just go inside," Wanda fretted, grabbing Nina's arm and pulling her away from Alger, but she tugged it back and continued to stalk her prey.

The air between the three of them was getting thicker, Alger's agitation growing by the second. Marty watched in fascination as his face displayed myriad emotions. He was fighting the urge to clock Nina. That much was clear from the way he clenched the fist that had held the flowers.

Marty was stupefied. She'd never seen him like this. Alger had always been so easygoing. So devil may care.

"Tell your friend to back off, Marty." His warning was clear, said with measured words, spoken in clipped spats.

"Nina! Cut it out. Both of you stop this. Alger," she said, looking at him with pleading eyes. "You have to go. It's over. We had a nice time together, and I appreciate the flowers, but I'm not changing my mind. Now please, before this gets out of hand, go home," she ordered more roughly than she would have liked to, but circumstance made it necessary.

Moving with a graceful speed she didn't know he possessed, Alger shoved Nina aside and backed Marty up against her apartment door. His body was lean and strong from many hours that he should have spent working, but instead had spent playing racquet ball at the country club. His breathing was shallow, fanning her face with the faint odor of whiskey. Muffin's desperate whine rang out as she began to dig under the door. *You'll miss me, Marty,* were the words that rang in her ears. They clung to them, and her discomfort began to escalate, settling in the pit of her belly.

"Do you hear me, Marty? *You'll miss me.* Don't fuck this up." He repeated the words again, jamming up against her and bracketing her thighs with his.

Marty's hands went to his chest to prevent him from getting any closer, when she heard a distinct growl that couldn't have come from Muffin. Muff could be a vicious, snarling bitch, but she couldn't create that much noisy menace, even on her best day. Then she saw Nina from just over the top of Alger's shoulder, her face angry, her hand ready to grab at his shoulder.

Marty's purse fell to the floor with a clatter. She heard the contents spill everywhere. That was the last thing she heard before a heavy gust of wind whipped between her and Alger, ruffling her hair and leaving Alger on the floor nearly ten feet away from her. The loud gasps of both Wanda and Nina mingled with hers. Muffin's barks became frantic with screeching howls from behind her door.

"The lady said go home, Alger," a familiar voice growled with controlled fury, standing over Alger's prone body, straddling his hips. His jean-clad thighs bulged and flexed, while he firmly planted his feet on either side of Alger. "That means you have to play nice and go away. Now be a man and do that, would ya?"

Alger had managed to gather enough air in his lungs to demand with a rasp, "Who the hell are you?"

Oh, shit, Marty thought, while Wanda and Nina rushed to her side, each clasping one of her arms with frantic fingers, pulling her toward the wall across from her apartment.

How nice. It was the werewolf.

The werewolf.

The very idea that she'd actually acknowledged him as such was absurd, even if it was only in her head.

What was his name again? Keegan. Yes, Keegan Flaherty.

Keegan reached down and yanked Alger upward by the lapels of his jacket, bringing his face to within mere inches of his own. The curtain of his dark hair was in stark contrast to Alger's blond perfection. "I'm her new boyfriend, and I don't like it when my girlfriend gets flowers from another guy. So it's time for you to hit the bricks. Got it?"

Alger's eyes narrowed. "Take your hands off me." The command seemed rather silly, in light of the fact that Keegan kind of had him by the short hairs.

"Or what?" Keegan clearly dared him to respond, gripping the lapels of his jacket tighter and hauling him up to his feet to shove him against the wall. The muscles in his back tensed and flexed with rippling waves of flesh beneath his light jacket. "Now you can go home with your ego intact, or I can wipe the floor with your ass. Your choice." That tic in his jaw worked again with a mesmerizing tempo. Marty remembered that look from this afternoon. It meant he was losing patience and the distinct pop of a can of whoop-ass opening wasn't far off in Alger's future.

Alger began to sputter a protest, but the look in Keegan's eyes thwarted any attempts at a response. It was dark, brooding, clearly confrontational.

Alger made one last manly effort by pushing at his chest with a solid thump. Keegan's feet remained rock solid beneath him, never wavering when he let go of Alger's suit jacket and shoved him backward.

Alger gave a final furious glare at an astonished Marty and hurried down the hallway. The flowers he'd brought were left scattered on the hallway floor in a colorful mess of leaves and petals.

"Wowwee, Marty. Where did you find the knight in shining armor? He's kind of to-die-for smokin'," Nina razzed with a nudge of her shoulder and a whisper.

"Yeahhh," Wanda acknowledged with a wistful sigh. "He's pretty dreamy. Sorta dark and ominous looking."

Marty's eyes raised and met Keegan's over the buzz between Nina and Wanda. All right, so he was cute, but that didn't *not* make him a whacked-out nut, and she certainly couldn't tell her friends that.

Keegan's lips lifted in a small smile, the indents on either side of his face deepening. Yet his eyes, hooded and coal black, remained unreadable.

The heat on Marty's face tickled her cheeks and flushed her neck. His smile made her stomach do a tumbling run any Olympic gold medalist would be proud of, twisting it into a knot.

"Are you okay, *honey*?" He was behaving all sticky sweet and concerned.

"I'm f-fine." So that was a lie, but she was caught off guard by his use of the endearment.

"Er, Marty? He's your boyfriend? Where do I get me one of those?" Nina joked. "And where did he come from? I thought you weren't dating anyone, so you could focus on this makeup hocking thing?"

"He's—he's not—um, my boyfriend . . ." She was stammering. How pathetic.

No, Marty, he's your werewolf. Howwwwwl.

Keegan stepped forward, taking her hand and twining his fingers through her limp, surprised ones. His smile was wider now when he said, "Aw, honey. You haven't told them yet, have you? That's okay, punkin, I understand. It takes time to adjust to finding your soul mate."

Her who? Marty thought it, but couldn't seem to gather the resources to say it.

"Your *what*?" Nina and Wanda said in unison.

Swinging their linked hands together, Keegan said, "I'll let Marty tell you all about it. It's just not my place. Anyway, I live right down the hall, girls. My name is Keegan Flaherty. If Alger comes back, give a holler. Apartment 24A. Now, how about I go, seeing as that jerk is taken care of, and let you have some girl time, sweetheart? Oh, and Muffin?" He rapped lightly on her door with his knuckles. "Knock that off, Princess. Be a good girl, and I'll bring you a treat tomorrow." He listened at the door for a moment until Muffin stopped her howling. With a smile of satisfaction, he kissed the tip of Marty's nose, winking at Nina and Wanda. "Bye, ladies," he said with that hot-chocolate honeyed tone, swaggering down to the end of the hallway, with three pairs of eyes glued to his fabulous butt.

Keegan disappeared into his apartment, and the opportunity to press Marty for info became wide open.

"Holy shit! Did you see his ass, Wanda?" Nina muttered, smoothing her hands down her nylon-covered legs.

"Uh-huh." She nodded distantly, her eyes still focused on Keegan's door.

"So, details, Marty," Nina demanded, kneeling to pick up Marty's spilled purse. "When did this all happen?"

"Yeah, how come you didn't tell us about him? And when did this happen? After you broke up with Alger?"

"He's . . . not my boyfriend." Her denial sounded off to her ears. What could she possibly say to his admission? If she told them the truth, they'd tar her with a crazy brush and call for the men with the butterfly nets. If she didn't go along with it, and she told them what he'd told her, Nina'd be knocking down his door with a battering ram and offering to duel him at dawn. In this case, Marty decided silence was golden.

"Well, he sure was pretty familiar with you, for someone who isn't your boyfriend," Nina persisted, running her fingers through her mussed tangle of dark curls. "You don't have to tell us about it if it's private. We can wait," she offered with a snippy tone.

"And did you see the way he jumped all over Alger? God, to have a man like that defend me," Wanda murmured, clearly still dazed from Keegan's yumminess.

Marty ignored their prattle and stooped to help pick up the contents of her purse. Her head was a swirl of crazy emotions and flashes of confusion. The one thing she could focus on was—Keegan Flaherty lived in her apartment building.

All this time she'd lived right down the hall from a werewolf.

Who'da thunk?

How could she have missed that little detail?

What the hell else lived here?

The Abominable Snowman?

Bigfoot?

Were there more just like him in her building who thought they were werewolves, too? How long had he been living right under her nose?

It could explain why Muffin didn't seem at all troubled when he'd come to the door earlier today. Then again, if he were a werewolf, he was kind of in Muffin's species. Like her cousin, right?

God, what was she thinking? Keegan Flaherty was no friggin' werewolf.

But maybe he was a part of some crazy cult. Like those people who thought they were vampires. They dressed in black all the time and wore all that white makeup and were—in Marty's modest opinion—sorely in need of a color consultation.

Yeah, sure. This was New York, after all. It could happen, she thought, sticking the key in the door to her apartment and bending to give Muffin her perfunctory greeting, but Muff had other ideas.

Ignoring Marty and the girls, she scooted between the three pairs of feet and headed straight down the hallway to Keegan's, scratching and whining at his door.

This madness grew curiouser and curiouser.

CHAPTER
4

Alana O'Brian absently stroked the shaft of the thickly muscled man who lay beside her on her silk-sheeted bed. He had become an afterthought now. Her attention was firmly elsewhere.

Like on Keegan Flaherty and the disaster he'd made of her life because he still refused to mate with her. Now, just when she'd thought she might have found a new way to capture his attention, he wanted to bring some strange female back to Buffalo to help her adjust, because he'd fucked up. Like some science project. Sloan said Keegan felt it was his duty to "fix" this.

Alana would have expected a careless mishap like this from Sloan, party boy and all-around fuckup, but never from Keegan. Her grip grew firmer as she thought of the injustice she'd suffer.

"Hey!" he yelped, his blue eyes looking up at her with confusion. "Do you want to rip it off or something?"

"Sorry," she mumbled, letting him go abruptly and sliding off the bed to grab her silk bathrobe. She slipped into it and tied it around her waist with a sharp twist.

"Um, I wasn't done yet." His moan was a protest, the protrusion between his thick, muscled legs a clear sign what he said was true.

But Alana cared little about what he wanted. "Well"— she smiled sweetly and threw a long blonde lock of hair over her shoulder—"I was." Ignoring him and his look of pathetic incompletion, she padded to her bathroom and flipped on the handles of the shower. When Sloan had sent word about Keegan's little accident, the rest of the week had turned into a real downer.

"How do you accidentally bite some pathetic human and then deem it your obligation to make them your personal charity case?" she'd asked Sloan.

"Because he's the boss," Sloan had said.

"Fuck the boss!" she'd screeched back.

Oh, wait, that's what she wanted to do.

Not that Keegan had ever cared much that she was next in line to mate, and it was her birthright as the most eligible female of her pack to be his mate. He'd made it abundantly clear that if he was forced to mate with Alana, he'd do it for the pack. Rather like taking one for the team, but he wouldn't do it willingly, and, well, that pissed her off.

Looking in the bathroom mirror, she just couldn't comprehend what it was about her that Keegan didn't want. What man in his right mind wouldn't want her?

Alana wasted no time with the ridiculous notion of modesty. It was for the weak and simpering. She was beautiful. Period. Plus, let's not forget, she had a killer bod. She spent an indecent amount of time at the gym, making sure her human form was in tip-top shape. How could Keegan ignore that? She hadn't met a man anywhere who didn't feel at least a small twinge of lust when he encountered her, and it didn't matter how faithful he was to his mate. He couldn't escape just one forbidden visual of her naked.

So what the hell was Keegan's problem?

Stepping under the spray of the shower, she squirted
some scented gel in her palm and began lathering her body,
starting with her toes, while she gave some thought to her
next plan of action. What was occurring between their
packs was unacceptable. She wouldn't be saddled with
some beta werewolf who didn't know his ass from his
elbow. She was meant for an alpha mate, and that mate was
Keegan Flaherty. It had been decided upon at birth. No one
was taking her rightful place beside Keegan if she had anything to say about it.

No one would take her shot at running that company
either.

But she digressed. Keegan hadn't dated anyone seriously
in ages.

However, Alana's senses were acute for some reason,
and this stupid, human bitch was the culprit. She couldn't
refocus Keegan's attention on her if he was all tied up in his
guilt over helping a pathetic were-wannabe. She didn't
want any woman, charity case or not, anywhere near her
man.

And Keegan *would* be hers.

Her face grew heated with her fury. She clenched the silver railing lining her shower stall to keep from slamming an
angry fist through the ceramic tile. As the water pelted over
her, raining down on her toned body, Alana decided it was
time to look into this human. She wanted to get a feel for the
council's reaction to Keegan bringing her back to Buffalo—
whom she was sure would want answers as to why she and
Keegan hadn't mated yet—and find out whatever she needed
to know to rid herself of this unexpected little roadblock.

THE sharp rap on Marty's door clanged in her head with a
vicious stab. Jesus, she felt like she'd been on an all-night
drinking spree. Her mouth had the pasty, dry feel of cotton
in it, and her head throbbed to the tune of an invisible
bongo player.

Popping the heavy steel door open, she squinted at her caller through the crack the chain lock on it allowed.

Oh, he was here again? How nice, another visit from her friendly resident werewolf. He was like Mr. Rogers.

Won't you be my neighbor?

Jesus, they were a persistent bunch, eh?

Keegan was holding a plastic supermarket bag and tapping his booted foot on the floor impatiently. His masculine aroma, whatever it was, drifted to her nose and hit her between the eyes. The scent was so clear and sharp it made her eyes tear in all its decadence.

His hair was still wet, gleaming in the darkened hallway, and he smiled a smile that didn't quite reach those black eyes when he saw her. The smile of the distantly polite. Keegan stuck his finger between the crack in the door and wiggled it at her. "Morning, Marty." He winked, waiting for her to open it, like it was his right to be let in.

At the sound of Keegan's voice, Muffin skidded across the room in a blaze of white glory, parking her small behind by Marty's feet, whining and wagging her poofy, little groomed tail. Marty scooped her up and tucked the wriggling dog under her arm. "You're being very obvious this morning, Muff. Men don't like girls who throw themselves at them," she whispered into Muffin's neck, chastising her blatant behavior. "It makes you look loose and cheap. Desperate even."

Keegan's fingers went immediately to Muffin's chin, scratching her through the door, making her wriggle and squirm frantically in Marty's arms. "Hey, Princess," he cooed, all sultry and seductive. "I've got something for you."

What could he possibly have for Muffin? A message from her people, perhaps? "What do you want?" Marty's question was sharp, making her press the heel of her hand to her forehead. Just the sound of her own voice made her want to crawl out of her skin. Enough was enough of this bullshit werewolf crap. Maybe it was time to look for another place to live. New York had its share of whackos, but they all seemed to be congregating in her building.

"I promised Muffin a treat last night, remember?" he reminded her. "And she did come right back home after she ran away. She deserves a reward, don't you, Muff?"

Marty ran a hand through her mussed hair and pondered that. Yeah, Muffin had come back home when Keegan had popped his door open and merely spoken to her. Both Nina and Wanda had thought that was a sure sign he was Prince Charming—like he was some kind of dog whisperer or something, and because Muff did whatever he told her to, it made him even more perfect than he'd been when he scared off Alger.

Muffin's adoration of this nut was uncanny—her exuberance over him, a glaring sign she was a traitorous wench. She hoped the adage was true that dogs were good judges of character, because Muffin didn't seem to see Keegan as anything but worthy of her worship. "She doesn't need anything from you." God, that sounded so petty. This was pathetic. To be jealous because Muffin liked the hot, mentally imbalanced guy was just absurd. What was even more absurd? Muffin merely tolerated other animals and humans. She'd never been terribly affectionate or warm except with Marty. She allowed people to pet her. No more, no less.

"Are we grumpy today, Marty?"

Shit yeah, she was grumpy. Her dog was deserting her for a man who thought he was a werewolf, and she felt like shit. She probably looked like shit, too. God, she was still in her nightgown. Thankfully it wasn't the one with the coffee stain on it. "Look, I'm not even dressed, and I don't know what Muffin's gig is with you, but she'll get over it. Thanks for the present for her. You can leave it by the door." Marty began to push the door shut, but Keegan jammed his hard, muscled arm against it.

"Let me in, Marty." His black eyes sought hers and locked with them, compelling her to do what he asked.

No, he hadn't asked, he'd demanded.

And she was becoming beyond aggravated by the stern set of his square jaw and the arrogant determination in his eyes. Sheesh, and Wanda and Nina thought she was rabid about selling eye shadow? They oughta try telling this guy they didn't want to be a werewolf. "I don't have all morning to spend with you talking about werewolves. I'm not listening to any more crazy, convoluted stories about dog bites and full moons. Go find someone else to initiate into your little society for lunar lovers. Oh, and besides, if I had my druthers, I'd never want to be a werewolf. The potential for fleas is enormous. Not to mention, you sniff each other's butts in the getting-to-know-you process. So tell all your little wolf friends I can't come out and play today—or any day."

His frown spoke volumes, while his arm remained wedged stubbornly in the door. "You can joke all you like, Marty, but this isn't a joke. I'm here to help you adjust. Now let me in," he said in that oh-so-irritating, do-as-I-say way of his.

"Tell me something?"

"Anything."

"Are you friends with like all sorts of other nuts who think they're things that don't exist outside of that world you've created in your mind? Like, say, fairies? You know any? Wings could be cool. Yes . . ." She nodded her head and clucked her tongue. "I think I'd rather be in that club. I mean, if you know any fairies, maybe you could send them my way? Do that on your way out, would you?"

His eyebrow rose, thick and arched, and his lips drew into a tight, thin line of anger. "Marty, open the door."

Alrighty then. His tone said he wasn't in the mood to play. Good, maybe now he'd understand how she felt. She was done with the ridiculous stories. She didn't feel well, and she just wanted to be left alone.

But Keegan wasn't budging, and neither was his all-male aroma. Lodged firmly in her nostrils, it clung to them, making her head swim.

Muffin was growing bored with their banter, unable to

take the temptation of her hero so close, yet so far away, any longer. So she took matters into her own hands and jumped from Marty's arms, slipping between the small opening of the door. One look down told Marty she was already begging like a sissy to be picked up by Mr. Yummylicious.

Marty tucked a toe under Muffin's backside and gave her a nudge, sending her a message with her eyes that screamed *deserter*. Muffin ignored her, scratching at the part of Keegan's leg she could reach.

Well, for crap's sake. Fine. Better than fine. How much more harm could he do than he'd already done by infecting her with his crazy stories? With a roll of her eyes and a slide of the chain lock, Marty flung open the door in defeat. So what if she looked like death? Who cared what the hunky werewolf thought? He didn't seem to pose a danger to her. He'd never tried to hurt her. Muffin sure liked him, and she'd never liked Alger. So what the hell? Why not indulge him while she nursed this mother of all headaches?

She padded over to her leather couch and plopped down carelessly without a thought to her appearance, tucking her nightgown under her. Rubbing her eyes, she realized she hadn't taken off her mascara last night before she'd fallen into bed like she'd just fought and won the Third World War single-handedly. God, surely the world was coming to an end, if she'd forgotten to cleanse and moisturize before going to bed.

"You look tired, Marty," Keegan noted, standing in the doorway with Muffin curled on his shoulder.

How very observant. Who wouldn't be tired after spending an afternoon with a guy who thought he'd turned her into a werewolf? Keeping up with the hair growth alone was exhausting on too many levels to count. Speaking of her bionic hair . . . She ran a discreet hand over her calves and realized she had major stubble again.

Well, fuck. She'd just shaved last night.

He continued to loom there, filling up the room, watching her intently, big and raw and—and—well, just *and*.

Marty couldn't find any words in her extensive vocabulary to describe him and how he made her emotions seesaw precariously.

Keegan Flaherty was many things that were indefinable. Well, except *fruitcake*. That word worked. *Let's not forget he's crazy, Marty.*

Her expression was wry when she finally looked up at him with smudged, weary eyes. "I had a long day yesterday, thanks to you, Wolfman Jack."

His chuckle spilled over her like warm caramel on vanilla ice cream, rippling and warm, leaving behind a strange, unfamiliar tingle along her spine. "C'mon, Princess, let's go see what I brought you." He ruffled Muffin's fur. She responded by nestling her head in his neck, blowing out a breath of contented air.

The rustle of the plastic bag in her small kitchen was like fingernails on a chalkboard to her ears, screaming along her sensitive nerve endings. She clapped her hands over them and moaned. For all the trouble she was having today, she should have at least gotten good and snockered out of it. "Could you be quiet? Pleeeeease!" she snapped, unable to hide the irritation clawing at her like talons.

Keegan poked his head out of the kitchen. His face remained impassive, but his tone was light. "Sensitive are we? Not a morning person?"

"According to you, I'm not a person at all," she answered snidely.

"Alger didn't come back, did he?"

Strangely, she'd mostly forgotten all about the incident with him and Keegan. She supposed a thanks was in order. "No, and thanks for getting him to go home last night. And do you know the trouble you've caused by telling Nina and Wanda you're my *boyfriend*? Are all you werewolves this presumptuous?"

He ignored her question and asked one of his own. "How long did you two date?"

"Long enough to know I didn't want to anymore."

"What made you break up with him?"

Her shoulders lifted in a tired shrug. "We just didn't want the same things."

"Like?"

Marty waved a dismissive hand at him. It was none of his business, damn it. "I don't know, and why do you care?"

He crossed the room in two confident strides and came to sit by her on the couch, nudging her over, and in the process, his thigh brushed hers. The crunch of the leather beneath his yummy butt crackled in her ears. The hard press of his leg against hers burned her right through her nightgown. Lifting her chin, he gave her a once-over glance, condemning but silent.

Marty squirmed self-consciously, twisting a strand of her hair with a shaky hand. "Okay, so I look like crap."

"Yep, you do." His confirmation was followed with a slight lift of his lips. In the crisp light of morning, he looked even better than he had the day before. The warm touch of his long fingers on her chin made her heart race and her mouth dryer than it had been when she'd first gotten up. Her nipples began to ache with a rhythmic throb that rivaled the pounding in her head. With a blink of her eyes, she tried to focus on something other than his lips—lips that were so close she could see every line in them. Her hands clenched together in her lap to keep from tracing the firm flesh.

Lawd, he was the shit. There was just no denying it. None.

And he's caaaa-razy, Marty. C-R-A-Z-Y.

Yeah, she answered her subconscious back, *he's crazy hot.*

Her gasp of disbelief was audible, wheezing on its way out of her lungs. Had she just thought that? Omigod, she had because he was, but that was no excuse. He wasn't up for discussion.

Marty took a deep breath of air and leaned away from the heat his body emanated. It overpowered her, leaving her winded and giddy. She pushed aside her sudden awareness of him and made a concerted effort to concentrate on anything other than the butterflies that were fluttering around in her stomach. Withdrawing to the other end of the couch, she curled her legs under her again and averted her eyes, staring sightlessly at a picture on her wall.

Muffin's stifled squeal as she lunged from the floor up onto the couch made her jump, forgetting she'd just—albeit only in her mind—admitted Keegan was hot. Muffin was dragging something cold and slimy, and it grazed Marty's foot, as Muffin settled in Keegan's lap. Marty's nose twitched, and she shoved her finger under it, pinching the bridge of it with her other hand.

Keegan slid a hand beneath Muffin's belly and placed her back on the floor. "No, Princess, you have to eat that on the floor," he reprimanded with another chuckle.

Muffin happily wagged her tail at him and went back to the task at hand with loud pleasure—snarfing down something that smelled divine to Marty's nose.

She peered over her knees to see what had Muffin so enraptured. Her small head bobbed up and down, while her tiny paws held a bone with a firm grasp.

God, she prayed, *please don't let that be a dog bone . . .*

Upon closer inspection, she realized it was a bone, with a large piece of meat still attached to it.

A piece of steak. An uncooked steak.

Mmmmmm, Marty thought before she could stop herself, then cringed inwardly at the clench of longing in her gut.

Muffin picked it up, throwing her head back and shaking the meat in the air with such joy, Marty just knew she'd grin from ear to ear if she could. She turned to proudly display it to Marty as if to say, "See?"

The sudden, loud churning of Marty's stomach took both her and Keegan by surprise. The crystal clear gurgle was unmistakable and sharp, piercing the quiet of the apartment. Her intestines roared like a pride of lions, caged and angry.

"You're hungry. You need protein, the red meat kind," Keegan stated simply, though his face had the smug look of a neener, neener, neener.

"I don't eat meat. I'm a vegan." Her protest was thin and weak, but she wasn't giving in to this crazy urge, because it would only support his wild notion. And his notion *was* wild. Outrageously so.

When Keegan looked at her, his face was clearly concerned, shaking Marty's insides all up. "Werewolves eat meat, and you're a werewolf. You need protein. A lot of it. The rare beef kind. It's why you don't feel well this morning. Your body is adjusting to the change, and meat will help nurture that change properly. You'll continue to be tired until you eat."

She wrinkled her nose and made a face at him. "What are you, a werewolf nutritionist or something? I don't eat meat. I'm not a werewolf, and now that you've given Miss Vixen here"—she pointed down at Muffin—"her little gift—something she's normally not allowed—you can go home."

Muffin's whimpers of decadent delight wafted to Marty's ears, and she found herself licking her dry lips with a gulp. Christ, that steak smelled good. She could almost taste it salted. Maybe with a little barbeque sauce . . . A.1.?

Keegan's brisk movement from the couch startled her. "Where's your cell phone?"

"Why?"

Keegan's expression was that of the clearly fed up. "Give it to me. I'll put my number in it. If you don't believe what I'm telling you now, there's going to come a time when you do, and I might not be in the direct vicinity to help. So you'll have to call me. You don't ever have to use it, but it's there if you need it. No harm, no foul. You see, I have things to do, too, Marty, and I'm trying to do the right thing, but you just won't let me. So you'll have to find out all on your own."

Again, her temper, the one that included an out-of-control potty mouth, flared, red and hot. Marty grabbed her purse from the end table beside the couch, hurling it at his head, but he caught it expertly, infuriating her further. "It's in there, and you know what? Why do you keep behaving as if I'm putting you out? If, in fact, you did turn me into a werewolf," she said with another exaggerated, disbelieving roll of her eyes, "that's not on me, buddy. It's on you. You bit me! So what's jammed up your ass?"

He thrust a hand into her purse and narrowed his eyes at her. "If you had better control of your dog, none of this would have happened," he said, his fingers punching numbers into her cell phone with vicious stabs.

"Are you on *crack*? I can't believe you just said that to me. I was innocently walking my dog. If that was you that night, what were you doing lurking in some dark alley? Picking through garbage?"

Leaning across her, he braced a hand on the back of the couch to look her in the eye and give her a hard stare.

Marty shivered. If only he knew how sexy that was . . . that whole flared nostril, heavy breathing thing. Hot. Very, very hot. No matter how crazy he was, he couldn't get away from being so hot.

She gulped.

He handed the cell phone back, sticking it under her nose with a jab before throwing it back in her purse. "That's what dogs do, isn't it?" Shoving off the back of the couch, Keegan stood, bending to ruffle Muffin's fur. "You be a good girl and eat that all up. Maybe you could share with your owner." He looked over his broad shoulder at Marty. "She could use the protein. She's too pale." Keegan shot her one last look. "I'll talk to you soon," were the last, confident, arrogant words he spoke before leaving her on the couch with a cold glance.

"You'll see me in hell first," she countered from behind, jumping off the couch and stalking off to the kitchen. The plastic-wrapped package he'd brought still sat on her countertop.

It called to her in all its bleeding, red yumminess.

There was some steak left.

She had to grip the handle of the fridge to keep from pitching forward. With slow, cautious feet, she went to the kitchen counter, her line of vision fixated on the package.

Her mouth watered when she placed a trembling hand on the cellophane, feeling the cool surface of the meat through it.

Look, if you're really going to do this, shouldn't you cook it first? her subconscious asked pointedly.

"Cooking it would imply I was going to eat it, and I'm not going to eat it," she said obstinately. She just wanted to look at it. Embrace her bizarre craving and let it pass. Looking couldn't hurt her. Like a smoker who'd recently quit smoking and had been subjected to her first smell of someone else's cigarette.

Willpower. She needed all the willpower she could gather. Her hands gripped the edge of the countertop— white-knuckled and achingly desperate.

Maybe just one small bite . . . The very idea had her stomach singing with joy.

That's like saying I'll just have one more sour cream Lays or just one more Godiva chocolate when there's a whole box left, Marty. Tsk-tsk.

Beads of sweat broke out on her forehead when she leaned forward and took a long, lingering whiff. The smell was intoxicating. Her mouth watered enough that she had to swipe a hand over it to keep from drooling. All she could think about was her lips wrapped around the soft, red meat, biting into it with reckless abandon.

Carnivore! her brain screamed.

She had no fight left in her when she grabbed the Styrofoam container and recklessly tore the plastic from the package. With violently shaking hands, Marty grabbed at the meat, tearing a small chunk of it off and placing it on her tongue without pausing to think.

Utopia was usually a word best used to describe a place, but in this case it was the word she'd use to describe the moment the meat hit her taste buds. What a head rush of tantalizing, euphoric flavor and texture. She didn't even bother to chew.

Her eyes rolled to the back of her head as the meat slid down her throat, and she gulped with a pleasure that came from so deep within her, she thought she'd die of it.

The moment it hit her stomach was the moment regret settled in. She hadn't had meat in almost five years, and even back when she'd indulged in a good burger it never tasted quite like this.

Tapping a finger against the countertop, she held the remainder of the steak in her hand. Decisions, decisions. To gorge or not to gorge. Scarf it all down, or walk away . . .

Fuck it, was her vague thought as she shoveled it into her mouth, stuffing as much of the remaining meat into her piehole as she could with gleeful snorts. With the back of her hand, she wiped the corners of her mouth.

She belched loud and proud, then gave a furtive glance around her small kitchen and quickly grabbed a napkin to cover her rude outburst.

Holy Angus cut.

She'd just eaten some poor cow.

But the good news was her stomach wasn't growling anymore.

Marty grinned.

That meant she could go buy some fresh vegetables without frightening people in a social setting and cleanse herself of the raw steak she'd eaten like it was the last granola bar on *Survivor*.

That left little time for remorse.

For the first time in over a week, her head felt clearer and she had a loosely formulated plan.

A few hours later, a long shower, some cute new sandals she'd bought a couple of weeks ago, and a mission had brought with them new perspective. She'd just go buy vegetables, and it would all be good. Maybe a nice salad with dandelion greens and wheat germ sprinkled on top was the answer. Suddenly, she felt better than she had in over a week. However, she refused to attribute that to Keegan's crazy theory that she'd needed protein. Marty made herself a promise in the shower to forget all about him and his hunkiness.

Sticking her cell phone in her skirt pocket, she grabbed her small purse and put a coupon in it she'd clipped for fresh vegetables from the bodega on Eighth.

Muffin's head bobbed upward for a brief moment; she gave a low snarl. Her eyes still glazed from eating her steak bone. Marty's stomach growled again, and she stooped to look Muff in the eye. "Look, Keegan may giveth, but I can and will taketh away. I'll fight you for that damned bone if I get desperate. Got that, precious?" Giving her a quick pat on the head, Marty reminded her not to get on the couch with her beloved steak bone and skipped out of her apartment with renewed hope.

Setting aside her guilt over consuming the steak like a rabid animal, Marty headed down the block, her stride purposeful. She'd decided to forgo the mixed-up message that damned animal protein had sent her stomach and make the best of this improved mood. She'd hit the bodega on Eighth Avenue—they always had the best tomatoes—and then she'd go home and enjoy a healthy salad. Maybe rent a movie, too.

As the day wore on, her frame of mind further improved, even as Keegan's words worried at the fringes of her brain.

A werewolf. Hah!

She was no stinking werewolf. That she'd even given credence to that idea simply because her body was experiencing some changes seemed completely moronic.

So her body had gone into like pre-pre-menopause. She was in her thirties now, and shit happened. Like having to wax more often.

But every day? Sometimes twice?

"Shut up," she warned the skeptic voice in her head. "Enough with the negativity, already. Don't piss on my parade."

Rounding the corner, Marty marched into the bodega and gave Mr. Gonzalez, the owner, a beaming smile as she headed for the cucumbers. "Hey, Mr. G. How goes it?"

His balding head bobbed, glossy and shining under the store lights. "Eees good, Miss Marty. Ju do someting wit ju hair? I liiiike," he crooned. His smile was teasingly lascivious and shone with approval. "I like de darker hair. Eees pretty on ju. Almost make ju a señorita, eh?" He chuckled at his own cleverness.

With a sigh, she grabbed a cucumber and ignored the comment about her hair. She was a blonde, not some brunette hot tamale. Tomorrow she'd call Steven and have her hair dyed. Tonight was reserved for good thoughts that didn't remotely include her friggin' delusional werewolf neighbor.

Gathering her purchases, Marty put them in a basket and placed them on the counter with disinterest, wishing she could summon the joy she normally gleaned from finding a good deal on fresh produce. The bountiful colors of Mr. Gonzalez's tomatoes and squash usually made her happy, but not tonight.

What was really floating her boat was the sign for the special on sirloin at six-ninety-nine a pound. The unrelenting urge to go to the meat counter and buy a whole damned side of beef was almost irresistible. But she fought it like her life depended on it, while her legs shook and her heart crashed in her chest.

A bead of sweat broke out on her upper lip.

"Ju ees okay, Miss Marty? Ju look bery tire." His warm eyes smiled in concern.

Yeah? See how you feel when you're stalked by a man who thinks he's a werewolf. Ju'd be bery tire, too.

Jesus Christ in a miniskirt. Was there a soul on the planet who didn't think she looked tired? Tamping down her sudden flare of exasperation, she bit the inside of her lip to keep her mouth shut. It wasn't his fault she was cranky because he had sirloin steaks on sale. "Been a busy day is all," she answered vaguely, handing him a twenty, while she helped bag the vegetables that did nothing to stir her palette. "You take care, Mr. G. I'll see you next week."

He waved a chubby hand in salute from behind the counter, then placed them on his abundant belly, settling back to watch the small black and white television above the counter.

Marty left feeling like a wet blanket had been thrown on her entire evening. As she stepped out into the cool night air, she was distracted by Mr. Gonzalez's comment about her hair.

She'd paid a small fortune at that swanky salon to be a blonde and this brunette-ness was unacceptable. A glance in a closed shop window told her that it wasn't just a couple of shades darker, it was nearing a medium brown.

All of a sudden she had like mood hair, a different color for every emotion. How could a simple dog bite have done this to her?

While she was in the process of a good dunk in the river of denial, she caught movement from the corner of her eye.

A smudge of a black figure, quick and skulking, followed by the unyielding pavement her head crashed against were the last things she saw.

CHAPTER
5

Wow, now this would officially be even more of a bummer than the whole werewolf thing, Marty thought as a hard jolt drove into her lower back. She figured it was time to open her eyes and face whatever the music was. It involved a moving car and the thick cloak of darkness she could virtually feel. Oh, and the crunch and squeal of tires, plus a new bongo player in her head. This drummer was far more active than the percussions genius who'd taken up residence in her brain this morning. His persistent rat-a-tat-tat in her head was violent and throbbing.

Her hand immediately flew to the spot on her temple that pounded with an ugly rhythm. Wet with a sticky substance she assumed was blood, it matted her hair, flattening it to her face.

Forcing herself to open her eyes, Marty encountered the suffocating, dark interior of the trunk of a car. Each detail of the car was crystalline, and if she had more time, she'd be freaked about this strange ability to see at night like the Bionic Man. Assessing the interior, she decided it was a large sedan, figuring from the trunk space. She could lay almost completely flat.

And older. The seats didn't seem like they folded down from the inside.

Maybe a Caddy?

Like it mattered.

The smell of motor oil weighed heavily in the claustrophobic air, cloying and thick. Terror rose in her chest, while panic threatened to take over any hope she might have of getting out of this mess if she didn't get a grip. She felt for an inside latch or anything that might help her escape. She could clearly remember reading an article about inside trunk releases, but this car didn't have one.

With each bump the car took on the winding, twisting road, she bounced uncontrollably. She heard nothing but the sound of the tires eating up the road. No horns. No sirens. Which led her frazzled mind to believe that she was no longer in the city.

Fuck. Who the hell had done this?

A serial killer . . . it really was the only obvious conclusion.

A sick, twisted individual who wanted to chop her up and—

Oh, good. That would be a fine way to balance out the end of this week of bloody hell.

Okay, think. She needed to think. Marty grappled with the constant stream of murderous acts that struck her randomly, forcing herself to battle her fears and take action.

First off, who gave a flying fuck who'd taken her? That wouldn't matter to anyone but some grizzled, tired homicide detective when she was found floating face down in the Hudson. There wasn't anyone else to care. Not like a super close friend or relative. She had business associates and acquaintances, nothing more. How depressing to know only Muffin would miss her, and really what she'd miss the most was the gourmet kibble she fed her at six sharp every night.

Second, she was in a trunk going to an unknown destination with little hope for escape. If whoever had her managed to get her alone, they'd hack her up into little pieces even a jigsaw puzzle genius couldn't put back together. What if he *Silence of the Lamb*-ed her and like wanted to skin her alive . . . ?

Oh. My. God.

Her breath quickened again, and her stomach plunged with a roll. Marty shoved a fist into her mouth to keep from screaming in terror. She was freaking herself out, and that wasn't going to be helpful. But—but what if he killed her and no one ever found her? Who would know she was gone besides Muffin? Would anyone even notice? Would anyone care? Her mother was gone. Wanda and Nina were the only women she spent much time with, and they didn't qualify as friends, if you didn't do anything with them except shove makeup-selling tips down their throats.

When push came to shove—and it certainly had— selling units of lavender eye shadow didn't seem so important anymore.

Oh, Jesus effin'. She had no friends.

No one was going to give a rat's ass if she was dead, because no one would know for days. Maybe weeks—even months . . .

Okay, she was thinking too much again.

Calling for help was in order. The fleeting thought that the gift of telepathy would be welcome right now came and went as she racked her brain for a way out.

Her purse! Where was her purse?

Marty felt the interior of the trunk bed with hands that knotted and trembled, twisting her body in as many possible ways in order to search it thoroughly.

Damn. No purse.

"God, Marty!" she muttered under her breath. "Of course, any good serial killer would take your purse. Every mass murderer needs some coupons and Lava Red Bobbie-Sue long-lasting lipstick." Clenching her fists at her sides, her hand hit a forgotten lump in her pocket.

The air she expelled from her lungs came in a rush of shaky relief.

Eureka! Her cell phone. She'd put it in her skirt pocket because her purse—the cute one she'd found on sale at Sax—was too small to hold much but a lipstick.

The fashion police should be locked up in their own jail cells for suggesting all you really needed when you went out was a tube of flippin' lipstick and a credit card. Thankfully, the moron who'd knocked her out didn't think to check her pockets.

Or tie her up.

Why hadn't he tied her up?

Marty gritted her teeth to stave off another wave of crazy, panicked thoughts and erratically jumping conclusions.

Jamming a hand into her skirt, she yanked out her phone and flipped it open. The blue light illuminated the face of it while she frantically sought her phone book, pressing buttons without thinking. Who should she call? She punched the auto dial for Nina in blind panic.

If there was anyone who could help her when a bully was needed, it was Nina.

Nina would kick the living crap out of whoever had her stuffed like some sardine into the trunk of this car just because. Nina'd take on Ted Bundy with only a butter knife for a weapon.

Three rings passed in agonizingly slow seconds that felt more like hours.

Oh, please, please, please pick up the phone.

"You've reached Nina. If you're that important, you'll leave a message. I'm too busy to answer you, because I'm out schlepping around Bobbie-Sue Cosmetics." Her message was followed by a loud snort.

Her voicemail. Arghhh. Could she have picked a better time than now to actually be out trying to make a sale?

"Ninaaaa!" she whispered hoarsely, pressing the phone to her lips—lips that stuck together against her teeth, trembling. "It's Marty. Hee—elp me. Someone's kidnapped me, and I'm in a—a—c-aaaaar! I mean the trunk of a car—I think. No, I'm sure. Yes, it's a trunk—a big trunk, and I don't know where I'm being taken. I've been kidnapped. Oh, God hurry. Please get me some hellllp!" She began to sob, hanging up and immediately searching her phone book for another number to call.

Her whole body shook as she hit the auto dial for Wanda, listening with a frustrated cry when she heard Wanda's voicemail, too. God, exactly when had the two of them decided to get on the stick and find some customers? "Hello, you've reached Wanda Schwartz, your Bobbie-Sue Cosmetics Independent Consultant. I'd love to hear from you. So please leave a message when you hear the tone." The tone was the theme song from *Love Story*.

Marty'd gotten it together enough to string a whole collective thought and leave a more coherent message this time. "Waaaaanda, it's Marty. I've been kidnapped. Help me. I don't know where I am. I'm in the trunk of a car, and he's taking me somewhere. Hurry, please!"

The car slowed with her last words, and Marty's heart banged against her ribs. Her throat was thick with fear. He was taking her to a place no one would ever find her, and he was going to whack her.

But what would he do to her before he killed her?

Did he have a gun? Crap, she didn't stand a chance against a gun. Unless she'd suddenly developed a new, as yet undiscovered super power that didn't involve hair growth at the speed of light.

The vehicle stopped with a lurch, and it was then she decided she was not leaving this world without a fucking fight a WWF champ would shed tears over. She clamped a hand over her mouth to keep from screaming while trying to tamp down her panic and listen to her surroundings. The door slammed, making the car shake.

"You want a cherry slurpee?" a man with a heavy New York accent asked.

"Why the fuck do you drink that shit? It'll kill ya," another man answered. His accent was definitely Jersey City.

Sweet mother, there were two of them? Her resolve to come out of this alive weakened.

Marty heard the first man's chuckled response as if he were right next to her ear. "The sugar keeps me awake, roid boy."

"Well, hurry it up, would ya? He ain't gonna like it if we're late."

Late? Marty cocked her head, clinging to the phone. Late for what? Who was *he*, and did serial killers travel in pairs?

Think the Hillside Stranglers, Marty.

A shiver skittered up her spine. Oh, yeah. Them.

"Screw him," the New Yorker spat. "He's a spoiled little asshole. You comin' in?"

Oh, please go in, Marty prayed. If they were both gone, she stood a better chance of making some noise and catching someone's attention.

"Nah, gotta watch the trunk. We don't need no trouble," Jersey City said.

"She's out cold. I knocked her pretty good. Besides, who the hell is out in Hooterville this late at night but the fucking raccoons? We was lucky to find a 7-Eleven in the first place."

Marty bit her fist again and clenched her eyes shut to ward off the fear. They were somewhere isolated. Sweat trickled between her breasts, her lungs heaving for air.

"We shoulda tied the dumb bitch up just in case."

Yeah, you shoulda.

"She's out, I'm tellin' ya. C'mon, relax would ya? Get a burrito or some crap and shut up."

Their grumbling continued, as their voices moved farther away.

It was now or never.

Panic, terror, the crash of her heart in her ears, and a stomach that threatened to make her yark all over herself, made for a rush of adrenalin that surged through her. The only obvious choice was to make some noise.

Yet she remained frozen. What if they caught her screaming bloody murder? Wouldn't the punishment they intended to dole out be far worse if she created a scene?

Marty? How much do you care, if in the end they're going to hack you up into little, unidentifiable pieces?

Well, there was that.

And they did call you a dumb bitch. Not just a bitch, but a dumb one.

Marty's eyes narrowed.

Anger became more than just an emotion. It became a filmy aftertaste in her mouth, lingering on her tongue, infuriating her, seeping into every pore of her body.

That fury, coupled with the idea that those freaks would make mincemeat out of her, set her in motion.

It was time to attract some attention.

So dumb bitch this.

Curling into a tight ball, she positioned her feet against the roof of the trunk, taking a long, deep breath. Marty began to kick upward, screaming for help. The leverage she had to work with was minimal, but she managed to get a good angle, and she went with it, focusing all her energy on hitting her target relentlessly.

Her haze of anger was ten different shades of red. She lost track of anything but the spot she'd planted her feet on and the hope that someone would hear her. She kicked at her target furiously. Her legs burned, screaming with sharp fissures of pain that gnawed at her thighs and calves. Her spine ached, and her arms threatened to give way as she held herself in place.

She almost missed the chilled, autumn breeze that wafted over the fresh blood trickling down her calf.

She stopped thrashing for a moment, bewildered. Her eyes opened and adjusted, squinting at what must be a streetlamp in the parking lot. There was a torn, jagged hole in the ceiling of the trunk that enabled her to see the black, starless sky.

Holy friggin' freaky.

She'd kicked her way out of the trunk of a car.

A. Car.

Fancy that.

MARTY clung to a tree waiting for Keegan to show up. Dried blood left uneven trails over the length of her legs, angry splotches of an ugly reminder.

And how nice. Her sandals were history. Obliterated.

Her stomach lurched again at the thought of her legs, cut and bleeding. They'd been pretty trashed when she'd first climbed out of the car and took off for the nearby woods. It had taken everything she had in her to keep from sobbing when she'd seen the two men exit the 7-Eleven and view the trunk. The air became rife with their rage, confusion, and finally, their horror at the condition she'd left the trunk in.

However, now her limbs had only faint, puckered marks to remind her of her escape and quite frankly, it was flipping her out.

If she'd ever had a WTF moment before, this was the mac-daddy of 'em all. She'd been a raw, torn, bloody mess, and now, an hour later, she had but mere scratches that looked like she'd fought with a thorny rosebush, not the steel trunk of a car.

Unfortunately, that wasn't the only sign that her life had run amok. Marty scrunched her eyes shut and shuddered. She would not dwell on what she'd discovered when she looked to see how much damage the back of her skirt had suffered.

Running her hands over her skirt pocket, she lingered over her out-of-charge cell phone. Why she hadn't dialed 911 instead of Wanda and Nina was a hindsight mystery to her. Her only explanation was panic had taken hold, and she hadn't been thinking clearly.

Looking at the back of her skirt, it was probably a good thing she hadn't called the police.

Never in a gazillion years did she ever think she'd be glad to see Keegan's number in her cell phone directory, until about an hour and a half ago, when she'd frantically called him and he'd answered with a gruff bark. He was the only logical call to make at that point, considering her newest predicament. She'd made that call, quaking with the idea that maybe Keegan Flaherty's wild tales weren't so wild after all.

Her uncontrollable sobs led to a fractured conversation

as Marty tried to help him locate her. Her fear of being found by her kidnappers kept her rooted to the spot in the woods she'd fled to for safety. The supersonic, bionic vision she'd suddenly acquired aided her in seeing the sign for the highway she was closest to. He'd talked to her until her cell phone battery had died, gently asking coaxing questions she couldn't answer for the mass of confusion and terror that plagued her.

Now she waited in the damp recesses of the woods riddled with gut-wrenching fear that the two men would come back and take another shot at her. The long branch she held in her grip for protection shook fiercely in her tight clutch. No one was stuffing her back in some frickin' trunk. If they came back, she'd crack their heads open.

And then, a thought, outrageous and forbidden, occurred to her.

She probably could because she was a—a . . .

No, Marty stopped her thoughts short. Do not go to the place called crazy now. You don't have time to dwell.

The night was cool and silky black, yet Marty could see every nuance of her hiding place, hear the crickets rub their legs together on the autumn air. The changing leaves on the trees were brilliant, lining the back road in thick groves. Her eyes scanned the deserted area for Keegan. Not a single car had pulled into the parking lot of the convenience store since the two men had left. They sure weren't kidding when they'd called this place Hooterville.

When Keegan's car pulled up with a roar, she flew from the edge of the woods straight into his arms, dropping the branch and forgetting that he was the cause of this newest predicament. He had to be. Her life had been pretty mundane before meeting Keegan.

His hard, muscled arms automatically wrapped around her, warm and protective. The comfort they brought flowed into her like a cup of warm chicken soup. Marty buried her face in the crisp white shirt he wore, inhaling his light cologne and fighting the urge to bawl open-mouthed like an infant.

"God, Marty, are you okay?" His question rumbled against the top of her head. Was that concern she heard?

That he hadn't yelled "I told you so" just yet made it harder for her to keep her tears in check. She rolled her head no on his chest in response. Words escaped her, while she clung to his tall frame. His hands were large and reassuring as they made soothing circles across the width of her back.

The nurturing gesture made her forget her resolve to stay strong. She began to cry in earnest with hysterical gulps for air. Fat, salty bubbles of water streamed down her face, leaving a puddle of mascara on his pristine, white shirt.

Keegan gripped her upper arms with big hands and made her look up at him. "I said, are you okay?" His fingers grazed the top of her head to touch the patch of dried blood on her scalp, now crusted over and beginning to heal.

Marty stiffened and swiped at her tear-reddened eyes, looking up at him, his face finally registered. The impact of what had just happened hit her all at once. Disbelief and anger took a firm hold. Did this look okay? What about this was okay? Anger came on in full swing again, and she found herself shouting, "You know what? That has to be the lamest question ever in a time of crisis. Who in their right mind asks someone who's just been kidnapped if they're okay? Do you think I'm okay after being knocked out, kidnapped, and finally kicking my way out of the trunk of the car owned—no doubt—by a couple of deranged murderers? I kicked my way out of that trunk like the Bionic Freaking Woman, Keegan. Not to mention my legs were torn to high hell when I climbed out of that trunk, and now I have scratches. Scratches! Do you have any idea how not okay that is? Nooo, I'm most definitely not okay."

Keegan's arms grew stiff, his body tensing against hers. "Why the hell didn't you call the police if you had a phone?"

She heard the disbelief in his husky tone, and it sent her

over the edge. How dare he question the means by which she chose to save her own life? Her hands pushed at his arms that held her imprisoned. She snapped her head back with a derisive snort to gaze into those black, unreadable eyes. "I don't know why I didn't at first. Fear? Panic? The fact that I wasn't exactly thinking clearly while in some serial killer's trunk? It does tend to make even the calmest in a crisis freak out. But tell me something. Would you call the police if you had this?" She pointed to her backside—her backside with the new, fuzzy appendage—and arched her eyebrow. "Do you see why you were the only logical choice? How the fuck am I supposed to walk around for the rest of my life with *this*?" she wailed.

Keegan's laughter boiled slowly, rippling along the hum of the cold evening air, swirling around her head and taunting her as it grew. The sudden quaking of his body suggested he was going to have a good laugh on her. "I—I'm soooor—rrry." He was literally cackling with a high-pitched keen. "I know I shouldn't—shouldn't—laaaaugh." He held his sides and bent over at the waist, taking deep, stuttering breaths to control his outburst. Standing up straight again, Keegan sucked in his cheeks and pasted on a serious frown. "I tried to tell you, Marty, but you just wouldn't listen." He'd managed to contain his laughter, but his grin became smug again, all dimples and teeth.

He was deriving far too much pleasure from her state of affairs, which she might consider comical if it were happening to anyone else but her. Another snort of disgust escaped her lips. "Yeah, I know. Forgive me for not falling for the 'you're a werewolf' bullshit. Who in a million friggin' years would confuse a statement like that with fiction?" she asked sarcastically, throwing her hands up in the air.

His hand went to the sprout of hair pushing through her ripped skirt. "So the shift has begun."

Shift, shmift. "Something has begun. Something that I'm not happy about. Something you say you did, and I want you to fix, so I can go back to my life!" Wait, did she really want to go back to her life, inaccessible to everything

and everyone but her career? Lord, and was now really the
time to have a reflective Dr. Phil moment?

Keegan's square jaw clenched, and he ran a hand
through his thick, black hair. Again, the cold mask he wore
so well replaced the one that had openly mocked her. "This
is your life now, Marty. There's nothing I can do to change
it. If I could, I would, believe me," he added with what
sounded suspiciously like disgust. Or was it disappoint-
ment? Like it was her fault he felt either way? "Look, right
now we have more important things to take care of than
you bitching at me about something I tried to tell you in the
first place. Like who did this and why? Have you pissed off
a customer or two lately? Maybe screwed up one of those
color wheels you babble about?"

That he would even suggest she had created dissatisfac-
tion in a customer made her blood boil. Marty circled her
face with a finger, glaring at him. "Does this look like the
face of a woman who has any clue who would knock her
out and stuff her in the trunk of a car? My life was pretty
'crazy-guy' free before you showed up talking about werewolves and raw meat."

Tears began to fill the corners of her eyes again when
she remembered just how alone she'd felt in that trunk. Her
life had indeed been pretty crazy free, but it also had been
isolated by her ambition, and there was no one to blame but
herself for that predicament. Marty shrugged off her lack
of girl's-night-out adventures and ignored the harsh ache of
realizing that she had no interests outside of work.

"Tell me what you saw. What you heard. What they
looked like. Where you were when this went down." The
determination in his voice was sharp as he pierced her with
his gaze. For whatever reason, that stare always left her
feeling like she'd been interrogated silently and with glaring disapproval.

Her mind's eye had plenty in its memory, but she
couldn't summon up what those men had looked like, even
though she knew she'd seen them when they came out to

find the car's trunk damaged. Marty rubbed the heel of her hand against her forehead. "I can't remember a whole lot. Forgive me for being immobilized by the fear I might be turned into some freak's idea of a jigsaw puzzle, tough guy. I was walking back from the bodega I always go to on Eighth, and the next thing I know, I wake up in the trunk of a car with only my cell phone. Thank God they didn't take my cell. I heard them when we stopped here at the 7-Eleven with the scenic view by the woods. There were two of them. One had a New York accent, the other Jersey City. That much I do know. They called me dumb—and a bitch if you want to haggle over words," she added with embarrassment.

Keegan gave another sharp bark of laughter.

She seethed. "I don't know what you think is so funny about . . ." Her words trailed off, and her mood took another turn. Suddenly, she remembered distinctly one of the last things New York had said. *Screw him. He's a spoiled little asshole.* "Wait, I do remember this." She gripped the sleeve of his shirt with excitement. "The one with the New York accent said, 'Screw him. He's a spoiled little asshole.' " She clapped her hands together, proud to have remembered even that much. "Yes, that's what he said. Whoever they were, they weren't the people who wanted me, I guess. They were talking about the person that thought kidnapping me was an adventure I'd lacked in my life up till now." Some spoiled asshole did, anyway. The idea that someone had intentionally done this left her more terrified than the problem she currently had sitting right on her ass. This hadn't been random.

That chiseled face grew harder still. Marty could see the wheels turning in his head, and it was making her uncomfortable.

"Well, that clears that up. You're coming back with me." Keegan's order was stern while he ushered her with a forceful hand to his car.

"Shouldn't we go to the police?"

"Yep, and we can call them from my cell phone on our way to my house upstate. I'm not taking you anywhere near your apartment."

Upstate? "Whoa, whoa, whoa," she yelped, digging her bare heels into the pavement. "What do you mean, coming with you? I'm going home to my apartment and my dog. Oh, and my life. You know, the one you say you stole?" She jabbed at him as a reminder.

"Marty, I'm not going to put up with any more of your shit tonight. If what you say is true, that your life was peachy before you met me, then your kidnapping has to be a result of my biting you."

Her mouth dropped open. "You aren't going to put up with any more of my shit? You, buddy"—she stuck a finger in his hard chest—"are nuts. I wasn't the one who did this. In the scheme of putting up with shit, I think I win." She pointed again to the protrusion from her ass.

"I told you—"

"Yeah, yeah. Fine. You gave me the heads-up. Whatever. If you know people who'd do this to me, I want nothing to do with you."

"I'm not some criminal. I just said it has to be related to me."

"Yeah, it's the 'has to be' part that's freaking me out."

"You're safer with me than with anyone else."

"I'm not going anywhere but home, and if you won't take me, maybe I'll flap my arms and see if I have wings now, too."

"Marty . . ."

There it was again, that warning that wasn't really a warning but a demand to do as she was told. She planted her hands on her hips and faced him with a defiant tilt of her head. "Yes?"

"Get in the car."

"No."

"Yes."

"Say please."

"Marty!" he shouted with a growl loud enough to make an echo.

Wow, he was so hot when he was mad. It made her tingle in all the right places.

She shook her head. "I am not getting in the car with you until you tell me where we're going and what your suspicions about this are. I have Muffin to think about." God, that sounded so pathetic. She didn't even have a plant she could claim she needed to water.

Keegan rolled his eyes heavenward, as if he were asking for the gift of patience. "We're going to my family's home. It's near Buffalo, and I'm not taking no for an answer. Not until the police figure out who shoved you in the trunk of a car. Unless you want to risk the chance that they might try it again and finally succeed."

Oh, yeah. There was that to consider. "Couldn't we just go back to your apartment in the city?"

"I'm needed at home, Marty."

"But the police—"

"They can question you anywhere. If I have to, I'll bring you back to the city myself for them to do it, but for now I'm not letting you out of my sight."

"But Muffin—"

"I'll send someone for her."

"But you don't have a key."

"I don't need a key."

"And her food. I can only get it at the specialty gourmet dog delicatessen."

"Tell me where it is, and I'll buy some."

"My clothes. I can't just leave without any clothes, and these are ruined."

"We'll buy more."

"Work. I can't just go off and leave my Bobbie-Sue customers without notice. They rely on me for deliveries and advice and—"

"We have Internet access. Email them."

"I prefer the personal touch."

"They can't get makeup tips from a dead woman."

Hmmmm. There was some truth to that statement. "My life—you want me to just leave my life for an indefinite period of time. I can't just leave everything."

"Marty, you don't have a life outside of work, and you won't have a life at all if whoever took you wants you dead."

Marty gulped hard. Dead. Death. He'd said those two words again. "Er, how did we decide that death was a part of their kidnapping plan? Why do I feel like you know something you're not telling me?" she countered with suspicion.

He shook his dark head. "I know nothing of the sort. But it's a logical conclusion, don't you think? You're not rich, so money wasn't the objective. You're not a public figure with any kind of pull in government or society, and kidnapping someone usually has some kind of motive in those areas, right? And to make matters worse, didn't you tell me on the phone they had your purse? Your identification was in it, wasn't it?"

She nodded.

"Then they can find your apartment."

Nothing irked her more than him knowing her financial status, and she couldn't say why she felt so irrationally upset by it. "How do you know I'm not rich?"

Keegan shoved a hand into the pocket of his jeans. "I know everything there is to know about you, Marty. I also know you probably like alive more than dead." His words were ominous and evasive.

"You know, I don't like the idea that you've been fishing around in my life without asking."

"It was for your own good, Marty."

"And this." She pointed again to the tuft of hair on her ass. "Is this for my own good?"

"There are a lot of changes you'll experience, and I've told you this repeatedly. You just chose not to listen."

Crossing her arms over her chest, Marty clucked her tongue. She'd grown a little tired of his ire over her unwillingness to simply accept his explanations without question. "I'm only going to say this one more time. Would you listen if some guy came to your door and declared you were a werewolf? Why not try to look at it from my perspective, Wolfman? It's completely absurd. It's like a Steven Spielberg movie or something. How about you walk a mile in my shoes and then get all pissy over my disbelief? It's not like you told me something people hear everyday. 'Surprise! You, Marty Andrews, are a werewolf. Wanna eat raw meat and bay at the moon?' I think you oughta ask yourself how feasible a revelation like that is to someone like me who never even considered that werewolves were anything more than a myth or a forensics case on *CSI*." As she finished, she let her irritation leak into her tone. How could he possibly question her haze of confusion and fear?

Keegan chuckled, his face relaxing a bit. His sleek, dark head dipped in agreement, followed by a sigh. "You're right. It does sound unbelievable I suppose. It's not something I've ever had to tell a person before either, so could I get a little credit for listening to you go on and on about that Bobbie-Sue and her color wheels? Really, there wasn't any other way to tell you, and it's obvious," he said, pointing his long finger at her butt, "you had to be told. I did try to do it before something like this happened."

Emotions Marty couldn't define washed over her in a flood of uncertainty. When Keegan wanted to, he could be anything but the abrasive shit he usually was, and she didn't like the way it made her pulse race. Their conversations thus far ranged from heated to the surreal and there was no in between. "Well, now you've told me, and I don't have a whole lot of choice but to trust you, do I?" She had no family to turn to, and, even if she did, how in the hell could she tell them something like this?

"You don't have any family." He stated a fact he clearly already knew, but it was delivered with a gentleness she'd only witnessed when he'd talked her down on the phone.

Sighing, Marty nodded. "No. Not anymore." Her mother

had passed away two years ago from leukemia. She'd raised Marty alone, determined to prove she could manage on her own without the support of an extended family who had shunned her when they'd found out she was pregnant with Marty. At least that was the story Marty had been told. Throughout most of her life, she'd never asked many questions about her father. She knew she didn't have one, and when she brought it up, her mother shut up. He was gone, and he wasn't coming back. Never one to push too far, Marty had let it go.

Her mother only spoke of her father once not long before she'd died. It was a somber recollection, tinged with a bittersweet memory of what had been a doomed affair from the start. He was married; her mother had been foolish. End of the affair.

When she'd discovered she was the product of an affair, it didn't break her stride or shame her in the least, but it did leave her wondering a great many things she'd probably never have answers for.

Keegan's hand brushed against hers, latching onto her pinky finger. "I'm sorry."

Marty smiled, fending off the butterflies his touch created in her stomach, and moved her hand away. "It's okay. I had a great mom, or did you already know that, too?"

"I only know the facts, not the emotions that go with them."

"Then you must know I can take care of myself." She attempted to keep the stubborn independence she so prided herself on out of her voice.

"I do, but that was before you were one of us. Now you have us to rely on."

"Define *us*." Her hesitance was clear when she lowered her eyes to her shredded sandals.

Keegan pulled her behind him, back toward his black Mustang. "It's not easy to define, but to sum it up in one word, *pack* would be it. You belong to a pack now, and you get all the glory being a pack member brings." She noted he said those words with a mixture of affection and irritation.

Christ. What was left? Packs and raw meat and hairy

legs and werewolves and whatever was on her ass. Her head spun from the implications this left her with. A pack represented a close-knit community in her mind. Sharing and all that other garbage she really sucked at. "Care to explain this glory?"

"You're never, ever alone. Ever." Keegan smiled and shrugged his broad shoulders. The collar of his shirt brushed the ends of his hair, and Marty wanted to reach out and wrap the ends of it around her finger. "For someone like you, I don't know if that's going to be a good thing, but we'll take care of you no matter what."

The warmth the idealistic notion of a family brought made her uncomfortable. She'd always been an only child, with a mother who'd worked full time and then some. Marty loved people from afar. Not in packs. "Is it like some kind of Waltons thing, where we all say goodnight to each other?" she joked, running a hand over her matted hair.

His full lower lip rolled upward. "I'd say we're more Ewing with only a splash of the Waltons. We know how to stick together when it counts."

"Why is it so important that I go with you?"

Again his eyes skimmed the wooded area, avoiding hers. "For your safety, of course."

She wasn't falling for that. Not totally. There was something else she just couldn't pinpoint. An underlying, unspoken thing Keegan wasn't ready to ante up. "I'm an intruder," she stated without dithering. Marty wasn't much for beating around the bush, and the idea that she was shoving her way into a place she didn't ask to be made her more than a little uncomfortable.

"No, you're mi—er, with me. I'm the alpha male of my pack. What I say goes. Well, it doesn't always go. Some just do what they want to drive me to drink, but overall, I'm the authority."

Marty wasn't so easily swayed. "That doesn't mean everyone has to like it because you deem it so. I mean, I bet they're not going to be happy about some strange ex-human turned were-woman showing up."

His eyes flashed an emotion Marty couldn't place. "They'll like it because I say they have to like it."

Oh, good. He was that kind of male whateverhe'dcalledit. The Neanderthal kind. "You can't shove me down people's throats."

"Yeah," he said with arrogance, "I can."

"Where does your family live again?"

"Near Buffalo."

"But you have an apartment in New York."

"When you meet the family, you'll see why."

"I don't understand how I could have missed you. You only live right down the hall."

Keegan shrugged. "I'd say it was a testament to your social life, but I only moved in a few weeks ago, and I'm not there as often as I'd like. It's really just a place for me to escape the pressures of running a pack."

Marty remained indecisive, though she realized her choices were severely limited. She could put on a tough, independent front and go back to her apartment, possibly be nabbed again, maybe even killed for whatever bizarre interest these men had in her. She couldn't afford a hotel, and again, that friend issue came up. She didn't have any. Not a close friend anyway. So it wasn't like she could borrow someone's couch. On the other hand, she could take his hand extended in trust and hope for the best. "How do I know you're not some crazy serial killer werewolf?"

His grin was cocky. "You don't."

"Does your family know I'm just dropping in? Do they know what happened?"

"They were forewarned, and yes, they know I accidentally bit you."

"And they feel how about that?"

"The bite?"

Marty nodded, her neck growing stiffer by the minute. Exhaustion was setting in, and her muscles were beginning to protest.

Keegan's eyes looked off into the distant woods again, once more avoiding her gaze. "They were shocked obviously. Something like this—a bite to another human—hasn't happened for a long time. I can only speak for my pack, but I'd venture to say no pack member has bitten anyone intentionally in many centuries. Yes, that's how we began, but we've evolved and learned to satisfy our needs in other ways. We do live by a fairly strict code, and biting—intentionally, anyway—just isn't allowed. We really don't go around trying to turn everyone into werewolves. In fact, most of us were born pure werewolf. So this unfortunate incident is something we don't know much about. But yeah, we did discuss it briefly and decided that of course you couldn't be left to your own devices with so many changes about to occur. We weren't sure what those changes would be, because you were one hundred percent human before I bit you, but so far they're pretty typical. Learning to shift will be your biggest challenge."

"Hah!" she barked. "Yeah, that and shaving my legs twice a day."

Keegan laughed again, and Marty found the sound pleasant to her ears. It was warm and rich and almost genuine. "That will lessen once you learn to control your body and make it do what you want it to do. Not the other way around."

Marty let her head fall back on her shoulders to ease the tension in her neck. "God, this really is crazy you know. I'd keep right on believing that if it weren't for this little factoid on my ass." She wiggled her butt in his direction, emitting a tired giggle born from stress and fatigue.

Keegan put his hand on her shoulder and gave it a squeeze. The tingle he'd evoked from her before returned, skipping along her spine. "It's been a helluva day, Marty. We have a long trip ahead of us."

"But I didn't say I'd go with you."

"Got other options?"

A long sigh let loose from her lips. "No. No, I don't, but I guess I don't have to stay if I hate it, right? I can always take my chances back in the city." She made the statement, hoping for reassurance.

"How about we talk about that tomorrow? We have a long drive ahead of us."

He was avoiding her questions, and if she weren't so tired and in need of a long, hot shower, she might pursue why. Because he was doing it badly. "Okay, but only until we figure out who's doing this. Then I'm going home."

His smile was as vague as his answer. "Sure you are."

"Where are we, anyway?"

"Poughkeepsie. A long way from Buffalo."

"You promise to get Muffin? By now she's probably crossing her legs to keep from making potties in my apartment."

"I promise." His answer was a solemn nod of consent.

Marty held up her finger. "Pinky swear?"

Keegan's chest heaved as he exhaled, but he wrapped his pinky around hers. "Pinky swear."

The touch of their fingers brought her comfort, and she had no explanation as to why. She also had no time to dwell on it. Her mental list of items she'd need from her apartment was growing. There were things a girl just couldn't live without, so Keegan would have to get them when he retrieved Muffin. "I need another purse. Can you get me my Prada knockoff? It's in my closet on the shelf. Pink. It's pink. I got it from a vendor in Manhattan. Jeez he was a tough negotiator, but it was worth the haggling. It's soooo cute."

Keegan sighed, raspy and long. "Okay."

"Oh! And my nail polish. I have two new bottles in the bathroom under the sink in one of those cute organizer baskets, you know? Like the ones you get at Bed Bath and Beyond? God, I love those. Anyway, I need Retro Red and Winsome Wisteria."

Another sigh followed, and then a nod of consent.

"My moisturizer. I never go anywhere, not even overnight, without my moisturizer. Not that I ever really go anywhere, but anyway I need it, or my skin will dehydrate and it could just be ugly. Top left side of my medicine cabinet."

"Er, okay."

"My shoes. I can't be without shoes. Let's see. I need my tennis shoes and my white sandals, because I don't think there's much hope for these, wouldn't you say?" Marty looked up at him and saw impatience written all over his face. "And my laptop. I can't check on my clients without my laptop, and they need me. Plus, there's that no-good bitch Linda Fisher. I have to watch that she's not stealing my accounts. Do you have all of that?"

He gave her that stern look again. The one that made her insides skedaddle around even if it was meant in reproach. "I'm going too far, huh?"

His smile was crooked. "Just a smidge."

"Okay, then. I guess I'll do without. Thank you for giving me a place to go."

When he turned to look at her, his eyes held hers again in that mystical, penetratingly fierce gaze. "You'll always have a place to go now, Marty. Always."

The seriousness of his words brought with them the rise of goose bumps on her arms. She ran her hands over them, smiling up at him to lighten the mood. "So, are we going to talk about how I came out of this with only scratches and this thing on my ass? Or are we going to pretend we don't really see it, like you would if someone had a big, pus-filled zit on their face?"

Walking her around to the passenger side of the car, Keegan put his hand at her waist, leaning into her ear to half whisper, "It's your tail, Marty. Or what will be your tail once you fully learn to shift. Your anger must trigger your shift, and among other things, I bet you were probably angry in the trunk of that car."

Just what every girl needed. A tail. How trendy.

Sliding into the passenger seat, Marty looked up at him. "I get the impression there's a whole lot more to this werewolf thing than you're letting on."

He nodded and grinned. "And then some."

"So spill it."

Keegan shut the car door and walked around to his side,

climbing in with ease for having such a large frame. "Small doses, Marty. It's better if the information comes in small doses."

Marty clicked her seat belt into place and leaned back on the headrest, letting her eyes close. "Look, I still say if I'm going to sprout wings it's only fair you tell me now."

Keegan started the car with a roar of the engine. "No wings. I promise."

"I think the shit in my life has officially hit the fan," she joked.

His dark profile, sharp and crisp, nodded. "Sorta."

"Keegan?"

"Marty?"

"I'm a werewolf, aren't I?"

"Yep, lock, stock, and full-moon howl."

Shit, meet fan.

CHAPTER
6

"I said find her and find her now!" he thundered, leaning against the cool glass of his penthouse suite window for support. The surrounding buildings and their random patterns of light left him without the pleasure he typically derived from them. Gut wrenching fear and anxiety built in his chest, tightening his throat. Desperation didn't suit him. It didn't suit him at all.

The shuffle of defeated feet on the marble floors reached his ears, grating and sharp. "We're doing our best," was the reply.

"No! Your best would have Marty standing here in front of me where she should be. How could you have possibly lost track of her?"

"Sir, I promise you, we'll find Ms. Andrews."

Reassurance. He didn't need reassurance. He needed results, and he needed them immediately.

"At all costs. You find her at all costs, and if you've left one stone unturned, it'll be your hide!" he spat.

Anger ripped through him, irrational and blinding, making him grip the expensive material of the curtains to slow the racing of his pulse. He straightened, gathering his wits and curbing his temper before it got the better of him.

This needed to be handled.

It needed to be handled promptly and without any unnecessary attention drawn to it.

Now.

A LONG, spiral staircase greeting her bleary eyes and the thump of Keegan's solid chest against her side before he'd deposited her on the cushiest of beds evah, with the order to "get some rest," were the last things she could remember before waking up in some crazy upstate New York version of Southfork.

Marty snorted.

It did look like Southfork, too—like the *Dallas* Southfork. Big, sprawling, with a chandelier and a fireplace in the frickin' bedroom, for crap's sake. Who had a fireplace in their bedroom? Werewolves clearly didn't mind a touch of opulence—a big touch. Stretching, she burrowed farther under the sheets, sheets that were clinging to the new stubble on her legs.

God save the queen. She had to shave again.

Groaning, she opted to snuggle under the warmth of the comforter and revel in these sheets very obviously not purchased at *Wal-Mart*. Soft as a summer breeze and hugging her every curve, they smelled of expensive scents.

Thankfully, they didn't smell like big dog.

Dog. She was a dog.

Jesus Christ in a miniskirt. There was no denying what had happened last night.

She was an honest-to-goodness, car-chasing, howl-at-the-moon, fur-shedding *dog*.

Woof-woof.

That thought brought with it a flush of panic, and she hurriedly rolled over, running her hand along her backside. Still in her torn clothes, she found the place on her ass that had had a bit more hair on it last night than she was comfortable admitting.

Thank God it was gone. Her fluffy stump of a pathetic tail had virtually disappeared. For now anyway, and who knew when it might pop back up. Rubbing the heel of her hand over her eyes, Marty sighed. She'd bet her bippy no one else in her *pack* had a tail that looked like hers.

And wouldn't all the other werewolves laugh at her because of it? Exclude her from werewolf games when they saw just how pitiful her tail really was? It was too Rudolph-esque for her tastes.

Last night came back to her in waves. Christ, she was in a strange man's house, who claimed he was a werewolf, after she had been hurled into the trunk of a car by unknown thugs who were going to deliver her with a *tail* to some *asshole* as yet unnamed.

How did she even really know Keegan was a werewolf? Yeah, she had some kooky shit goin' on from her caboose, but had she seen him do that shift thing to prove what he said was true?

Er, no. Of all the gullible, retarded, dipshit things to do, she'd gone home with him.

But then, he'd known far more about the conversation she'd had with Wanda and Nina that night in the alleyway than was possible if he were lying.

A grip was decidedly in order here.

She'd almost fall for the idea this was some kind of cosmic joke but for the evidence that had popped out of her ass last night. That was no fabrication. Even if Keegan Flaherty was an ace liar, there was no denying her tail.

Omigod—she had a tail. And not a nice plush one either. It was a little nub of nothing in comparison to what she remembered of Keegan's. It wasn't even as nice as Muffin's. Maybe if it filled in she could get one of those poofy hairdos the groomer gave Muff. Tie a bow on it? A bow in her color wheel of course.

Mary Mother and all twelve apostles, she was considering flattering styles for her tail. Her *tail*.

Marty, Marty, Marty. What's next? A pink collar and matching leash?

A squeal of panic slipped from her lips, and she clapped a hand over her mouth to keep from being heard.

Her ears perked to the sound of Keegan's deep voice from behind the heavy, oak door, and if she was hearing correctly, his tone was less than thrilled.

Wow, what a surprise. It seemed he was always impatient about something.

Her supersonic ears picked up another voice too—an angry, hushed one. Curiosity made her slide from the warmth of the bed, planting her feet on the floor and digging her toes into the thick carpeting. Crossing the large expanse of the bedroom, she tiptoed to the door. God, she really *was* the Bionic Woman now. She'd just clearly heard the words *Pack Cosmetics* come from the lips of the Mantasy known as Keegan.

The single largest retail cosmetics company in the world.

What in theee hell?

While Pack was retail-based and Bobbie-Sue was door-to-door, multilevel, they were still the name to be reckoned with in the industry. Not to mention, a competitor to a degree.

So wait like one Bobbie-Sue minute. What did Keegan have to do with Pack Cosmetics?

Her door popped open, and Keegan stuck his midnight dark head around it. "Look who's up." He smiled with his disarming, pearly white grin.

Yeah, up and looking like she'd been on a three-day bender, involving some booze and a running bar tab. Yep. She was up. Marty ran a hand over her mussed hair, skimming a finger beneath her eyes to wipe away the residue of mascara caked under them. A tantalizing scent wafted up from those crazy long stairs, distracting her momentarily. Was that Eggs Benedict she smelled? With bacon? Bacon. Ohhhhh, bacon! Glorious in its promise to slap some cellulite directly on her tail-licious ass. She sniffed again. It was definitely bacon and hash browns, probably browned to perfection country style in butter even . . .

"Hey, I brought your clothes." He nudged her with a suitcase, pushing his way into the bedroom and leaving someone who looked suspiciously like him to stand in the hallway.

Her nose swiftly changed gears, inhaling Keegan's scent. It was unique, and strangely, she'd have known it was Keegan's special blend blindfolded with duct tape jammed in her nostrils. It settled in her nose like an old friend, enveloping her senses. Marty tried to focus on the suitcase and not his chiseled, freshly shaven jaw.

Her stuff. He had her stuff. "Ohhhh, thank you! Is Muffin okay?"

He smiled. "Yep."

She blew out a relief-filled breath. "Did you get my Prada knockoff?"

Keegan nodded and rolled his eyes. "I guess that's what it is."

"Oh, and my moisturizer?"

He blew out that long-winded sigh of exasperation he'd mastered and cracked his jaw. His nostrils flared, and again Marty couldn't help but think how crazy-sexy he was when he was agitated. "Yes, Marty. I have the moisturizer. I have the whole damned bathroom and bedroom closet and some bunch of crap from the hall closet. Shoes, purses, and more makeup than Marilyn Manson ever had. There's more downstairs." He pointed over his shoulder for reference.

"You know," she said with the cluck of her tongue, tilting her head to look up at him, "I'm not one hundred percent in love with your sarcasm about my makeup. I sell it for a living, FYI. Remember the whole lavender deal you screwed up so royally by biting me? Having Marilyn Manson-like booty is my job, you sky blue convertible wrecker. You probably brought some of the samples I keep. Any good Bobbie-Sue rep knows makeup should be an enhancer not a mask of goop. You really only need four or five things to express your color aura properly."

"Is that the conclusion to the Bobbie-Sue sermon for today?" He rolled his tongue along the inside of his cheek and rocked back on his heels.

Now it was her turn to sigh in exasperation. "I don't wear everything you brought, Wolfman Jack. And that brings me to this—what do you, a mere man, er, were-whatever, know about something like Pack Cosmetics?" Crossing her arms over her torn shirt, she waited for an answer.

His large shoulders bunched up nonchalantly beneath his tailored, dark blue–striped shirt when he shrugged. "Huh?"

Her eyes narrowed with suspicion. "You heard me. I heard you and whoever that is skulking outside the door say Pack Cosmetics, and don't tell me I didn't, because I do, thanks to you, have that bionic hearing thing happening. I'm so hoping more perks are involved in this were-wolf gig, too. Time will tell, eh? But for now I know what I heard. So what gives?"

"Um, my family owns it?" He gave her a sheepish grin with his admission.

"They *what*?"

"We own it. Keegan's Pack's CEO," the man outside her door said. He smiled as a way of introduction, sticking his long tapered hand out for her to shake. Tall and as dark as Keegan, he was leaner than Keegan, but still as impressively good looking. His hair was shorter and maybe a shade lighter than wolfman's, but just as thick and luxurious. Definitely an autumn.

The deep grooves on either side of his mouth deepened when he grinned, just like Keegan's. "I'm Sloan. Keegan's younger brother. It's a pleasure to meet my first hu—er, never mind. It's just a pleasure."

She held out her hand for Sloan and absentmindedly smiled. The Flaherty brothers had been hit with a tsunami of hotness by the hottie Gods.

And they owned Pack Cosmetics.

Werewolves owned a major cosmetics company.

Did that mean vampires owned Sax Fifth Avenue?

The world had surely tipped on its axis as far as she was concerned, but it all made sense with a name like Pack.

Keegan put a finger under her chin and pushed upward, closing her gaping mouth and relieving her from the firm grip Sloan had on her hand. "I have to bet your mouth hanging open like that isn't very Bobbie-Sue-ish," he joked.

"I gotta go." Sloan slapped Keegan on the back good-naturedly. "Seeing as my big brother here has been slacking off to bite humans, work's gotten all backed up." He smiled a grin that was similar to his brother's and took his leave, his deep-throated chuckle following him out.

Marty remained rooted in place, astounded. "You do not either own Pack Cosmetics."

Dropping the suitcase on the floor by the bed, he nodded his slick, black head. The tendrils of hair, evidently still damp from his shower, curled against the collar of his shirt. Hair that would probably feel like silk on her fingertips . . . brush seductively against her naked breasts, whisper across her abdomen, slide along her . . .

Whoa, Nellie.

Tart. Jezebel. Hoo-chie.

"Do so, too. It's not some big secret. You could have found that out by looking on the Internet if you were interested enough. In fact, I'm surprised you didn't at least look up my name. Like Google me, you know? Then you would have seen I'm not the nut you thought I was," he finished smugly. "Oh, and I called your friends. Wanda and Nina, right? I let them know you were with me here in Buffalo."

"How did you find their numbers?"

"On your fridge, according to Victor."

"Victor?"

"Yeah, Victor. He works for us. He's who picked up Princess and your things."

"Her name is Muffin, and is he a werewolf, too, or some other crazy supernormal species? Like say a warlock or maybe a genie? How cool would a genie be? Maybe he could grant me a wish—like a wish that includes me going back to the way I was before you lopped off a piece of my hand."

"I didn't lop. I mistakenly bit you, and we're *paranormal*," he corrected haughtily.

"A who?"

"Paranormal. We're considered paranormal if you go by what The Discovery Channel labels us. Not supernormal. That would imply that we're all obscenely average," he said on a husky chuckle.

That very chuckle set her teeth on edge. It was scrumptiously sinful, washing along her spine like cascades of warm water. And she wasn't having it. It was too easy to find herself lost in the dark chocolate of his deep brown eyes, or the way his ass fit a pair of jeans like a second skin. "So that means I'm paranormal now, too. Oh, yippee skippee. You know, all this time I was just an average Anglo Saxon, and really, I was happy that way. All I know is I have a tail now. Not much of one either. How utterly fucked up that I should become a werewolf and not be able to change, er, shift or whatever it is that I'm supposed to do properly. Only *I* could manage to accomplish that. I bet if you were a vampire and had bitten me I'd be like allergic to blood or some such crazy shit." She clapped a hand over her mouth. God, she was swearing like a drunken sailor lately.

He cocked an eyebrow at her and chose to ignore her wisecrack, moving to stand in front of her. His presence alone was daunting enough. Up close and personal it made her thighs clench together to thwart the ache that had begun to build. "Wanda said to remember to moisturize, and Nina's mouth is still just as big as it was the other night. God that woman must be a handful for some poor schmuck, and what is it about you women and face cream?"

"Well, Mr. Lip Gloss—you oughta know, being a makeup mogul and all. How could you forget to mention this little detail to me? You own a major cosmetics company! That's not like forgetting to tell me you like *Coke* rather than *Pepsi*. I mean, really. You'd already told me you were a friggin' werewolf. Why not give me a little icing with my cake?"

"You were on overload. I didn't want to overwhelm you."

"Overwhelm me? O-ver-whelm me? All this time you've known I worked for Bobbie-Sue, clearly a competitor to your company. A competitor you should make it your business to know and you didn't want to overwhelm me?" Her voice rose with the question. "Short of telling me you were God, I don't think there's much left that can overwhelm me." She shoved a hand into her matted hair and found it was stuck together with dried blood from the blow to her head, but oddly without any wound to speak of.

She mustn't dwell on that or she'd simply tip right over the edge of insanity into the dark never-never-land of there's no coming back.

Keegan shoved his hands into the pockets of his jeans and blew out another breath of air. The breath of air that screamed he was losing patience with her. "I don't know that I'd call them a competitor, per se. We're in very different markets. How about we discuss this in its entirety later?" His mood changed then and his eyes held amusement, obviously flashing his laughter at her comparison to the two companies.

With a finger directed at the solid wall of his chest, she poked him. "Oh, no, you, you paranormal person! I'm not waiting anymore. I want to know everything, and I mean everything, there is to know about this canine—"

"Lupine. We're lupine."

"Fine, *lupine* lifestyle so rudely thrust upon me. If my urges are going to lead me to pissing on trees sometime in the near future, I wanna know. I also wanna know about your company. I better get full disclosure—no more secrets. You know everything there is to know about me, because you have the kind of money to hire someone to poke around in my life, but I don't, and you wouldn't have had to poke if you'd have kept your snarling, drooling muzzle to yourself! So, in the interest of me being out in public somewhere and say, sprouting my new doggie ears, I think I deserve to know everything there is to know about this werewolf gig."

He leaned into her, the heat of his body wreaking havoc with her raw nerves, making them dance frantically. She'd pushed him too far, and although she'd wondered what would happen if she actually accomplished that task, at the same time there was that sexy, intense pulse of heat when he was agitated that made her mouth water and her nipples tighten. His lips lingered so close to hers she could see the tip of his tongue.

Her hand instinctively went to the sculpted hardness of his chest, flattening against it, and she wasn't sure if she wanted to thwart what could happen next, or encourage it. She found herself wondering what it would be like to kiss those lips that were forever compressed into a thin line of impatience. She found herself wondering what it would be like to have those hard thighs surround her with those fancy Egyptian cotton sheets at her back.

She found herself not liking where she was wanting to find herself . . .

Voices outside the door interrupted her rant. Several voices. Clearly they wanted a peek at their first ever human turned were-woman.

Marty groaned and backed away from him. How was she going to face all these people? This pack . . .

Keegan stuck his head out the door and yelled gruffly, "Family members! Go downstairs and quit being so damned nosy. I'll introduce you all as soon as Marty's had time to shower and change." With a firm hand, he shut the door and leaned back against it, crossing one ankle over the other.

Despite the confusion, his tall, sculpted frame made her pause, her breath hitching. God, these lunar-tics were del-ish. The tug of awareness she'd experienced since she'd met him was simmering just below the surface of her emotional cauldron. However, now was absolutely not the time to troll for dates.

"Marty?"

"What?"

"I'm losing you again. You distract easily, you know. I need you to focus long enough to grab a shower and change, then come downstairs to meet everyone. Muffin's down there, too. Safe and sound."

Yeah, the Judas was probably curled up in some other damned hunky werewolf's lap.

"I can't hold this pack off for long. They're curious, as I'm sure you are. Stop looking like Little Red Riding Hood. I promise we don't bite. Not on purpose anyway." He wiggled a raven-tipped eyebrow at her.

Marty giggled—genuinely laughed for the first time in over a week as he slipped out the door with a wave of his hand.

Grabbing her suitcase, she hauled it up onto the bed and sifted through it. She could do this. She didn't have a choice. There was no going back to the city right now—not after last night. Why she'd suddenly come to that conclusion must be due to how serious she'd come to believe this really was.

Straightening her shoulders, Marty cupped the back of her neck and rubbed it. Okay, a shower. She needed a shower, a good cleansing cucumber scrub and everything would be right with the world again. Reaching into the suitcase she pulled out her black pumps.

Thank the shoe fairies he'd brought her pumps.

There was nothing she couldn't face without her pumps.

Not even a pack of cosmetic company-owning werewolves.

MARTY took her time descending the winding staircase, clinging to the oak railing and fighting the trembling in her knees. Showered, shaved for like the twentieth time in a week and moisturized, she was still so not ready for this.

Closing her eyes, she took a ragged breath and smoothed a hand over the only silk skirt she owned, double-checking the buttons on her red, cheesy copy of a Liz Clairborne sweater she'd picked up at the discount designer outlet mall.

Hell's bells. Anyone with any sense of fashion would know this was a designer knockoff and surely, these pack people knew the real thing when they saw it. They had butt-loads of money.

Oy and vey. She wasn't wearing this insecure crap well at all. Where was the confident woman of a week ago, who'd just achieved her year-long goal of lavender?

You mean the salon-perfect blonde who lived and breathed nothing but her career and had no friends?

She's kaput, snookums. Done. Finito.

If the need for food hadn't overridden all else, she might have considered hiding up in that room until she could go home again. However, the obnoxious rumble in her stomach roared like a caged animal. It needed food.

Actually, it had given a lot of thought to a side of beef—rare, with maybe some barbeque sauce to dunk it in.

Fuck. A. Duck.

Raucous laughter came from the big room off the oval, high-ceilinged entryway, and so did that enticing smell of bacon. She smoothed a hand over her skirt before covering the short distance to the dining room. The clack of her heels alerted everyone to her arrival. She took a deep breath, letting it out with a shudder, and strolled in on legs of jelly.

Upon her entry, the group grew instantly silent. Marty cleared her throat and fought the rush of heat to her cheeks. The beauty of the room was in its hominess, not the pretentious designer furniture she'd expected. The long table was made of a lightly finished oak wood, warm and comforting. Each chair had thick backs with simple lines, and the seat pads were made of a plaid material. An old, wooden buffet spanned nearly the length of the wall behind the table, holding a large bowl of assorted fruits. Wall sconces that looked like lanterns bracketed each wall on either side.

Her eyes scanned the chairs filled with people with expectant faces, each as good looking as the next.

Oh, and look. Over in the corner. It was Muffin. Doing exactly as she'd thought.

Curling up in some hunky werewolf's lap, snoring contentedly. Never once did she even look up and acknowledge the woman who'd brought her friggin' gourmet dog food from that shi-shi-foo-foo deli every blessed night for the last two years.

Philistine.

Keegan pushed his chair back with a scrape of wood on expensive flooring. She was beginning to feel smaller by the moment, but Keegan held his hand out to her, and she took it in the hopes he'd hold her up if her legs gave way.

The silence engulfed her while looking upon all those bewildered werewolf faces. Funny, they didn't at all look like werewolves. The expectant pause in conversation made for an awkward moment. Seriously, what did you say at a time like this? *Family—meet Marty. You know, the chick with the rabid poodle who nearly gnawed the living shit out of me before Marty got in the way and I took a hunk out of her hand? She's one of us now. Marty—meet family. The people you'll shift with, run by the light of a full moon with, eat angus cuts of beef with.*

Fucking fabulous.

She didn't belong here. She was a freak among people she'd so callously in her delirium called freaks.

Keegan squeezed her hand, and warmth infused it, sizzling all the way up to her elbow. What the hell was that about anyway? Who said he could wander around dripping raw sexuality from every pore on his body and just get away with it? He winked one dark chocolate brown eye at her with reassurance before saying, "Everyone, this is Marty. Marty, this is my sister Mara. Victor is the man responsible for pampering the tiny tornado better known as Muffin, and well, you've met my younger brother, Sloan."

She took a hard swallow before speaking. "Hi. It's nice to meet you." Good. That was good, and she'd done it without too much tremor in her voice. Meet and greet could officially be over.

"Holy shit, Mara," Sloan said to his sister. "We got us a real live human."

"Sloan!" Keegan erupted, but Mara nudged her brother, slapping him on the arm. "Shut up, dumb ass. Like you've never screwed up? You just don't get caught." Mara rose from her seat and smiled at Marty apologetically. Her blue eyes, so unlike her brothers', held sympathy. "Sorry. I don't mean Keegan screwed up by biting you. I mean, he did, but, well, whatever. This is awkward for you, I'm sure. It's just weird all round, but I promise not to gawk at my first ever human turned were too much, okay?" She smiled again, and Marty couldn't help but think this family had hit the lottery when it came to fabulous-ness.

Keegan's sister was maybe all of twenty-five, if Marty judged by the condition of her skin alone. Even in jeans and an old, stained, oversized T-shirt, Mara had perfect skin, perfect hair, and an even more perfect body. Her skin was like ivory, her cheeks colored with no help from a jar of blush. Thick lashes like fringe surrounded each sapphire eye. All of that shining, gloriously chestnut colored hair was scraped back in a ponytail, but it didn't seem to matter. Whatever Mara did with it, Marty suspected she'd look casual chic without even trying.

If this was what happened to you when you were a werewolf, then, hoorah, baby.

Bring it, she thought ridiculously, accepting Mara's hand and smiling back. "It's okay. I understand, believe me. I appreciate your letting me stay here while, well, while things settle down."

"That was some scary stuff last night, huh?" Mara asked, taking Marty's hand from Keegan and plunking her down in the chair next to hers.

"Yes. It was definitely scary." Marty eyed the platters of food scattered on the table, coughing to keep the growl in her stomach from being heard.

"Do you have any clue who did it?" Sloan asked, shoveling a forkful of eggs into his mouth.

Marty shook her head, frowning. "No. I led a pretty quiet life before—I mean—"

Sloan held up his hand and shot her a crooked grin. "You mean before Keegan took a chunk out of your hand?" He chuckled, hunching over his plate, his shoulders shaking as he snorted.

"Ach!" a robust woman from the far side of the room chided, pushing past the double swinging doors with a generous hip. Crossing the expanse of floor, she took her dish towel and swatted Sloan on the head while setting a plate in front of Marty. "You have no room to talk!" she accused with an accent Marty would guess was German. Placing a meaty, weathered hand on Marty's shoulder, she gave it a thump. "I am Helga of Stuttgart," she offered in a stern, no-nonsense tone.

"Um, Marty of, uh, Piscataway. I mean I was born there. Now I live in Manhattan."

Keegan chuckled from across the table and covered his mouth with a napkin. Leaning back in his chair, he folded his fingers behind his head.

Helga grunted and pointed to the food. "I make ze food for you. Is gute. You eat." It was a demand rather than a request.

Her body was stout, her face round and red from cooking, but her smile, missing some teeth, was almost warm. Almost. If you didn't count the effort it appeared to take to get her to crack one.

"Thank you," Marty mumbled, too busy eyeballing the plate brimming with eggs, bacon, those country fried hash browns she'd identified, like she'd been rattling off the name of a well-known perfume by smell alone, and steak.

Oh, lo and behold. A hunk of glistening, red meat. Her vegan stomach didn't protest even a little when she grabbed a knife, slicing into the meat and jamming a forkful into her mouth.

Cheerist, it was like Nirvana on her tongue. Seasoned to perfection, it melted in her mouth like butter.

Forgetting her manners Marty dug in, shoveling mouthful after mouthful between her lips to appease her ravenous stomach.

Helga stood with her arms crossed over her large bosom and nodded, clearly pleased. "Is gute, yah?"

Marty looked up guiltily and said, "Yah—um, yes. It's delicious. Thank you for taking the time to make me a plate."

"Gute." Her response was gruff before thumping Marty one last time on the shoulder and departing for the kitchen.

"What do you say we take a ride over to Pack today, Marty? We can get to know each other, and I'll show you the plant and corporate headquarters, okay?" Mara's question followed a tentative smile. "If you're up to it, I mean. If you're too tired I'd understand."

Too tired to see a cosmetics company run by mythical creatures who were only supposed to exist in some movie producer's mind? Hell, no. Not on your life. She wasn't going to miss something like that. Besides, it would help pass the time until she could go home. Maybe she'd learn something and garner helpful information for her own cosmetics quest to glory. "I'd enjoy that. Thanks, Mara."

"It's the least I can do, seeing as you're going to be my new sist—um, my friend. Right? I mean, of course we'll be friends." Mara's words tumbled from her mouth in an anxious jumble.

Had she been less aware of the food she was literally slapping on her thighs like cold cream, and more alert, she might have questioned Mara's slip. However, the delicacies on her plate could only be done justice by giving them her undivided attention. So Marty just nodded her head and sent Mara a distracted smile.

Pushing away from the long table, Keegan rose, glancing at Mara. "I'd appreciate that, kiddo. I have a lot to catch up on."

Marty's ears burned simply because she knew she was the reason he was so far behind. Well, if he'd have just kept his teeth to himself . . . Leaning down over her shoulder, he whispered in that tone reserved just to make her insane, "You enjoy that, Marty. Eat it *all*. You'll need the nourishment. I'll see you tonight, and we'll talk about calling the police."

A chill zinged up her spine, and she straightened in her chair, shaking it off. "Sure. Tonight." Maybe tonight they could grab some of those rawhide bones and gnaw on them in companionable silence, while they mulled over exactly how to explain her medal-worthy escape to the police? How cozy.

Marty grabbed the napkin from her lap, swiping daintily at her mouth, after eating like it was the Last Supper, and glanced at Muffin, who still lay in Victor's lap. "Would it be all right if I left her here? I don't want to be an imposition."

Helga popped through the door, waving a large hand covered with flour in Muffin's direction. "You leave wis Helga. I taken ze gute care of ze princess."

Princess. Marty fought a snort. Helga definitely had Muffin's number calling her princess, but Marty was hesitant. Muffin was a wench and a half with strangers. Well, typically anyway. Clearly, she wasn't much minding Victor's big, barrel chest as a pillow. "She can be kind of difficult." Surely an understatement on behalf of her precious who'd gotten her into this mess in the first place.

"Ach. Not wis Helga. She is gute girl." She waved her hand in the air again, dismissing her. "Go now. Is gute."

Gute then. Wunderbar, even.

Mara pushed her chair back and grabbed Marty by the arm. "It's settled then. Grab your purse, and let's go."

Twenty minutes later, established in Mara's car, they headed to Pack Cosmetics. Marty was trying to figure out exactly where a plant the size of Pack would be in an area as isolated as this. Tree after tree lined each road they took, with barely a house in between. It was obvious there'd be no caramel low-fat soy latte at a Starbucks for her today.

Not in Sherwood Forest.

"So, how do you feel today?"

Feel? She felt like a Schnauzer. She'd eaten a meal fit for a linebacker and had a tail that might pop out at any given time. "I'm okay, I guess. I don't know that I've quite wrapped my head around this just yet."

Mara shook her dark head. "I can't even imagine. For what it's worth, I'm sorry you were dragged into this—our way of life, I mean. It can't be easy. I'll help you to adjust if it makes you feel any better."

"Will you be nicer than Keegan is about it?"

Her laughter filled the compact car with a tinkling lilt. "He can be a shithead sometimes, I know. He's a good guy, really. Just impatient and stubborn as hell, but he means well, and when he says he'll take care of something, you can bet he'll do it."

Marty laid her head against the window, letting the cool glass graze her cheek. That ever-present vibration in her head was back. "There's not a whole lot going on here, is there? It's pretty Sherwood Forest."

"Lots of wide open space."

"Space?"

"So we can run. When we shift, we need to run, and we sort of need to do it in a place where no one will catch us, if you get my drift."

Marty's mood instantly soured. Yeah, that thing she couldn't do, but everyone else seemed to with the ease of changing their underwear.

Shift.

And how had that become so important in the scheme of things? What suddenly made her want to be a part of the canine in crowd?

The hunk? a sinisterly gleeful voice whispered.

Shaddup.

It had nothing to do with the hunk. Yes, he was yummy, yummy, yummy. No, she would not allow those thoughts to seep from her lips. There were more important issues to deal with besides her over-the-top hormones. It had to do with accepting what fate had doled out to her. If she'd had her druthers, werewolf wouldn't have been her first pick of lifestyles, but such was the way of the universe. When life handed you lemons, you just had to make lemonade.

In this case it was a buttload of lemonade, but whatever. Turning to Mara, she watched her profile behind hooded eyelids. "Can I ask you something?"

"Of course. Ask me anything."

"Is there anything else I need to be aware of? I mean, I guess you heard about the tail thing, right?"

Mara's nod was in the affirmative, as was her playful smirk. "I did, and I'm really totally trying not to laugh. That would be obnoxious of me, but you have to admit it's sorta quirky."

Yeah, quirky. "Is anything else going to happen to me? Like more surprises. I'm having a really hard time controlling my moods, my hairy legs, and of course, there's my tail that is, but isn't."

Her sigh was deep and choppy on the way out. "You'll have urges. Strong urges. You've already experienced the urge for protein. Eventually, you'll need to run with the pack at the full moon. It's not something that can be denied. You'll also want to mate—"

"Mate?"

Mara bit her lip, running a tongue over it before speaking. "Sex is an important part of anyone's life. It's a natural instinct, but for a werewolf it's a necessity."

Hookay. That was just it! If she was going to go around humping anything that would remain immobile long enough for her to get a good thigh master grip on it—she wanted out. Couldn't she be spayed? Muff was . . .

Her panic must have been evident. Mara immediately patted her hand. "I see that freaked-out look on your face, Marty. Relax. Yes, you'll want to mate, but it doesn't mean you'll go around indiscriminately banging everything that moves. It just means you'll be at your peak during the full moon. Like any other woman say in her later thirties who experiences her prime, you'll want to have sex. It's not so far from what human women experience, but it can be very intense—especially with your life mate."

Now she was peaking. Hadn't she peaked enough with the hair on her legs alone? If that wasn't peaking, she didn't know what was. And what the fuck was a life mate? Was that a soul mate in human-speak like the kind you found on eHarmony? "Tell me something. Do the male members peak, too?"

"Ooooh, yeah. They peak."

"So that means Keegan's going to peak? Or has he peaked, and I just missed it in all this craziness? Because if he peaked, I sure didn't see it." And what would it be like to peak with Keegan—mate—whatever. Her face flushed like a teenager's at the thought, and her fixation for this man swelled.

"Keegan's very in control of everything," she said almost disdainfully. "His life, Pack, and especially his shifting. He needs to lighten up. Forget Keegan. He can't give you a female perspective. Like I said, we don't screw anything that moves, but in a pack it's natural to mate."

"At the full moon . . ."

"Not only then, but that's when your urge to do so will be strongest. You'll learn to control it along with everything else."

So ho-ing it wasn't essential to pack life. She was no prude, but she certainly didn't boink just to boink. She'd had three lovers in her thirty years, and she sure as hell hadn't met them while running under a full moon. Nor had she done them date one—or even date four or five. She wasn't going to start slamming just any old guy. Um, dog. *Werewolf.*

Oh, Jesus.

"Marty?"

"What?"

"You're panicking. I only told you because a full moon will be coming up soon, and I wanted you to know what to expect."

So did that mean it was like orgy time when the moon was full? Would naked bodies abound across these empty fields of green? Marty blanched and bit the inside of her lip.

"This mating . . . is it a pre-req to being accepted into the inner werewolf sanctum or something?" Would she have to mate with just anyone? Or could she mate with Keegan? A mental hand slapped her forehead. What the frig was that about? What was this fascination with him? She'd never been hot quite like this for anyone else. She'd never paid this much attention to a guy's ass. Sure, sex was a good thing, and she'd enjoyed it a time or twenty, but she never had the kind of mental images Keegan brought to mind. Naked, writhing with beads of sweat on those brawny shoulders as he ravished every last inch of her.

Marty closed her eyes briefly, praying the heat between her thighs would lessen. Opening her eyes, she saw Mara grin.

Mara flashed her dimples and flipped the turn signal on. "No. It's not like that. It's just a phase of the shift. Everything becomes sort of magnified. Your hunger, your senses, your hormones. You won't turn into a nymph. All of the morals and values you possess now won't just go the way of the slut. Promise. In fact, your urge to mate will be strongest when you mate for life."

Life? Whoa, now. Hold on right there. Nobody said anything about doing life. This wasn't prison.

"Hey," Mara said, cutting off Marty's unspoken anxieties. "You haven't even fully shifted. Let's focus on that first. The rest will happen naturally, I bet. You'll learn the ways of the pack—our laws—the Lunar Council will make sure of that."

Lunar Council. "You have a council?"

"Yep. In simple terms, they're rather like the paranormal government. They keep us in line, so anarchy doesn't reign, and they sure want to know about you . . ." Immediately after letting that bit of info spill, Mara clamped her mouth shut with a look that said she'd gone further than she'd intended to. Her profile, highlighted by the sun, paled ever so slightly. "I have a big mouth. Don't worry about anything but you. Keegan will look out for you and explain everything you need to know. We all will."

Tucking her purse under her arm, Marty let the mating, ritualistic boinking, supernatural government, Keegan naked obsession thing go in favor of her current hyper-focused subject and asked, "What is my problem, anyway? I don't feel much when this shifting thing starts—except for the anger, which seems to be what triggered it last night. But looking back at how I felt, it's almost like it's right on the tip of my tongue. Yet it slips away before I can get a grip on it," she said with frustration. "I felt it last night when I was so angry at being thrown into the trunk of a car, but I was too scared to focus on much else. Yet there I was with a tail."

Mara's nod was sympathetic. "I was born with the ability to shift. Our pack cultivates that from birth. You weren't. I think it's just a matter of time and patience. I know it's a stupid thing to say, but don't get all freaked out about it. We'll all help you figure it out. This has never happened in the history of our pack. I'd bet Keegan probably told you, but it bears repeating. Our pack has been around awhile, but we've never had a biting incident as long as most of us have been around. We were all born full were. In fact, I don't know anyone who isn't full were. We don't have a clue what it's like to be human. So we have some learning to do right along with you."

Mara pulled the car to a stop in a spacious parking lot. Large, brick buildings dotted the horizon, and in the middle of the cluster stood a taller one with soaring, glass windows. Cement benches lay on either side of a patterned, brick walkway. A fountain bubbled, the water crystalline and shimmering under the sun as it poured into the pool surrounding it. "Here we are," Mara announced with satisfaction.

Marty forgot about her shifting issues as her heart began to pound. Insecurity began to claw at her gut again. Did these people know about her predicament? What if Pack and all its employees knew about her tail trauma? They were all werewolves, too, weren't they? "Is every employee here a werewolf?"

"Yeah. It's a merge of many packs, and we're all were-wolves. But the Flahertys are the founders of the company."

Capturing Mara's searching gaze, Marty nodded, determined to make the best of this. "Okay, then. Let's do this."

Her stomach lurched. A good yark couldn't be too far off, if she didn't get a handle on her ever-changing emotions. She was good with people. She loved people. Even were-people. They couldn't be much different than humans. They'd love her back, too.

If it frickin' killed her.

Or them.

Whichever came first.

CHAPTER
7

Hookay, so *love* was a strong word, and when defined, it could have many interpretations. None of which apparently applied to her where the Pack employees were concerned.

Many a hard stare were cast her way, as she and Mara entered the crisp, white halls of Pack Cosmetics. Marty sank lower in her jacket, pulling the collar over her chin and busying herself looking at the pumps she'd thought she could leap tall buildings in.

When Mara stopped at the reception area to introduce her to the secretary, the glacial winds of contempt blew with a fierce howl. Her loose, auburn curls shuddered as she peered at them over the top of her glasses, giving Marty nothing more than a cool hello.

Mara leaned over the receptionist's desk and whispered something to her with a hiss before taking Marty sharply by the arm and leading her down another long corridor. Piercing eyes glanced their way from various open office doors, and they were none too friendly. Marty literally smelled their anger—distaste. It was heavy and mingled with the scent of foundation and blusher.

It didn't go unnoticed by Mara either. "Ignore this bunch of stuck-up snobs, Marty." Her voice was loud, her words spoken between clenched teeth. She pulled her arms out of her down jacket and tied it around her waist with choppy movements. Her words swept down the long hallway, echoing against the walls lined with pictures of Pack products.

"Mara!" she hissed in her ear. "Please, it's okay. I'm a party crasher. An outsider. I knew that coming in. Don't make a scene on my behalf." There was nothing she hated more than being the center of attention—especially when it was plain as the cellulite on her ass that no one at Pack was going to pick her to be on the kickball team.

Shaking her head abruptly, she said none too softly, "No. I won't let them persecute you for something you had no control over. You didn't ask for this—it happened. So stop being a bunch of discriminatory assholes and get over it!"

Oh, God. Red definitely came in many shades, and Marty was probably wearing all of them on her face. "Please, please," she implored, flashing Mara a frantic glance. "It's okay. Just take me on the tour and let it go." Straightening her spine—the one that seemed to have a permanent slump in it these days—she spoke with more conviction than she felt. "I can ignore it, if you can."

Mara scoffed, her voice rising with each word she spoke. Her nose wrinkled in distaste. "This would be only one of the things I hate about the elder pack members. They're so stuck on the old way of doing things. All the secrecy involved in trying to blend with society. The paranoia. It's ridiculous, and it's not like you found us out and revealed our dirty little secrets. Keegan bit *you*. The council knows that. So what all the hoopla is about is beyond me. C'mon, I'll show you the factory." She turned to Marty with a huff, stomping down the hallway, her messy ponytail bobbing behind her head.

Marty trailed behind her, caught up in the pictures of
staff members and products. Oh, the product to be had
here. She felt almost guilty for deriving so much pleasure
from another cosmetics line. Bobbie-Sue would probably
shit liquid eyeliner for a week, but even she'd have to
admit, Pack's packaging was outstanding. The copper
shine to each powdered eye shadow case and lipstick made
her eyes glaze over.

Makeup slut, Nina's voice whispered in her head.

Yeah. She loved girly crap. Nina might have been ac-
curate when she'd said Marty was rabid about selling
Bobbie-Sue, but it was only because she genuinely loved
anything that had to do with being pretty. In hindsight, she
suspected what Nina had meant was not everyone shared
her desire to play dress up, and you couldn't force them to
find their color potential if they weren't looking.

She was so enthralled with the inner workings of Pack
and the beauty of the various shades of lipstick, she slipped
on the slick floor, bumping into the watercooler at the end
of the corridor.

Water sloshed in the tank, her legs splitting awkwardly
as she grabbed at the top of it to keep it from tipping over.
Mara rushed to aid her, while a sleek blonde giggled from
the corner.

"You okay?" Mara asked with concern.

Peachy. She was just peachy. Her eyes caught a glimpse
from Blondie as she righted herself and what she read in
them, what her newly acquired senses screamed, was more
of the same. *You're an interloper. A clumsy human with a
tail even a terrier would mock. We laugh at you behind
your back in the break room while we dine on steak tartare
and sip sparkling water.*

There was something else, too. Something . . . well, just
something. Marty couldn't pinpoint it, but it existed just the
same. Her cool, hard features were immaculate as she
sipped water from a paper cup, leaning back against the far
wall and raising one perfectly waxed eyebrow. "Who's
that?" she whispered to Mara.

"Oh, that's Alana O'Brian. She's slated to be Keegan's ma—forget it." She stopped short, waving her hand and averting her eyes.

Mate—his life mate? That's what Mara had been about to say. That's what that look was for. It was the look of the green-eyed monster. So Keegan had a mate. Or once did. There had been no mention of mates in any of their convoluted conversations. So if Keegan and Alana had been involved, did that look mean Alana's panties were twisted because he was spending so much time with Marty? And what did *slated* to be Keegan's mean? Did this pack slash life mate thing mean you had arranged marriages or something? Betrothals?

Alana didn't make a move to introduce herself, and that was okay by Marty. All this scorn was wearing way thin. Okay, so they didn't like her. She got it. Proving herself was clearly going to be something that didn't happen easily. Mere mortal that she was—had been. Her internal war over why it was so important to her to be accepted left her confounded.

She could just be a werewolf in the city, couldn't she? Once she learned how to shift, and if her urge for sex became a problem, well, she'd just buy a battery operated boyfriend, aka BOB, and mate with it. Thus eliminating the possibility of little BOBs, right? No muss, no fuss. Was there a rule about who you mated with?

And this Alana chick. If she wanted Keegan, no one was stopping her. Although, that twinge in her belly wherever Keegan was concerned began chomping at her intestines like Pac-Man. Marty glanced up one last time to find the lovely Ms. O'Brian—hard bodied, dressed to the nines, in a cute dress Marty was sure wasn't from some discount mall, and primped to within an inch of her long, blonde tresses—glaring at her.

Biotch.

Marty's anger began to build, crawling for mere moments until a starburst of fury flushed her face. Her fingers curled into fists at her sides, and then she realized—she had the potential tail problem to consider.

Whoa, Nellie. Pressing her forehead to the top of the watercooler, she sucked in a deep breath of air. Mara's hand rested on her arm, squeezing it. "Do you feel all right?"

"I'm fine. I think I'm just worn out. Would you mind if we went back to the house? I really appreciate your bringing me here though. We can finish the tour another time." Hide. She just wanted to hide in that big, luxurious bed at Southfork and stay there until this was over and she could go back home to her apartment and be left alone.

Alone.

The word stung, clanging around in her head like loose change in a can. She'd always been alone. Why that should stab at her heart now was just another question left to be answered in the gazillion she was busy compiling as they spoke.

"Yeah. Don't forget to thank me for bringing you. That was really bright of me. I've introduced you to a bunch of stuck-up shitheads." She spoke out of the corner of her mouth, but in Alana's general direction.

Marty put a hand on Mara's shoulder and gave her a tight smile. "Please, don't say anything more on my behalf, Mara. I don't want you to get yourself in trouble, and I don't want you to be angry over something you have no control over. Let's just go. Please," she said once more with feeling. This experience reminded her of the time Joanne Ledbetter had announced to everyone on the playground that Marty didn't have a father. She'd never forget the flush of humiliation she'd felt being singled out for being different. Back in the day, single parenting wasn't as prevalent, and her classmates took the opportunity to treat her as if she'd had a disease and she'd pass it on to them if they so much as touched her. She'd been thrust under a spotlight of criticism then, and the same thing was happening now. That same rush of unease, embarrassment for something she had no control over, clung to her.

And she wanted to flip everyone the bird because of it.

It was definitely time to go back to Southfork.

Besides, she had clients to check on, and she mustn't forget that account-nabbing wench, Linda Fisher.

Surely by now, after Marty's two-day absence, Linda must practically own Bobbie-Sue.

Her eyes narrowed at that thought. She needed email and a quiet place to think about what to do from here.

"I'm sorry, Marty. I really am. C'mon, I'll take you back." Mara's voice was tinged with regret, her face filled with sympathy. A sympathy Marty knew was concern, but instead found uncomfortable. She didn't want pity. She wanted to figure this out without the added pressure of a bunch of strangers making her feel like she had two heads.

Thank God this werewolf thing didn't include two heads.

The ride back in the mid-afternoon sunlight was quiet. Marty lost in her thoughts, Mara steeping in her anger. The aroma of turmoil was clear, and she decided she'd had enough discord for one day. When they pulled into the long driveway at Southfork, Marty thanked Mara again and took off to her room.

Victor had done as requested when she'd given Keegan her long list of needs and brought her laptop. It was on the big overstuffed chair, just waiting for her to open it and find out Linda Fisher had been recently elected president or something. Her phone, complete with charger, sat neatly on the nightstand, and my, my, look who'd come to visit.

Flopping down on the bed, she wriggled a finger at her long-lost dog. "Well, well, Miss *Princess*. Where's your hunky were-sitter, huh?" Muffin's ears rose. She scurried over to Marty, burying her face in her hand. Tears stung Marty's eyes at the simple, familiar gesture. "I think we've got a real problem, Muff. I know you like it here at were central, but I gotta tell ya—nobody likes mommy." Muffin rolled over, exposing her fluffy, white belly for Marty to scratch. "I think we've bitten off more than we can chew, you troublemaker."

Muffin whined in response, rolling over once more and jamming her nose between her paws.

"Contrite looks good on you, Muff. How about we keep those chops to ourselves from here on out? Who knows what I could turn into next."

Flipping open her laptop, she hooked up to the wireless network and opened her email, one eye shut in hesitance. There were many emails emphasized with exclamation points and subject headers with caps, from Wanda and Nina, demanding she call them.

And say what? She couldn't tell Nina she'd kicked her way out of the trunk of a car. First of all, Nina'd never fall for that from Marty. She'd once called her a pansy-ass for not knocking some guy's teeth out who'd looked down her shirt on Surf and Turf night at the Seafood Palace. How could she explain she was a werewolf and now possessed the strength of ten men?

Nina's "I don't give a shit what the hotter than Hades hunk says—you'd better call us, or I'll come get your ass" email made her grin. You could always count on Nina to be anything but subtle. Marty popped open her cell phone and found Nina's number, pressing the speed dial before thoroughly hashing out her story.

She picked up on the first ring. "Where the fuck have you been? Do you have any idea how worried we've been about you?"

"I know. Keegan told me. I'm sorry."

"Sorry? Sorryyy?"

"Well, of course I am."

"Sorry? Oh, nuh-uh. Sorry doesn't cut it."

"How about a limb? Want a limb? Will that make up for it?" Jeez.

"Don't you get smart with me," Nina warned. "I don't know what's gotten into you lately. You've been acting like a pit bull ever since our last Bobbie-Sue meeting, and you're upstaging me. So cut it the fuck out!"

No, no. Nina had the wrong breed. She was a werewolf. Not AKC approved, but still in the same general family. "Don't you get pissy with me, Nina Blackman. I'm tired, and I've had a rough couple of days. So lay off!"

Nina changed tactics, lowering her voice. "Ya know, Marty, when you do it, you do it big. You couldn't just go and get a hot boyfriend and take him off to some deserted place to give him a good slam. You have to get yourself kidnapped? What the fuck is going on?"

A trickle of warmth infused her veins, flowing to create a smile on her lips. If she didn't know better, she'd think Nina of the "fuck everyone" attitude had been worried about her. Imagine that. Marty softened, tugging the bed's comforter around her legs. "If I had an answer for that, I'd be back in my apartment right now. I don't know what's going on or why anyone would want to kidnap me. Of all people. I was klunked on the head at the bodega on Eighth, stuffed in a trunk, and somehow, I managed to escape. I—I called—um, Keegan in a panic, and he brought me here to his house in Buffalo."

"Esssss-scape?" Nina rasped. "Who the hell escapes from the trunk of a *car*, Marty?"

Werewolves with superhuman strength? No, that would be the wrong answer, wouldn't it? Typically, that'd probably freak out the humans. Think, Marty . . .

"Wonder Woman, maybe," she continued. "But you're no superhero."

No, she was par-a-normal. "Some trunks still have inside latches, Nina. When they stopped at a 7-Eleven, I popped it from the inside and hid in the woods until Keegan came and got me. They didn't tie me up or anything. I guess they figured I wouldn't put up much of a fight with that blow to my head." There. That wasn't so bad. It could happen.

"Motherfuckers!" she shouted. "Did they hurt you? I'll damn well rip their balls off!" she growled savagely.

Very Nina-esque. She should be upset that Nina didn't believe she could take care of herself, but then, friends stuck up for friends, didn't they? Maybe she did have a friend. Maybe. "I'm not hurt. Er, just some scratches and a lump on my head." That was gone now. Like it had never happened.

"Do you have any idea who'd do this?"

"I don't know, Nina. If I knew they'd be locked up and I'd be back in the city right now, doing what I do best. Selling Bobbie-Sue. I know two men were involved, but I only heard their voices. I never saw them."

"Did the hunk with the hot derriere call the police yet? He told us you panicked and called him instead of 911, but he said he'd take care of it. He'd better, or I'm coming up there to get you, and we're going to the police ourselves."

Marty ran a tired hand over her eyes. Now she had to lie. She couldn't tell her why she didn't call them in the first place. Oh, would Nina have a field day if she knew about her tail . . .

A long pause crackled in her ear and then the rustle of the phone. "Give me the phone, Nina! Stop grilling her already. And quit being such a potty mouth! We're out in public, for Heaven's sake. She's been through an," a muffle of hands over the receiver and the whispered word *ordeal*, spoken like it was a dirty word. Marty could just picture Wanda's face harried and nervous while she cupped her mouth with her hand and hushed out the word *ordeal*.

"Wanda?"

"Marty?" Wanda squealed. "Omigod! Are you okay? Do you have any idea how sick with worry we've been over you? I mean, talk about scary. Who would want to hurt you?"

Her concern touched Marty, and she wasn't sure how to deal with that amidst all the other emotions she was experiencing. "I'm fine, Wanda," she soothed. "Really. I'm with Keegan and his pac—family, and everything is okay."

More rustling occurred and then, "Give me back the frickin' phone, Wanda. God damn it! What was I thinking when I said I'd go to bingo with you?" A sigh followed while they apparently struggled for rights to the phone, and what a surprise—Nina won. "Marty? Look, we just want you to be okay. We needed to hear your voice to make sure everything was all right."

Marty whistled into the phone and hid her warm fuzzy with sarcasm. "Okay, so now it's my turn. What the hell is wrong with *you*? Did the pod people come and take over your body? Cuz the Nina I know is never this nice to me."

"Shut your makeup whoring yap, Marty Andrews," she crowed into the phone. "I'm not heartless, and just because I'm checking on you doesn't mean I like you. Not even a little. You *are* my supervisor. My guide to all things color coordinated, remember?"

Speaking of colors . . . she needed to check her Bobbie-Sue email account. "Yeah, I remember. So have you sold anything yet, Nina?" She couldn't help but taunt.

"Shut up, Marty! You know as well as I do I suck at this shit. I'm only hanging on until I can find something better. Something that has absolutely nothing to do with bullshit colors like lavender and some retarded sky blue makeup machine."

Marty burst into giggles. Now that was the Nina she'd come to depend on to make her utterly miserable with her complaints. Yet today, it wasn't having the same effect on her it once had. Once upon a time it had made her crazy. Today, she realized with sudden clarity, it was simply Nina's way of showing she cared. Abrasive and crass as it was. "Oh, just admit it, Nina. You liiiike me," she sang into the phone.

"I no such thing you," she denied gruffly. "Now pay attention to me, you color wheel freak. You keep in touch with us. Don't make me come to the sticks and friggin' dig you out. I will, you know. I want an email a day—if not a phone call. Got it?"

"Got it. I promise to keep in touch," she said before saying her good-byes and clicking the phone off. A glance out the window told her it was getting late. The afternoon was slipping into early evening, and she'd spent the better part of it holed up in her room, battered after her Pack Cosmetics debacle.

Marty shrugged off the bad vibes, letting her thoughts return to her email. When she spied one from Alger, her stomach curled into a tight ball of knots. Reading his words sent a cold chill up her spine.

The tone was desperate, begging her to answer her door or at least her phone. According to him, he'd left countless messages on her cell and home phones and had dropped by her apartment a dozen times. He wanted to know why she wasn't answering him, and then he became apologetic, asking for forgiveness for his behavior that night at her apartment. The entire email was erratic and jarring.

Could he have done this? Was Alger really capable of masterminding a kidnapping? Marty just couldn't picture him summoning up the energy to do something that required so much thought and creative input. Alger was motivated by little unless it involved suntan lotion and a lounge chair.

Rolling her head on her neck she made a mental note to tell Keegan about it and then set about checking her Bobbie-Sue email.

Her independent consultant supervisor had sent an email titled: Warning.

Hoo boy, that couldn't be good. Not good at all. Her stomach took another nosedive, and she clicked it open, with her heart in her throat. As she read, her face flushed and her eyes narrowed.

It would seem if she made another scene like she had the other night, she was going to have her accounts taken away and be asked to leave Bobbie-Sue. Clearly she'd made a serious faux pas. Conduct unbecoming of a cosmetics whore. And if she didn't regain her Bobbie-Sue attitude pronto, she'd have to go.

Regain this, you bitch!

That shitty account-stealing Linda Fisher would pay for this, if it was the last thing she did. Marty jumped up off the bed and paced the length of the floor, her hands fisted in tight wads of anger. The vibration in her head grew, pounding out the staccato rhythm of her rage.

Which always led to very bad things at the backend of her. *Bloody hell*, she thought, catching a glimpse of her ass in the freestanding mirror in the corner of her plush room.

Her tail was struggling to make an encore presentation.

The back of her silk skirt rippled, and the stretch of her skin tugged at her backside.

"Arghhhhh!" she screamed in total frustration, pressing her hand to her butt.

"Marty?" Keegan called from behind the door.

Shit, shit, and shit. Sucking air into her lungs, she fought for calm. "Yes?"

"Can I come in?"

She ran a self-conscious hand over her ass. What did it matter? It wasn't like he hadn't seen her sorry excuse of a tail. She made her way over to the door and popped it open. "Sure. C'mon in." Backing away, she clasped her hands behind her back and rocked on her heels.

He gave her a once-over, scanning her from head to toe warily. "What's up?"

Looking away, she directed her vision squarely at his shoulder. "Nothing, absolutely nothing. Just checking some emails and you know—just nothing," she replied, trying to keep the guilt out of her voice. "What's up with you?"

"The police are here."

"Now?"

"More like finally."

The mere mention of law enforcement rattled her. "What the hell am I going to say to them, Keegan? I can't tell them how I got away from those goons unless I lie like I did to Nina and Wanda. I told them I got out of the trunk because there was an inside latch, but there wasn't. It was an older car. If I don't tell them the car was an older model they won't be looking in the right places!"

The twitch in his jaw snapped up and down beneath the tightly stretched skin. "We'll figure it out. There's no way I'm going to let this go, Marty. I want to know who's responsible for this, and I want to know sooner rather than later. We have to protect you. If an incident similar to this occurred in the area recently, then we can at least chalk it up to something other than the bite. But I don't know that, and I want it on record that you were accosted." His tone said that was definitely that. No discussion. Period.

She'd be infuriated if he wasn't such a damned sweet package. Was there anything about this man—even when he was demanding and pushy—that wasn't kick-ass hot to her?

She raked a hand through her hair and rolled her eyes. "I can't go downstairs like *this*." Turning around she stuck her backside out at him.

Keegan snorted a laugh, his Adam's apple bobbing up and down his bronzed throat. "We really have to do something about that. And we will. But first, we have to do something about this. Put on your bathrobe, something heavy, and I'll take care of the rest. I don't do it often, but I'll use my influence if it's necessary to make the police listen."

That was probably the only reason they'd agreed to come in the first place. Because he was Keegan Flaherty. A multimillion-dollar cosmetic company's CEO.

Digging through her still unpacked suitcase, Marty found her robe and jammed her arms into it. Cocking a glance at him, she muttered, "I hope you're good at this. P.S., I'm a sucky liar. You've probably had more experience hiding this kind of thing, huh?"

His posture grew stiff, and the set of his mouth was tight. "When the situation calls for it, I do what I have to, to protect the pack," he replied with sarcasm and a stern set to his jaw. "It's a necessity for the safety of our kind."

There he went getting all offended and uptight. Marty made a face at him. "Don't go getting all wiggy. Quit being offended. I'm just giving you a heads-up. I've never pretended to be a human who's not really a human but a werewolf, paranormal whatever. I'm not a good liar at all. I get flustered. So if I screw up, I'm just giving you a warning, and it doesn't help that I have this thing sticking out of my ass."

He swatted her rear end with a flat palm, and chuckled. "Say as little as possible. Stick to as much of the truth as you can, and it'll be okay. Just stay in front of me, and I'll follow."

"If you say so."

"I say so. You in?"

"Yeah, I'm all in." She gave him a thumbs-up, though her stomach churned.

Raising his hand, he made a fist, his knuckles facing her. "Ready, partner?"

This would be a part of her life from now on. Hiding. Secrets. Mystery. She'd better get ready—so suck it up, girly.

She knocked fists with him and winked. "Ready."

Marty reluctantly meandered out the door and along the hallway, taking the steps one at a time. When they hit the bottom of the stairs she felt Keegan firmly plant himself behind her, wrapping an arm around her waist from behind. She relaxed a bit then. The sculpted press of his chest on her back soothed her frazzled nerves. Muffin had skipped merrily down the stairs beside them.

The officers were in the family room, standing by the stone fireplace, taking in the grandeur that was Southfork. The fireplace alone covered the entire middle of the wall and had a hearth that could seat twenty. Marty hadn't had the chance to explore much since she'd arrived, but the overstuffed furniture was warm and welcoming, with cozy quilts strewn haphazardly over the arms of the furniture. It would be an awesome place to curl up and read a good book—if it weren't for the police officers who were crisp in their uniforms and wore the faces of boredom.

Keegan stayed true to his word, firmly planting his feet in a wide stance and gathering her to his chest possessively.

Craning her neck, she asked him, "You'll stay?"

"Yep."

"Ms. Andrews?" the taller officer queried from across the room. "We're from the Poughkeepsie Police Department. I'm Officer Johansson and this is Officer Withers."

"Um, yep. That's me. Marty. Marty Andrews. From Manhattan. The victim here. The kidnapp-ee. The kidnapped. The nabbed. The assaul—ow!" Keegan yanked on her tail to silence her. She was rambling, because she knew she had to lie.

Officer Johansson tipped his hat in greeting and nodded. "Right. You were kidnapped. Mr. Flaherty told us. Can you tell us what you remember about it?"

"Uh-huh."

The officer poised pen over paper and waited, taking in Marty's bathrobe with eyes that were distantly amused.

Keegan nuzzled her neck and whispered, "I think they mean now, *honeybuns*."

"Who?" *Honeybuns?*

"Mar-ty." Keegan called her by name rather than using the endearment. "Answer the nice police officer."

"Oh, right. Sorry. I'm still a little flustered. Well, let's see. I was leaving the bodega on Eighth Avenue. They have the best ever vegetables, and I stopped to look in a store window—" What the hell had she stopped for anyway? Oh, yes. Her hair color. She'd caught a glimpse of it, and it had troubled her because she'd spent an ungodly amount of cash to have it lightened. She'd been thinking about having Steven her hairdresser fix it, and then, whamo. Right. "So I was looking in this window, and after that . . . I—I woke up." There. All done.

"*Where* did you wake up, Miss Andrews?" Joe cop two asked. She couldn't remember if he was Withers or Johansson.

"Uhhhh, in a trunk?"

"Are you sure?"

Was he frigging kidding? How could she ever forget that? Indignation took over, and she frowned. "Of course I'm sure. Why wouldn't I be sure? I should know where I woke up, and I'm positive it was in the trunk of a car." Keegan's fingers bit into her waist. That meant shut up. She'd forgotten the keep it simple rule.

"Do you know what kind of car?"

Yeah. She was so into cars. It wasn't like she read *Car and Driver* with any religion. The only reason she'd known about inside latches on newer car trunks was because she'd read an article on it in *Good Housekeeping* at the dentist. Pure luck. "Um, no. I have no idea."

"Was it big? Could you move around in it?"

Oh, yeah. Ginormous. "Yep. It was big. Super big. Like super-sized. So big I probably could have done jumping jacks in it. Big enough to fit a whole herd of cattle. Probably bigger than the fine state of Montana. Biiiiig. Very big—"

"Ms. Andrews—I get it. It was a *big* car. So you were hit on the head, right?"

"Yes. The head."

"Do you have any marks from the blow?"

"On my head?"

"Yes. On your head."

"No. No marks."

"If the blow to your head was enough to knock you out, you must have a lump or something. The incident only occurred last night."

What was this? Flippin' *ER?* "Well, I don't. I guess it doesn't take much to knock me out. I keel over easily."

Officer one sucked his cheeks in. "Right. How did you get out of the trunk?"

"Out?"

"As opposed to *in,* pumpkin," Keegan said jovially, pulling her tighter to him.

"I—I can't remember. I mean, it's all such a huge blur, you know? I think I have post mortem—partum—traumatic stress syndrome. Yes. I'm traumatized, and I can't think straight. That's called a blackout. Or amnesia, right?"

"Sometimes," was the guarded reply. "Do you know how long you were in there?"

A bloody millennia. "I don't know how long it was before I woke up. But I woke up in Poughkeepsie. Right, *precious*?" She knocked the back of her head against the solid wall of Keegan's chest, sending a glance upward at him for confirmation. *Take that, sweetums, sugarplum, angel face.*

"That's right. I came and picked her up in Poughkeepsie." He slithered a palm down her shoulder, running it along her forearm, until he clasped her hand at her hip.

Her face warmed, and without will, she found herself relaxing into him. Christ, he had the strongest arms . . .

"Poughkeepsie," officer one stated flatly. "Did you hear anything? Anything you think might be helpful to aid us in finding who did this?"

. . . and a hard abdomen. The ripples of his stomach rubbed against the top of her waist. Wow, he was pretty tall. Marty knew he was tall, but she hadn't realized how tall until just now.

"Sweetness?"

"Uh-huhhh?" Was that her voice all dreamy and wistful?

"The police officer asked if you remember hearing anything last night that might help them in identifying who did this."

Her haze of acute sexual awareness cleared momentarily. "Oh, yes! When the car stopped, they went into the 7-Eleven to get slushies—slurpees. Something like that. They both had heavy accents. One was clearly a New Yorker, and the other Jersey City. One of them didn't want to go in. He said sugar was bad for you. He wanted to stay and watch the trunk, but the other one called him a roid boy. Then he said that whoever had this done wasn't going to like it if they were late. Then the other guy said 'Screw him' and called this person—I guess the person who had me kidnapped—a spoiled asshole and then—then . . ." She paused for a moment when Keegan placed his hands on her neck and massaged her shoulders. Ahhhh, that was sooo nice. He nudged her from behind again. "Then the guy who wanted the slurpee said his partner didn't have to watch the trunk because he'd knocked me over the head pretty good. And then he said, 'We should have tied the bitch up.' Well, truth be told he called me a dumb bitch. Which is kinda mean. I'm not dumb. I guess I couldn't be that dumb if I managed to get away—"

"How *did* you escape, Ms. Andrews?"

That was the sixty-four-thousand-dollar question, wasn't it? "I don't remember," she said vaguely, avoiding his eyes and focusing on the paintings hanging above the fireplace.

"You don't remember." That was definitely disbelief mixed with some suspicion on the side she heard in his tone.

"Nuh-uh. Like I said, it's all such a blur. Blurry, very, very blurry. Like looking through prescription lenses that aren't yours. It was *that* blurry."

"You have no idea how you got out of the trunk of a car? That's quite a feat, Ms. Andrews," Officer number two piped up with definite skepticism.

Tell me about it. "I'm sorry. I wish I could remember."

Columbo number one suddenly nodded briskly, as if he'd just solved the Jack the Ripper murders. "The trunk probably had an inside latch on it. Most cars do nowadays for just that reason. In your panic and fear you must have used the opportunity when they went into the 7-Eleven to pop the latch."

Yeah. That worked. Marty only nodded with a slight bob to her head, zipping her lips shut. No good could come from the flap of her gums.

"What happened next?" Johansson prodded.

I ruined a perfectly good pair of sandals, that's what happened next. "I hid in the woods nearby. When I discovered I still had my cell phone in my skirt pocket—they'd taken my purse—I called Keegan."

"Why didn't you call 911?"

Because I had a fucking tail, you moron! Keegan felt the bunch of her shoulders tense and rubbed them harder. *Calm, soothing breaths, Marty,* she mentally ordered. "Well, I think it's like you said. I was panicked and confused, and he was the first person I thought to call. I mean, he is my *boyfriend*." Snort. "He talked to me until the charge on my cell phone ran out."

"Is that right, Mr. Flaherty?"

"Yes, that's correct." Keegan's tone grew commanding and succinct.

"So you didn't see these men at all?"

"No. I ran into the woods. I was too afraid to even go into the 7-Eleven for help. That's where I waited until Keegan came and picked me up."

"And you and Mr. Flaherty know each other how?"

Because he bit me. Right on my hand. And now I'm a werewolf just like him.

"We're neighbors. I have an apartment right down the hall from Marty in the city. That's how we met."

"Right," she murmured. "We're neigh-bors," she repeated with emphasis.

"Any ideas about why someone would want to kidnap you?"

Cop-inator said "you" like she was too insignificant to be worthy of a kidnapping. She bristled at that, but Keegan cut in with a stern answer.

"I'm a rich man, officer. Marty's my *girlfriend*. I'd say that could be a motivating factor, wouldn't you?" His voice was steady, firm, laced with an underlying anger.

She'd lay bets his nostrils were flaring. Not a good sign.

Marty didn't much like where this was going at all. The tone of the two officers ranged from disbelief to boredom during their conversation, and truth be told, how could she blame them for questioning her? Not only was her story off kilter, all of the dots didn't connect without the full explanation.

"Right, sir. I didn't mean to imply—"

"I don't care what you imply. I care that you find who did this to *Ms. Andrews*." He whipped the words out through tight lips. The rumble of his voice vibrated against her chest. She didn't have to see Keegan to know he was growing impatient. Fierce. He could be pretty fierce when he needed to be.

Hot.

That was definitely a big *X* in his hot category.

"Well, Mr. Flaherty, we've been to the scene where Ms. Andrews claims this occurred, and unfortunately, we don't have any witnesses to speak of. The New York City police have no reports of kidnappings involving brunettes that match a description of Ms. Andrews. With so little to go on, no make or model of the car, nothing other than what Ms.

Andrews heard that night, I'm afraid we can't be of much help."

God damn it all to hell. She was not a brunette! She was a damned blonde. Blonde, blonde, blonde. St. Tropez blonde with Tapioca highlights and Banana Pudding lowlights, to be precise. Christ on a cracker.

"I understand, officer. However, this matter is very serious and had to be reported. Thank you both for coming all the way out here to hear our story. I trust you'll keep us informed."

Dismissed. Keegan had dismissed them without a backward glance. Helga came out of nowhere to show them the door, nodding at Marty and Keegan as she flew back to the deep, dark bowels of the kitchen.

Marty let out a long sigh of relief. "I talked a lot, didn't I?"

Turning her to face him, he grinned. "Ya think? You have a tendency to sort of just keep going and going when you're nervous."

"You do realize they don't believe me, don't you? They only indulged you because you're a rich, influential man and they think I'm your crazy, eccentric girlfriend. No cop from Poughkeepsie is coming all the way to Buffalo to hear some half-baked story about a kidnapping, otherwise. They think I've recently had my meds upped is what they think."

Keegan shrugged with indifference. "I don't care why they came, just that they did. I won't allow anything to happen to you."

He'd taken a tremendous risk, allowing those police officers to come here. There was so much to be discovered by prying, human eyes. It made her heart twist in her chest. "Oh, the power of greenbacks," she snarked.

"Whaddaya say we do something about that?" He pointed to her butt. The firelight spilled over his five o'clock shadow, making his features softer somehow and giving her nipples another reason to salute him.

This could not go on. This wonky hormonal flux. Marty,

you must focus on the task at hand. Achieving tail-dom. Stop fucking around. "Question is, is there something that can be done?"

"I think we'll have to see. I say we go for a walk and find out."

"Outside? Are we going outside because it's—it's a *messy* process?"

"Nah, I just figured I'd show you the stables while we're at it."

Planting her hands on her hips, she had to ask, "Do you seriously think this is going to work? Maybe I'm just destined to be half human, half werewolf. Which, of course, means I'll *never* fit in. I'll be like the redheaded stepchild of your pack. The black sheep of the family. I won't be allowed to run with you at the full moon, because I won't be able to keep up. I feel certain the other pack members won't much appreciate me bringing my Schwinn on a ride-along."

Keegan's laughter erupted, and the corners of his deep brown eyes crinkled. "We'll never know unless we try."

"And you're going to show me."

"I'm your man of the hour. Let's call it a date?"

How many women could lay claim to a date involving a good metamorphosis?

One in a million, baby. You're one in a million.

CHAPTER
8

After changing into jeans and a top and finding her tail had subsided, Marty threw on a jacket and met Keegan downstairs.

This was it.

The big moment. No going back. She was going to shift. Turn into a dog. Sport a tail. God willing a real one the others wouldn't mock.

She shivered just thinking about it, and Keegan put his arm around her as they made their way to the stables.

"You think you're ready to go all the way?"

All the way. Even half the way would be better than nothing. "As ready as you can get when you're going to turn into a walking allergy." Marty giggled into the night. Crisp and clear, the stars hung like bright Christmas tree ornaments from the sky. The scent of other animals reached her nose. Yet it wasn't the typical smell of horse droppings and hay. She could literally smell the blood coursing through the animals' veins. The strong coppery odor sank into her nostrils, settling there. Her keen senses could even pick up one gelding's agitation.

God, of all the fucked-up-ness in the world, this had to top her list. She ran a finger under her nose, scrubbing it briskly. Her eyes didn't need to adjust to the inky black night anymore. Her vision was sharp, and every detail of the vast acreage at Southfork was crystal clear.

Keegan grabbed her hand, pulling her through a patch of trees as they made their way to a clearing with an old but well-kept barn. "Let's go. I'll introduce you to Dexter."

"Who's Dexter?"

"One of our studs."

Keegan let go of her hand, making a direct path through the wide-open barn doors. A large, black horse stood proudly in the farthest stall, burring softly. Four more stalls contained horses in various colors. Keegan stooped to scoop some oats out of an old bucket to feed Dexter, and Marty's eyes zeroed in on his ass, still in those tight jeans.

Mary mother of all things tight and compact.

Her gulp was hard, forcing its way down her throat like thick molasses. Heat rushed to her nipples, turning them almost painfully rigid. Waves of electricity shot to every sensitive nerve ending in her body. Her panties dampened, and her mouth grew dry. Marty clung to the edge of an empty stall and fought the crazy impulse to hurl herself at him. All that man in one place put her lust on overload.

If he could just not be so damned hard everywhere. So perfectly proportioned with his slender hips, tapered waist, and thick thighs. Keegan's scent seemed to intensify, swirling around her in thick clouds of rugged, primitive man. The memory of his chest imprinted on her spine left little room for breathing. Her knuckles tightened their grip when wave after wave of need, wanton and hot, ripped through her.

It was that mating thing Mara had talked about like it was so natural to want to rip someone's clothes off and ride them to orgasmic glory. That intensified need to do the humpbacked beast. Marty heard the whimper escape her lips, and she doubled over, hugging her lower abdomen and crossing her thighs.

Fortunately Keegan had his back to her while she sucked in gulps of air.

"So tell me about your family." He rose to his full height, twisting on his heel to face her. "I know about your mother."

She popped up. Instantly, her heart slowed, thinking about her mother. Sweet, gentle, funny, and determined to care for her daughter without any outside help. Even if it meant she'd kept Marty isolated from an extended family her mother would only describe as unsupportive. "I can assure you, I don't have the kind of lineage you do. You already know my mom raised me alone. I don't know who my father is, and my mother's parents died shortly after I was born, according to my mom."

"Sounds lonely," he commented, coming to stand closer to her, leaning a casual arm on the horse stall. His eyes sought hers. Eyes that always made her feel he was trying to get into her head and pull up a chair so he could get comfortable while he dug around her brain.

The stark comparison of her family and Keegan's brought with it an awareness she'd never paid much attention to. Her mother had kept them from inviting anyone into their lives. For the first time, she wondered why her mother had never dated, hung out with the girls from work, and why she'd kept Marty so close to her. "This coming from a man who has more family than he knows what to do with and an apartment in New York City to escape to?"

"Yeah." He grinned crookedly. It was so natural, he had to have done it without thinking about it. When he wasn't considering his next move, his appeal took on a whole new layer of yummy. "They can be a lot. Someone's always getting into something. They're loud. They're opinionated. They're nosy. But they're mine."

Keegan clearly loved his family, and the possessiveness in his voice made her smile. It had been a long time since she was loved by anyone without condition. It also made her wonder where his parents were. Someone had done one hell of a job teaching him to be so protective, but she didn't ask who.

Shrugging her shoulders, she folded her hands together and shook her head. "It was definitely different than the way you were raised. Aside from the werewolf thing. It was mostly just Mom and me. She was a good mother, even if she was a bit overprotective." That came out sounding like an apology, and it wasn't what she wanted to convey. Her childhood had been fairly healthy, if unremarkable. Her mother had taught her strength and determination to succeed. She could take care of herself as a result. Maybe she took the taking-care-of-herself spiel to a whole new level with her ambition. Bobbie-Sue and her sky blue convertible seemed light years away right now.

"I was never prom queen or a cheerleader. I didn't date much either, until I was in my mid-twenties. After graduation I took a couple of courses in economics before I dropped out of a local college and went to work. I found Bobbie-Sue while working in the mail room of an advertising company, and here I am." She curtsied, finishing her life history with a smile.

"I guess that explains why we're so overwhelming for you. You were an only child, and we're a three ring circus."

Marty watched Keegan's lips move, felt his breath fan her face, and she almost lost her train of thought. "The circus isn't so bad, I suppose, even if I definitely qualify as a side show."

He winked one luscious, dark eye at her. "I can't imagine them not in my life even when I'm knee-deep in their shit. I did tell you we're always there for each other, especially when times get tough." For a fleeting moment, his expression changed, and his hard face went from light to dark in an instant.

A memory of something painful, she supposed. She wanted to ask, but found herself hesitant to dredge up what was undoubtedly a personal event. When he'd said she'd never be alone, he'd been adamant, but at the time, she didn't want anyone's help. The trouble was she found herself both intrigued and a little afraid of the tight-knit bond they shared. It meant a buttload of accountability. "I like Mara. She can be pretty lively."

"I heard what happened at Pack today, Marty. Mara told me. I won't allow them to treat you that way." Again, his expression changed, turning to a cold mask of stone.

She rolled her eyes. It was so not cool for him to interfere. She was getting the impression he acted first, talked later, but her troubles weren't so cut and dried. She didn't need anyone to protect her, though if she allowed herself to dwell on it, it wasn't a horrible thing that Keegan wanted to. "Don't go all Neanderthal on me with them, Keegan. Please. I can't blame them for being wary of an ex-human, and you can't either. Your world is filled with secrets, and humans are usually kept at bay. It's a wall that's long been in place. You can't exactly expect them to welcome me with open arms, if I'm a precedent."

"Wow, that was pretty insightful, Color Guru," he teased, gifting her with a sudden smile and running a finger down the length of her nose.

"I watch a lot of Oprah."

"Why didn't *you* tell me what happened at Pack today?" His jaw clenched, his nostrils flared.

"It wasn't like I had a lot of time to do it, and for what? So you can throw your alpha weight around and make everyone more miserable than they already are? Nuh-uh. I'm no tattletale, buddy. I don't want to end up fighting for my lunch money at recess."

"You know you can always come to me if there's a problem."

"While I appreciate the gesture, I think time is crucial here. I didn't accept my fate overnight, and neither will the people in your company. It was just some angry glances and the silent treatment. Sticks and stones, ya know?"

"This wasn't your fault."

"Established."

"They should be angry with me."

Placing a hand on his arm, she shot him a smile. "Look,

it's okay. I say we forget it and move on. Don't go sending mass memos to your employees titled "Be nice to Marty, or else" on my behalf. I'll never be invited to join the Chess Club that way. It'll only make things worse for me, and I have far bigger issues at hand than some dirty looks."

"I think you're tougher than I thought, Cupcake."

"I think you didn't notice because you caught me at a bad time. I'm pretty skilled at taking care of myself." That she had to make that crystal clear only exposed her desire to keep Keegan from feeling like she was his obligation.

"I know, I know. You're a tough nut, Marty Andrews."

A real walnut. "So when are you going to tell me about the Moon Council?'

"The *Lunar* Council," he corrected with a shake of his glossy head.

"Yeah, them. The people who are like the super species government. They don't like me, do they? I mean, I guess I can't blame them any more than I can blame the people at Pack, but is it making things harder for you?"

"You let me worry about the council."

"You know, if I let you worry about everything that's been a problem for me since this happened, you'd get wrinkles. You already frown enough for two people. Why don't you tell me why they don't like me, and we can make a list—you know, the one that's as long as the infamous red carpet? It can go right below—was once a human." She grinned at him, brushing a strand of her hair away from her face.

Keegan pushed her hand out of the way and tucked the stray hair behind her ear. "How about we give shifting a shot?" Amusement flickered in his eyes, dancing in his deep, dark orbs.

How about I give you a shot? At me.

Naked.

Oh, mercy.

She rubbed her sweaty palms down the legs of her jeans. "Okay, so clearly we're going to avoid yet another subject. I can live with that for now. So what do I have to do?"

"For now all you have to do is watch. I know this is easier said than done, but at least you'll have the opportunity to see firsthand what occurs during the shift."

Yee and haw. Marty was riding the fence between excitement and terror. Finally she'd see what would happen when she was able to fully shift. Did she want to see how it happened? Would it hurt? She blanched. "Does it hurt?" Surely it had to hurt. Her body was going to distort, bones would be displaced, she'd have more hair.

Fab. Just what she needed. More hair. New razors. A trough full of wax.

"No. It doesn't hurt. In some cases it's a relief. Freeing, I guess. It's like shedding a skin."

"Oh, good. I can't wait to find my inner werewolf by exfoliating and setting it free. What if I can't do it? Will you yell at me?"

"Yell?"

He acted as if he didn't know he was the most impatient, demanding man on planet Earth. "You're not exactly the most patient man, Keegan Flaherty. You yell aaaa lot."

"I do not."

"You do, too."

He sighed his discontent.

"See?" She placed a hand on his lips, trying to ignore the soft, full flesh beneath her fingertips. "There it is. That big ole huff of wind you expel when you're getting bent because I have so many questions."

"I'm sorry. I promise not to yell if you can't shift."

"Do you mean it?"

"Of course I do, Marty." The lines around his mouth tightened.

"Swear?"

"Marty . . ."

"And that, too. You Marty me all the time. It's my signal I'm pushing your buttons."

"You don't push my buttons."

"I do, too."

"Okay, *sometimes* you push my buttons."

"I do it an average of three times per conversation. That's more than sometimes."

"I promise not to yell or let you push my buttons. How's that?"

"Can I get that in writing?"

"No."

"Pinky swear?"

"Fine."

"Say it."

"Pinky—swear," he ground out, sticking his finger under her nose.

They latched fingers, and Marty smiled at him. "Okay, Rover. Do your thang."

"You are the most infuriating—"

"Pain in the ass. I know. You've conveyed that upon occasion. But in case you were of the mind-set that you're easy to get along with—get over it. You're just as much of a pain in *my* tuchis. Now shoo—go show me your magic." Marty waved him away, taking his coat when he stripped it off and handed it to her. He strode out of the barn and stepped behind a large maple tree, kicking off his shoes.

The pounding of her heart thumped in her ears, but her eyes were glued to the tree. Keegan stood under the sliver of moon, his dark hair thick and glossy, his body rigid and so still she could hear his heartbeat mingled with hers.

The crisp air thickened, growing heavy with his unique scent. The leaves once stirring with the faint, chilled breeze stilled. The horses in the barn whinnied, then quieted. Marty tensed, every fiber of her body, waiting, on edge, rife with anticipation.

"It's about focus, Marty," he called, the ripple of his voice reaching her ears with sharp clarity. "You have to harness all of your energy, your emotions, and focus on making your body comply."

And then it happened.

Like a thousand pieces through the lens of a kaleidoscope, the colors of his clothes blended, falling away to reveal bronzed skin and muscle, then were just as swiftly replaced with a blur of black that melted into the background of the night.

Keegan's large frame folded in half, as he fell to what should have been his hands, but were now paws. His drop to the ground was met with the crunch of leaves and a cloud of dirt. He lifted his head, capturing her blue eyes with his deeper, darker ones.

Holy crap.

Marty couldn't move. In her imagination she'd created many scenarios for when this finally occurred. She'd thought she'd prepared herself for this insane reality that was now hers.

However, nothing could compare to witnessing it. Seeing firsthand the kind of transformation you only saw after you'd paid seven bucks to see a Steven Spielberg movie. Silhouetted against the moon, Keegan stretched his length, shuddering until the midnight black hair covering his body fanned out.

Oh.

My.

Hell.

This was real.

OhmyGodohmyGodohmyGod.

Keegan trotted over to her on light paws, his huge head reaching her waist when he came to stand beside her. He nudged her lifeless hand with his muzzle, the cold wet of his nose jarring her out of her cloud of mystification. The cloud that was one part freaked, one part awed.

Instinctively, due to Muffin, she cupped his muzzle, caressing it. He burrowed his nose into her hand, letting her fingers roam over his head, scratch his ears freely.

He must feel like some kind of guinea pig, but she couldn't get over the idea that this was the man who was always irritated with her. The man whose body made hers behave like she was a nymphomaniac on a celibacy diet. The man who catered to her snarling teacup poodle like she was a queen.

Her memory of the night he'd bitten her was vague but

for the visual of him. She would never forget what he'd
looked like then, even in the jumbled confusion of tearing
Muffin off his jaw. He was as beautiful to look at up close
as he'd been while Muffin was clinging to his muzzle.

Sleek, lean, tremendous in stature, he was striking.
When she caught her breath, Marty placed a hand on the
top of his head and said, "You know, if you were a dog in
the pound, I'd adopt you just because I live in the big, bad
city and you look like you could take on a backhoe."

Keegan sat back on his haunches, gazing up at her with
eyes that sought hers.

She knelt down in front of him and cocked her head, staring at him head on. "Can you even understand me in werewolf form? I mean, do you still understand English?
Human-speak? This is crazy, Keegan. At first I thought you
were just talking smack, like bullshitting me. Then I sort of
began to believe you. Really, what choice did I have after a
tail popped out on my ass? But this—this is incredible. It's
cool and scary and wigging me out and well . . . wigging me
out. What if I can't do it? What if I look like a beagle if I do?"

His silence disturbed her.

So she filled it with nervous words. "Well, don't just sit
there looking at me, Wolfman. Work with me here, would
ya? I need answers. Maybe I'm only meant to shift partially, and I could almost live with that if it weren't for
these crazy uncontrollable urges. Like an itch that needs
scratching but I just can't reach it. I felt it tonight when I
was angry over some emails I'd received. It tingled,
stretched, but then, nothing." Marty covered her face with
her hands, pushing the heels of them into her eye sockets.
The pounding that had begun in her ears reached her temples. Forcing herself to stand, she popped up and began to
pace, while Keegan watched with those soulful puppy dog
eyes.

All right. No more pansy-ass bullshit. It was time to take
control of this situation and own it. Determination to succeed,
something she'd never lacked, reared its head. Clapping her
hands together, she spoke with an under-no-uncertain-terms

attitude. "Okay, I'm going to focus just like you said. You just stay there, and I dunno, focus with me. Ya know, like be my cheerleader or something. Think good werewolf thoughts."

Clasping her hands together she raised them above her head and stretched, rolling her tongue over her lips. "Okay, here we go," she announced.

If anger was what really triggered her shift, then she'd have to center her rage. Find what truly made her want to beat the snot out of someone and use it. Hmmm, what really pissed her off?

"Linda Fisher," she muttered. Yeah, she made her batshit. The bitch. She'd taken her account from the secretarial pool of the prestigious Fogarty, Ross, and Carruci, and she'd done it with ease. Then she'd announced her coup in front of all of Bobbie-Sue, humiliating her with her green suit and Marty's ticket to a sky blue convertible.

Fuckwit.

Now she was a thousand bucks a month poorer. Which meant she'd have to give up her bimonthly highlight/lowlight sessions with Steven and quite possibly her therapeutic, seaweed wrap massage.

God, she loved that seaweed wrap. It was an indulgence she'd waited for for well over a year while she'd beaten down door after door, selling makeup to get it. And that infuriated her.

That absolutely did it.

She adored her seaweed wrap, and Linda Fisher had taken it like a red ball on the playground.

The tingle now familiar in her spine swept over her, racing along her skin, leaving behind it the scent of her rage. Her face flushed with heat, her hands clenched into tight balls. Every nerve in her body was alight with a raw, tangible energy, sizzling along her veins. Her skin began to pull and stretch, so she pushed.

Hard.

And voilà.

A tail and little else.

"Arghhhhh!" Her shout came from deep in her throat,

frightening the barn animals when she stomped her feet, throwing her arms up in helplessness. "That's it? For fuck's sake! Whaaaat? What do I have to do?" she screeched, rolling her eyes skyward, looking for anything that might guide her to all things werewolf.

Looking down, she caught Keegan, still in were form pensively watching her. Jesus, the stress of this werewolf shit was going to kill her. If all these werewolves couldn't remember how long it'd been since they'd bitten a human, then they couldn't know if she was going to ever be able to accomplish what they did with a little focus and a tree for cover. What about this shifting thing was so important to her anyway? She'd never been the kind of person who needed to fit in, and maybe that had left her isolated, but she'd never felt more alone than she did right now while she was trying to do just that—fit in.

What a freakin' conundrum.

This wasn't like not being able to hang out with the popular girls at school. This was a way of life. A life she didn't ask for, but had nonetheless and couldn't live to its fullest if she was only going to end up a wannabe werewolf. The theory she might whip up a batch of lemonade out of this mess was rapidly souring.

Marty was so absorbed in her misery over her futile efforts, she didn't notice Keegan padding away, until he took her by the arm and hauled her up to face him. With no warning, her mood shifted once again.

Go figure.

Instead of rage slicing through her, she was now left with that acute, sexual awareness it seemed only Keegan's body brought.

He was dressed in the clothes he'd brought in the beach bag. Gripping her by her upper arms and penetrating her with his stoic gaze, he wrapped his arms around her and hugged her.

She hung from his arms, her own arms dangling loosely at her sides, her feet suspended but an inch above the ground.

Marty's eyebrow rose.

Well, huh.

Fancy that. The beast did have a sympathetic bone.

"I'm sorry, Marty," he whispered into her hair harsh and low.

She didn't fight the tidal wave of heat. Instead she embraced it, slinging her arms around his neck and tipping her head back to get a better look at him. "Not nearly as sorry as I am, Rover."

"I can understand every word you say when I'm in were form. I know this is frustrating," he offered, his eyes turning dark, glazed.

"I'm never going to fit in here, Keegan. Not like this."

His hands splayed over her waist, curving into her hip, molding her to him. Their thighs rubbed each other's, leaving her to experience every last bulge in his. "Whether the shift happens or not, you're one of us. Period." He spoke adamant words, punctuated with the flare of his nostrils.

And for Marty, that was that. She couldn't take it anymore. That nostril-flare thing was so hot. His possessive words, his arms holding her unbearably close, all made for a very naughty thought in her head.

Well, it made for more than one, but they eluded her when she laid one on him. It wasn't just any old kiss either. She meant every tongue lashing, lip bruising ounce of it. Yet Keegan didn't allow her control for long. When he adjusted to her surprise attack, he took the wheel with the speed of an expert and the forceful, commanding presence he wore like his own skin.

Their lips clung to each other, parting only to allow the thrust of Keegan's tongue, hot and silken, exploring her mouth. Moist, sweet, full on their lips meshed. The explosion of flesh upon flesh left her clinging to him, reeling with need that pulsed like the beat of her heart.

Their breathing grew ragged, and their kiss only deepened. She suckled his tongue, drawing it back into her mouth over and over, relishing the male taste of him.

His knuckles brushed the underside of her breasts, making her nipples greedy for more. Her heart slammed against her ribs in time with her pulse crashing in her ears. She found herself wrapping her legs around his waist until his hands settled under her ass, kneading the globes of flesh, drawing her deeper against him.

Somehow they made their way to the wall of the barn, and Keegan held her against it hard. Her breath was lost when the impact of solid wood hit her back. The thrust of his lean hips pressed against her jeans, allowing her clit the delicious friction of his hard cock pushing her closer to a place she'd never been. Rigid and solid, he rubbed between her thighs, keeping her lower body flush to his. It was raw, primitive, a desperate desire to get closer to him until his body absorbed hers.

He groaned into her mouth, kissing his way along her jaw, finding the sensitive spot on her neck just below her ear and nipping it.

Marty's hands jammed into his hair, luxuriating in the silken feel of the strands playing over her fingers. Her hands made fists against his scalp when Keegan slid under her shirt, shoving her bra up with forceful hands. Low in the pit of her belly, the fire he'd created raged, boiling, making her squirm. Her sex grew heavy, swollen with an ache needing fulfillment.

The moment his thumb grazed her nipple, Marty stopped breathing altogether. Moisture flooded her panties, her neck arched, pushing her breasts into the solid strength of his hand. His skin was rough, calloused against her softer flesh.

The top button of her jeans popped open, her zipper slid down with slow deliberateness, and suddenly his hands were on her, his mouth enveloping her nipple, his fingers parting her wet, swollen folds, slick with desire.

Marty bucked into his hand as he teased the hard nub of her clit, tightening her hold on his waist with legs that threatened to collapse from trembling.

Keegan's moans, husky, feral, called to the core of her deepest, most primal urges, begging her to answer. His breathing was ragged, harsh as he swirled his tongue over the expanse of her nipple, tugging it hard into the heat of his mouth.

The cool air of the night mingled with his hot breath made her grind against his hand, seeking relief from the almost painful ache of pleasure.

He cupped her sex, grinding the heel of his hand against it, making her back arch and her hands find the tops of his shoulders. She dug her fingers into the muscled roundness of them, gritting her teeth as her chest heaved against his lips and her hands clawed at his back.

"We have to stop," were the ragged words she heard, torn from his lips. Yet she didn't feel their impact until Keegan pulled his lips from her breast and drew his hand from her jeans.

Stop?

"Stop, we have to stop, Marty," he said against her neck, panting.

She was just about to feel the earth fucking move and he wanted to *stop*?

"There's more I have to tell you," he spoke between harsh breaths, letting her body slide down along his until she stood limply on her own feet.

He bracketed her head with his arms, placing his hands flat on the wall above her. The top of her head burned from his stare. "Look at me, Marty." His order was hoarse as he fought for breath.

Oh, hell no. She'd just thrown herself at him like some whore in an all-male frat house, then, as if that weren't enough, she'd writhed against him like some freakin' pole dancer. She was not going to look at him. No looking. Looking at him ever again was out. "No."

"Marty. I said *look at me*. We have something else to discuss."

There was always something else, wasn't there? What now, for Christ's sake? Global warming and its effects on the cycle of the werewolf?

Her eyes lifted slowly, meeting his with apprehension,

while she fought the tremors wracking her body. "Now what?"

He raked a hand through his thick hair, while he formulated his words. Words she just knew she didn't want to hear. His gaze pinned her to the barn wall. "There are other things about our lifestyle you need to know."

"Yeah. Like?"

"Like we're cyclical."

This was a reason to abort their mission? "You mean the moon thing? I know that. Mara already told me," she rasped, still fighting to draw breath into her lungs.

"There's more—especially for a female."

Ohhhhh. He meant the mating game. Hormones raging, et cetera, et cetera. Her hormones were definitely raging. "So I guess you're going to share this with me *now*? After all, sharing is caring." Her remark was dry, and she was feeling edgy and irritable. Unfulfilled . . . "I already told you, Mara warned me."

"She didn't tell you everything. I wouldn't allow it."

"You're way into being the boss of everyone, aren't you?"

"This is a crucial part of our way of life, Marty. It isn't something you talk about in a casual conversation."

Marty's breath shuddered on its way out. "So spill it."

"Like I said, we're cyclical. Females especially. You're going to go into heat, Marty."

"*Heat.*" She let her head wrap around that word. Heat like a dog heat?

"Yes. Your urge to mate will be strong."

Relief washed over her. Those had been Mara's words, too. "I know that. Mara explained some of it to me. She didn't call it heat, but she said—"

"Did she explain when it would happen?"

"Um, no. She just said that I'd have urges that were intensified. I'm okay with that. There's nothing wrong with a healthy need to—to you know, *do it*, is there?" she joked, because she had the sinking feeling it was more than just a magnification of lust.

"She's right, but what she didn't tell you was you'll go into heat. Between January and April." There was never any buffer between Keegan and his words. He candy coated nothing. He just said them and let the chips fall where they may, which was usually in her lap.

"So what's the big deal about January through April? Do you schedule your mating?" That was so callous—so calculated—so OCD.

His head shook as he frowned. "No, Marty. I'm not talk-ing about sex for pleasure. Though yes, you'll definitely have a healthy appetite for sex."

After that blatant exhibition a resounding duh was in order.

"I'm talking about your fertility. Between January and April, as a part of the pack, you'll be expected to eventually not only mate, but choose a partner for life and . . ."

"And?"

"Create pups." He dropped the words like a bomb. No warning, just bam! Everything exploded around her, leav-ing the word *pups* at her feet.

Pups.

You, Marty Andrews are the procreate-a-nator.

"It's for the good of the pack."

Of course it was. Everything everyone did around Southfork was for the good of the pack—to protect the pack. The pack, pack, pack. Well, she wasn't some damned baby-maker for a bunch of men who had traditions that were as old as Methuselah. This was getting to be more like a Jim Jones cult thing with each passing second. And Nina thought Bobbie-Sue was cult-like. Hah! "So what you're saying is, in order for me to be a part of this pack I not only have to be able to do the magical thing called shift, but I have to have puppies, er, babies? What the fuck kind of deal are you all running around here? Are the females in the pack nothing more than brood mares?"

"It isn't like that, Marty. The pack doesn't expect you to do anything before you're ready, but it will happen."

"I'm not even ready to be a werewolf! I don't even have

one of those lifer things you crazy people keep talking about!"

"Life mate."

"I don't give a shit what you call it. I don't have one, and how do I determine who it is anyway? Do I pick a name out of a hat?"

His gaze grew distant, hard. His chiseled chin lifted when he said, "In most cases you'll just know instinctively."

Marty's snort was scathing. She was just shy of flipping her nut here. "Yeah. That's very Match.com. This is all too much, Keegan. Every time I turn around there's something more to this deal. Councils and steak and litters of puppies. Any ritualistic sacrifices I need to know about?"

The air between them became thick with tension, and it only served to make her angrier. They had no middle ground. They were either high or low, and it just wasn't something she was used to. Her mundane life had been turned upside down and what she really wanted was the truth. *All of it.*

"I know this isn't easy."

Her eyes widened in disbelief. "Easy? Eassssyy? No, it's anything but easy, Keegan. I can't shift without producing anything more than a lame version of a tail. My job, you know, the one that pays my rent—is in severe jeopardy because of my behavior at Bobbie-Sue. I was kidnapped for no good reason, knocked over the head, and dumped into the trunk of a car by two thugs, and the police think I'm a half-wit they only indulged because you're rich. My moods are like a swinging pendulum. They change with the slightest provocation. I fucking swear now. I hardly ever had a potty mouth until this happened, and now on top of everything else, I'm expected to produce babies for the good of a pack that doesn't even like me? Forgive me for thinking you're all just a little schizoid. Forgive me for behaving badly about it, too. If you could just be honest and upfront about *all* of it instead of nailing me in bits and pieces, I might be less inclined to get my freak on. What is it with you and all these secrets?"

Keegan pushed himself off the wall with his hands, crossing his arms over his broad chest. Now he was pissed. She could see it in the set of his mouth and the scent his body flung around like invisible beads of sweat. "You know, not everything is just about you, Marty. You're no longer in the world alone. You're in it with *us*. We're doing our goddamnedest to make you comfortable, and you don't make it easy. This is an adjustment for my family, too—for me. Yes, I created this, and I've apologized, but I'm not going to apologize anymore. It is what it is, and the days of your self-indulgence are over. Deal with it," he barked.

For the merest of seconds, remorse set in. His immediate family had been nothing but nice to her, but it was quickly washed away by the idea that a hedonistic law like creating more pack members was in play in this day and age. This was nucking futs. When she finally spoke, her words were calculated, measured, so she wouldn't fly off the handle and make more of a mess of this than it already was. "I think I'm going to go do that now. You know, deal with it, and when you're ready to tell me whatever else it is that I have to do to be an upstanding pack member, you just let me know."

With that, she ducked under his arm, flying out of the barn, pounding out her discontent with heavy feet, her stump of a tail wagging behind her.

THE loud, high-pitched wail of an ambulance siren pierced the cool evening air of the city. It startled him from deep thought. No one took what was his. Especially not some nobody who hadn't earned her place. Bitter anger ate at his gut, wrenching his stomach.

Marty Andrews needed to die.

It wasn't like anyone would miss her . . .

Picking up the phone beside his couch, he pressed speed dial.

The call-ee answered on the first ring, his heavy breath the only answer, crackling and wheezing on its way out.

"She's disappeared, but I have a lead. Interested?"

The reply came in the form of a grunt.

"Good. Pay close attention. We need to move quickly and quietly. I don't need anyone finding out about this. The scandal would ruin us. Take care of it and take care of it quickly."

He hung up the phone, a smug smile of satisfaction creasing his thin lips.

CHAPTER
9

Keegan crumpled the anonymous note in his hand, balling it up and hurling it across the room with a snap of his arm. It caught the cold glare of the morning sun when it landed on the floor next to Sloan, who sat across from him. The hell he'd allow anyone to threaten Marty's well-being. No matter how crazy she made him. "Whoever did this better hope I don't find them," he warned with a hiss. His chest was tight with anger, every muscle in his body poised to do some damage.

Sloan picked up the note and glanced at it, his brow furrowing. "Any idea who dropped that little bomb?" he asked him from the other side of his desk.

When Keegan had arrived at Pack today, a letter, unsigned, lying folded on his desk, awaited him. His already bad mood had plummeted. "I'm going to take a wild stab in the dark and guess it's someone from the Lunar Council who doesn't approve of Marty. Self-righteous assholes," he muttered. "They threatened her life on paper, for Christ's sake. If one hair on her head is harmed—I'll see someone in hell." His temper flared, boiling hot.

"I'd bet it was Alana. She's not exactly thrilled about this Marty thing. Everyone knows she was supposed to be your mate."

"Alana was hot to own a part of Pack, not me, and ask me if I give a fuck what she wants," Keegan growled, narrowing his eyes in his brother's direction.

Sloan held up his hands in defeat. "Hey, big brother. Take that stick out of your ass. I'm all about whatever you want, but you know the council. Marty's an outsider, and they're afraid of what could happen if, in her fear of the unknown, she reveals us. We definitely don't need that kind of shit hitting the fan."

He clamped his teeth together, flicking the stack of papers on his desk. "It's not like I don't know that, Sloan. And the council might want to keep in mind, Marty's a were-wolf now, too. Our secret is officially her secret. But she's not at fault here. I am. Any result of that is on me."

"I know." He began to cackle with laughter, slapping his hand on his thigh. "And it's a pretty awesome fuckup. Nothing I've done compares to this. Even I'm still impressed."

Sloan's joking was meant to be good-natured, but today, and after last night with Marty, it was rubbing him the wrong way.

"I'm glad I could offer some amusement," Keegan said distractedly, staring out the tall glass windows of his office.

"Dude, you did it bigger than I ever could. This will go down in were history."

"Dude, enough!" He wasn't going to put up with Sloan's flippant crap today. Especially not today.

"What the hell is wrong with you? Usually you're cranky, but Jesus, Keegan, you're off the charts since this thing happened with Marty. What's up with that?"

Keegan ran a hand over his chin and sighed. "I don't know. She drives me insane."

Sloan nodded his head, all knowing. "Ahhhh, you wanna bag her. I get it."

"I don't want to just bag her, asshole. Stop talking about her like she's just some piece of ass."

"Hoo boy." Sloan let out a whistle.

"What's that supposed to mean?"

"You're in, buddy."

"In?"

"Yeah. You want her bad."

Keegan's eyes drifted to his lap. If his nether regions were any indication, *bad* was an understatement. "So?"

"So I'd bet the council and our fair Alana are going to have something to say about that. Does Marty even know about Alana and the fact that she's supposed to be your mate?"

Keegan shifted in his chair, grabbing a pencil and twirling it between his fingers. "The council can deal with *me*. I'm not going to let them decide who I'll mate with for life, and it wouldn't have been Alana whether Marty showed up or not. It's bullshit for them to try and dictate who you should spend the rest of your life with. I know it's council law to mate with whomever they choose, but that's never sat well with me, and I refuse to mate with someone I don't even like. I think Marty has an idea, but I don't know if she really understands the impact of it. She comes from a very different world than we do."

Sloan made a face. "Big words, brother. No one has ever defied the council's choices. You know how the council feels about pure bloodlines and offspring. It's tradition. You and Alana were going to make that dream come true. You're risking your place as alpha if what you're considering is what I think you're considering, and I know you don't want to have to hand that title off to me. Shit, I don't want you to hand that title off to me."

Keegan ignored Sloan's warning. He knew the risk he was taking, but what had drawn him to Marty that first night in the alleyway was what continued to keep him captivated. He wanted the chance to get to know her. He wanted every independent, color-coordinated, neurotic, headed-for-disaster inch of her, and he didn't care who knew it. Least of all the council. "They've bent the rules before, Sloan. They can bend them again."

"She's a human, Keegan. Or was one until you sank your canines into her. There isn't even a rule about something like that yet to bend. There aren't many left who weren't born pure in our pack and you know that. You also know how the council feels about pure bloodlines. The biting of a human with specific intent hasn't happened in centuries and it doesn't because the threat of being booted or labeled an outcast is pretty real. When the pack set about keeping the peace with the world at large, they meant it. So they're bound to be freaked about this, accident or not. You know the council. They have to make a big deal about calling a meeting of the elders to determine what to do. Protocol and all that jazz. There's nothing the council likes more than to add another rule to their long list of do's and don'ts."

"I know what she was, Sloan, and the council is just going to have to figure it out. She's staying. End of discussion."

Sloan raised his chin and lifted one dark eyebrow. "Okay, so you've known this chick for a couple of weeks, and you're already acting like she's your territory. You don't have to piss on my tree to make your point. What I don't get is why are you being so territorial? Your obligation to her only extends to teaching her our ways. The council will handle the rest. They'll mate her off. So wanna explain what gives?"

"She's a nightmare," he said, the corner of his mouth lifting in amusement.

"And that's good how?"

"There's no explanation for Marty. It turns me on. *She* turns me on. Every neurotic fucked-up inch of her turns me on. She didn't know anything about my money and didn't care when she found out. She's all about colors of life and her makeup career with Bobbie-Sue, so you'd think that I'm the CEO of the largest retail cosmetics company in the world would at least interest her while she adjusts to her new were form. But she doesn't care about it at all. She cares more about standing on her own two feet. She's incredibly independent and totally overwhelmed by the lot of us, yet there she was in the barn with me last night trying to shift so she can fit in. She's as girly as they come with her makeup and knock-off designer handbags. She's got a mouth that runs nonstop, and when I'm not busy trying to answer her endless questions, I'm busy thinking about kissing the shit out of her." He slid farther under his desk to hide the emphasis his crotch seemed to want to make about that point. Every curve on her body, the way she rolled her eyes at him when she was bent out of shape with him, her scent, the sprinkle of freckles across her nose, which she tried to hide with makeup, all made him want to do a multitude of things to her. Protect her, stuff a sock in her mouth, make love to her until she was weak from it.

Sloan sat for a moment, obviously digesting Keegan's admission. "I've been meaning to ask you, what the hell got you caught that night? You're usually so careful when you shift."

Keegan's focus became hazy. "Her scent," he murmured.

"But you smelled her *before* you bit her?"

Keegan shook his head with the memory of how foolish and careless he'd been. "I did, and I don't know why her particular scent appealed to me, but I knew it the moment I took a good whiff. Her scent is what got me into this mess. I was distracted by it, something I rarely, if ever am. If I'd been paying more attention to my surroundings and less time scoping Marty's ass, I might have seen that little fluff ball full of teeth coming at me." Christ, the guilt he'd suffered for one moment of preoccupation. He'd dragged her into something bigger than either of them. He'd be sorrier if it hadn't led him to Marty and bringing her here. Where she belonged.

With him.

"Everything happens for a reason. Have you told Marty the council will expect her to mate with someone of their choice?"

"Sort of," he answered vaguely.

"But you don't want that, do you? That's what this delay in calling a meeting of the council is about, you shit. *You* want Marty." Sloan's remark was filled with smug confidence.

Keegan ignored Sloan's reference to why he hadn't contacted the council. "What worries me more now is the rogue members of the council. We've all heard the stories about them taking matters into their own hands. If that note was from a disgruntled member of the council and they go after Marty, I'll see someone dead." He spoke the words with a calm certainty.

"They want a meeting with you, you know. It's all over the office."

"Yeah, I know, and if they think they're just going to assign Marty a mate, they've got another think coming. She will not end up with some loser beta from a pack of cavemen who just want to fuck." His voice was tight with anger, and he knew it. He heard the furious spew of his words, experienced it in every ounce of his flesh, yet had no control over it. There was no doubt he liked to be in control, and Marty made him lose control more times than he cared to admit. It was part of her charm, and while it should piss him the fuck off, it only made him want her more.

Sloan picked up on it and chuckled. "Dude, again I say, you are so gone."

Keegan said nothing. He didn't know what he was after last night. Marty was right. He should have told her everything, but doing so would result in her being more freaked out than she already was. His timing was sunk no matter how he sliced it. There was just no easy way to tell Marty the council would require she mate and carry on the bloodline. If that's what the council's intent was where she was concerned. *If.*

She wasn't pure were. What that would mean for her future in the pack worried him.

And the council . . . They'd been so damned sure he'd

mate with Alana without issue. When he'd made it clear he
didn't want to, they hadn't liked it, but they hadn't enforced
it either.

Yet.

While Alana was the obvious choice and next in line in
her pack to merge, she'd left Keegan cold for as long as
he'd known her. Marty, on the other hand, left him hotter
than Texas in July. The council had never had to enforce a
mating. No one went against the council, but they'd have to
clobber him and take him hostage before he ended up with
a viper like Alana.

"So what will you do when the council wants answers?
When they expect to hear about Marty's intentions?"

"I'll put in formal notice when I'm good and ready."

"I hate to say it, but I'm damned glad the council is so
focused on you. They've been so busy they haven't once
asked me about *my* life mate."

Keegan pointed an accusatory finger at him. "You got
off too easy, and don't think for a minute this grief-stricken
shit you play up so well about your intended life mate
being hit by a train is going to keep pulling the wool over
everyone's eyes much longer. The council will come for
you, too, eventually." Sloan's life mate, the one the council
had handpicked for him, had been tragically killed in her
were form. Run over by a train. A bitch for sure. Though
Keegan knew the news had upset Sloan, he also knew he
wasn't sorry he didn't have to go through with the mating.
Sloan mated plenty without a life mate.

"Do you think Marty's the one?"

"I think it's none of your business."

"Chicken shit," Sloan taunted with a lopsided grin.

Keegan flipped Sloan the bird and grabbed his office
phone, punching in some numbers. "Yvette? Please have
Alana come to my office."

Sloan frowned. "Do I want to stay for this?"

Keegan didn't have time to answer. Alana poked her
sleek blonde head around the corner, the curve of her hip
holding the door open. "You rang?"

Sloan rose from his chair and motioned for Alana to have a seat.

Keegan stared at her, long and hard, taking in her cool features filled with obvious discomfort. Alana visibly squirmed. "Did you just call me in here to glare at me?" she asked curtly. "Because I have better things to do than sit here while you give me the look." She crossed her long legs, letting the tip of her toe bounce with impatience. Her slender arms crossed over her chest while she glared right back at him.

"I want answers, Alana."

"For?"

Keegan rose and swiped the crumpled letter from Sloan's hand, shoving it at her. "This."

"And *that* is?"

"A threat. An anonymous threat, because whoever dropped this little grenade on my desk today was too cowardly to say it to my face." He spat the words like bullets from a gun.

Alana whipped forward in her chair, gripping the arms. The length of her long hair swung around her face. "I did no such thing!" Her denial was filled with her fury. "Surely you must have known when you brought *her* here there would be trouble. She was a *human*." She said the word as if it made Marty inferior. "Whatever happens after that is on you!"

Leaning over her chair, Keegan eyeballed her with a venomous glower. "Her name is *Marty*, Alana, and you'd better get used to it. If this," he held the letter up, "has anything to do with you, I'll find out, and if I find out it was you, I can promise you, there'll be hell to pay." There was no rise to his voice, yet his low growl held menace.

Alana jumped up from her chair, facing off with Keegan, her pert breasts heaving at the top of her suit's low neckline. "How dare you accuse me of something like this! How dare you threaten me! Who the hell do you think you are?"

"The man you thought you'd drag to the altar," he replied with cool succinctness. "The man you thought you'd mate with and by marriage, own and manage a chunk of this company." Keegan knew where he stood with Alana. He'd always known, and her desire to rule Pack was no great mystery. "If anyone has motivation, Alana, it's you."

Her green eyes flashed myriad emotions, shooting fury and fire all aimed at him. "Our fate was sealed long ago, Keegan. The council demands it. We were set to be mated from birth. You're disregarding what the council wants—not me."

"Fuck the council!" Keegan thundered back harshly.

Her face twisted into a hard mask. Her body language screamed rabid rage. Yet she kept her ruby red lips clamped shut.

Sloan stepped between them, taking Alana by the arm and whispering, "Enough. I say you and me go get some coffee," he said to Alana, then placed a hand on Keegan's shoulder. "Back up, brother, and cool down." With a thump, he patted Keegan's chest and tugged Alana out the door.

Two long strides and he was back at his desk where he shoved his chair into place and sat down hard. He picked up the phone again and punched in some numbers. There was only one person he could involve in this, and it had to be someone he trusted, yet wasn't too closely involved with his immediate family.

"What's up, Keegan?" a voice like aged leather answered.

"I need a favor."

"Hit me."

"I need you to look after Marty, but I need you to do it quietly. She'll give me hell if she knows she's being followed."

A bark of laughter shouted in his ear. "I hear she's a feisty one."

Keegan couldn't help but smile. "That she is. Will you do it?"

"You know it."

He hung up. Feeling a little better, he steepled his hands under his chin in thought. Alana's fury over being accused

was nothing less than he'd expected. She wanted in, and
she had the council to back her, but would she resort to
kidnapping and threatening notes? Was she capable of for-
going a trip to the manicurist for it?

Maybe it was Marty's ex-boyfriend, Alger? He definitely had the kind of money it would take to orchestrate it,
but was he really that hung up on Marty? Alger struck
Keegan as a lazy rich boy who couldn't get out of his own
way.

There was no better way to find out than to pay Alger a
little visit. If he was responsible for throwing Marty in the
trunk of that car, he'd fucking rip him apart.

With his own hands.

MARTY slumped on the big couch in the family room,
stroking an absent hand over Muffin's spine. She was bored
and confined. She needed something to do.

Soon or she'd go out of her mind.

She'd given Wanda and Nina full access to her accounts
for the time being, putting in for a leave of absence with her
supervisor. The only explanation she could feasibly give
was a severe health-related issue.

She had a tail, for shit's sake. That had to be considered
a medical issue, if there ever was one.

Her Bobbie-Sue clients were content enough to allow
Wanda and Nina to make their deliveries on Marty's behalf
and thankfully, so far Nina hadn't insulted anyone. In fact,
it seemed Wanda was getting the hang of things, and according to Nina, her Bobbie-Sue attitude was so much like
Marty's she wanted to puke.

Marty couldn't help but giggle when she'd read Nina's
email. Wanda would be okay, and it seemed while Nina
was still trying to slap lip gloss on unsuspecting women at
the IHOP to make ends meet, she was studying to become
a dental hygienist at night.

Marty sighed. Some people just didn't grasp the concept
of Bobbie-Sue and finding your season of life. If this were-

wolf thing had taught her anything, it was shoving something down anyone's throat only made them defensive.

Just ask her and her wannabe tail.

So she'd probably end up losing Nina as a recruit, and that should truly disrupt her ever-spinning color wheel, but there was so much more now than just the goal of a sky blue convertible at stake. Losing Nina as a recruit only saddened her. It meant they surely wouldn't spend as much time together if she ultimately left Bobbie-Sue.

Helga disrupted her pity party by plopping a tray of sandwiches in front of her, flicking her fingers in their direction. "You eat. Is gute. I make ze new recipe for you."

Marty smiled up at the big, imposing woman and warmed instantly. She and Helga had spent some time together these last few days and she wasn't nearly as gruff as Marty had first thought. Though she was as tight-lipped about this werewolf thing as everyone else. She'd deduced Keegan had ordered everyone to keep their mouths shut around the ex-human, and it would piss her off but for the fact that he'd clearly planned to take his level of responsibility in this very seriously. He obviously wasn't going to let anyone pick up the slack for his mistake.

You couldn't buy the kind of loyalty Helga had for the Flahertys, and Marty wouldn't dream of encroaching. So she'd let things lie, but there was more. Of that she was sure.

Helga reached down and scooped up Muffin who went with nary a complaint. She laid her on her broad shoulder and ruffled her fur. "I take ze princess. You eat. Come," she said to Muffin. "I have ze treat for you."

Marty chuckled. Muffin had been the joyful recipient of many treats since entering the Flaherty household. Everyone doted on her, including Keegan.

Speaking of the lycanthrope of the hour . . . they hadn't spoken much since the other night in the barn. They'd passed in the halls of this pseudo Southfork; the slightest brush of flesh between them, and Marty was on fire all over again, calling up the memory of his lips on hers, taking possession of them like he'd always had the right.

Keegan felt it, too. She could smell it on him. Arousal, desire, unadulterated lust leaped off him each time they were in a room together.

Testosterone. Keegan oozed it, and with her new nose, there was just no hiding it from her. Which meant he could smell her, too.

Nice. Very fucking nice. She wondered if desperate was a scent. If it were, she was certain she dripped it.

When he'd glanced her way over dinner, she felt the flames of it to her very toes. But he made no move to bring that to fruition. Why she'd want him to left her baffled. It wasn't like they were involved, and she'd never been a one-night-stand kind of girl. Yet, she couldn't get him out of her head. The image of his lips on her breasts, his hands stroking the most intimate parts of her. No one had ever taken her so close to the edge with such forceful finesse in such a short amount of time.

And that scared the bejesus out of her. Keegan had once been slated for Alana. Maybe she'd been treading on someone else's territory? The details of that potential match were eating her from the inside out. She wanted to know every sordid detail, and then she didn't.

She had a million questions, like why weren't Keegan and Alana together now? Had they ever been? Mara had hinted at something between them before she'd clammed up. The council must have ordered it, like they ordered everything else. Wasn't ignoring the council's orders like a big no-no in the werewolf world? Why was it so important they mate to begin with?

One thing was irrefutable, Alana clearly didn't like Marty. Words weren't necessary between them for her to figure that out, but was it because she was once human or because of Keegan's involvement with her, period? Keegan's interest in her had more to do with his sense of obligation, or so she'd thought until the other night.

He'd wanted her, too. Maybe he was just a decent enough guy not to take advantage of a woman in a weak state. Yeah, he was sexy as hell, and there was no denying it, but again, so what? There were loads of sexy guys out there. This crazy yearning she had for him, a longing like nothing else she'd ever experienced, had to be a part of the mixed-up mess her head was in. She was fragile— vulnerable. That state of mind could lead to all sorts of bad choices.

Yet when the image of one of his rare smiles came to mind—one she'd been responsible for—it made her stomach flip-flop, and it had nothing to do with throwing him to the ground and riding him to orgasmic glory.

How pathetic.

Grabbing a throw pillow, Marty pressed her forehead into it and groaned. At this point in time she just wanted to go home and resume what was left of her life.

Or did she?

Why was it that whenever she thought about going home her heart seized with flutters of anxiety?

At least for now, she and Keegan had declared a truce. It was silent, but evident, and peace between them, for the moment anyway, was a good thing.

After the other night, she didn't know what to expect.

Her behavior that evening, on all levels, appalled her. She'd thrown herself at him like Joe Montana threw a football, and when he'd drawn a halt to it, obviously because he wasn't into taking advantage of nymphomaniacs, she'd pitched a hissy.

She'd reacted badly.

An understatement if there ever was one. Yet, if Keegan were just a scumbag, looking to hook up, would he have stopped what clearly would have been a mating session to end all just to tell her about some more crazy pack laws?

Maybe. She was living under his roof, and whether he'd loved 'em and left 'em in the past, he did have to coexist with her until this was over. That could make for some very uncomfortable circumstances in the aftermath. So maybe his sense of right and wrong had nothing to do with him turning on the cold water.

It was too hard to cling to any reason when her moods

swung high and low. She was having more and more trouble controlling them. However, Keegan hadn't been honest with her. Not totally.

Though he had said he'd tell her what she needed to know in small doses and truthfully, he was due some credit. Some of these pack laws were downright fucked up. To nail her with them all at once would have been too much info in just one conversation. Then again, she was a little tired of not having the full picture. Fair was fair, and if she was expected to do all of these bizarre things this unknown council wanted her to do—she'd better know all of it and soon.

Who were these council members anyway, and how did you get an appointment with them? Cuz she had some sharing she'd like to indulge in. And who the fuck did they think they were telling people who they had to spend the rest of their lives with? Let alone have children . . . um, pups with.

As far as she was concerned it was as archaic as it got. The idea made her want to go back to New York even if the crazy motherfuckers who'd kidnapped her did know where she lived.

But she couldn't do that. She knew she couldn't, and it wasn't just because someone had nabbed her.

"Marty?"

Her eyes lifted to see Keegan's broad frame, blocking out the light coming in from the corner window. Her nose smelled him before he'd ever entered the room but the sight of him was always like a jab in her gut. He was definitely an impact player. Dressed in khaki colored silk trousers complemented by a light blue shirt and dark blue tie, he looked like he'd just stepped out of *GQ*. Yet there was a ruggedness about him that couldn't be hidden with tailored clothing and fine silk. It made for a heady combination of restrained sexuality. A wolf in sheep's clothing.

Catching her breath she sent him a flirtatious grin. "Wow. Do you mean me, Marty? Like the one sitting here on the couch? Cuz you haven't said boo to me in a couple of days. So I want to be sure we have the right Marty. Marty Andrews. The jacked-up werewolf-in-training Marty."

His hand cupped her chin, giving her face a once-over with a teasing grin. "You look like her. Are you the one with the tail trouble?"

Marty grinned, giving him a flash of teeth. "That'd be me."

"Then you're the right Marty."

"What's up? More werewolf stuff?" She tried to keep the angst that thought brought from her voice.

He took a seat beside her and grabbed one of the sandwiches Helga had left. His heavy weight made the couch sag and her body lean closer to his.

Definitely not something she needed today. God knew she was a hormone waiting to happen, and with the way her moods had been swinging, she didn't want a repeat of the other night. With as much subtlety as she could muster, she inched toward the arm of the couch, draping herself over it.

His expression darkened for a moment, and then he seemed to reconsider. "Nope. No werewolf stuff."

Marty expelled a sigh and bit into her sandwich. "So what's up?"

"I was just wondering what you've been doing."

She held up the thick sandwich. "Eating. Helga keeps me well fed. If I keep this up, I'm going to have to add diet to my color wheel," she joked, giving him a teasing grin.

"How are the mood swings?"

She shrugged her shoulders. "I'm managing, I guess. Most of the time I think I have it under control. There hasn't been much to be angry over lately either, so maybe I'm adjusting?"

"You're bored?"

"I think I'm just not used to having so much time on my hands. I work full-full-time to keep my Bobbie-Sue clients happy, and in my spare time I work at finding more clients." Which gave her an idea out of the clear blue. Why she hadn't thought of this before eluded her. Most likely because everyone hated her at Pack and she wasn't about to shove herself down anyone's throat, seeking acceptance, but she was tougher than the likes of some bunch of snobs who hated her ex-human guts.

What better way to show them she was trying to make this work than to work *with* them? Besides, who knew her color wheels like Cole Haan knew shoes? Without thought for the consequences, or the sure trial by fire they'd give her, she blurted out a request. "You know, I do know a thing or two about makeup, and I do have a lot of time on my hands until we decide it's safe for me to go back to my apartment. So put me to good use. Give me a job at Pack."

His posture stiffened for a moment, and he stopped chewing his sandwich.

A "No, Marty" was on the way—she felt it.

But he surprised her. "Okay. I think I can arrange that. But I need you to promise me something."

A lung? Kidney? "Sure," she agreed with a tentative smile.

"I want you to come and go to Pack via a driver I'll arrange."

Her antenna went up. "Why?"

"Because I said so."

And he was, after all, the second coming. So naturally his word was on par with the Almighty's. "Wanna tell me what's going on?"

His face became cloaked again. That granite mask of unreadable emotions he wore so well spread across his handsome face. She was getting better at gauging his moods, looking for the subtle signs he gave off when something was askew. "Nothing has changed where you're concerned. I'm still as worried about your safety as I was when this kidnapping happened, and if you want me to find you something to do at Pack, then you have to follow my instructions."

Okay, so she could pick a fight with him just so she could watch his nostrils flare—which wasn't a bad thing in her mind, cuz it was killa sexy—or she could shut up and have something to do with this endless stretch of days that seemed to be on her agenda. "Fine."

"Fine?"

"Yeah. Fine."

"No argument. No endless stream of questions?"

"Nuh-uh."

"Not even a 'Keegan, you're being a pain in my ass, you arrogant shithead'?"

"Not a one."

He pressed a hand to her forehead and gave her a look of comical confusion. "You're not the Marty Andrews I know. The Marty Andrews I know asks a million questions, refuses to listen to logic before she's dragged me through the mud first, and she definitely doesn't just give in when I tell her to do something. My Marty has a fresh mouth and an answer for everything. So who the hell are you?" He grinned, making the creases on either side of his mouth deepen.

His Marty . . .

Marty swatted at his hand, mostly because it felt way too good against her skin, and going to the place called overactive libido was not a good thing right now. "I am the one and only Marty Andrews, and I need something to do before I lose my mind. So for now, I'm shutting up about how pushy and dictator-like you are and hedging my bets. I need something to pass the time until I can go home. I know makeup—at least the Bobbie-Sue kind anyway, and well, my having some knowledge of the cosmetics industry should definitely be put to use. So before I say something I just know I'll regret, I agree to your terms. Don't push your luck. It can only hold out for so long." She smiled, popping up off the couch, holding out a hand to him and yanking him upward when he took it.

Keegan clipped the end of her nose with the tip of his finger while looking down at her. "Are you scamming me?"

Her expression was coy and playful. "Would I talk smack to you? Of course I'm not scamming you. I'll come and go with the babysitter—um, driver."

"You promise not to go anywhere without the driver?"

"I draw the line at the bathroom. Some things must be treated delicately."

"You know what I mean, Marty."

She grabbed a handful of his tie and tugged. "I said okay. Now quit pushing."

"Pinky swear?" He held up his finger with a glib smile.

With a sigh, mocking the one Keegan was known for, she replied, "Fine. Pinky swear." She locked fingers with him, feeling that same odd connection to him that made no sense.

They stood like that far longer than was necessary to seal a pact, fingers intertwined, eyes locked. The air circulating between them stilled, their connected flesh one entity.

And that was all it took for her to experience the same dizzying, compelling rush of need. The need to burrow against his thick chest, bury her face in the vast expanse of muscle residing there.

This time the surge of emotion had nothing to do with sex. It had to do with wanting comfort from another person—Keegan specifically. It was a plethora of wants and needs—a minefield of sensations she was too afraid to explore.

Alrighty then.

Marty broke the spell first by releasing the grip her pinky finger had on his. The loss of contact left her feeling very alone.

She covered up this newest discovery by sending him a cocky smile, taking a step backward. "So, what do you have in mind for me, Mr. Flaherty? Because I have to tell you, if you leave me with that witchi-fied woman who answers Pack's phones, I think I might end up clobbering her with my fake designer shoes, and then I'll never be invited to play on the monkey bars at recess."

Keegan laughed, rich and deep. "Would I do that? I'll hand you over to Yvette. She's my personal secretary and not nearly as scary as our receptionist. You ready?" he asked, holding his fist out, knuckles forward.

"As I'll ever be," she responded, her tone too husky for her own liking when she knocked fists with him.

But was she really ready? Who was ever ready for the kind of scorn those Pack members felt for her? She set her lips in a firm line of determination while following Keegan from behind. They didn't have to love her. They didn't even have to like her. She could live with that, but no one was going to make her feel like she wasn't good enough.

She had sufficient grit to weather this storm until the tide turned. There were two clear choices here. Either these rough waters would take her back to her apartment in New York alone, or she'd manage to find some kind of acceptance from these were-people.

Out of the frying pan and into the fire you go, Marty Andrews.

CHAPTER
10

Oh, to be a fly on the wall when Alana O'Brian hit the break room, skidding in on her sassy, little pumps to come to a halt in front of her salivating coworkers with the news that she'd been assigned to the ex-human. Marty would love to hear that conversation.

When she'd arrived at Pack to the resounding silence she'd left last week, Keegan had doled out some fierce glances to his employees on her behalf, then handed her off to his secretary, Yvette, because he had a production meeting.

Harried and clearly not having a good day, Yvette had given her to her assistant, Claudia.

Who'd given her to Alana like a trussed-up Christmas goose.

A smiling Alana behaved as if the daggers of death they'd exchanged over the watercooler had never occurred.

But by now, Marty knew bitch when she smelled bitch, and Alana was the reincarnation of the word.

"So, how's it going at Keegan's?" Alana asked too

pleasantly, while they headed to wherever it was her idle hands were going to be put to good use.

Good. Things are very good. I've accosted him on one occasion, making lewd sexually laden passes at him and unsuccessfully tried to turn into a dog. Everything is so fabulous I could just shed tears from the beauty of it. "It's been an adjustment," was all she said from stiff lips that didn't seem to want to work properly. Hiking her purse over her shoulder, she rolled her head on her neck.

"I can only imagine," Alana rebutted, walking nearly two steps ahead of Marty. When asses were handed out, Marty had to admit, the gods had shown Alana some serious love. The low-waist black trousers she wore accented her long legs and torso. Her flat belly, concave and probably ripped, led to pert, high breasts jutting out from the red tuxedo shirt she wore. The collar was casually flipped upward, highlighting the large, gold hoop earrings in her ears that swayed in time with the swish of her ass.

And she was very, very blonde.

How come Alana could keep her blondeness and she couldn't?

Who the fuck did she have to talk to about that?

The quick glimpse she'd given the hall mirror before leaving told her if she didn't get to Steven some time soon, all bets were brunette. Her hair grew darker every day. Marty ran a hand over her head, smoothing out her shoulder-length hair self-consciously. Though it was thick and full, it didn't part seductively over her eye or fall in waves down her back like Miss Clairol's did.

Alana was like one of the Coors Light poster girls and Grace Kelly all rolled into one.

Even Marty'd call Keegan a dumb ass if he'd dumped Miss America here, and that was pissing her off.

She had no business, even if it was only mentally, shoving Keegan off on Alana. She had no definitive answer about what might have passed between them or if anything even had. If nothing had, Marty sure couldn't find a good reason why not. Alana had the kind of va-va-voom every woman yearned for. That kittenish quality—the mark of every good vixen and the sort of sensuality men started wars over. Meow.

Bitch.

Enough already with these crazy spikes of jealousy, she chided herself. She had no right to question what had made Keegan give up a hot broad like Alana—if he had. She shouldn't give a rat's ass what he did with his personal life.

But noooo, here she was churning possibility after possibility around in her taxed brain. If Alana wanted Keegan, then have at it.

She'd dare the hard-bodied slut to try.

Hellafino.

Marty squeezed her temples, as if that might wring her possessive Keegan thoughts from her mind. What the hell kind of attitude was this? She'd never in her life fought over a man. Especially before she even knew if a fight had to ensue to begin with.

But she'd kick the bitch's ass from here to eternity if she had to . . .

You so want him, that sinister voice whispered through the endless halls of her head.

So?

God, this was ridiculous. Just flat out nuts. What a perfect time to have a revelation. Yeah, all right, she wanted Keegan. He was arrogant, impatient, difficult, and bossy, but yes, yes, yes, she wanted his lupine ass.

Okay?

Apparently so did Alana. Or had. Or might have.

What-the-fuck-ever.

Glimpsing Alana's cool, collected presence had obviously irked her. She was feeling insecure in her gray sweaterdress—no longer in her color wheel, thanks to the werewolf—that hugged much curvier curves than Alana's sleek planes. Somehow, her boobs just didn't have the kind of bounce and lift Alana's did. Marty hid a breath while sucking in her gut. Her belly could be flat like that, too, if she held her breath like forever. But on the up side, she did have cute boots and a low-slung belt around her hips that was just to die for. Even Alana, fashionista that she was, couldn't deny that.

Score!

Marty—one.

Barbie—one.

They stopped at an elevator, Alana's perfectly manicured red nail punching the down button. She stretched, highlighting her firm breasts as she arched her back. "So you work for Bobbie-Sue, right?"

So your ta-tas are made of silicone, right? "I do." Marty kept her reply light, clasping her hands behind her back so her breasts would look perkier. *So don't make me break out my color wheel and give you what for, you man-eater.* Not that Alana needed any help finding her season of life. She was spot on, securely planted on the calendar in the category of spring.

Again, another reason to hate her immaculate, unruffled guts.

"I know a little about the company. The levels of color and such. Lavender, blue, et cetera. Oh, and cars. Don't you get a car or something?"

Her inner saleswoman wept silently for the tragic loss of her sky blue convertible. It seemed pretty far away and totally unobtainable now. "If you sell enough, then yes."

"Do you enjoy your work?" she asked like she gave a shit, but Marty knew better. Alana thought she was far superior in every way to Marty no matter how outwardly agreeable she tried to pretend she was. She reeked of it.

"I do."

"Door-to-door, newspaper ads, multilevel, right?" She tossed a clipboard between her two hands absently, making her bangle bracelets jingle and catch the fluorescent lighting.

Yes, yes, yes, you snotty, silicone-implanted bitch. I bang down people's doors to make a living. God that sounded so cheap when she said it in her head. Marty nodded. "Yep. Door-to-door." Many, many doors. So many doors she'd lost count.

"Low overhead. You don't even need an office. How interesting," she drawled, flipping a length of hair over her shoulder.

Says the woman who has an office the size of my apartment.

Damn it all. How dare she allow this woman make her feel inferior. "It's definitely interesting." *Beyond interesting, you condescending witch.* Ugh. Marty shifted from foot to foot to hide her discomfort.

She assessed Marty's face with eyes that to most would look like she was interested, but masked tightly reined contempt. "So you know a little something about makeup then?"

Oh, Barbie. Do I know a little something . . . well, duh. Look at me. I don't want to brag, but hellllloooo. Is it me, or are you missing my perfectly applied foundation, followed by a light matte powder that lasts all day and never shines? No one could fault her makeup technique. If there was anything she knew, it was fucking makeup. "Yeah, a *little.*" She fought to keep the sarcasm from her tone as they stepped into the elevator.

Alana smiled, the corners of her mouth tilting upward ever so slightly to reveal—yeah, go figure—perfectly straight teeth. "Perfect," she crooned. "Then you'll be thrilled with your assignment."

Yippee and skippee. Whatever it was, it was pretty far away from the upstairs offices, because the elevator ride was long. When the doors popped open to reveal a dimly lit hallway painted in dark shades of gray, Marty frowned.

They were in the basement.

Now how in theee hell could she create color wheels if she was in the basement and from the looks of it, alone?

Alana grabbed what looked like surgical scrubs from a metal utility shelf along the hall wall and draped them over her shoulder while they continued to walk to the end of the corridor. A long row of large, metal doors marked with letters of the alphabet stood before them.

Alana chose door B, pushing it open with the weight of

her slender body. Row after row of round, black vats lay before her. "So here we are," she said with a satisfied smile, spreading her arms like she was showing her where the Hope diamond was stashed.

"And where is here?" Cuz "here" was looking a little sketchy to Marty.

"Here is where Pack makeup is made. In those vats."

Oh. "And what's my job?"

"Scrubbing them." She said it as if Marty should know something so vital to the creation of Pack Cosmetics.

Puulease, bitch. Her eyes narrowed. How charming. You know, they really should just have a bitch-slap fest and get all this pent-up bent-out-of-shape out of the way. It would make things so much more pleasant between them after Marty kicked the fucking perfect out of her.

But this was the putting-her-in-her-place portion of the Alana show, wasn't it? Well, fine. Fucking ducky. She wasn't going to have people saying she was anything but a lady. She'd be damned if she was going to let this ethereal vision of loveliness see her crack like fine China. Marty dropped her purse and took the scrubs from Alana's tapered fingers, shrugging into them.

The chirp of Alana's cell phone had her digging in the pocket of her pants to answer it while Marty counted the vats. She gave up after forty-two and went to the table Alana was pointing out in the far corner of the vast room while she yakked on the phone in hushed, low tones.

Rubber gloves and industrial bottles of cleanser lined the table. A list, laminated and hanging from the wall of measurements for the solutions for each numbered vat, told her all she needed to know to get started.

Cradling the phone to her shoulder, Alana absently addressed her one last time before leaving her in the dank recesses of the basement. "I see you've found all you need to get started. I'll trust you don't need much direction because you're a *smart* girl, who knows her makeup." She winked one green eye at her and pointed to the phone, covering the mouthpiece. "I really have to take this call. It's been"—she paused and rolled her tongue along the inside of her cheek—"lovely to meet you. Bye now," she cooed, sauntering out of the big room with a sultry sway to her ass.

Yeah. Buh-bye.

Marty rolled up her sleeves. Okay, then. If this was Alana's way of insulting her, so be it. Bring it, Blondie. She'd scrub those fucking vats until they shined like Barbie's perfect fucking teeth.

ALANA smiled smugly, leaving Marty and hopping with light feet onto the elevator, pressing the phone tighter to her ear. "We are clear, aren't we, darling?"

"As the day is long," the male voice, hard as nails, replied.

"Good. Because messy entanglements at this point in my life aren't my thing. I have a goal. You scratch my back, and I'll scratch yours, so to speak." She used a hushed, kittenish tone reserved for men who were doing as they were told before she clicked the phone shut. She had no intention of taking this relationship further than ridding herself of that classless tramp Marty. This man was a means to an end and a good fuck to occupy her while she figured out, with his help, exactly how to eliminate the competition.

If only Keegan were as easily manipulated as her cohort, her life would certainly be far less trying.

No one was taking this opportunity from her, least of all some disgusting ex-human from Piscataway. She shuddered. Of all the places to be born and bred. Word was Keegan behaved a little more than just obligated to Marty, and she wasn't having that. He could fuck whomever he liked after he did the council's bidding and mated with her. She'd be too busy owning a piece of Pack to care.

Well, it mattered not at this point. When all was said and done, Marty wouldn't be a problem much longer, and then she could set her sights on consoling poor Keegan over his loss. In the meantime, she'd amuse herself and her insatiable libido with whatshisface. Thank God they'd crossed paths . . .

SIX hours later, easily a million cleaning solutions mixed, twenty rubber glove changes, and the sweat of her brow, Marty had cleaned every last vat. Her back ached from lugging buckets of water, and her head throbbed from the odor of heavy cleansers.

But she'd done it.

No one could ever say Marty Andrews wasn't a team player. She could only imagine what tomorrow's job would be. Maybe toilet scrubbing? Surely that had to be a step up from this grueling work. She could borrow Barbie's toothbrush and have it back before she ever knew it was gone.

Alana had done this to demean her. To put her in her place.

Marty grabbed a stool with rollers and plunked down on it, sucking in a deep breath. That was okay, too. Marty could take whatever that windup Barbie doll could dish out. She'd clean vats until the Apocalypse just to show Alana she wasn't going to let her beat her down.

"Marty?" Mara's fresh face peeked in the door, her long, chestnut hair flowing to the middle of her arm when she nodded her head in Marty's direction. She looked upset.

Marty smiled and motioned for her to come join her, shoving another stool at Mara. "Have a seat."

Her oversized sweatshirt hung to her slender thighs, and her hands clasped the outside of sleeves that were too long for her arms. Her cheeks were flushed, and her pretty mouth pinched. "No. I'm not sitting, because when you're done telling me what the hell you're doing down here, I'm going to go give someone a piece of my mind. Who brought you down here?"

"Uh—"

Pointing a finger at Marty, she shook it. "Never mind, you don't have to tell me. I already know. Alana, right?

God, she's such a jealous, mean bitch! She couldn't just have put you in filing—or even the mail room. She had to prove a point. Well, guess what? I'm not going to let this go without telling Keegan. He'll be furious, and you can believe, when he's mad, no one crosses him."

Marty pulled her to a sitting position on the opposite chair and shook her head. "Relax. Please don't tell him. I know you told him about last week, and I appreciate your looking out for me, but I think this was about me having to prove myself. It wasn't so bad. He knew when he brought me here I'd be subject to this sort of discrimination. But I get the feeling no one tells him what to do, and if someone had told him not to bring me to Buffalo, that'd just be one more reason why he would. He could have left me to my own devices, yet he didn't. Even knowing it wouldn't be easy." Was that her defending the big, bad wolf? Wow. Talk about defining moments. Nonetheless, she found she believed Keegan's intentions about looking out for her were good. The rest—like the hootchie-kootchie in the barn—was still a bit fuzzy.

Mara's voice rose in her insistence. "That's really decent of you, Marty, but it isn't him down here cleaning vats. No one even does that by hand anymore. It's done by machine."

Aha. Well, score another one for Miss Wonder Butt. She guessed no one could call her a pussy then, could they? No, because you're a *dog* . . .

"And why should you have to prove anything—especially to Alana? She's just jealous of you because—"

Marty pulled the scrubs off and lifted her shoulders upward, cutting her off. She wasn't sure she wanted to know why Alana might be jealous just yet. If Keegan was spending less time with Alana because he felt obligated to Marty, she didn't want to know today. "Because I wasn't born a werewolf? I'm sure people are as afraid of me as I was of them. You guys have a hella big secret to keep. I'd worry, too, if some freaked-out human came along and barged in. Speaking of secrets, isn't it hard to keep this from outsiders? Don't you have to meet with investors for Pack who are human?" There was so much more she wanted to ask, but didn't. It would mean Mara might be put in an uncomfortable position, and she didn't want that.

"First of all, you didn't barge in. Keegan was at the root of this problem. Honestly, when Sloan told us, we were in shock. He's usually the one in some kind of trouble. Second, you'd be surprised how many of us there are in the world with you. We deal with humans all the time. We have a select group of people who handle things like that, and they're very careful. Pack wouldn't be what it is today if we weren't."

Marty held up her hands. "Look, I don't know what the deal is with Alana, and I don't want you to tell me. I know it would put you in a bad position with Keegan. So let's let it go. He's doing his best, and it seems to me he has enough on his plate without adding more."

Mara's grin was knowing. "You like my big, bossy brother, don't you?"

Marty remained silent, unable to commit to the words out loud just yet.

"I figured as much. You don't have to say the words for me to know. I can smell it whenever you two are together."

God, could everyone smell her? There just wasn't enough deodorant in the world to hide from these ultrasensitive noses.

Mara's laugh tinkled when she patted Marty on the thigh. "Sorry, I don't mean I can literally smell it. I just meant it's obvious."

Great, now she was flaunting her lust. "He's okay," was all she begrudgingly admitted to.

Mara screwed up her face and nodded. "Uh-huh. I can see that. I want you to listen to me. Don't let a bitch like Alana get in your way if Keegan is who you want. Don't let any of the pack members, employees, relatives—whatever, get in the way of what you want. Ever. Some risks are worth it—even when it means you have to rearrange your whole life to take one." Emotions played across her face in rapid fire, and if Marty were to define them, she'd have to say Mara looked almost wistful, yet her words held conviction.

For whatever reason, Marty felt the need to explain her laid-back attitude about Alana and everyone else who'd snubbed her. Alone wasn't something she'd ever minded—acceptance even less. Even though she wanted these people to like her, she would live if they didn't.

"I don't want you to get the wrong impression about me, Mara. I'm not the kind of person to leave something alone if I want it badly enough, but I am the kind of person who understands what it is to bide my time. I'm pushy to a degree. Like when it comes to selling makeup—if you believe my friends Wanda and Nina—but I've never been one to get too close to anyone. I realize that now after spending time with all of you. I was into my career, and nothing was going to stop me from selling buttloads of Bobbie-Sue. I didn't spend a lot of time making friends, and I regret it because I have no family left to speak of, and in this craziness, it would have been nice to have someone to turn to."

Her words were wry, punctuated by the loneliness she'd been feeling lately. "But I'm also definitely not the kind of person who's going to foist myself on a bunch of people who don't understand me any more than I understand them. Pack—your pack is afraid of change. I represent a huge change. I also bring to mind the idea that I might, in my panic over this, tell someone who could create havoc for all of you. You've lived this way all of your lives. Me? Not so much. All of this contempt for me is rooted in fear. I know better than anyone what it is to be afraid. I mean, I sprouted a tail. Scary stuff for us humans," she joked with unease.

Mara twisted a strand of her hair around her finger. "I know we're a lot, Marty. I mean, a lot. I can see how we might overwhelm you, but that's no reason for the elders of the council or anyone else to make it harder for you. A little understanding would go a long way in your adjusting to this. Keegan's approach to it is to make everyone accept you, and while normally I don't agree with his Neanderthal attitude, in this case, I do. He made the mistake, and you shouldn't suffer because of it. As long as I'm around, you won't."

Where was this coming from? This righteous indignation toward the council? Hadn't they always lived by these outdated rules and regulations? Marty wanted to ask, but again, she found herself clamming up. This would be where the pushy in her stopped and the caution began. Asking meant the chance she'd have information that would bring her closer to another person. Knowing someone's secrets, their deepest desires, meant, in some cases, you were obligated to return the favor, and if there was anything she wasn't good at, it was sharing her innermost thoughts. The things that kept her awake at night—her dreams. Dreams that had begun to take a vastly different path than they had a month ago. "Okay, so now that I know you'll kick Barbie's ass on my behalf, I say we call it a day. I'm beat, and I think I broke a couple of nails. I simply can't go on with a chipped nail." She held her hand up for Mara to see with a giggle.

Mara pursed her lips, rolling up the sleeves of her sweatshirt. "I'm telling you, all you have to do is say the word, and I'm on her."

Marty rose, her limbs sore and aching. She needed a bath and a soothing facial mask. Grabbing her purse, she said, "I know. But violence is so ugly and very, very unbabe-like." Her smile held the hint of a tease. "C'mon. Evander, put away the gloves and let's hit the road."

On their way out the heavy, metal door, Mara's cell phone rang, her brow lifting when she looked at the number. It looked important.

"You go. I can find my way upstairs. I promise you can trust me to find my babysitter so he can drive me home." Marty grinned, patting her on the back.

Mara's smile was vague and appreciative. She waved her fingers in affirmation, then scurried down the hall in the opposite direction.

Marty wrapped her arms around her waist, while she waited for the elevator. If she weren't so tired, she'd be pretty tweaked that Alana had done something so shitty. But after cleaning a gazillon vats like some scullery maid, all she wanted to do was eat and go to bed.

She wandered the secluded halls of Pack, pushing her way out the revolving door with tired hands, while she wondered where Keegan was. The night air smelled clean, and the scent of wood-burning fireplaces warmed her. Though a glance upward told her it was cloudy and overcast. Tut-tut, smelled like snow.

Jesus. Who was she now? Doppler 5000?

The parking lot was well lit, illuminating the spot her driver had said he'd wait for her in.

However, the space was empty, and so was the parking lot. At least on this end.

Scanning the vast area, she couldn't see anything past the edge of the building but darkness, so she took off in the other direction, her boots crunching on the cold pavement. You know, she really was trying to follow all these rules, but you couldn't get a lift home from someone who was flippin' invisible.

She spied a long, dark sedan and headed for it. It looked like the car that had dropped her off. Approaching the vehicle, she saw the tags were the same vanity plates Keegan had told her to look for—*PACKONE*.

Excellent. Rounding the corner of the car, Marty went straight for the driver's side to give her babysitter what for. Rule number one—never leave your charge alone. God only knew the trouble they could get into if you took your eyes off them for a second.

She giggled, but her amusement with her thoughts turned to horror in the blink of an eye. Her driver, Les was his name, was slumped against the car door, his face pressed to the glass, lifeless.

Marty reacted without thinking, digging in her purse for her cell phone to call Keegan with one hand and yanking open the car door with the other.

The weight of the driver's body fell to her hip just as she was pressing speed dial. Her hand flew to the spot on his neck just below his ear, trying to locate a pulse. His skin was cold and clammy. She took a huge, shaky breath of air. He was out cold, but he wasn't dead.

Just as Keegan's phone began to ring, a hand, gloved and rough, clapped over her mouth from behind. Her cell phone and purse flew to the ground, Les's body left in a heap on the pavement.

Whoever it was, dragging her backward, smelled of Pierre Cardin and expensive soap. Her nostrils flared, taking in the scent and memorizing it.

He was strong. She was no lightweight, yet he was brawny enough to lift her off her feet with only a hand over her mouth and one around her waist. She couldn't get a grip with the heels of her boots to stop him from pulling her.

And with that thought, came another.

What the hell was it with these people anyway? Always klunking her on the head and stuffing her into confined spaces.

It sent a thunderbolt of fiery wrath on an all-points bulletin to every cell in her body. Her heart crashed. Her head throbbed. Her mouth grew dry. Her lungs burned from fighting for air through her nose. Her stomach plummeted, then rose to rebel against these unwanted hands on her.

The fuck she was going to let someone clobber her over the head and stuff her into some trunk again! Rage, fury, fear, panic seeped into every pore, bubbling over until she thought her head would explode.

And in a split second, she made a very clear, conscious choice.

She'd sever the motherfucker's hand and eat it for breakfast with some béarnaise sauce before she'd let him drag her to parts unknown and do God knew what with her.

She clawed at the hand that clamped over her mouth with stiff, cold fingers, pulling it far enough down over her lip so she could latch onto it and bite.

Hard.

She clenched her jaw, preparing to sink her teeth into the hand of her attacker, tasting the leather of his glove. The material was thick and gooey on her tongue. Huh. Tasted like Gucci.

Soft, supple. Like butter.

Definitely Gucci . . .

She shook her head violently, heard the crunch of bone as she tore into him, but she couldn't breathe from the mouthful of hand. Marty spat the glove from her mouth and howled her fury. The eerie scream erupted from her throat and to her ears, sounded spookily like the wild cry of a werewolf. With a hard jab, she nailed him in the ribs. The force of the blow amazed even her.

With an ear-splitting, agonizing shriek, he let go, thrusting her to the ground with the force of a quarterback. Footsteps crashing against the pavement resounded in her ears, as she hit the hard ground on her hands, skidding and tearing the flesh of her palms before she rolled to her back.

Her head slammed against the pavement and bounced back up, leaving her dizzy and disoriented. She lay there for a moment, gasping for breath, running a hand over her forehead with a wince.

More footsteps greeted her ears.

She groaned. Cheerist. If there were more of them, they could bloody well take her. She'd figure it out later.

"Marty!" Ah, Keegan. His voice was like manna from Heaven.

Then Mara's. "Oh, my God!"

Marty scrunched her eyes shut, fighting a wave of nausea. "Les . . . go get Les. He's breathing, but I don't know if he's just knocked out or seriously injured."

Mara's feet left her line of blurry vision with quick beats on the pavement. Jesus effin', her head hurt.

She fought to come to a sitting position, but Keegan was on all fours beside her before she could even lift her head, his hunky body blocking out the glare of the streetlamp.

He bracketed her head with big, solid hands. "Are

you—wait, never mind," he quipped, obviously remembering her last rant about asking her if she was okay, when it was more than obvious she wasn't. "I know you're not all right. What the hell happened?"

"Could we have this conversation standing? Really, it's cold down here, and I'm tired of being knocked around by strange men."

With hands she didn't know could be so gentle, Keegan pulled her to her feet, cradling her against him. She swayed for a moment, trying to catch her balance.

"So you know it was a man? Can you be sure?"

"I smelled his cologne. Pierre Cardin, and if that was a woman, she could definitely take Helga with one hand tied behind her back."

"Did you get a look at him?"

Marty leaned over his arm and covered the side of her mouth, spitting. "Sorry. I hate the taste of leather. I tried to bite him, but I gagged."

"What?" His voice thundered with a roar that left her already aching head pounding. His hands grabbed each side of her face, tilting her head up under the light. "Did he fucking have his hands on you? I'll find him and *kill* him."

"No. He never had the chance. I guess I should be glad I didn't go all Hannibal Lector on him, or we could have had another case of me," she reminded him sheepishly, digging in her coat pocket for a tissue to wipe the taste from her mouth. "That's *if* he's not already a werewolf friend of yours. I did give him a good one to the ribs, though. There's something to be said for this superhuman strength."

"Who, Marty? *Who* did you hit? Do you have any idea?" His voice held an anxious edge to it, and he cradled her closer to him.

"Well, if I knew that all our cares would just melt away, wouldn't they? I just don't know. I came outside to find Les, just like you said. The car wasn't in the spot I was supposed to meet him in. So I wandered down to this end of the parking lot and found Supernanny knocked out. I went to help him, and someone grabbed me from behind. I tried calling you on your cell phone. Where were you?"

His eyebrows rose. "I was leaving for the day. My voice-mail must have picked up."

"Well, I can tell you one very distinct thing. He had on Gucci gloves."

"And you'd know that how?" He cupped her chin, running his thumb over her lower lip.

Silly, silly man. She'd know the taste of Gucci any-where. "I know Gucci like the mob knows cement blocks, is how. Oh, and he smelled of Pierre Cardin cologne. Not that a million people in the naked city don't wear Pierre Cardin cologne and Gucci gloves—I realize it's not much help." She glanced downward and with that, another wave of fury swept over her. "Oh, and by the way, I have to tell you, I'm really, really sick of being accosted. And god-damn it, would you just look!" Marty held up her hand under the light. "Not only are my hands blacktop burned, but I broke another fucking nail. Fuck, fuck, fuck!" she hollered, exasperated and utterly fed up.

"Marty!" Keegan grabbed her around the waist, pulling her back to his hard chest, cupping the back of her aching head. "Cupcake?"

"What?" God, couldn't he see she was in manicure crisis?

"It's a nail. In the scheme of things, like you being dead, not such a big deal, babe. And your hands will—"

"Heal. I know. The magic of being a werewolf." Marty slumped against him. He was right, but even though it was only a nail, it represented someone invading her personal space, and she'd kinda like to know who was responsible for that. "You're right. I know you're right. I'm just tired and frustrated."

From the dark night she heard Mara call out, "Les is okay. I'm going to take him home."

Thank God he hadn't been seriously hurt simply be-cause Keegan had asked him to look out for her ass.

"So you hit him, huh?" She heard the chuckle in his voice, restrained, but still there.

Marty nodded her head against his chest, letting her cheek rest against it, snuggling nearer to his warmth. The crinkle of his long leather jacket as he put his arms around her made her smile. "I did. I was so pissed, I just nailed him. Almost tore into him like he was a T-bone. I didn't know I had it in me."

"Ahhh, grasshopper." His grumble came from deep in his chest, vibrating against hers. "You've learned well. What about our tail troubles?"

Her giggle was light when her hand went to her butt. She sighed. There it was, pushing through the back of her sweaterdress like the eyesore it was. "Sure enough. I was really pissed that someone was doing this to me *again*. Hey, how did you know I was here?"

He slid his hands inside her coat, running his thumbs in circles over her waist. "I think half of Buffalo knows you're here. I heard you howl—um, scream just as I was coming out of the building."

"I howled, didn't I? Like a bonafide werewolf." Marty grinned. She couldn't help but feel a sense of pride about that. If she couldn't turn into a four-legged hairball, at the very least she was a screamer. A good one.

Keegan leaned down, placing a kiss on her forehead. "Uh-yeah. That's a mighty set of lungs ya got there, human."

"Ex-human. So I guess we still have a mystery." She was deflated, her tone flat.

"Indeed we do, but it might help if you come clean about things instead of letting me hear it from someone else. You have anything you want to tell me? Any bad experiences you won't share because you've gone all kung fu on me?"

"Experiences?" she asked guardedly.

Resting his chin on the top of her head, he scoffed, "Yeah. Like the one where all the Pack employees treat you like shit, and you just take it because you don't want to cause a scene?"

"We went over that already."

"They could just as likely be suspects, Marty. Everyone is suspect now. So was anyone overtly difficult? Rude?"

"Actually, today everyone was pretty nice." And that was a truism. Alana had been very pleasant when she'd dumped her tuchis in the basement with some rubber gloves and Mr. Clean.

"Okay, so anything else you want to share? Like where you were all day?"

"I was busy." Which wasn't a lie. She had been busy. Ultra busy. So, so busy.

"Wanna tell me what *kind* of busy?"

"Nope." That could only cause more unwanted trouble.

"Marty . . ."

"Yes?"

"Do I have to ask Mara?"

She nudged his chest with her shoulder, closing her eyes. Why couldn't he just let her suck up his yumminess in peace? "Oh, come on. That's not fair. She shouldn't be in the middle of this."

"Look, I can't even begin to figure out who might want to hurt you if I don't have all the information. What if it's someone from Pack? I can't look into it if you don't tell me if anyone's bothered you or treated you unfairly. So now who's being unfair? Don't you want to figure this out so you can go back to your apartment and New York?"

I don't know, she wanted to whine, but instead said, "That's very sly. Okay, fine. I was cleaning . . ." She pressed her lips to his chest to muffle her words and finished with, "Vats."

"Say again?"

"No."

"Marty."

Ahhh, the official calling of her name in vain. "Vats. I cleaned all those vats in the basement."

"*All* of them?"

"All of them."

"If you tell me by hand—"

"Okay, so I won't tell you it was by hand."

"Who sent you down there? Was it Yvette?"

"No."

"Claudia?"

"Nuh-uh."

"Marty, damn it. Tell me," he demanded, surrounding her shoulders with his hands and levering her body away from his, so he could lock gazes with her.

Oh, the look. Intense, penetrating, just waiting for her to fumble. It got her every time.

She smiled to defuse the moment, walking a finger up his arm flirtatiously. "Only if you promise not to make a scene."

Keegan shook his dark head, his expression chiseled, his black eyes narrowed. "No, I won't promise that. Tell me, or I'll beat it out of Mara." He followed that statement up with a cockeyed grin.

"You will not."

"Yeah, I will. She told me to ask you what you did today, and I did. Now spill."

There was no time like the present to get this out of the way. The time for answers had come—before she became more attached to him than not. Throwing caution to the wind, her reply was cool. "I spent some time with your girlfriend."

"My *who*?"

"Barbie," she insisted impatiently.

"Like Barbie the doll?"

"No. Like your girlfriend Barbie."

His look was of the truly perplexed, thus warming the cockles of her heart. "Who the hell is Barbie?"

"Your *girlfriend*." Stopping now was out of the question. She seemed to garner the most information from him when she goaded him.

"I don't have a girlfriend, Marty."

Weee doggie. "Really?" She fought the squeal in her voice, but her heart raced.

"Really."

But wait . . . "*Did* you have one?"

"Sure, I've had girlfriends."

"How many?"

"I didn't count."

"Sure you didn't. Okay, so how many were serious?"

"Define serious."

She sighed. "Serious is like a relationship that lasts more than one night in caveman-speak."

He grunted. "Aha. Then I've had two."

"How long did they last?"

"I don't remember."

Naturally. "Like a week? Or longer than a whole moon cycle?"

Here it came . . . right on cue, his nostrils flared. Hot, hot, hot. She tried to keep her face unreadable.

"Marty, where are we going with this?"

"Answer the question."

"I think one was at least a month."

"That's like forever in Neanderthal time, huh? And why did you break up?"

"I can't remember."

"Were you in love?"

"Um, no. But I liked her *a lot*. She was ho—uh, really nice."

Marty frowned. Oh. "Define a lot."

He was growing impatient. It was in the set of his mouth and the lift of his eyes. "Do you want me to warn you one of my long-winded, impatient sighs is coming—or should I just nail you with one?"

A giggle bubbled from her throat. "Bear with me."

"Could we get to the heart of the matter here?"

"So your girlfriends . . ."

"What about them, Marty?"

"Did they all look like Barbie?"

"Okay. Enough. *Who* is Barbie?"

"Alana."

"She put you in the basement? Goddamn it. When I get my hands on her—"

"No! Stop it. Forget it."

"Mara told you we have machines to clean the vats, didn't she?"

"She did."

His jaw pulsed. "Then Alana needs to be checked."

"Oh, Keegan," she crooned. "Be nice to Barbie. She can't help being a bitch. You're spending too much time with me, helping me adjust. Your girlfriend's jealous."

"I'll do whatever the hell I please and she's *not my girlfriend.*"

"Was she?"

"Nope. Not on your life."

"Never? Like ever?"

"Never," he said firmly.

Well, okay then. Things were definitely looking up. That he hadn't dated Alana and had never wanted to did mushy, fuzzy things to her insides. It spoke volumes about his character. Alana was the Mona Lisa of women. Beautiful, flawless, perfect, but apparently Keegan wasn't just interested in looks because, if honesty were to play a role in her surmising, Marty was more like a kindergartner's stick figure portrait in comparison.

She smiled the smile of the truly wicked.

Neener, neener, neener that, Barbie.

Suddenly, she was exhausted, her legs weak, her eyes grainy.

Keegan must have sensed the tension leave her body and the wobble of her legs. He wrapped a strong arm around her waist, the muscles pressing securely against her waist. He planted a soft kiss on her cheek, making her forget how tired she was, and making her lean into the smooth warmth of his lips. "C'mon, tiger, let's get you home."

Home.

Where *was* home?

New York and her cute apartment felt light years away.

The good-natured ribbing and unity of the Flahertys, Helga's to-die-for meals, Muffin's star treatment, and Keegan, so much closer.

Clearer.

There was no denying her attraction to Keegan. There was no denying her desire to fit in anymore. She wanted to be a part of this. This family that hadn't asked for her, but had done their best to include her.

And she wanted Keegan.

Arrogant, pushy, domineering, impatient, crazy-sexy, smart, overprotective, totally wrong for her in every way, slated to mate with someone else, Keegan Flaherty.

The mental admission took her breath away, but she felt it as if she'd always felt it. Like it had never been any other way.

Deep.

Like way.

CHAPTER
11

"Is Les okay?" Keegan asked Mara, who'd followed him and Marty home with Les in her car. He took a long pull of his beer and stretched his neck, bending his head to let his chin touch his chest. He'd taken Marty upstairs, leaving her with strict orders to eat what Helga brought her and sleep. Naturally, because she was Marty, she'd had a million more questions for him, but he'd demanded she rest. The idea that someone had hurt her enraged him, and he was fighting the urge to break things.

"Yeah. Just knocked out. He'll heal. So what happened? Is Marty all right?" Mara plunked down on the couch beside him in the family room.

"She's pretty tough, I'll give her that. Someone grabbed her from behind. Probably the same person who knocked Les out." And when he found the bastard, he'd eat him for lunch with a side of fries.

"How did she get away?"

He grinned wryly with the admission. "She bit him. She didn't break his skin, but she latched on."

Mara laughed and crossed her legs to sit Indian style. "I guess she is pretty tough. So, thoughts on who's doing this? Sloan told me about the note."

Keegan's face hardened as he set his beer down on the coffee table. "I don't have a clue. We bat around the idea that it could be a rogue member of the council."

Mara blanched, turning pale. "Oh, that's just great. Just what we need. You've heard the rumors about those questionable rogue members." Her shiver was visible. "What are you going to do, Keegan? You can't keep putting the council off, you know. They'll want answers."

"I'll answer them when I'm ready," he spoke between clenched teeth.

She hurled a pillow at him, knocking the side of his head with it. "That's great, Keegan. Let your arrogance get Marty hurt, dumb ass! Maybe if you called a meeting with the council and tried to straighten things out, whatever the hell is going on would stop. Quit being such a jackass about your pride and think of Marty."

"That's all I do," he said with a murmur. Day and fucking night he thought about her. His attention turned to her every evening when he climbed between sheets that were uninviting and cold. Marty and her soft, full body. What her luscious lips, glossed in her favorite Winsome Wisteria lipstick, would look like wrapped around his cock. What it would be like to drive into her when she was wet and slick with desire for him.

And *only* him.

She was going to drive him out of his mind if he didn't discover every inch of her soon. But she deserved to know what would happen with the council if he went against a decision made for him at birth.

Most likely, he'd have to choose between Marty and his family. The company he'd worked all these years to build with them.

He'd kept his hands to himself for as long as he could, but that night in the barn, the way she'd latched onto him like he was the last man on Earth, made his gut ache—his body burn for her.

"Duh. Like we all couldn't see that, brother. We knew something was up when you said you wanted to bring her back here. Now you have to tell the council your intentions where she's concerned. If you do that, at the very least, if these attacks on her keep happening, you can rule the council out."

"Not necessarily, Mara," Sloan added from the lounge chair in the far corner of the room. "If it's a rogue member who's acting out of fear and the need to protect the pack, we may never know."

"You do realize what this means, Keegan. If you choose Marty and don't mate with Alana, the council could decide to strip you of your alpha status. That means Sloan," she snorted, "takes over."

"I know what it means, Mara," he said on a growl, his anger pulling him in one direction, his sense of loyalty to his family dragging him in another.

Mara winced. "Don't get excited with me. I'm just pointing out the obvious because it needed to be said out loud. We need to stop beating around the bush and get to the point. Marty's life is in an uproar, and it isn't just your future at stake here, Keegan. It's ours, too."

Raking his hand through his hair, he realized Mara was right. There was no more time to waste. He couldn't keep putting off the council or his intentions.

"Is Marty who you want to mate with for life?" Mara's question was tempered with hesitance. As if she was afraid she'd step on his toes just by asking. Marty's assessment of his impatience was obviously right.

"She is." He grew solemn. He must have known it that night when he'd seen her near the alleyway. He'd found something in her natural scent that had spoken to him, drifting on the New York City air and wrapping an imaginary lasso around all his senses. At the time, he'd been too lost in the moment to pay attention to Muffin.

"Oh, fuck," Sloan croaked. "Dude, I thought you were just hot for her. I mean, I knew you didn't want Alana, but I seriously thought you'd reconsider if you knew the council would take your alpha status away. This is serious shit."

Mara winged another pillow in Sloan's direction, nailing him in the chest. "Yeah, it's serious to you, because it might mean you'll have to take over the pack and quit fucking around. What's serious here is our brother is falling in love or at least well on his way, and he's found his mate. A mate he wants more than he wants to yield to the council's ridiculous laws. His happiness should be more important to you than the possible end of your philandering. Stop being so damned selfish, Sloan Flaherty, and try to be supportive!"

Sloan gripped the pillow with his fingers, kneading the fabric, and dipped his head. "Sorry, Keegan. I just don't think I'm cut out for the kind of tasks you undertake every day. I'd disappoint the council, not to mention our pack. I'm just sayin' . . ."

Mara folded her hands in her lap and gazed at Keegan with thoughtful eyes that implored him. "You have to be honest with Marty, Keegan. You can't keep giving orders for us all to keep our mouths closed, when she deserves to know the truth about everything involved in being a part of the pack. You don't have the luxury of time anymore. Someone wants her dead or gone or whatever, and that someone could be part of the council. Your future is at risk, and it isn't just your future. It's ours, too . . ."

MARTY sat at the top of the stairs, her hands gripping the edges of her bathrobe as she curled her knees to her chest, resting her chin on them.

You're eavesdropping, her conscience sang.

No shit. Shut up so I can hear.

This isn't the way to hear sensitive information about your future. You should be ashamed. Instead of asking direct questions to the man in charge of this gig, you're skulking in stairwells. Very upstanding.

Marty rose on heavy legs, heading back to her bedroom. She should be ashamed, but the snippet of their conversation had prevented her from going downstairs when she'd caught Mara's last words.

Toe up in the morgue was a bad thing. A very bad thing, but it made a great deal of sense that the person who was doing this was from the council. She evoked fear just by being. Understood. But to want to knock her off because of it was a little over the top.

And Keegan could lose everything because of her . . . but what would he lose? She hadn't heard the entire conversation. She couldn't allow him to keep trying to make her a part of his family—his life—if it meant she was the cause of whatever trouble he was headed for. People were getting hurt because of her, too.

With a tug of the covers, she climbed between the cool sheets, staring up at the vaulted ceiling. Her eyelids began to droop. This threat hanging over her head, a death warrant she had no control over, had become information overload.

Would it satisfy the council if she just went away, or would they continue to stalk her because she had a secret so enormous it left them subject to trusting her to keep it?

Were her only options dead and dead?

Cuz that would suck.

Maybe a werewolf witness protection program was the answer?

The heavy veil of sleep beckoned, and with it came a cloak of blissful silence in her head.

She'd just sleep on it.

Her eyes drifted open sometime later, heavy and grainy. The sag of something weighty beside her had awakened her.

The light of the half moon streamed in from the trio of windows, revealing Keegan, somber, stoic, his eyes pinning hers. His crisp, white T-shirt fit snugly over his broad chest, making her heart skip a beat and her stomach flutter erratically.

She could fill up this moment with nervous words, or she could do what she'd wanted to from the moment she began to see him as more than a disruption in her life.

Keegan said nothing when the compulsive need to touch him brought her to lay a flat palm against the firmness of his pecs. His hard face softened a bit, his hand capturing hers, and bringing her fingers to his lips, he kissed each tip.

Marty's breathing stopped for a fraction of a second when his dark eyes closed, the fringe of his thick lashes grazing his cheeks as he moaned low. Her body trembled, waiting, nearly jumping out of her skin at the slight gesture.

His eyes darkened when she arched her back involuntarily. "It's time, Marty," he said thickly, his voice like warm caramel. "I don't think I can stop myself."

Her throat tightened; her mouth grew instantly dry. Her nostrils were the ones to flare this time, absorbing his musky, male aroma. Letting the heavy scent envelop her, tantalize her in all its rich fullness, she replied, "Then don't."

It was a statement of acquiescence.

A declaration of pent-up desire.

A plea to fulfill this burning, aching need.

His hands slid beneath her, tugging her upward, molding her hard-tipped breasts to his chest, gathering her to settle on his lap.

Breathing became an unbearable battle of short, raspy breaths. When she tilted her head back, Keegan nuzzled her neck with his stubbled chin, skimming the length of it with his hot tongue.

Her arms encircled his neck, her hands digging into his scalp, the sensation of his tongue sharp with pleasure. He nipped at the skin of her throat, moving in agonizing increments until his lips hovered near hers. The heat of his breath fanned her face, the corners of their lips barely touching.

Silence became a sound, crashing around them. Marty heard nothing but Keegan's breathing, felt nothing but each inch of sculpted muscle in his chest and arms melding with her own flesh.

His tongue snaked out, whispering over the outline of her mouth, making her jolt and cling to his shoulders. When he parted her lips with his own, driving his tongue against hers, Marty moaned. It was slick, hot, darting over her teeth while his hands sought the buttons of her nightgown, popping each one with deft skill. The muscles of her back flexed, arched, reaching for more.

His mouth devoured her, suckling her lips, cupping the back of her head until their lips became one fluid movement. She let her own hands roam over his chest, testing each rung of his abs, slipping beneath the crisp cotton of his shirt to feel the heated skin of his back.

Rigid planes met her fingertips, hard curves under softer skin. She dug her hands into his skin, savoring it, memorizing the sculpted perfection.

Keegan cupped his hands under her armpits, lifting her off his lap to lay her back on the bed, never taking his lips from hers. Instantly her arms were back around him, coasting over his shoulders as he brought his chest down on hers.

His heavy weight was delicious, his scent wanton, wicked. When he tore his lips from hers, she whimpered, missing the intimate press of them immediately. He parted her nightgown, slipping each side over her shoulders, down along her arms until she was naked from the waist up.

Marty shivered, unable to tear her gaze from his, consuming her bare breasts. Her nipples tightened almost painfully, swelling and burning. Keegan's stare grew molten as he traced a calloused fingertip across each bud, bringing the digit to his mouth and wetting it with his tongue, then circling each nipple again.

The cool air mingled with his saliva left her squirming. Her hips began a rhythmic pulse against the bed, but she couldn't tear her eyes from the mesmerizing patterns he made along her body. His dark head bent, trailing kisses over her collarbone, licking at the soft flesh of her neck, then sipping each breast, letting his knuckles skirt the globes on each underside. Her heart bounced erratically in her chest, a moan escaping her lips when he tugged hard on a turgid bud, swirling his tongue over it, tugging on it with his lips. Sweeping away her nightgown, he shoved it to her feet, then hooked his thumbs into her panties, pulling them down, too.

Though she was exposed, vulnerable, she didn't shy away from his piercing eyes. She stared back at him, willing him to finish what he'd begun.

There was nowhere else on planet Earth she wanted to be right now. No one else left her breathless, wanting, needing the way Keegan did. She'd never been terribly bold, but this moment had captured her, this man intrigued her, and now she wanted it all.

Keegan's large hands slid under her waist, lifting her torso to his mouth. He planted wet, hot kisses over her ribs, tracing her navel, burying his head in the curve of her body where her thigh and pelvis met.

Marty gasped when his hands spread her thighs, then glided through the soft, swollen lips of her femininity. Sharp longing coursed through her, silky hot and slick with desire. He circled her clit, letting his thumb graze it, taunt the hard nub until her hands reached out blindly for his head, dragging him closer.

He took a deep breath of air, groaning when his mouth drew nearer to the vee between her thighs.

His dark head dipped lower, his breath scorching, carnal against her exposed flesh. Marty raised her thighs, spreading herself wider for him, bucking when his tongue finally found her core. The lash of his tongue, sweeping, rasping against her sensitive flesh, brought with it a wave of shudders, leaving goose bumps over her arms, tightening her nipples. The pit of her belly fluttered, her fingers clinging to his silken locks.

Keegan inserted a finger into her aching passage, using the cream of her body to lubricate his path. As he licked her, he withdrew the digit, then thrust back once more, reaching the sweet spot of her womb.

Her breathing was ragged, wheezing from her chest as she rolled her hips, keeping him flush to her lower body. The wicked sound of his mouth on the most intimate part of her reached her ears. Forbidden and decadent, she luxuriated in his skillful tongue, making love to her with firm strokes.

Keegan hummed against her, moaning low and feral.

The sinful sound of his appreciation pushed her over the cliff she hung on. That delicate limbo just before orgasm. Tears stung her eyes, bolts of electricity sizzled along her every nerve, and then she cried out—a sharp howl of completion as she tumbled over the edge into a fulfillment she'd never known.

Her hips crashed against his face, her thighs tense and aching from lifting her hips to meet his finger's forceful thrusts. She came with a crash of blinding heat, a kaleidoscope of lights and colors behind her eyelids.

Keegan rode the wave of her orgasm until her body grew weak, trembling, melting into his mouth. He raised his head and held himself up on his arms, skating along her body until he hovered over her.

Marty's hands cupped his face, running a thumb over the lips that had brought her such acute pleasure. She drew his mouth to hers, placing a soft kiss on his lips, tasting her essence on them.

His shoulders heaved with the effort to breathe as she tugged his shirt up and over his head, then reached for the buckle of his belt, yanking it open and popping the button on the top of his jeans.

He rose from the bed, pushing his jeans along his thighs and taking his boxer-briefs with them. Kicking his shoes off, he stood in the light of the moon, his bronze skin glistening over taut muscles. His cock jutted between his legs, thick, long, hard. The utter beauty of him stopped the loud pounding of her heart for a moment.

Wide shoulders led to a broad chest with just a sprinkling of hair over each nipple and between his pecs. His waist was tapered, lean, and his abdomen sharply defined. The muscles at his hips, cut and distinct, made her mouth water.

Now. She wanted him now. Like no one before him, with a heart-wrenching tear of her gut.

Keegan took two small steps back to the bed and parted her thighs, seating himself on his haunches between them, his hands exploring the skin of her inner thighs. His head fell back on his shoulders for a moment, his breaths shuddering on their way out. His hands gripped her legs, shaking as he dug his fingers into her legs.

The force with which he held her, the contorted mask of his face when he lifted his head, led Marty to believe he was holding back.

And she didn't want that. She wanted him to take her in whatever way he wanted. Ruggedly, with the force of passion to back each thrust—softly, with the thick glide of his cock slowly driving into her.

Her hands reached for him. Taking his shaft in both hands, she circled it, encompassing it with a slight twist of her wrist. It was hot, rigid, rock-hard and pulsing against her hands. She traced each vein along it with her thumb, spiraled her hand along the hard length, felt the bit of pre-come gathered at the head. Cupping his testicles, she rolled each orb between her fingers as she stroked him.

His hiss of breath was all the evidence she needed to know she was bringing him closer to the edge of his own completion.

"Stop," he ground out, pulling his cock from her hands. "I need you, Marty. I need you *now*. But this kind of lust—I couldn't live with myself if I hurt you." His jaw pulsed, working with that rhythmic tic.

Wrapping her legs around his waist, Marty scooted down to center herself between his thighs. Placing both hands on his forearms, she looked up into those dark, deep eyes and whispered, "You won't hurt me, Keegan. I want this. I want *you*." She took the small step out on a very shaky limb with her heart lodged firmly in her throat, but she'd taken it.

Her words obviously triggered something in him. Whatever had held him back let go and he let his arms go slack, covering her body with his, letting his cock slip into the moist warmth between her thighs.

The skin-on-skin contact was dizzying. Her breasts scraping against the crisp hairs on his chest made her light-headed. Slipping her arms under his, Marty lifted her hips in wicked invitation.

She felt no hesitation, no fear, as she locked her ankles at his lower back and closed her eyes. The head of his cock teased her entrance, slick with her body's juice.

Keegan levered his hips, positioning himself, then entered her in agonizingly slow increments. The width of his shaft stretched her, burned her tight entrance until she clung to him in anticipation.

When he finally thrust into her, Marty gasped, pressing her lips against his ear, biting her lower lip to keep from screaming out her satisfaction. Keegan muttered something incoherent, grunting his pleasure when he was finally deep within her. He settled in her, stilling, his body rigid, each muscle quivering, holding back. His arms shook, the muscles visibly quivering as he fought for control.

But Marty needed to feel him move within her. She craved the thick invasion. With a twist of her hips, she thrust upward, making Keegan moan low and sweet against her cheek. Laying her hands on his lower back, she pressed the heels of them against the hard, muscled globes of his ass, kneading the flesh, encouraging him to pick up the pace.

He began a slow glide, thrusting in, then drawing back until only the tip of his cock remained in her. Her breath shuddered with each withdrawal. With each slick stroke, she almost sobbed, arching upward, drawing him closer until her arms were again around his neck. He gathered her to him until she hung with her back hovering an inch or so over the bed.

Her legs fell away, and she let them spread wider to allow him deeper penetration. Keegan ground his hips against hers, creating a delicious friction against her clit. His strokes grew bolder, wilder, quicker, pushing her to meet him thrust for thrust.

Capturing her lips, he slid his tongue between them, adding another element of agonizing, erotic pleasure.

She was close to orgasm once more, the head of his cock hitting her womb, drawing back in a wet glide, the slap of their flesh ringing throughout the room.

Her lungs burned, ached, her nipples scraped against his chest, her body bucked in time with his forceful strokes until she didn't think she could hold on a moment longer.

The starburst of pleasure began low in the heavy weight between her legs, spiraling, creeping along every nerve in her body, dragging wave after wave of scorching heat with it. Her womb clenched, milking his cock, gripping it like a glove, making Keegan throw his head back.

The sight of his strong throat, the sinew and muscles working, bronzed and hard, made her dig her fingers into his skin. He was a forceful lover, bending her to his will, making her want him on a whole other level.

Her sanity gone, Marty came, clutching at him, rearing up against his hard frame rolling her hips, trying to absorb every last sensation, savor his heavy weight.

Keegan came, too, with a long, feral moan, his cock pulsing in her, his seed coursing through her.

They collapsed, he still inside her, clinging to one another, gasping, chests heaving.

His hair was damp as she burrowed her fingers into it. Sweat trickled from his face, their bodies glued together from perspiration. Keegan's arms clamped around her back, holding her close.

As their breathing slowed, her heart returning to normal beats, she clenched her eyes shut.

Wow and wow.

She was afraid to move, speak for fear she'd ruin this complete peace that had settled in her chest. Her body was replete, as was her mind. Making love to Keegan had been as amazing as she'd anticipated. Everything about his touch made her crave more.

How could she want someone who drove her so crazy, so much?

Maybe it was just the magnified hormones thing?

Oh, no, Marty. You're falling, and you can't get up.

Oh, hell she was in really, really deep now. Like eyeball deep.

Snuggling closer, she decided she didn't want to over-analyze it. She did that far too often with too many words.

When Keegan lifted his head, he grinned at her. "Well, Ms. Andrews, I think we spun that color wheel right off its hinges, huh?"

"Indeed," she replied coyly with the lift of one eyebrow. "I—"

She saw the look of an explanation written all over his face. She didn't want to know where this was going right now. She didn't want to think about tomorrow or how she was going to confront him about the very real possibility that he could lose his place in the pack because of her. Not tonight.

"How about we don't talk?" She purposely cut him off, casting a furtive glance at him. "We always end up getting into trouble when we do that, and right now, I think we should just afterglow, whaddya say?"

His smile was playful, his white teeth glowing in the moonlight. "Afterglow, huh?"

"Yeah. We women are needy like that."

Withdrawing from her, he padded to the bathroom and brought back a warm, wet cloth, taking special care to clean her. "Okay, Cupcake. I think I can do that."

Of course he could do that. It meant he didn't have to have her pestering him for answers.

He took the cloth from her and went back to the bath-room, wandering across the floor, completely unembar-rassed by his nudity. It was a sight all women should experience at least once in their lives. His raw beauty, bronzed, sculpted, rippling, took her breath away.

Upon his return, Keegan nudged her. "Scoot over there, bed hog." He climbed in beside her, gathering her back into his arms.

Her ear pressed against his chest, absorbing the steady, slow beat of his heart. He ran his fingers over her head in a soft caress, lulling her.

"Keegan?" she murmured sleepily.

"I thought we weren't going to talk?" He stroked her arm with lazy fingers. "Because you're right, you know. It does get us into trouble. I say something obnoxious, you say something *completely ridiculous*—"

She tugged at the hair on his chest. "Hey! I do not. I just ask a lot of questions. I have every right to ask questions. I mean, this is my life we're always fighting about. It's my head that keeps getting whacked. So I don't know what's wrong—"

Pulling her up to eye level, he silenced her with a kiss. "Shut up," he growled and smiled when he was done. "No more talking. Now lie down and be a good girl and get some sleep."

She gasped, but he thwarted her outburst with a finger to her lips. "Enough."

She slid back down his body and slung a leg over his. He was right, she thought, sighing.

Tomorrow she'd ask about the council and this alpha title and when they could do what they'd just done again. And again.

Cuz what had happened between them warranted some serious do-overs.

And like she'd said to Mara, she wasn't the kind of girl to back down from a challenge when she wanted something.

And if she hadn't been sure before about the entirety of this situation, she was now.

She wanted Keegan Flaherty.

Marty wanted the chance to explore that life option package with an upgrade to long-term relationship.

But Keegan had to want it, too, and if it meant he'd get

grief in return, would he even consider such a foolish move? Mara had said they'd take everything away from him.

What would these invisible people take away?

Why would he risk whatever he was risking for some nobody from Piscataway? She couldn't let him keep challenging these people on her behalf.

And it wasn't like he was asking her if she wanted him to. He did whatever he pleased with arrogance and a take-charge attitude. He'd asked her to come stay with him because he'd felt obligated to help her with the drastic changes she was going to experience.

He didn't invite you to set up housekeeping, cookie. Might not want to get out that frilly apron just yet.

This was exactly the kind of rock and a hard place she'd avoided all her life—messy entanglements with people you allowed to get too close who could let you down in one way or another. Her mother had taught her well . . .

But she couldn't deny the feelings she had for Keegan and his family. She didn't have the energy to even try anymore.

Tears stung her eyelids, and she clenched them tighter to prevent them from falling to her cheeks.

This was like the Rubik's Cube of life.

One big glob of scattered, multicolored possibilities she had to sort out and line up in the appropriate manner by twisting endless scenario after scenario in her head.

And it sucked.

Big, fat wankers.

KEEGAN stared down at Marty's sleeping form in the pre-dawn light. The slight rise and fall of her luscious breasts told him she was sound asleep. Leaving the warmth of her curves was the last thing he wanted to do. The memory of last night made his cock stiffen again. There was nothing he wanted more than to take her over and over. Every ounce of restraint had been necessary when driving into her soft, yielding body. Staying inside her was what he'd wanted, but his appetite for her, his insatiable need to consume her, would scare the shit out of even the toughest of people.

Marty was every fantasy realized, but his fantasy would come to an abrupt halt if he didn't first, find out who was stalking her and second, confront the council.

There was no way he was going to mate with Alana, and if he'd been sure of that before he'd made love to Marty, he was even surer now.

Marty and he didn't get along. She bombarded him with her constant chatter, made his head ache right along with his cock. Yet there was no one who intrigued him more. No one who cajoled him out of a bad mood with her unwarranted opinions and quirks. No one who'd taken up so much time in his thoughts or infuriated him with her stubbornness the way Marty did.

And now he had to tell her everything.

He placed a soft kiss on her forehead, and she stirred. His gut tightened, twisting up his insides. Muffin's head popped up, her eyes blinking drowsily.

He put a finger to his lips to keep her quiet, and immediately she lay back down. Chucking her under the chin, he ran his hand over the swell of Marty's hip, tucking the blanket around her, then silently padded out of the bedroom.

It was time to see what he could do, if anything, about keeping this fucking council from taking everything because he wanted Marty.

And he wanted her that much.

CHAPTER
12

Breakfast called to her in the way of steak and eggs, the smell drifting up the stairs as she made her way down the hall and headed for the dining room.

She could eat a cow.

And that was probably, however bizarre, a literal statement nowadays for her.

She'd awakened minus Keegan, half content, half more confused than she'd ever been, and ravenous, with Muffin snoring softly beside her. After a hot shower to soothe the long underused, pleasantly sore spots on her body, she'd dressed and decided to head downstairs, hoping to go back to Pack and like maybe get lucky enough to count paper clips today. She'd taken extra care with her appearance, trying to convince herself the snug faux cashmere sweater she'd chosen had absolutely nothing to do with Keegan.

Of course, she was delusional. It had everything to do with Keegan. So did the extra layer of stay-all-day lip shine.

But whatever.

When she strolled into the dining room, Muffin lagging behind her, a pause in conversation greeted her. Each Flaherty, including her hunky love doctor from last night, looked at her expectantly. "What?" She wrinkled her nose, expressing her discomfort.

"How do you feel?" Mara questioned from the far end of the table next to Keegan, her face wrinkled with concern.

Feel. Omigod. Had the whole family heard them last night? A blush of red tinted her cheeks, and she nervously wiped her hands on her linen trousers.

"Your *head,* Marty." Keegan gave her a brief, smoldering gaze before glancing back at his plate.

As always, the sight of him made her pause. The simmering sensuality, mingled with the ready-to-explode-at-any-second aura, was even more appealing after last night.

"Marty? Your head. How's your head?" Keegan pressed again, looking away when she found his gaze.

Ohhhhh. Yes. Her head. *Not* her nether parts. Pulling out a chair next to Sloan, she shrugged her shoulders and smiled. "All better. I'm a werewolf, right? Healed right up just like magic."

Mara nodded her head and grinned. "Now you're getting the hang of it."

Scooping some eggs from the large platter in the middle of the table, Marty inclined her head toward Keegan. "So, what's my job today? Maybe buffing the upper floors with my toothbrush? Oh, wait, I know." Her chuckle was mischievous. "How about I reorganize the supply closet alphabetically or spit shine the windows?"

Sloan's laughter filled the room. "I could use some help cleaning my office," he joked, dark circles ringing his eyes.

"You could use some help showing up at your office." Mara gave Sloan a pointed gaze.

"What is it you do for Pack, anyway, Sloan?" Marty wondered out loud, taking a piece of steak from the platter and cutting into the juicy seasoned thickness of it. She'd been so dazed since her arrival, the details of Keegan's family's role at Pack had escaped her.

"He occasionally shows up after a long, hard night of partying. So we keep his tasks simple due to hangovers." Mara's snort held derision. She ran a napkin over her lipstick-free lips.

"Sloan has a degree in biochemistry. He works in research. Er, when he shows up." Keegan watched Sloan's face when it screwed up in clear indignation.

"I'm head of packaging and design," Mara offered.

Mara was responsible for all that glorious gold packaging and more surprising still, Sloan had helped create the velvety smooth moisturizer she'd snuck a dollop of.

"You're not going to Pack today, Marty." Keegan interrupted her musings with his distant, stalwart tone of voice.

She stopped chewing the medium-rare, tasty morsel. "Why?"

"Do I need to remind you about last night?"

She flushed again, knowing full well he was talking about the person who'd attacked her, but she couldn't help the tingle in her stomach the memory their lovemaking brought. "Well, where's Supernanny? Is he feeling well enough to babysit today? He's a werewolf, too, right? That means he healed right up just like me. I know I'm a handful, but I bet if you up his hourly wage and offer to let him talk on the phone all he wants, he'd do it."

The look he gave her rooted her to her chair. "Les is fine, but I'm not taking any more chances. You're like trying to corral greased cats. So today you're staying here with Helga. Period."

And again, the word of God as handed down by Keegan Flaherty. We were back to the Keegan of old. The one who ran everything in his life like a dictatorship and left no room for bargaining. She opened her mouth to protest, but he stopped her with his palm. "I said no, Marty. Enough is enough, until we figure this out."

"The figuring out part might be a good plan of attack.

Like *soon*," Mara said in Keegan's direction with a hint of sarcasm.

Clearly today wasn't the day for *Let's Make a Deal*. It also wasn't a time for her to argue simply because she was bored. Her boredom had left someone hurt. Her appetite was suddenly gone. "Okay. I understand." She offered the words with no enthusiasm.

"But," Keegan said with the first hint of a smile he'd given her since she'd entered the room, "I do have a little surprise for you, and it should be here pretty soon. So you stay put, hear me?" he warned, his gaze capturing hers for only a moment. "The moon is full tonight. I have things I have to clear up before then," he said to everyone else before he rose and told everyone to have a good day.

His eyes were unreadable as he left—remote. Maybe he regretted last night? Well, fine by her. If the most incredible mattress stomp she'd ever had in her life meant so little to him, then—then fine. More than fine. This surprise he'd arranged barely registered. She was too busy pouting, because she was going to be stuck in the house doing nothing again.

And the moon was full tonight.

Brilliant.

She bristled in her seat, stuffing more steak in her mouth to keep from climbing over the table and going after Keegan, wrapping her fingers around his brawny neck and choking him.

Was this what the morning after a one-night stand was like—except she was living with the one-night stand?

Fucktard.

"Hey," Mara called. "I've got a light day today. I'll try to come back later this afternoon, and we can hang out or something, all right?"

Marty smiled. She liked Mara. In fact, she liked her a lot. More than she liked stupidhead right now for sure. "Sure, that'd be great. Well, I guess I'll go answer some emails and try to keep busy. You guys have a good day," she

said with the wave of her hand, traipsing back up the stairs
to her jail cell, with Muffin following closely behind.

*That's so not fair, Marty. Keegan's right. Too much trou-
ble is had when you're not contained.*

Striding across the floor of her bedroom, she grabbed
her laptop and logged on. The attempt was halfhearted, and
that alone should have made her pause. Not so long ago,
nothing in the world excited her more than checking her
Bobbie-Sue email.

But it didn't mean she didn't have obligations to
clients—even if that encapsulated world seemed so distant
now.

As she attempted to log in, her efforts failed. Had she
forgotten her password? No. Never. She typed in "Rich-
isinmycolorwheel" again.

The message said her password was invalid.

Marty frowned and tried one more time.

Same message.

What in the frig was going on?

The knock at her door kept her from hurling the laptop
across the room. "Come in," she yelled absently, staring at
the computer screen and frowning.

"Well, look at you. A fucking brunette. What happened
to all those vanilla pudding highlights?"

"Banana. They were banana pudding," Marty said before the words registered and she looked up to see who was
speaking them. Her eyes lifted to find Nina and Wanda
smiling at her. Nina in a long, dark trench coat, her wavy
dark chocolate curls hanging down her back and wearing
Laffy Taffy pink lipstick. Wanda was in a bone-colored
jacket with a wide, belted tie and matching pumps. They
were a sight for her very sore, bionic eyes.

"Oh, my God!" Marty squealed, dropping her laptop on
the bed and throwing herself at them. She planted a kiss on
each of their cheeks, hurling her arms around their necks to
draw them close for a group hug.

Nina was the first to protest, disentangling herself from

Marty's grip with fast hands. "All right already. Get off me." Her expression was uncomfortable, though she said it with a smile.

Wanda hugged her hard, pulling back to inspect her closer. "You look awesome, Marty! You glow."

"How did you two get here?"

"Mr. Ass-tastic flew us in on his private jet. Boy, you color wheel freak, when you do it, you do it big, huh?" Nina cracked, punching Marty's arm playfully.

That statement made Marty pause for a minute. Would someone who thought you were nothing more than a one-night stand do something like this for you? The guilt . . . Ohhhh, and she'd called him a fucktard in her head. For shame. "He has a private jet?" She was in disbelief. There were still so many things she didn't know about him.

Nina scoffed, pulling off her coat and plunking down in one of the chairs by the trio of windows. "Like you didn't know. Yeah, he has a private jet and a limousine and a hottie for a pilot. It beat the shit out of driving here. How could you not tell us he owned Pack Cosmetics? Jesus, Marty, your color wheels must be orgasmic by now."

There'd been a time when Marty would have chided Nina for her crass assessment of Keegan and his apparent riches, but she found she'd missed Nina's big mouth and inability to shut her trap when it was inappropriate to speak. "I guess it wasn't as important as the bigger picture," she sidestepped the question. "It all happened so fast—my coming here. When someone tries to kidnap you, it kind of takes precedent, ya know?"

"This is sooooo exciting." Wanda was glowing and chirping, while she hung her coat neatly on the rack in the corner and took Marty to sit with her on the bed. "You have a rich boyfriend! I want to hear everything. You guys met in your apartment building, right? Are you in *loooove*? Is he?"

Oh, so innocent Wanda, behaving like a teenager. It made Marty smile. And was she in *love*? That was such a heavy word. Was love never wanting to let someone out of your sight? Did love involve the most incredible lovemak-

ing like ever? Or was that her hormones raging with magnification? "We did meet in my apartment building, and I
don't know if I'm—" Marty kept it vague, stopping at the
L word. "Never mind me. Tell me about you guys. What's
going on at Bobbie-Sue?"

Nina's face grew dark, and her hands clenched into fists.
She planted them on her jean-covered thighs with a thump,
her hair curtaining her supermodel features.

Wanda gulped and worried the hem of her conservative
skirt, gnawing her bottom lip.

"So?" She looked from one woman to the other.

"Those fuckers," Nina muttered, scowling.

"Nina! Mind your mouth." Wanda's eyes widened with
a scold, while giving Nina a shut-up look.

Nina flicked her fingers at Wanda. "Oh, the fuck I will,
Wanda. What they're doing to Marty is crappy. I should
have beat the shit out of that pasty white asshole Terrence!"
Nina's dark, almond eyes narrowed, her jaw setting firmly.

"Terrence Bradford? Bobbie-Sue's son Terrence?"
Marty spewed in surprise.

Wanda nodded her dark brown head and reached behind
her to pull Muffin closer. Her worried gaze flitted between
Marty and Nina, the wrinkles on her normally smooth,
creamy brow deepening.

Marty put a reassuring hand on Wanda's leg and patted
it. "So who's going to tell me what's going on? I couldn't
get into my Bobbie-Sue account today, and I know I typed
the password in correctly. So what gives?" Her stomach
had this sinking feeling her career as a color specialist was
circling the drain.

Nina slid to the end of the chair, a venomous look darkening her face. "I'll tell her, Wanda. Those motherfuckers
took your accounts away. Terrence found us at last week's
corporate meeting and informed both Wanda and me that
we'd have a new rep shortly, and he did it with no explanation, citing some privacy bullshit."

Marty's heart plummeted. Her stomach did a backflip.
"A new rep?" Her eyes narrowed. "*Who's* your new rep?"

"Um, Linda Fisher . . ." Wanda squeaked, clutching
Muffin closer to her chest.

Anger, in all its red glory, swooshed over Marty. "Linda
Fisher?" she shouted, pushing off the bed with a hard shove
and springing to her feet.

Nina nodded, sucking in her cheeks. "I told the little shit
he could fuck off and die. I'd be Linda Fisher's bitch the
day I could ice skate in Hell."

Wanda bobbed her head furiously. "She did, too. You
should have seen the look on Terrence's face when she
yelled at him. I don't think he liked it. You know Nina.
She's not one to beat around the bush, and she let him have
it—in front of everyone—even Linda Fisher!" Her tone
had evident pride in it.

A brief moment of gratitude for Nina's loyalty made
Marty send her a smile before her anger took over. Sizzling
along her veins, it clutched at her, slicing through her like a
red-hot bolt of lightening.

"I'll kill that fucking bitch!" Marty screamed, bending
over at the waist, fighting for air as she wrapped her arms
around her waist.

Wanda's gasp hissed from her lips. "Marty!"

Nina scrambled from her chair, snapping a hand up to
quiet Wanda. "Enough is enough. What the hell is up with
you, Marty? You're always so calm, but that last night we
saw you, you were on friggin' fire. And I know we didn't
talk about it, but your teeth did some bizarre shit that night.
The Marty I knew was like buttah. She would melt in your
mouth. Now you're yelling at me, in a very un-Bobbie-Sue-
like manner, I might add. Your eyes get all glassy and possessed looking. All of a sudden you need anger management.
This is not the Marty I signed on with. So what the hell?"
Her question was a demand for an answer. She pushed Marty
up by her shoulders to look her in the eye.

Linda Fisher had taken everything from her, that's what
the fuck. Though she couldn't seem to say the words. All
she could see was a haze in shades of red.

Nina shook her so hard, her head bobbed. "Marty! Look,

I told Terrence he could fuck off and die, and Wanda'd do the same if you want. I know Bobbie-Sue meant a lot to you, but there are other things in life besides fucking color auras."

She hadn't meant to, but Nina's touch sent her brain-waves on overdrive, and she reacted. Marty suddenly couldn't bear the feel of her hands on her ultrasensitive skin.

In hindsight, this werewolf thing could be very wrestle-mania, given the wrong setting.

The next thing she knew, Nina was scrambling back up off the floor, coming at her both barrels loaded, her face an infuriated mask of outrage. "I will kick your ass, you color ho!" she yelped.

Marty's hand clapped over her mouth in astonishment. She'd knocked Nina to the ground with nothing more than a shove.

Muffin yipped with discontent when Wanda launched from the bed.

Wanda flew between them, placing a flat palm on each of their shoulders. "That is absolutely enough! Damn you both! Do you have any idea the kinds of pins and needles I walk on when you two are together? It's not good for my stress levels, and it definitely isn't going to keep me from getting wrinkles! Now, you"—she pointed to Nina with a hard shove of her finger—"back to your corner, and you"—she pointed to Marty—"in a corner far, far away from Nina. I don't know where this is coming from, Marty, but Nina, albeit she went about telling you the wrong way, is abso-lutely correct. You are not the Marty Andrews we signed on with. To quote a favorite phrase of yours—you are very, very red today. Now knock—it—off!" Wanda's mouth was pinched, her eyes wide with frustration and anger. They held conviction and for the first time, Marty saw something else—a take-charge attitude she didn't know Wanda had in her.

The air of anger surrounding her dissipated as quickly as it had arrived. Like turning off a vacuum, it swirled and deflated. "I'm sorry, Nina. Oh, shit, shit, shit." She stuck a knuckle between her teeth. "I'm sorry. I—" Well, now, she couldn't tell them why she was having these awful mood swings, could she? "Linda Fisher just—just her name makes me crazy." And that was true . . . "I don't know what's wrong with me." Her eyes conveyed an apology.

"The fuck you don't, Marty." Nina spit the words out. "I should beat the living snot out of you, but I won't because you're obviously facing some sort of *challenge*. I know you know better than to screw with me, sistah." She lowered her tone, a tone fairly dripping perilous danger.

Wanda huffed from her place in the middle of the room, expelling a long lungful of air. "Better." Her compliment was aimed at both of them. "Now, let's talk Bobbie-Sue, and let's do it like adults, agreed?"

Each woman nodded her head, though the hard set to Nina's face didn't ease.

Closing her eyes, Wanda breathed deeply again, then opened them. "Okay, so here's the word. Terrence came to us last week and said you'd left Bobbie-Sue and Linda was our new rep. He didn't say why, though he did say he couldn't get in touch with you, and if we had a number or address to reach you, then was the time to tell him."

Marty shook her head in disbelief, pinching her temples. "I don't get it. How did Terrence get involved? We hardly ever see him around. Since when does he care where anyone is? Especially me?"

"Well, he is the head of Consulting. So I guess he's finally decided to do his job and handle the consultants," Nina replied testily.

Yeah, Terrence all of a sudden wanted to earn his money instead of having it brought to him slathered on his breakfast bagel? The rumors about Terrence were rampant and often bandied about the consultants. Speculation was he was a playboy. A mama's boy, and he liked to party—not earn a living. She couldn't even remember seeing him the night she'd wanted to kill Linda. So how very strange he should have decided to speak to Nina and Wanda himself, and stranger still was the idea that he wanted to know *where* Marty was. Why should he give a rat's ass where she was if he was going to boot her from Bobbie-Sue? He could have just sent her an email. Or left her a message on her cell. "Why didn't you email me or call me? You've known for a week," she accused, her last mode of defense waning.

"Because, you whacked-out lunatic, Wanda said it would be *insensitive* to just call you or email, seeing as Bobbie-Sue is your whole world. We were going to drive up here and find you if we had to, but we wanted to tell you in person." Nina said the word *insensitive* with a Dr. Phil lilt.

Instantly, her mood swung again. "Ohhhhh, that's so sweeeet." Marty's chest welled up with affection for them.

Nina snorted sharply. "And see where nice got me? Knocked on my ass. I should kick the shit out of you for even *thinking* you could take me."

"I said I was sorry, Nina." Marty was feeling huffy, jamming a shaky hand into her hair. "Now back off, or I'll kick the shit out of *you*!" She pointed a threatening finger and fought the wild seesaw of emotion creeping along her spine.

Nina sought Wanda's eyes, rolling hers as if she were bored with the idea Marty could take her. "She *has* lost her mind. I'm going to take a deep breath and ignore any crazy ramblings about beating me up. You do not want to throw down with my ass. Now, on to more pressing shit like that weirdo Terrence. The dude is seriously caa-reepy."

Wanda shuddered for effect. "Definitely creepy."

"Did you tell him where I was?"

"Are you kidding me? Um, no. We told him we didn't know anything more than he did. We told him we hadn't seen you and all we had was your cell phone number and your Bobbie-Sue email account address. Fuck him if he thinks I'm going to let him harass you. After we told him that, he went away. Scurried on back to his rich mama, I guess," Nina said with a shrug of her slender shoulders.

Christ on a stick. How had it all come to this? She had no job. She'd lose her apartment, her leather couch . . . "I'm sorry this has happened. I feel responsible for letting you down, and now you have Linda for a consultant. I dragged you two into this Bobbie-Sue thing and made you try to do something neither of you were good at or happy about. I see that now, and the pressure I put on you was unfair."

Suddenly, Nina's face relaxed, her posture slumping ever so slightly. "You were just doing what the color cult wanted you to, Marty. You were successful, and you wanted that for us, too. Besides, I'm all good. I'm ditching Bobbie-Sue. I can't take any more of those wing-nut color consultants. Those courses I was taking as a hygienist are kinda cool, and I can move in with my grandmother until I'm done. Then I can find another job."

Was that understanding in Nina's voice? Compassion? *Oh, the horror.*

"I'll leave, too, Marty, straight away. I'd rather have the devil as my consultant than Linda Fisher," Wanda piped in, her soft eyes smiling her loyalty to Marty.

"Well, before you do that, why don't you tell Marty how many units you sold this month since she's been gone?" Nina goaded.

Marty clapped her hands with excitement and squealed. "You sold something?"

"Not just something, but *many* somethings." Nina winked.

Wanda's smile was sheepish. She lowered her head to her chest and peeked up at Marty with bashful eyes. "I sold four units. I didn't want to tell you that over the phone either. I thought it was due the personal touch."

Marty hugged her. "Four? Holy cow! That's awesome! But listen . . ." She paused, looking Wanda in the eye with heartfelt sincerity. "Don't leave Bobbie-Sue because of me, Wanda. You're well on your way to becoming a lavender. To be honest, I'm not sure if I'm even coming back to Bobbie-Sue, but you're doing so well. Don't give up now."

"Oh, now I know you've flipped a lug nut if you're not even considering giving Terrence shit for fucking with your beloved Bobbie-Sue-ness." Nina's laugh no longer had a tinge of anger, but taunted her nonetheless.

Marty ignored her. She'd officially flipped all her lug nuts. She didn't know what she'd do about Terrence and Bobbie-Sue. Appealing to a higher order at corporate might be her only recourse, and right now, she didn't have the energy with everything else that was going on. "I'm serious, Wanda. If anyone can get along with Linda, it's you."

"But *Linda Fisher*?" she protested with a wrinkle of her pert nose.

"Forget it, and I'm sure you can have my old accounts. I mean, I don't see why not, right? You two have been making all the deliveries for me. You have a rapport with the customers now."

Silence, crisp and heavy, greeted her.

Wanda worried the bottom of her full lip.

Nina crossed her long legs and clucked her tongue, squinting her eyes.

No. No fucking way.

Marty folded her arms over her chest and gave them a suspicious glance. "There's more, right?"

"Um, yes. But it's okay," Wanda's voice soothed.

"The hell it is," Nina cut her off. "That freaky fuck Terrence gave all of your old accounts to Linda Fisher."

Fury rose like a tsunami, exploding in her chest, billowing from her ears until she could see nothing but that red haze again.

And then, she lost it.

She felt the elongation of her teeth, the stretch of her skin in her linen pants, heard the sound of them ripping as her tail announced itself.

And then there was Wanda's scream.

Loud, wailing, high-pitched, ripping through Marty's sensitive ears like a gunshot to the head.

Oh. Fuck.

Rucy had some splainin' to do . . .

* * *

MARTY wet the cloth under the cool water for a third time and trudged back in to Wanda, who lay prone on the bed, her pretty face a pasty white, her body trembling.

Nina skirted around Marty, moving as far away as she could as fast as she could. Under any other circumstance, that kind of command over Nina would have been euphoric. A rather "Who Da Man?" kind of power.

Today, it just left Marty feeling like an outsider again.

Marty laid the cloth on Wanda's head and pressed it with gentle fingers. "I told you I could kick your ass," she joked over her shoulder at Nina, trying to make an uncomfortable situation less tense.

Nina had no response for that. Instead, she asked for a direct answer. "So explain this again. Keegan was the dog who bit you that night?"

"Yep."

"Okay, okay. Hold the fuck on," Nina grunted, holding a palm up at Marty. "His biting you did—did—that thing that just happened."

"Again, yep. A lot of things happened because of the bite. I didn't choose for my hair to be this color. It just got darker because of the bite. Not to mention the hair on my legs grows like weeds in a lawn, I'm moody as hell, I could out-cuss Ms. Blackman here on my worst day, and my hormones are like those of an out-of-control thirteen-year-old male."

Nina put two fists to her eyes and rubbed. "I wanna believe this is some fucked-up joke, but that . . ." She stammered off into silence, pointing to Marty's tail.

"Yeah, I know. It's a long story. In a nutshell, I can't shift fully, and when I get angry, I grow a tail, but I must be getting better, because my teeth popped out, too. They've never happened at the same time. Keegan said sometimes emotions—like the kind that are really extreme—can trigger a shift. Nothing pisses me off more than knowing Linda

has the accounts I worked a year for. That's my only explanation. It's also how I got out of the trunk of that car. It was
an older model. It didn't have an inside latch. I'm sorry I
lied. I really kicked my way out."

"Do you hear yourself, Marty?"

"Do you see my ass, Nina?"

"For the love of all things shiny, I do, and I can't fucking
believe it. This is crazy!"

"I know exactly how you feel. It's exactly what I said
when Keegan came to tell me he was the one who'd bitten
me. I thought he was a dog back then, too. Believe me, this
has been a month to end all."

"Marty?" Wanda stirred, pushing the cloth from her
face and sitting up, scooting to the head of the bed as if
Marty had a disease.

Tugging on her legs, she pulled Wanda back down the bed,
ruffling her skirt up around her thighs. "I don't have a disease,
Wanda. You can't get werewolf cooties from me." She chuckled, finding it totally ironic that she was now almost in the very
same position Keegan had once been in with her.

"Marty?" Wanda whispered, fear edging her tone.

"Yeah?"

Wanda pulled the comforter up to her chin, hanging on
to the edge of it, kneading it with her fingers. "We need to
get you he—he—*help*. There must be something we can do
to reverse this. I can't deny what I see, but you have a tail!
A tail. It's—well, it's—"

"Nuts." Marty nodded. "I know, and the worst part about
this is you can't tell a soul. No one. I already have enough
trouble with the Lunar Council breathing down my neck."

"Um, the who?" Nina's question was husky and harsh.

"The Lunar Council. It seems werewolves have a sort of
code they live by and people who govern them." Marty
went into a brief explanation about the council's duties,
while Wanda and Nina nodded, dazed. She omitted the bit
about baby-making. Nina would do her best Gloria Stein-
hem impression, and she really wasn't up to it today.

Nina spoke first. "Do you really think these elder people sent out a hit man to do this to you?"

"I don't know. Keegan hardly talks about it. I overheard that tidbit when he was talking to his family. I didn't mean to eavesdrop . . ."

"You have every freakin' right to eavesdrop, Marty! You'd better get your shit together and make him tell you everything right now. What are you waiting for? To get yourself killed? And why didn't you come to us? We would have helped you. You could have stayed with me or Wanda until you figured this out. Is he making you stay here? Like forcing you? Brainwashing you? I don't give a shit how hot he is, if he hurts you—"

"Noooooo! No." She jumped to his defense. Keegan had done something far worse. He'd made her like him. Want him . . . "He hasn't hurt me or brainwashed me. It's just complicated, Nina." Marty heaved a groan of frustration.

"It's not complicated at all. You're falling in love." Wanda spoke up on a wistful sigh.

"No—" she began, a litany of denial at the ready, but Wanda stopped her.

She grabbed her arm and squeezed it. "Don't deny it, Marty. It's a good thing. It's written all over your face, and I think it's wonderful, even if he is a wereman."

"Wolf. He's a werewolf," Marty corrected.

"I don't give a flying Dutchman if he's the bogeyman, he owes you some answers."

Nina was right. Keegan owed her answers, about last night, about her future, about what she was going to do now that she had no job.

"Listen, my life is clearly in jeopardy. I don't want yours to be, too. Please, don't tell a soul. *No one.* If something happened to either one of you, I don't know what I'd do. I don't know how these werewolves go around hiding this from everyone. It ain't easy."

"Oh, Marty." Wanda sighed. "We *are* more than just rungs on your mental color ladder, aren't we?"

"Jesus, Nina. Where do you come up with some of this crap you fill Wanda's head with?"

Nina rolled her eyes. "Well, it's not like I wasn't telling her the truth—or what was the truth at the time. Whatever. I've had enough of this warm, fuzzy bullshit. So cut it out and let's get to the business at hand."

"Which is?" Marty cocked an eyebrow.

"What you're going to do about that?" She motioned to her tail. "And these people who want to kill you?"

"I have no answers. I've just sort of been riding a wave here. It's been an adjustment. Keegan has a big family, and sometimes I feel so overwhelmed by them. But mostly I like them. I like them a lot. I think I might want to try and fit in as crazy as that sounds. Know why that's crazy, don't you? Because all of the people at Pack hate my ex-human guts, and that's uncomfortable at best."

"They snubbed ya, didn't they?"

Marty nodded at Nina in the affirmative.

"Assholes. I guess discrimination comes in all species."

"And Keegan?" Wanda prompted.

"What about him?"

"Don't be silly, Marty, and stop avoiding the question. Are you going to tell him you're falling in love with him?"

Love was a big word. Too big to contemplate right now. She hadn't thought past the really, really liking him stage of things. And today, she'd warred with even that. He'd done something so sweet by bringing Nina and Wanda here, but this morning at breakfast, he'd behaved like they hadn't boinked the life out of each other. "I think for right now I just want to find out who isn't so hyped on me being here—what I'm going to do about that, and how I'm going to earn a living now that Bobbie-Sue is pretty much over."

There would be no sky blue anything in her future.

And Linda Fisher had her recruits *and* her accounts.

Marty had a bunch of people who hated her guts, the hots for a man who could lose everything because she existed, and a tail that was pathetic.

Oh, and the full moon was tonight.

That's when this running with the pack thing would occur.

It was also when she'd have to suffer group humiliation because she couldn't shift like everyone else.

This was a pickle of epic proportions.

CHAPTER
13

The full moon hung low like a pregnant belly on the verge of birth. Swollen and round, it called to her. Her nose flared, taking in the scent of a change in the atmosphere. Thick and heavy, like inhaling molasses.

Marty stared out the window of the kitchen, the white, majestic glow of the moon holding her captive. The race of emotions she'd felt earlier today weren't as frenetic tonight. She felt an invisible tug of unity. Solace in the mess that was now her life.

She desperately wanted to be outside, beneath it, at one with it.

And she wasn't going to let a bunch of werewolf bigots stop her. Her knees quivered.

Well, wait. Okay, maybe they could stop her *this* full moon, but she was all in next cycle, both guns blazing. She'd show them what shifting was all about.

Nina and Wanda had left her with concerned looks and the promise mum was the word. Marty had sat quietly after she'd watched them fade into a small dot as they'd driven away, absorbing this new friendship she'd begun with them. Grateful they'd cared enough to come all this way to see her. Worried for their safety and Wanda's future at Bobbie-Sue. Wondering what in theee hell Terrence wanted with her.

And now, several hours later, she was faced with the possibility of this new life—terrifying, yet exhilarating at the same time.

The pack had gathered just as the sun faded—there were at least thirty people milling about Keegan's backyard, laughing, talking, and in general treating this like it was some kind of family barbeque minus the ribs and potato salad. She saw lots of faces from Pack and some who were unfamiliar. Almost all of these people were a part of Keegan's extended family, and if she was going to make nice, she *had* to go outside.

Instead, Marty hovered inside, lost, cagey, gnawing on a piece of beef jerky.

"You go out," Helga demanded as she hauled Muffin up in her meaty arms, blowing air in her ear to tease her fur. Muffin squirmed, snuggling against Helga's neck with a soft, contented sigh.

"Oh, I dunno, H. They don't much like me."

"Ach! Do not let them vin."

"Vin?"

"Yah!" She raised a pudgy fist. "Is like game. You show dem who is chompion."

Ah. The agony of defeat speech. Easy for Helga to say. She had no trouble shifting. "I think they'll laugh at me, Helga. My tail is pretty sorry."

"Is gute tail! Small, but gute. Like da Princess here. Floofy." She tweaked Muffin's tail with thick fingers and grunted.

Not as gute as it could be and definitely not very floofy. Certainly not the tail of a chompion.

Keegan poked his head in from the sliding glass doors that led out to the brick patio in the backyard. He was dressed casually in jeans and a black pullover sweater that clung to his sinfully lickable abs. He'd scraped his hair back from his face, accentuating his razor-sharp cheek-bones.

He wiggled a finger at her and smirked.

She shook her head no so she wouldn't whine out loud. He'd probably warned everyone to be kind to her in that Keegan way, and it left her embarrassed.

Keegan shook his head yes, cocking it in that stop-being-a-baby manner and held out a hand to her. His eyes were warm, deep, almost gentle.

Well, shit. How could she turn him down when he smiled like that? How could she turn him down when he just breathed?

With a long, suffering sigh, she crossed the floor, her feet dragging out every inch, and took his hand. Instantly she was at ease, relishing the contact, feeling every brush of his skin on hers.

Her nipples tightened despite the fact that she was on her way to a good stoning.

He held up his fist, knuckles forward with a questioning look.

Marty sighed one more shuddering breath and knocked her fist against his.

Their unspoken deal complete.

When they stepped out onto the patio, the crowd that had gathered grew silent.

Which was, after all, golden, yes?

Some faces were curious, some held disdain. The majority narrowly assessed her.

Good Christ, she just couldn't catch a break. Hovering behind Keegan's broad back, she let her eyes stray to the ground.

"So," a familiar voice from the back of the crowd called, "are we going to do this?" Parting, the mass allowed the voice to come to the forefront.

Oh, look. How apropos. It was Barbie. It just wasn't enough that she had a dream house and a shiny red Corvette, she shifted, too. Flawlessly, no doubt.

Marty rolled her eyes. She couldn't help it.

Alana was, of course, beautiful. She wore a long, flowing, white dress, scooped at the neckline, revealing her rounded, plastic boobs. Bare feet, small and perfectly pedicured, peeked out from beneath the billowy material. Her silhouette had the ultimate backdrop. The moon shone behind her, kissing her nakedness beneath the filmy fabric.

The slight swell of her hip attached to long legs, led to a tiny waist. She wore her hair up, though ringlets of sausage curls escaped the ribbon tying her hair back.

"Everyone, go on without us." Keegan's order was spoken with nary a glance to Alana-licious.

Marty straightened and smiled smugly right at Alana. She *could* have helped that, but she didn't want to.

The assembly began to depart in groups of three or four, muttering Marty's name. Her keen hearing caught several rather naughty words Nina would be proud of.

"Do you think you're ready?" Keegan's words floated against her ear. He was edgy, tense, ready to shed his human form and free the were in him. Marty smelled it all over him.

"No. I think I should just go in."

"And give up?" He gave her a challenging gaze with those black eyes.

She bit her lip and lifted her chin. "Look, don't start goading me, okay? I have a killa headache, and everyone laughing at me won't help it."

"No one will laugh. Promise." He held up two fingers in a scouts honor.

"Because you told them to be nice to the new girl. Stop doing that! You can't *make* them like me."

His mouth set in a firm line. Clearly he'd decided he could.

Marty softened a bit. He was trying to gain her acceptance into the He-Wolf Human Haters Club, and she had to appreciate that. "It isn't that I don't appreciate it. You just—well, you just can't be so pushy. They'll only resent me more."

He changed tactics, ignoring her plea. And instead reminding her that shifting was now vital to her, too. "You *need* to shift, too, Cupcake. That's why you have a headache. It's gravity, the moon. You know, eighth grade science class."

She just couldn't try this with a group of people waiting for her to fail. "Go ahead without me. I can feel how edgy you are. You need to bay at the moon or something."

"I can smell how edgy you are, too. I'm not the only one who needs this."

He was right. She wanted out of her skin. Skin that felt like a tightly wrapped cocoon. "I'll try. I do feel whatever it is you feel. I just don't know what it'll take for me to accomplish what you do. Now go—run and play with your friends and stop worrying about me."

He kissed the tip of her nose. "Good enough. If you need me, just call. I'll hear you." He offered up a rare grin, walking off into the velvety cloak of night.

Marty followed behind him, her steps slow. She found a rambling oak tree a few hundred yards from the house and backed up against it. As her eyes adjusted to the blackness, her heart slammed in her chest. She could see everything as clearly as if it were daylight.

Several of the pack had gathered just over a small crest, necks arched, howling the freedom from their human forms. They nudged one another playfully, rising high on their hind legs only to drop to the ground again.

It riveted her as she watched them frolic.

She yearned, longed, burned to do the same.

In the midst of the huddle, the largest of the small group rose on his back legs, a deep midnight black with slashes of blue along his thickly coated back. His eyes beckoned hers.

Keegan.

Beautiful, dark, compelling Keegan, willing her to join him.

Marty closed her eyes, calling on her deep desire to kick the fucking snot out of Linda Fisher as motivation to shift.

The familiar, overpowering rage assaulted her like a

punch to the gut, clawing under her skin, begging for release.

Every ounce of her focus was spent on producing something more than a tail and big teeth. Sweat trickled between her breasts, heat rose and fell from her toes to the top of her head. Her hands clenched into tight balls at her sides, willing this incredible act to happen.

And there it was.

Bada-bing, bada-boom, baby.

Her tail.

With a sob, she opened her eyes and hopped around in a circle. Fuck, fuck, fucker!

"Having some trouble, I see. How can I help you see the error of your ways?" a cultured voice mocked.

Marty stiffened, backing away from Alana, wanting nothing more than to run back to the house and hide.

Alana held the dress she'd worn at her chest. Unashamed, she dropped it to the ground, stepping into it and pulling it up over her lithe, tight body. Her stare was cold, brazen. "So, you can't shift? That's too bad. Definitely a dilemma."

Marty lifted her chin, as more of the pack members returned from their run, staring at her with faces that ranged from scorn to amusement. "State the obvious much?" she replied coolly.

Alana approached her with menace, her green eyes slanted and laughing. "You do realize you'll never fit in here, don't you? And even if you could shift, the council will never recognize you as one of us."

"You do realize your boobs are fake and you're a bitch, don't you?" Marty shot back, crossing her arms over her chest and eyeballing Alana. Oh, snap! Had she said that out loud? When had she grown balls? She must have, because they were clanging around like church bells. Jesus. Heat rose to her cheeks with a sweep of warmth that she'd retorted so crassly. And then, anger that she was being singled out became bigger than her fear she'd come across too shamelessly.

The fuck she'd take this kind of crap anymore. Barbie needed a good smack down. Marty planned to be the metaphoric hand that helped her out.

The crowd grew, the buzz hissing in Marty's ears.

Alana's neck lengthened as she stuck it out, her red lips scrunching up. "You little wannabe! I'll be damned if I'll let some nobody from nowhere take what's rightfully mine by pack law! Do you hear me, you half-wit?" Her feet shifted, moving her closer to Marty. So close Marty could count the hairs in her nostrils.

"Loud and proud, Barbie," she snarled, jamming her face back at her.

The crowd snickered.

"Who the hell do you think you are?" Alana shrieked so loudly it blew the hair out of Marty's face.

Sloan pushed his way through the gathering people and gave Alana's arm a good yank. "Stop right now, Alana!" His shout had such authority it stunned even Marty. Her encounters with him had always been so playful, carefree. With the flip of a switch, he was a force to be reckoned with.

"Get off of me, Sloan!" She tried to pry his fingers from her upper arm, to no avail.

"You come with me—now." His order brooked no bullshit. Looking to the rest of his pack, his usually easygoing countenance darkened. "What are you all standing around looking at? Get the fuck gone. *Now.*"

Dispersion was rapid at Sloan's command, leaving just the three of them in a thick pot of tension, until out of nowhere, Keegan strode from the darkness. "What's going on?" He looked to Sloan and Alana, his eyes hardening when they landed on Miss Clairol.

Sloan shook his head and slapped him on the back. "Nothing. I'm taking the feisty one with me." His nod was directed at Alana, seething in all of her perfectness. "You take care of your own." Sloan dragged a snarling Alana behind him, but not before Marty mouthed a thank-you to him. He smiled then, broad and mischievous.

"What happened?" Keegan took her by the hand and rubbed her skin to warm her.

"I think Barbie is tweaked." Marty blew out a breath she didn't know she'd been holding.

"Oh, really," he drawled with sarcasm. "Well, I guess Barbie will just have to get over it."

What did she have to get over, and what was Marty taking from Alana if Keegan hadn't wanted her in the first place? "I sure hope so. She can get a little riled up, eh? All teeth and frothing at the mouth. Very unattractive in a girl."

His nod was curt, but his expression changed when he looked around her body. "No luck, huh?"

Her response was dry, almost defensive. "Obviously."

His dark head dipped, eyeing her thoughtfully. "I'm sorry."

Marty waved a hand, dismissing his apology. "Forget it. It's hardly your fault. Wait, it *is* your fault, but consider yourself forgiven for making me an outcast," she teased, patting his chest. "So those were your family members?"

"I'm ashamed to admit it after the way they've treated you, but yep. That's them, in all their furry glory."

Marty giggled. "Nice bunch. Can I ask you a question?"

"Shoot."

"Where are your parents? I feel like I'm intruding—being nosy, and if you don't want to tell me, it's okay, but you've never mentioned them—"

"They're gone. They died on a skiing trip in the mountains when I was in my twenties."

Her heart tightened. She knew so well the grief he must have suffered. "Oh, Keegan. I'm sorry. I didn't mean to pry . . ."

"My family is your family now, too, Marty. You're not prying, and I miss them very much."

Her family. She'd never been a part of that kind of equation. It came with heavy responsibility—emotional baggage—dinners shared with real, live people instead of Muffin and *Seinfeld* reruns . . . "Your twenties, huh? So it wasn't that long ago." He looked like he was in his thirties.

"You know I don't even know how old you are. I don't know many details about you period. I'm thirty. I'll be thirty-one in June. The eleventh, in case you wanted to like surprise me with a car."

Keegan laughed. "Are you ready for some more freaky werewolf factoids?"

"I don't know. Does it involve me having to sacrifice a lung to the pack?"

"Nah. No lungs. The occasional ovary, but nothing vital." He sent her a wry grin.

"Then hit me."

He hesitated for a moment then launched what she hoped was his final rocket. "Okay, I'm just going to say it. No beating around the bush. Another werewolf secret. We're immortal. I'm eighty-three." His face didn't change; he eyed her solemnly, no-holds-barred.

"That's funny. You're really funny. Full of shit, but funny."

"I'm not joking."

"But your parents are . . . dead . . ."

"Oh, we can definitely be killed. Blunt trauma to the head so severe it damages the brain, a silver bullet of course, but it takes *a lot* of doing." He looked at her, clearly watching to see if she'd have another conniption.

She rolled her eyes and cracked her knuckles. "I know you're just dying for me to freak out, but I can't seem to summon the will. I'm a lot harder to shock these days," she said, shivering.

The night had grown cooler, and seeing as she only had the new batch of hair on her legs to keep her warm, she was cold. Marty tightened the long sweater around her and pulled the collar over her nose, peeking up at him and waiting to see his response to her cool, calm reaction.

Immortality. How utterly go figure.

It would have to sit for now. She'd worry about living an eternity some other time.

Keegan reached for her, putting an arm around her waist and dragging her to him, molding her hips to his. "We need to talk." He cupped the fullness of her breast, grazing a knuckle over the underside of it.

The hardness of his body, the ridged outline between his legs made her shudder with awareness. "Haven't we discussed this talking thing?" She rose on her toes, letting her lips linger close to his, arching against him wantonly without realizing she had. "It *always* gets us in trouble. We don't talk, we spar. Or I spar, you huff."

A low hum in his chest made her nipples tighten when he crushed her to the thick expanse. "We can't avoid it," he muttered, snaking his tongue over her lower lip, drawing it into his mouth to stroke it. "We have to straighten some things out between us, but first there's this one little thing we have to take care of." He wiggled his eyebrows and looked down between their bodies.

Little. Hah. There was nothing little about him down there, or anywhere else.

She sighed, letting her weight fall into his. The race of her pulse, the tingle between her thighs told her there was no denying him, even if he had brushed her off this morning.

"Yeah, like why you were so cranky this morning for starters." She gave him a questioning glance.

"Hey, you two." Mara sauntered across the brown patches of grass toward them, effectively making them both jump.

Marty stumbled backward, folding her arms over her chest while Keegan growled his irritation just low enough for her to hear him.

"How'd it go, Marty?" Her question was given with a hopeful smile. "I would have come to help, but I couldn't seem to find you in the mess of people."

"The way it always does, unfortunately," Marty said flatly.

"Well, shit." She made a face and ran a hand through her long, dark hair. "Look, how about a break from all this ritualistic crap, and we just hang out? Just us girl werewolves.

I'm borrowing Marty, Keegan. Go do man things, and I'll send her back when I'm done."

Keegan's look to Marty was dark, heated, but he quickly recovered and nodded his consent to Mara. "I'll go grab a shower." His amused chuckle tickled her ears as he headed off back to the house.

Marty smiled a secret smile. That she could create the same kind of fire in him that he created in her left her feeling omnipotent, empowered.

A real vixen.

Mara motioned her head to the patio where a chiminea burned aromatic wood. A string of lanterns outlined the spacious decorative brick, and tables with lit candles were scattered here and there. "Let's sit and talk. This has been a rough few weeks, and I imagine you're doing the insecure thing after tonight."

Marty shrugged her shoulders, grabbing a lounge chair and sitting down hard. "I don't get it, Mara. I was this close." She put her thumb and index finger together. "I felt it tonight. I really did." God. She hadn't expected this overwhelming sadness to engulf her like it was.

Mara sat opposite her, throwing her feet up on a small glass table. "I get it, Marty. I do. I know you just want to fit in. I want that for you, too."

And Marty believed she did get it. Why or how was what she didn't get, and Mara offered nothing else in the way of explanation. Running her hands over her face, Marty groaned. "I'm so—so overwhelmed."

"I know you're not used to a crowd of family members—especially a crowd of gawkers. You know, if you ever want some down time, Keegan would kill me for doing this, seeing as you're never supposed to leave the house alone, but I'll leave my spare keys in the kitchen in an envelope. Somewhere no one will look. Take them if you ever need to just get the hell away from us. Just promise you'll be careful. I'll leave the envelope in the pantry right behind Muff's gourmet chow."

"Keegan would shit a whole cow if I did that, wouldn't he?" The irony of it made her laugh. "But I appreciate the offer. Some days I'd just like to do normal things again. Like grocery shop. Get a manicure. I'd lop off my own arm for a Starbucks."

"Keegan," Mara murmured distantly. "I hate to state the obvious, but you really like my big brother." It wasn't a question, more a statement of fact.

Marty stared off into the distant hills. "A little." Her concession led to the familiar fear that gripped at her intestines. What was she going to do about Keegan?

Mara giggled with a soft snort. "Yeah, a little."

Mara's observation brought with it the flood of this afternoon and her doomed career at Bobbie-Sue. Wanda's words also reared their ugly head, and suddenly, she just needed to sort her thoughts out. "Listen, would you mind if we did girl time later? I think I just need to—to—"

"Get the hell away from us? I don't mind at all, Marty." She smiled sympathetically. "Just know I'm here if you need to talk, okay?"

Marty's eyes welled up with tears of gratitude. "I think I'll just walk a little, maybe go to the barn." She rose and stretched her arms. Blissfully, her tail seemed to have subsided. Though it hadn't been because she'd willed it to. "I'll catch you later, okay? Maybe we could have that lunch tomorrow that we missed today. You know, like in public," she joked.

"You're on."

She desperately needed to clear her head and think. So many things were falling apart at once, yet the realizations that had evolved as a result left her not just enlightened, but winded.

Her reflection brought her back to Wanda's earlier statement. Was she right? Was she falling in love with Keegan?

She'd never been in love. She couldn't compare other relationships to the one she shared with Keegan. None of them had ever been this intense, this precariously teetering between infuriation and euphoria.

However, when she examined it, she made some startling discoveries.

If wanting to spend every last moment of every day with him, even though they fought like opponents in a mud pit, was love, then check. If love was wanting to be included in every aspect of someone's life, then double check. If love was considering giving up everything you'd worked so hard for to live a lifestyle that wasn't just a change of locale, triple check. If love was wanting to be a part of his family, wanting to shift like she'd once wanted a sky blue convertible, then quadruple check.

If love was thinking about ripping the head off another woman because she'd dared consider merely looking at your man, then watching it roll to the ground while you yelled with the high-pitched cry of the warrior, then fuckin' A—there was nothing left to check.

Well, okay.

Fine.

Groovy.

Grand.

She was falling in love.

For fuck's sake.

CHAPTER
14

•

"Wanna tell me what the hell you were thinking putting Marty in the basement to clean vats when we have machines to do that?"

"Well, darling, it isn't like she's qualified for much else, now is it?" Alana draped her lithe body against the arm of the couch in the Flaherty family room. She'd changed into a slinky little sapphire blue number that showed off every inch of available flesh. Her hair fell in those long waves down her back, and she smelled of expensive perfume.

"And it isn't like you bothered to find out, is it, Alana?" Keegan hovered over her with eyes Marty couldn't see. "You wanted to humiliate her, and I won't have it. Are we clear?" Oh, Hell's bells. If that wasn't a threat that seethed, then she didn't know what was.

Alana slid upward to her feet, pushing her breasts forward, running her hand along Keegan's forearm, giving him a seductive gaze.

Wow, was that ever slinky, Marty thought upon returning from her walk, stopping dead in her tracks, and silently stepping back around the corner of the kitchen when she'd heard Alana and Keegan's voices raised. Dayum, Alana knew how to work it.

She'd have to see the bitch dead for being so damned good at it, but Marty definitely admired her seduction skills.

Her heart pinged in time with her pulse. She couldn't see Keegan's face, but she could see Barbie's, and Marty wasn't much liking what she read there. Desperation, anguish, fear, and a whole lot of desire.

Keegan stood statue-like, unmoving. He wasn't responding, but it wasn't like he was running away from her either.

Which meant he was going to do what?

Marty's first instinct when she'd come upon them was to run the other way, instead of sticking around to watch Alana hurl her Lucky Charms at Keegan. Or she could find out once and for all if he was telling the truth when he said he didn't want Alana.

But you're eavesdropping again, Marty. It's impolite. Her conscience tap-tap-tapped her guilt with a metaphoric finger for listening to another conversation she had no business listening to.

Oh, for fuck's sake, it's not like I find anything out when I just ask. Do you see my rock and a hard place here? Give me a flippin' break.

So here she was skulking like some Peeping Tom in the corner of the kitchen, waiting. Her heart pounded so hard, she was sure she'd be caught from the sound of it alone.

Sure, she could turn tail and run. Make up all sorts of crazy shit about Keegan and Alana in her head, or she could take whatever his response to this viper was like a man.

She gulped. She wasn't sure if she was ready to be manly. Though God knew she had enough hair on her body these days to give any guy a good run for his money.

"I say we don't talk about *her* anymore. I've had enough of that woman to last me a lifetime," Alana said slyly.

"What do you want, Alana?" Keegan's question was gruff.

"What I've always wanted." Her smile was slow. "You."

See? Marty mentally sent Keegan an "I told you so." Her breath stalled.

It was now or never. If he'd been telling the truth, now was the time to shit or get off the pot.

He'd better get off the pot, or Marty would sever his fucking balls.

Hauling Alana up by her arms, Keegan loomed over her, leaving Her Blonde-ness looking small and waif-like. He held her wrists in his grip. She took the opportunity to mold herself to his frame.

Marty's stomach clenched, while she fought the urge to either yark or gouge out Alana's eyes.

Choices, choices . . .

Seconds ticked by like watching molasses run uphill in the wintertime. If he didn't answer Alana soon, Marty was going to lose it and end up getting caught. She needed to know what Alana wanted so badly from Keegan.

But do you really want to know?

Hell, *did* she really want to know?

Well, of course she did. That was silly. She couldn't go around crushing on some man who really wanted someone else, but was a lying puke, could she?

No. No. That wasn't acceptable at all.

But if she left and Keegan hadn't been lying, she'd have this image in her head forever of him holding Alana, and she'd never know why.

That would be called one of those classic misunderstandings she watched all the time on Soap Net.

No go.

So the fuck she was going anywhere. She'd stick around for the Barbie show.

"But," he said with malice reeking from his tone, "I don't want *you*, and I never have."

Woot!

Marty smiled, creeping farther into the shadows of the kitchen.

Alana's face fell, her eyes narrowing.

Oh, too bad, so sad, Barbie. Tissue?

There, there. No more tears. Maybe GI Joe's still on the market, and he has a tank—not just any old stupid Ken-car, but a bad-ass tank.

Marty wanted to whoop her relief, scream her joy. Instead she clamped a hand over her mouth to keep from rasping out a noisy breath of air she'd been holding.

Keegan thrust Alana away from him, his stance wide, defensive.

"You'll pay, Keegan." Her threat came out a whimper. "The council says you're my mate. We've been slated to mate since birth. I won't let that bitch take what's mine!"

In a swift move of motion and flesh, Keegan took her by the shoulders, making her neck arch as she held her head up to look at him. "Fuck the council." Whoa, he was really steaming. His shoulders flexed the muscles rigid as he gripped Alana's upper arms. "I wouldn't mate with you if you were the last were on Earth. Whether Marty had shown up or not, I wouldn't have mated with you. You never wanted me, Alana, you want Pack, and if it's the last breath I take, I'll be goddamned if you'll get it through me!" His roar aimed at Alana's incredulous, fearful face.

Yeah, that's the way, Barbie, Marty cheered her blonde rival. *Go on with yer bad self and piss him off.* She'd bet her uterus Keegan's nostrils were flaring.

A sob escaped Alana's pouty, red lips. "The council will stop you, Keegan! They won't allow her into the pack." Her voice rose with hysteria when she shoved him away from her.

"I guess we'll have to wait and see, won't we? I've called a meeting of the council, and I totally intend to denounce any merger between the Flahertys and the O'Brians if you're involved. Your underhanded tactics and bullshit deals are going to kill Pack, and I won't let you do that," were the final words he spoke before whipping around and storming up the steps.

"I know what you want from her, and I'll tell the council before you ever get the chance!" Alana finished her angry threat by flying to the front door and throwing it open, exiting in a flurry of blue skimpy dress and a cloud of blonde hair.

Keegan turned for a moment in Marty's direction, sniffing, then shook his head and took long, rigid strides to the staircase.

Marty released another breath of air, pressing her hand to her heart to thwart the pounding.

Holy fur and kibble.

Keegan had been ordered by the council to mate with Alana.

Since birth.

But he didn't want to mate with Alana.

Nah-nah nah-nah-nah-nah.

But what would happen if he didn't mate with Alana? What happened when you disobeyed the almighty Lunar Council?

She might be pleased as punch that Keegan didn't want to mate with Barbie, but she had to know what would occur if he didn't. Was this the lose-everything deal Mara had been talking about?

Marty raced up the stairs to Keegan's room and rapped sharply on the door. When it popped open, Keegan was shirtless and smiling. "Well, well. It's my little Color Guru. C'mon in." He pulled her inside, but she brushed him off, shoving him toward the bed, fighting to ignore the sensual pull of his naked chest and well-defined abs. He'd just had a pretty intense fight with Alana, and now he was all smiles? And men thought women's moods changed on a dime . . .

"Er, yeah and remember you said we had to talk?"

"You said we suck at talking, and if you remember, I said we had a little something to take care of before we did?" His eyebrows rose, and he winked, backing up to the bed and sitting at the edge of it.

She'd never been to the wolf's lair, but it screamed Keegan. It was painted in bold, deep colors—burgundies and lighter beiges for accents. Darkly stained walnut furniture, rich in detail, were his bed and dresser. The light cream carpet was thick under her feet, allowing them to sink into it as she stood in front of him, ready to get this confrontation over with.

"Stop that right now and pay attention." Her reprimand was followed by a stern shake of her finger, letting him know she knew what he was thinking. "Look, I was coming back from a walk, and I heard what Alana said, werewolf. How could you not have told me *she* was supposed to be your life mate as ordered by those heathens? That was grossly unfair of you to put me in a position I had no idea I was even in, bucko, and I want some answers. No wonder she hates my guts. I didn't know it ran that deep. I thought she was just tweaked because you didn't return her undying devotion. Jesus . . ."

He didn't bother to deny it. Instead he looked her calmly in the eye and owned up to it. "You're right, but in my mind it didn't really matter. I wouldn't mate with Alana if she were the last—"

"*Were on Earth.* I heard. So tell me what happens if you don't mate with her. I'm assuming it's some outdated bullshit rule I'll scoff at."

The gleam in his eyes was wicked. His bronzed hand patted the place beside him on the bed. "Come sit down next to me, and I promise to tell you—everything."

So he could avoid her questions? Not gonna happen this time. "Oh, no, Keegan Flaherty. When we get too close, stuff happens, and it has nothing to do with coherent sentences and good grammar."

"I promise to keep my hands to myself." He smiled devilishly.

"Pinky swear?"

He stuck out his pinky and latched it with hers.

Marty sat next to him on his big bed, turning to face him so she could watch his face. "Okay, so what happens if you don't mate with Alana?"

He pondered her question for a moment, his face becoming glacial. "The ugly truth?"

"All of it. I heard Alana say you could lose your alpha status. Is that true?"

"I could lose both Pack and my alpha-male status."

The gasp of shock she expelled was raspy. "You know, I have one thing to say." She swatted his arm. "You can be such a stubborn dumb ass! *Why* are you doing this?"

His raven-tipped eyebrow lifted. "Would *you* marry Barbie?"

Point. "All right, there is that, but you could lose everything, Keegan. You have Mara and Sloan to think of, too. This isn't just about you."

He took her hand in his, tracing the light veins on the back of it. "Wow, we've had some serious personal growth, haven't we? I remember saying those very words to you."

"Would you forget about me and my part in this? Think about your family, Keegan! You only get one of those." No truer words were spoken. God, epiphany was a bitch.

Drawing her palm to his mouth, he grazed it with hot lips. "I wouldn't have mated with Alana at gunpoint. It has nothing to do with you and never did. I was only putting off the inevitable, and then you turned up. It's been chaos ever since." He grinned at her over her hand, making her insides turn to overcooked spaghetti.

"How can you joke about something so serious? What happens if they boot you? How can they possibly take things from you that aren't theirs?"

"First, I'll be an outcast. Anything that's part of the pack isn't technically all mine, whether it was founded by my family or not. It's cumulative. Sort of a what's mine is yours thing. Like a big pot that everyone contributes to. I have a modicum of control over what people like Alana do, and I've found as of late, her business practices are far from ethical. I've been successful as the head of Pack, so the council lets me do as I see fit." He shifted positions, letting his thigh rub against hers.

"Now, as to my alpha status, it means I'm sort of the authority on what flies and what doesn't. I guide, if you will," he said. "It can be a heavy burden sometimes. It's why I got the apartment in New York."

"And what happens if you lose that position?"

"In the event I'm stripped of my alpha status, if pack members communicate with me, they risk being eradicated. Second, I won't allow someone to dictate to me whom I mate with. Period." Pulling her closer, he murmured against her cheek, "Now, are we done talking, because I have something so much more pleasant in mind? I can talk during it, if that's what turns you on." His grin was wicked.

Her hand cupped his jaw, reluctantly removing the mouth that drove her to distraction and shoving him back to his space. "Cut it the hell out! Tell me something. Do you think Alana might have had something to do with these attempts to kidnap me?"

"She denies it, which is no big surprise."

"What about someone else from the pack?" she prodded, knowing full well her nosiness had revealed something he didn't want to share.

"I've given that a great deal of thought. I didn't tell you because you have so much on your plate, and I had a pretty good eye on you. Or I thought I did. We have rogue members of the council who aren't above handling things in their own way."

"How about you let me decide what items I choose to put on my plate at the buffet line, okay? There might be plenty on my plate, like babies and mating and eternal life. I'm just picking at each item for now instead of gobbling them whole. I have a right to know everything. There isn't much I can't handle. At least I don't think there is."

"Then yes, it could be a rogue member."

"And? What else do I need to know about the council?"

"The council will want you to mate, too."

"Yeah, yeah. The baby-making thing. I know all about it."

"That's not all of it. If they let you stay, I'm going to

assume they'll want the same thing they want for all females of the pack."

"That being?"

"They'll choose a mate for you, too, and you'll be expected to carry on the bloodline."

"I have no say in who I choose?" she squealed.

"No one's ever questioned it as far as I can remember. So I couldn't say for sure if you do or you don't. Traditionally, we know from a very young age what's expected of us and who we're expected to do it with. It's a choice made at birth. Just like Alana and me."

"Which means I could end up someone's bitch . . ."

"Not if I have anything to say about it." He had that icy determined look on his face.

"No, no, no! I will not allow you to lose everything because of me, Keegan. I won't. It's bad enough you won't bend to their will where Alana's concerned, but I won't be a part of that. Jesus! Who the hell are these people anyway? This is like communist Russia."

Keegan raked a hand through his hair. "They're the elders of the pack. Some have been around for centuries. Their job is to protect the integrity of the pack. You were right about one thing. They're afraid of you. Afraid you might leak something to the outside world."

She blanched.

"Marty . . ."

She skirted the warning call of her name. "Did I tell you how wonderful it was of you to fly my friends here? I think it slipped my mind after 'When Barbies Attack' showed up to shift, but it was so great to see them. Oh, God, we talked and laughed and had the best time—"

"You told them . . ."

She peered at him hesitantly. "Shit. I didn't mean to, but they had some info about Bobbie-Sue that made me nuts, and I got angry, and well, you know how that goes. Whamo! Like there it was. My teeth got big, too. I swear, if I could have prevented it I would, and besides, whose fault is it anyway that I have that poor excuse of a tail?" She quickly reversed the blame to save herself his wrath.

"I know it's not your fault. Let's not get into another pissing match over that again."

"I've endangered them, haven't I? Oh, God. What kind of friend am I? I made them swear not to tell. Let's just hope the council doesn't find out."

"What made you so angry?"

There was no way she was going to tell him about Terrence and Linda. She was a jobless loser right now. Her shame was more than she could put into words. "Oh, just Nina. You know what a big mouth she is. She just made me mad. Forget that. What will we do? I mean about the council. Do they have a hotline or maybe an email address? Like heathens@stupidheadrules.com?"

He laughed huskily. "No, no email address. I say we'll just have to wait and see. We aren't going to get the answers we need tonight." He grinned, dragging her closer and pulling her onto his lap. "But, I think there are other things we can do to help pass the time."

The rigid outline of his cock pressed against her ass, the heat of it through his jeans searing her. He moved her hair, nibbling at her neck, teasing the flesh with his teeth.

"You know, I was thinking."

He sighed that sigh of aggravation while turning her so her back faced his chest and, cupping her breasts, lightly pinched her nipples through her sweater. "What were you thinking, Marty?"

A moan, long and low slipped from her lips. She turned and found her arms slipping upward around his neck, her back arching, encouraging his exploration when he lifted her sweater and pushed her bra upward. "I was think—ohhhh—ing that you werewolves are more like a cult than Bobbie-Sue ever could—ohhhhh—beeeee," she whimpered on a breathy sigh.

His hand cupped her chin, tilting her head back so her eyes aligned with his. "I say we don't talk about it anymore." Keegan captured her lips then, driving his tongue between them, leaving her shivering, aching to feel his naked flesh. The moment he was near, she was on fire. Thoughts, carnal and scrumptiously sinful, blotted out everything else.

She couldn't think clearly when he touched her. Reason went the way of the dodo bird. It became extinct. If there was anything she had to do at this point, it was find a way to prevent Keegan from giving up everything. Her mind raced, struggling to think of a plan of action while his hands tortured her deliciously.

One thing was certain, she wanted to make love to him again, and, when all was said and done, whatever happened with the council, she'd have this moment. She refused to waste it on anything else but the two of them.

Marty stirred in his embrace, rising to stand between his legs, pushing him down to lie on the bed. Her heart hammered in her chest when she lifted her arms, pulling her sweater off, then unhooking her bra and letting it fall to the floor. She followed with her jeans, leaving nothing on but her pink, lace panties.

His eyes were stormy, tumultuous. They filled with surprise when she slid her jeans down along her thighs, kicking off her shoes and tossing them away. His nostrils flared, his gaze deepening, devouring her seminudity.

Marty returned his gaze, openly scanning the length of his bronzed chest, leaning forward to run her tongue along the wicked definition of his abs. Her fingers didn't fumble when she tugged his belt apart and unzipped his jeans, shrugging them over his thick thighs, tangling her fingers in the fine hair sprinkled over muscle and sinew.

Her head bent, her lips skimming the top of his underwear as her hands removed them, too. She felt the shuffle of his feet when he kicked them aside, the tug of his hands as he tried to pull her up his chest, but she had other ideas.

Keegan's cock jutted upward, nested in dark pubic hair crisp to her fingertips. His big hands went to her head, wrapping his hands in her hair and hissing when she traced the head of his shaft with her tongue.

Smooth, silky, hot, he tasted salty and delicious. Her stomach clenched when he said her name, as her lips wrapped around him, drawing him deep into her mouth. Keegan bucked, clenching her head, cupping her jaw, following the slow up and down motion she made. She made pass after pass, a glide of tongue and lips, swirling her hand over his thickness and caressing the soft orbs of his testicles.

His feral cry and the thrust of his hips empowered her, but he pulled her from him, the sinful sound of flesh popping as his cock left her mouth. Dragging her upward, he wrapped his arms around her waist, devouring her lips with the hard crush of his mouth.

Their skin slid together, hot, wanton, leaving her sharp gasps an echo against his mouth. Her pulse skittered to a stop when he turned her on her belly and, removing her panties, ran his palms over the indentation of her waist, slipping between her legs to caress the swollen lips of her center.

Marty raised her hips in response, lifting herself to her knees seeking his fingers, crying out when he circled her clit with his thumb. Hot kisses were planted along her spine, a mix of tongue and gentle teeth when he pressed his head between her thighs and swiped his tongue along them.

The silk of his hair, combined with his tongue slipping between her aching thighs made her nipples tighten painfully. She clenched the bedcovers between her fingers, burying her face in them to keep a scream from escaping her lips.

And then he was behind her, the rigid press of his abs hot on her ass, his hands roaming over her with forceful passes, cupping her breasts, kneading her spine.

There was no pause when he entered her. A swift drive of his cock left him embedded deeply within, touching her womb, and this time she did cry out, followed by a long whimper.

Keegan filled her, stretched her to accommodate him, bracing himself with a hand on her lower back, thrusting over and over. He reached his other hand around to fondle her clit, slowly circling it, leaving her chest tight, the place between her legs wet and slick.

Marty wanted all of him, every last inch to consume her. The need clawed at her so she reared back farther on her knees, raising her hips higher, silently begging Keegan to push her over the edge into climax.

Keegan stiffened, the slick slide of his cock becoming frantic as he pumped his hips against her. His abdomen pulled away from her body, and she felt him arch backward, gripping her hips. The pulse of his shaft raced when he found release.

The slap of their flesh rang in her ears, and it was her undoing. The swift rise of orgasm dragged her over the edge like high tide. Her body went rigid, tightly strung, heat attacking every intimate place on her body, and with a hoarse cry, she came.

It was so sharp, so sweet, and came from a place so deep it brought tears to her eyes.

They collapsed together, the heavy weight of his frame capturing her beneath him. Keegan's chest heaved hard breaths, pressing against her back, the air from his lungs ringing in her ears.

Turning her to face him, he caught her jaw between his large hands, kissing her forehead. "You just wanna afterglow again, or are we going to do the girly thing and talk." He was obviously lighthearted, though his breathing was still choppy.

That he could speak after that was a feat as far as she was concerned. No, she didn't want to talk. Not now when she had to gather her thoughts, think of what to do to stop these unseen council members from taking anything away from Keegan. "I think afterglow is good enough for now, but that doesn't mean I might not want to talk later. I know you get mad about it, but it's essential to good communication skills, Caveman."

"Yeah, yeah." His muttering was colored with a slight slur.

He tucked her against him and propped his chin on the top of her head.

When she heard a soft rumble of a snore leave his lips, she knew she was safe to try and think.

What to do, what to do?

Staying here was only going to make things worse for Keegan and his family. If she just disappeared the council would leave him alone. But then there was Alana. So that didn't entirely solve the problem.

Yet, if nothing else, she could eliminate at least her part in it, right?

Her heart rebelled against that. Why should she have to give up this family because of an accident? Why the fuck should these people, people she'd never even seen, be allowed to dictate who she mated with? Who Keegan mated with? She'd only been a werewolf for just over a month—so who said she had to adhere to traditions that had never applied to her before now?

The hard realization that this wasn't just about her now gnawed at her gut. It involved Mara, Sloan, Nina, and Wanda, too, if the council got wind of the fact that she'd blown their cover.

She had to find this council before Keegan had his big powwow. She'd bow out, go into hiding, do whatever they wanted, if they'd just let Keegan keep his alpha status and Pack. The rest she'd figure out later. Because she'd have this man if it killed her.

Her eyes narrowed. Where was the first place the council would go looking for her if she left Southfork unprotected?

Her apartment.

If whoever had kidnapped her still had her purse, even if by some remote chance it wasn't the council, they knew where she lived, and when she turned up missing, it would be the first place they'd look.

Hey, live bait! What if they don't come to your apartment?

Then I'll have a whole bloody moment to myself to decide what to do next.

Slipping from Keegan's embrace, she ran a quick hand over his hair and smiled. He was out cold. Just like a man. Marty said a silent prayer this wouldn't be the last time she saw him. The chiseled lines of his jaw, the dark smattering of stubble across his chin and cheeks made her want him again.

Now was not the time to get herself caught. If Keegan found out where she was going—he'd put her under lock and key.

Grabbing her clothes, she threw them on with haste, while her mind raced. It wasn't such a brilliant plan if she couldn't execute it. Execution meant transportation.

Damn these werewolves for not having wings. How the hell was she going to get to her apartment six hours away in the city?

Mara's car! She'd offered it to her. Crap, where had she said the keys would be?

Behind Muff's food in the pantry.

Thank you.

Have you forgotten the directionally challenged part of your brain? You'll never find the city from here in the rolling hills of Sherwood Forest.

A map. She needed a map and a gas station.

Before she had the time to linger, wish she could remain in the safe haven Keegan's arms offered, she opened the door quietly and ran to the end of the hall, heading for her room.

She grabbed her cell phone, car charger, and a credit card that hadn't been stolen when she was nabbed the first time. Flying down the stairs, she stopped short. Helga had fallen asleep in front of the fireplace, Muffin curled on her round belly.

Muff's head popped up, and Marty held a finger to her lips, indicating for her to remain quiet.

In less than five minutes she had the keys Mara had promised, and she was out the door on quiet feet. Rounding the side of the house, she found Mara's compact car and climbed in.

For a moment, she clung to the steering wheel, bracing her head against it and taking deep breaths.

Jesus Christ in a miniskirt, this was crazy. It was insane to will these people to find her in the hopes they'd listen to reason. What the fuck was reasonable about wanting someone dead because of an accident?

Her hand shook when she turned the key in the ignition and pulled away. She vaguely remembered signs for the highway when she and Mara had driven to Pack, and for crap's sake, could it be any darker?

Surely there was a gas station in Clampetville?

Headlights glared in the rearview mirror, blinding her for a moment. The beams shot through her head, stabbing her eyes. Whoever it was had their high beams on, and they were in a hella rush, because if they came any closer, an introduction was in order. Were people in the country even up at this hour? A glance at the car clock told her it was after midnight. What could Bubba and Jeb possibly be doing out this late at night? Cow tipping?

That was her last coherent thought before a screech of metal and tires blocked out everything else. The grind of her brakes screeched in the silence of the car like a banshee. The harsh beat of her heart and her scream of panic echoed in the small space.

Her hands grabbed frantically at the wheel, yet she couldn't seem to control the sideways spin.

The two passenger side wheels reared up, and then the last sound she heard was the sickening crunch of the car slamming into something hard and unyielding.

Her last frantic thought before unconsciousness overtook her was of Keegan and how much she wished she'd stayed where oddly, she felt more than ever, she belonged.

Safe beside him in his big, warm bed. As a part of his family—a part of his life.

"Do you have her?" a silky, cultured voice asked.

"I do. Thanks for the heads-up."

"Remember our deal."

"Don't you worry your pretty, greedy little head." His chuckle was glib, his breathing through the phone harsh with excitement.

"Make sure you make this all disappear, or I *will* make you wish it was you that was dead."

"So this is good-bye?"

"I do believe it is."

"Ah, then, later."

She clicked the phone shut with a snap of satisfied fingers, turning to make her way around to her car.

"Ya wanna tell me who's making who disappear?" Sloan asked, coming out of the dark night to face Alana, leaning against the hood of her car.

"I have no idea what you mean," she replied, keeping her tone light. "And what are you doing here so late?"

"Um, I live here, and I just got home. I think the more appropriate question is, what are *you* doing here, Alana, and who was that on the phone?"

Her smile was crafty. "I left my purse here after the shift. I came back to get it."

Sloan peered into her passenger side window and sucked in his cheeks. "Okay, and now the real reason you're here?"

With a huff of air that steamed in the cold air, she said, "Fine, I came to talk to Keegan, all right? To beg him to reconsider our mating." She offered the lie without a single stutter, her face passive.

Sloan jammed his hands into his pockets and slanted his head, moving in to let his face hover near Alana's. "Nuh-uh. I ain't buyin' it. So I say we go on inside and find Keegan, and while we're at it, I think you'd better give me the cell phone." He held his hand out, waiting for her to place it in his palm.

When she hesitated, he grabbed her by her upper arm. *"Now,"* he ground out.

Alana swallowed hard.

This just might be the part of the Marty Andrews story where she got caught.

CHAPTER
15

For the love of Tylenol, her head throbbed. It wasn't the throb of her inner werewolf though. This was the kind of throb yet another klunk to the head brought.

As she came to, her eyelids fighting to peel themselves apart, the jam she was in became clear in slow increments.

She moved each portion of her body with care. If she could fully open her eyes, she'd roll them over the very idea that she was being held captive—*again*.

In fact, there were many agains.

Again she was somewhere she didn't want to be.

Again she was in a big pickle.

Only this again included duct tape—over her mouth, her wrists, and ankles.

Wherever she was, it was cold, damp, and smelled old. It was early morning. A slant of weak light gleamed from above her head and shone on her bound feet. As she pried her eyes open further, she took note of her surroundings. For sure a basement, judging from the stark gray of the cement walls and stacks of boxes that were wet and sagging.

"Hello, Marty." A rich, thick voice came from the far corner of the dark, small cellar.

Well, she didn't want to be rude, but she couldn't exactly respond with her mouth glued shut, so she nodded.

A lean body came forward, the light through the small window above her head revealing a well-kept, trendy man. His dark navy suit was Kenneth Cole, his tie a deep lavender, his shoes real leather, judging by the smell, and his hair blond, artfully arranged with that careless tousled, but totally calculated look. His face was pleasant enough, though his lips were just a bit too thin for Marty's tastes. It could be that he was scowling at her, but overall he did nothing for her physically.

Now she was rating her kidnapper on a wet panty scale of one to ten?

"Do you know who I am?" His question was gleeful. Rather one a stalker might take great pleasure in asking his prey after a long hunt.

She shook her head no. Though, as he stepped farther into the light, he did look familiar. Why, she couldn't say. On the assumption he was another werewolf, Marty then decided she definitely couldn't possibly recognize him.

Placing his hands behind his back, he rocked on his heels. "I'm Terrence. Terrence Douglas Bradford."

Her head reeled for a moment. Bobbie-Sue's Terrence Douglas? Yeah . . . her vague recollection of him the night she'd gone all freaky on Linda Fisher clicked. But why did he have her tied up? Her confusion must have shown on her face.

"Yes, that's right. I'm the, ah, shithead, I believe your foul friend Nina called me, who took away your Bobbie-Sue accounts. You were a good rep for Bobbie-Sue. It was a pity."

Huh? Again, what did Terrence have to do with her?

"Do you know *why* you're here, Marty?"

He wanted a custom color wheel?

Marty vehemently shook her head no, wriggling her

hands behind her back to see if she could grab an edge of the tape.

"Because I have some very, very interesting news for you. It's gonna rock your world."

For the love of Pete—her world was plenty rocked, thanks. No more rocking.

"Wanna know why?"

On a scale of one to ten? She was maybe feeling a four. Peaked interest, but not a must have information situation. She skeptically nodded her head yes, knowing full well it was the right thing to do.

He stood silent for a moment, perusing her trussed-up form, cocking his head, clearly gauging her mood.

Drum roll, please.

"Are you sure you're ready for news of this magnitude?"

Again, on a scale of one to ten, now she was maybe a seven. He apparently held the key to all this kidnapping, but she wasn't one hundred percent sure she wanted to know why he'd kidnapped her. However, she dutifully shook her head yes.

He licked his lips with a nervous tongue. "Then I'll just say it. I'm your brother. Well, half brother, if you're into technicalities, and I've waited well over a month to meet you."

Um, okay. Hold on. Her half brother? So he wasn't a werewolf from the council? And hang the fuck on! She didn't have a half anything. The only half she had was a tail.

"It's true," he responded to the evident look of the lost on her face. "My father, Donald Bradford, is your father, too. He did a very bad thing once upon a time. He had an affair with your mother, *Lucinda*."

Now that was strange. He knew her mother's name.

"Do you believe me?"

In the scheme of things, did that really mean a rat's ass to him? She had no answer.

"Know what?"

"Mmm-mmm?" she pushed out from behind the duct tape, shaking her head.

"I don't care if you believe me, but I figured you at least deserved an explanation before you die a tragic, untimely death. So, here we go. Your mother met my father over thirty-two years ago. They had an affair. She broke it off when she discovered he was married. I know, because I overheard my father tell a longtime friend the night we saw you at the corporate meeting. He was pretty shaken up. He said you looked just like her, and he was going to do some digging. So I hacked into his private email account, read all about you, and voilà—here you are."

Marty's eyes widened. Was this some kind of joke?

He rifled in his pocket, pulling out a worn, faded scrap of paper that immediately caught her attention. Her mother's stationery had looked just like that. She'd never forget it, because anything personal her mother had written, she always put on that very stationery.

"Here, look," he said, shoving the paper under her nose. It was a letter to a Donald, scrawled in her mother's handwriting. Snatching it back, he gave her a satisfied flash of teeth and lips. "See? It's true. It took me a while to find any hard evidence, but it was enough for me to believe. You know what that means, don't you?"

Her head made a slow, sluggish dip. *Enlighten me.*

"It means you own a good deal of Bobbie-Sue, and I can't have that. I hope death becomes you."

Whoaaaa.

Forget the death thing.

Donald Bradford was her father?

Who's yer daddy?

"I own Bobbie-Sue?" came out in a muffled string of hard-won grunts, as the tape over her mouth puffed out with each word she tried to speak. For a moment she forgot she was hog-tied in an unknown dark, dank basement, with some lunatic salivating at the mere thought of her death. For a moment, her color wheel of life spun in glorious shades of gold and silver. Product after product flew across the window of her mind's eye. She'd hit the palettes of life bonanza!

Holy color wheel Heaven.

Marty Andrews owned a piece of Bobbie-Sue.

Booyah, baby.

Marty Andrews from nowhere Piscataway. The product of a single parent and an affair.

An affair her mother'd apparently indulged in with Bobbie-Sue's husband, Donald.

Christ on a stick.

"So I can see you get the big picture." His expression jeered at her, dripping venom and a hatred so tangible she felt it in every pore.

Oh, indeed. She owned a part of Bobbie-Sue. What else in life was there? She saw the picture—through a big, fucking panoramic vista of blusher and foundation. She felt it in the winds rushing through her hair when she hopped into her cute, sky blue convertible to take it for a spin.

"Like I said, my father said you look just like her. He saw you that night after you accosted Linda Fisher."

Ahhh, the lovely Linda.

Poor, poor disillusioned, account-stealing, lying, cheating, back-stabbing Linda. Now wouldn't she be in for a fucking slap upside her head when she found out who owned a piece of her ass? Oh, happy, happy, joy, joy. There'd be no more stealing anything from her or Wanda when Marty was done reading her the riot act. Despite her situation, Marty smiled, wicked and slow—or to the best of her ability, in light of her mouth being duct taped to high Heaven.

If she had time to relish this moment, she'd ponder it longer. Savor it. Roll the words *cosmetic windfall* around on her tongue, like they were buttered toffee, chocolate-covered candies. Of all the crazy things to find out *now*. However, this information was clearly going to be followed by her brutal death at the hands of her psychotic half brother.

How totally *Psycho*.

That was how it always happened in the movies.

Just before your death you find out you're entitled to an

entire empire of lip gloss and eyeliner, and *splat*, the killer shares this information just as he's preparing to attach the cement blocks to your feet and dump you in the drink.

Wasn't that just the fucking way her life would go?

Yet Terrence's agitation seemed to be centered right now. He needed her to hear his fury. He needed validation before he whacked her.

Which, in this case, was a bit over the top for Marty's taste and just a smidge over her threshold for crazy.

How very *Jerry Springer*.

Grabbing her by the shoulders, he dug his fingers into her flesh. "Do you have any idea how much I *despise* you? How much I stand to lose if word gets out that you're my father's indiscretion? Not to mention the scandal it would bring to all of my mother's hard work!"

Well, judging by the amount of duct tape he'd used on her mouth, wrists, and ankles, *despise* was probably a word subject to interpretation, and as to the indiscretion part, well, fuck him. She was no one's indiscretion. That her father was Donald Bradford was mind-boggling, but it didn't change who she was. How she'd come to be the woman she was.

She was still the product of Lucinda Andrews's upbringing. It had left her self-sufficient, determined, and a little alone.

Until lately.

And she'd be dipped in shit if some mad half brother was going to take away what she'd found because he didn't want to part with some cash.

With a vicious swipe, Terrence ripped the duct tape from her mouth, tearing at the soft flesh of her lips.

She struggled with all she had not to scream her surprise and rage, tasting blood seeping into her mouth from her cracked lips. Instead she let her eyes narrow, lifting her chin to challenge Terrence's wild eyes.

"You didn't think I'd let you fuck me out of millions of dollars, did you?"

Her gaze was defiant. "Ya know, Terrence," she said

through lips that were numb and sticking to her teeth. "Here's the funny thing about all that cash." She ran her tongue over her teeth. "I had no clue I was entitled to it. If you'd just left me alone, I'd have never been the wiser." She'd tack on a *dumb ass* for good measure, but at this point, the point of no return for Terrence, she suspected, giving him that last little shove probably wasn't genius-level problem solving.

His spiked hair, styled in that purposefully salon-tousled look, bounced on his head when he threw it back and laughed with abandon. "You didn't think my father was going to let his spawn from some whore go, did you? No, Donald is just too niiiice. He's all about doing the right thing, and his guilt over not knowing you existed just wouldn't let him sleep at night. So he had to go and do something foolish like find you. *Big mistake,*" he spat, the spittle that came with his words striking Marty in the eye.

So Donald had looked for her? Oh, God, maybe he was looking right now. If she could just keep this lunatic talking to her . . . *you'll what, Marty? Create a color aura for him?* Shit, shit, shit. What next?

And had he just called her mother a whore?

Oh, no, no, no.

Tsk, tsk.

Now—now it was on. Screw the fact that he'd probably slice her to ribbons. Nobody called her mother a whore. In the midst of this lunacy, her mother's protective nature, keeping Marty so close to her, all made sense. She'd been afraid to lose Marty to the wealth of Donald Bradford. The familiar tingle of fury skittered along her spine, urging her to speak before thinking.

"I'm sorry. I believe the word you used in reference to my mother was *whore*. That's not nice, Terrence. Not nice at all. I mean, you didn't know my mother, and she never did anything to you. Okay, so she had an affair with your father, and technically that's a sin. A big one. But she didn't ask for anything from you or your family. What Donald did was his choice. I had no idea who my father was, and that you have the unmitigated gall to tie me up like some animal over something as trivial as money is appalling. You should be ashamed of yourself—do you hear me? Ashamed. Shall I spell it—"

His hand snaked out and crashed against her cheek before she had time to finish her sentence. Her head whipped back on her shoulders, then snapped back up. "Shut—the—fuck—up, you dumb-ass bitch!"

Really, was it necessary to call names? How had she been labeled a dumb-ass bitch? So utterly and totally uncalled for. That was twice in less than a month . . .

Oh, my. Now she got it. That she hadn't put it together sooner left her reeling. "It was *you*? You hired those two idiots to kidnap me? You've got to be kidding. With all of your money, surely you could have hired professionals! They did the worst job, Terrence. I mean, look, I got away! I hope you didn't put out too much for that job gone awry."

Terrence's eyes grew dark with rage.

Okay. So telling him how to go about having her murdered properly might be called overkill.

Shutting up.

"I didn't put out anything. They took off, and I never heard from them again." He said it as if he were trying to one-up her. "It doesn't much matter now, does it? Because here you are, and not a soul knows. So I say we just get this over with now."

Now was so final.

So over.

A buildup to this dirty deed was in order. He should be savoring his coup, and instead he wanted to rush headlong into her death. Were all spoiled, rich kids so impulsive? She wet her lips and tried to think clearly. "Murder is a tough rap to beat. Even for someone like you who can afford the best attorneys. Why does it even matter that I exist, Terrence? What if I signed something that said I wanted nothing from you or your family?"

His laughter filled the room, insane, dark, downright freaky. "My father the do-gooder would never allow that.

He needs to pacify his guilt. He wants to make up for everything you didn't have growing up, and he wants to do it with *my* money." His voice rose to a maniacal pitch, droplets of sweat dotting his upper lip.

That she was going to say these next words should astonish her. It should feel like someone had stabbed her in the eye with a mascara wand, but she didn't need pity from a man she didn't know. Nor did she . . . need . . . his . . . she fought a sob . . . cosmetics company. Christ that had hurt. "Well, then you can just tell him I had everything I ever needed, and I don't want his money. See? Everything is all better now. Now cut this tape off me, and let's go spread some glad tidings. What say you?"

"I say, fuck you!"

Such unpleasant words. If he weren't an utter loon he'd be Nina's knight in shining Kenneth Cole. "I really think we can work this out, Terrence. And besides, even if your father gave me a share in Bobbie-Sue, you people make so much money you wouldn't even miss it. What's a couple mill in the scheme of billions?"

"Because it's mine, damn you. It's mine, and you have no right to it."

And everyone thought she was a bad sharer . . . Terrence displayed the typical only child syndrome to the nth degree.

"If your mother had just kept her legs closed. If she hadn't been such a whore, none of this would be happening."

Oookay. Now that was just about enough. He could call her whatever he liked, but she'd be fucked and feathered if she'd allow him to continue to bandy about words like *whore* in reference to her mother. A strange vibration clung to her spine, working its way along and spreading outward. Her head pounded from the crash of her pulse in her ears. "Terrence? I'm going to just give you a little heads-up here. Calling my mother a whore is making me a wee bit upset. So I'm going to ask you nicely to please refrain from being such a potty mouth." *You spineless fuck.*

"Or you'll do what? From where I'm standing, you're a little tied up, and your mother *is* a whore. A cheap slut. A home wrecker!" he sing-songed in a puppet-like parody.

The muscles of her back flexed, tensing, pushing at her skin in the strangest manner. Marty felt the compelling need to warn Terrence he was treading on sacred ground. Yet she had no clue why she thought she had the balls to back up a statement like that.

However, she was unable to stop the threat coming from her mouth. She heard her voice, recognized the words, and was suitably astonished by them. "I said shut up, Terrence, or I'll beat the fucking life out of you for all the times I missed knocking the crap out of you when we were growing up. For every time I missed out on stealing your GI Joe doll and dressing it in Barbie's clothes, I promise you, the payback will be times infinity." How odd that her tone was so cool and calm, while her insides were in a complete uproar. Electric bolts of heat made her skin prickle almost unbearably.

Grabbing her by her hair, he yanked her upward, forcing her eyeball-to-eyeball with him. His breath smelled of hard liquor, his wrath of dank, decaying bitterness. "I'm going to fucking kill you, and I'm going to smile when I do it, knowing I've probably eliminated another whore in the making."

She tilted her chin up with arrogant insolence, squarely meeting his wild eyes. "I dare you, you skinny, spineless, pansy-assed motherfucker." Her challenge was clear, not once doubting her newly acquired balls had just clanged like church bells. The words came easily, her rage rising and falling in deep swells.

Terrence's scream was filled with a desperate frustration as he threw her to the basement wall where she hit with a force that knocked the wind out of her, leaving her to crumple awkwardly to the ground.

And that was when she saw the silver gleam of the knife.

Well, if nothing else, his threats weren't empty. Apparently, his balls were clanging, too.

* * *

"YOU'RE sure it was Mara's car?" Keegan fought the impulse to put his fist through the nearest wall.

"Yeah, boss. I'm sure," Victor said with a curt nod. "It was pretty smashed up, but I didn't find her at all. No sign of her. I'm sorry. We'll keep searching, though. I'll gather the pack." He glanced sympathetically at his longtime employer.

Goddamn it, Marty, where the fuck are you? He wanted to scream the words. When he'd awakened to find her gone, he hadn't panicked at first. Not until he couldn't find her anywhere. And not only was she gone, but so were her cell phone and the stupid pink purse she'd been so hot for him to remember to get. Immediately he'd been on the phone, summoning the pack to search the grounds for her. When he'd found Mara and she'd confessed to allowing Marty the keys to her car, it was all he could do not to rage at her. When they'd found the keys gone, he'd lost it.

If someone had hurt her, touched one pretty hair on her not-so-blonde head, he'd fucking rip them apart.

Then everything unfolded at a pace that became a blur of motion and sound, and now Mara's car was on the side of a road, broken and battered, and Marty was nowhere to be found.

His cell phone chirped, and he flipped it open, praying it was Marty, but he didn't recognize the phone number on the voicemail message. As he dialed his voicemail and listened, his heart slammed against his ribs in time with the roar of his pulse in his ears.

A frantic, frightened Nina and Wanda had left him a message, and it had to do with Donald Bradford. He frowned. He'd briefly met Donald a time or two, because they moved in the same circles. What in the hell could Bobbie-Sue's husband possibly know about who'd kidnapped Marty?

"Victor!" Rage, fear for Marty's life, and the idea that

she could be dead tore at his gut. "Get that damned plane
ready. *Now!*"

"Yes, sir. Our destination?"

"New York and Bobbie-Sue corporate." His reply was
curt, tight. Turning on his heel, he broke into a run, with
Victor hot on his heels.

God save Donald Bradford if he'd had a hand in hurting
Marty.

Keegan would watch him bleed to death after he ripped
his throat out.

TERRENCE held the knife in front of Marty's eyeball, slicing it through the air with short, quick thrusts. He knelt in
front of her, dragging the blade over her cheek, pricking
her skin, and all the while instead of feeling the utter terror
she'd felt in the trunk of that car, the kind of fear one felt
when death was imminent, instead Marty seethed. She
wanted to live, and she wanted to do that with Keegan. She
wanted to spend time with him minus the stress of this kidnapping bullshit hanging over her head.

Maybe have a burger—go to a movie—do normal couple shit, and she'd be fucked and feathered if she was going
to let this maniacal whack-job take that from her.

He could keep his flippin' money.

Who needed a sky blue convertible any-the-frig-ol'-
way?

The air became thick with her fury.

It simmered like a pot of sauce, reaching a frenzied boiling point.

The aroma stormed her senses, seeking, waiting, dancing along her spine, begging for release.

The scrape of the blade along her flesh was distant, ab-
stract, as her focus found the core of her rage.

No, fear no longer played a factor in this game of cat and
mouse. Control did, and she wanted to harness this beast
tearing at her from the inside, howling a cry for autonomy.

Terrence's ranting became muted, and when he let the

knife graze her throat, when she felt a slick stream of blood trickle down her throat, was when a multicolored haze of light and muffled sound blotted out everything else.

A snap and crunch of bone resounded in the damp of the basement. Her skin, momentarily excruciatingly taut, loosened, stretched. Her pores opened, allowing for the distinct feel of needle-pricking jabs sprouting from every inch of her body.

Tape, so tightly bound she'd surely be numb, tore, snapping with little effort.

And she continued to call upon her fury, visualizing it like a living, breathing entity. Cultivating it, nurturing it, honing the sweet hum of freedom, until it slithered along each of her veins, searing her until she could no longer breathe from it.

When the final, furious thrust of limbs and flesh contorted, shifted, jutting in all directions, Marty saw one last thing before this raw, animal instinct coursing through her took over.

Well, actually two.

She saw the terrified, silent scream of Terrence's mouth.

And paws.

Great, big, hairy paws.

Paws that were a sandy color mixed with stray splotches of chocolate.

Well, thank God *someone* had the good sense to realize she was a blonde.

Even if it was the shifting gods.

"YOU do realize I'll kill you if you don't tell me where she is, don't you?" Donald Bradford held his wife of almost forty years by the lapels of her sky blue, Bobbie-Sue suit. The petite blonde shook; her porcelain skin creased.

"How dare you threaten me, Donald!" she shouted up into the weathered, tanned face of her husband. Her voice held disbelief, desperation. "You had an affair with that

filthy tramp! Her spawn deserves nothing—nothing from
the coffers I've worked so hard to fill!"

Keegan stood behind them, both unaware he'd stormed
his way past a receptionist and three security guards with
a flash of his canines to get to the illustrious offices of
Bobbie-Sue Bradford.

"Don't for a minute forget *whose money* funded this!"
Donald snarled with such vicious anger, it shocked Keegan.
"And don't for a minute forget your name may be on this
company, but I own every bit as much as you do!"

Keegan smelled panic mingled with Donald's fury and
Bobbie-Sue's horror. The combination was explosive, and
before things got too far gone, he stepped in, moving on
silent feet to come up behind Donald and tear him from
his wife. Bobbie-Sue scrambled backward, nearly falling
to the floor before righting herself. Her face filled with
confusion when Keegan dragged Donald back, securing
his neck with an arm he fought to keep from strangling
the life from him.

"Where's Marty?" His whisper was sinister in the ear of
the man who knew where his mate was.

"You know my daughter?" Donald choked out, clawing
at the hands that firmly held him in a death grip.

Keegan kept his surprise in check, but his mind mentally
fought to put those words together. His daughter? "I said
tell me where she is. Tell me, or I'll rip you limb from limb.
Literally." Fury assaulted Keegan, and he had to clench his
teeth to keep from tearing Donald's throat out.

"Who are you?" His question was a hiss, while he
gasped for breath.

Keegan hurled him to the floor with a force so hard,
Donald crashed into the far wall, leaving a dent in the sheet
rock. He was on him like a starved animal, gripping his
bone white suit jacket, hauling him upward to flatten him
against the wall. Keegan narrowed his eyes, warring with
the beast inside him that wanted Donald dead. "Where—
is—she?"

Bobbie-Sue had regained her senses, coming at Keegan

from behind and tearing at his back, screeching, but Keegan tossed her from him without a backward glance. "What do you know about Marty?" he bellowed in Donald's face, relishing the terror he saw there.

"She's my daughter!"

"That *whore's* daughter!" Bobbie-Sue shouted with desperation. "Did you think I didn't know, Donald? I've known about that woman for a very long time. What I didn't know was you'd created a child. I won't allow the scandal to ruin a name I've worked for years to create. Bobbie-Sue Cosmetics commands respect, and nothing—not even your guilt over some illegitimate child—is going to take that away!"

In his rage, it occurred to Keegan, his target wasn't Donald at all. It was Bobbie-Sue, and she knew something. His angry hands thrust Donald from him, and with a growl of rage, he turned his wrath on Bobbie-Sue.

Stalking her, he backed her up against the edge of her mahogany desk, looming over her, bending her slight frame until his arms bracketed her body. "Where is Marty?" He flashed his canines with seething fury.

She cowered with revulsion. Her face filled with horror, her hand flew to her slender throat, her mouth opened, but no words formed.

Suddenly Donald was between them, imploring his wife, "Where is she? Tell me where she is! Do it now, before I let him finish you off." He was insistent, frantic, urgent, the soft sweep of his stark white hair falling to his brow.

"Terrence—she's with Terrence—at the house in Queens," she whimpered with a drawn-out whine, looking to Donald with tears in her eyes.

"Who's Terrence?" Keegan cut in.

Donald shoved at Keegan. "Stop! I'll deal with her later. We have to get to Marty," he pleaded, his urgent tone laced with tension. The leathered skin of his face was drawn and worried, his eyes frantic.

Keegan smelled his anxiety and decided he had little to

go on other than what Bobbie-Sue had just revealed. As much as he wanted to gnaw the life out of her, he had to take the chance that Donald was being truthful.

Pivoting on his heel, he hunkered over Donald and warned with maliciousness, "If you've lied to me, when I'm done with you, you'll wish I had killed you. Now take me to the house in Queens."

Donald's eyes, so like Marty's, were sincere, genuine, with a plea Keegan had no choice but to believe. "I'll get my driver."

"No." Keegan sniped a command, taking hold of his arm and marching him to the door. "We'll take my car, and you can tell me all about this Terrence."

Whoever this asshole Terrence was, he'd better pray Hell didn't really exist.

WHAT a mind fuck, Marty thought while running her long, pink tongue over her muzzle. She could definitely understand the joy it brought Keegan and the pack to shift. She rolled her jaw, licking her chops. Dayum, now those were teeth.

Christ, when her face had exploded during the shift, it had felt like the jaws of life prying her apart, but when all was said and done—this was some pretty radical shit.

Heady and powerful, with a dab of exhilaration for good measure.

Niiiiiiice.

Stretching her limbs, she let a shudder run the length of her body, shaking out the last vestiges of her human form. Rolling to her back, Marty rubbed it against the hard cement with glee, admiring her new paws while she wriggled.

God, that was fabulous. If only she had a mirror.

Werewolf was soooooo in her color wheel.

A whimper from the corner of the basement caught her attention and reminded her why she was where she was.

Tsk, tsk. Poor Terrence. Her *half brother* Terrence. Her

half brother who didn't want her to have anything because he was a gluttonous, spoiled, big, fat baby.

And he's your brother . . . family. You know, like the one you've grown so attached to? A unit of people who support one another.

Marty let her head roll to her right side, taking in the crumpled heap Terrence was in.

Dude looked seriously freaked out.

She could totally relate, and if he hadn't been such a raving lunatic, she'd tell him so. However, he hadn't exactly welcomed her to the fold with open arms, now had he? All waving a knife around like he was Jeffrey Dahmer—and over some money.

How uncouth.

Marty sauntered over to him, letting a low grumble loose from her chest and spill from her mouth. She planted her paws on either side of his body now in the fetal position.

"Ple—eeee—ase," he whispered with a sob, a tear falling from his eye. "I don't know whaaaa—aaat the—the—hell you are, but pleeee—ase leeee—leeeeave me alone."

Marty cocked her wolven head and eyeballed him. Terrence cringed, curling tighter into his protective ball, clenching his eyes shut. Sweat stained his dark suit, and his hair was mashed to one side of his face.

He looked way scared. Gee, this was probably the exact look of terror she'd had all over her face when she was locked in a fucking trunk not knowing where she was or why someone would do something so heinous.

Funny how life was sometimes like a mirror.

Asswipe.

She dipped her head low, sniffing his collar, because she knew it would make him squeal like the pig he was, and that brought a certain sort of maniacal hilarity to her.

Which was freakishly like Terrence's glee over capturing her and keeping his millions.

Oh, Marty . . . do unto others and all.

But would just one more little poke with a stick really be so wrong? He'd terrorized her first . . . and honestly, he'd taken everything from her. Her job, her apartment, her accounts. Would a little healthy sense of fear kill him in the long run?

Marty, you're being terribly spiteful. Look at him, for Christ's sake. He looks like he's just seen the second coming. How can you possibly claim to possess the Bobbie-Sue spirit if you behave so badly? Hell, the Bobbie-Sue spirit is partially your heritage. Is this any way to treat a beloved— albeit an "I love me jacket" candidate—member of your family?

"Cupcake?"

Huh. How odd. Her conscience sounded just like Keegan. Caa-razy.

"Marty . . ."

Now that was definitely the Keegan warning tone with the big trail-off sigh. It meant he was mad, and while under normal circumstances she'd worry it was with her, she wasn't so worried right now. She'd torn duct tape like it was frickin' toilet paper, for crap's sake. Who could do that? She'd felt like Xena Warrior Princess and the Hulk all in one shift. Seriously, she was pretty kick-ass right now— not a whole lot was likely to scare her.

Even the head honcho werewolf.

"Marty, c'mon, honey." His voice coaxed while placing a comforting hand on her back, stroking her fur, pulling her from Terrence with gentle hands.

She snarled, letting drool drip from her teeth to plunk on Terrence's quivering cheek.

Terrence suddenly sagged, passing out and deflating her power trip.

She growled again.

"Now, Marty, don't be like that. C'mon, look, your dad's here."

She swung her big head awkwardly, eyeing the tall figure behind Keegan. Stately, white-haired, and tan, he was everything she'd always pictured a dad would be. He looked scared, too. The wonder, awe, and terror on his face made her remorseful for being so petty.

Her anger ebbed, easing some, dulling the roar in her head.

Keegan leaned down to whisper in her ear, making it twitch from his gravelly compliment. "Look at you, huh? Not only did you manage a full shift, but you're a blonde to boot. Now let go of the anger, honey. It's time to learn to shift back. You'll be a pro in no time." His assurance led to a chuckle.

That was all it took for her human form to want to make an appearance. It happened more rapidly than shifting to were form, and she was thankful she remembered to rise to her back legs while everything that had distorted righted itself.

In a matter of seconds, she was human again.

And naked.

Which was undoubtedly awkward for all concerned.

Keegan tore his coat off and covered her with it, hauling her to his side and lifting her chin. "Do you have any idea how goddamned stupid this was? I swear to Christ, Marty, do you ever listen when I tell you to do something? I told you to stay put, woman! Do you see what happens when you don't listen to me?"

Marty looked at him for a brief moment. She saw the anger he was so good at spewing, but she also saw fear. The fear that he would find her toe-up in the morgue, and that held a secret, womanly power she could no longer resist.

Throwing her arms around his neck, she rained kisses on his face, bear hugging him. "Do you have any idea how glad I am to see you? I didn't do this to make you mad, I swear. Okay, so it was impulsive, but I just knew if I didn't do something, I'd lose my mind. I did it because I couldn't let you give up everything without at least trying to help. And look," she nodded in Terrence's direction, "I helped." She smiled in victory. "And I did it all by myself."

"Honey?"

"What?"

"We have *a lot* to talk about."

"No shit! I mean, did you hear? I, *me*, Marty Andrews, owns a piece of Bobbie-Sue."

His dark head nodded, and he smiled, kissing her nose. "I did hear. Your color wheel must have spun and spun, huh?"

Marty giggled, then sobered. More than a piece of Bobbie-Sue, she had a father. A father, who, according to Terrence, had looked for her. Her head popped up from the warmth of Keegan's embrace, and she eyed the man who knelt beside his unconscious son.

It was rather a "Luke, I am your father" kind of moment.

Slipping from Keegan's warmth, she pushed her arms through the sleeves of his jacket and approached Donald Bradford with tentative steps. She held her hand out to him when he took note of her presence. "I'm Marty Andrews. It's nice to meet you. Weird—like way weird—but nice."

Donald's face held countless emotions she could read like a book. Worry clearly lined his eyes. Tension grooved the firm set of his mouth, and there was fear. Probably because he'd just witnessed something rare and frighteningly unbelievable. Yet he managed a smile in her direction. "And I'm Donald Bradford—your—the—"

"Father I never knew I had, but apparently my half brother did," she finished without a bit of ill will in her tone.

His head bowed for a moment. "I'm sorry about this. Terrence . . . well, he's—" He shook his head again, a look of sorrow on his face. "There is *no* excuse for what he's done. I—will he be all right?"

Keegan spoke up then, his voice tight and barely under control. "I think he'll be fine. However, I'd suggest you get him out of my sight before I finish what Marty started."

Donald rose and took in both Marty and Keegan with befuddled eyes. "Uh . . . what was *that*?"

Marty had to give him kudos for his amazing composure. That he wasn't indulging in the same fate Terrence was, owed some credit to his strength. She gave him an uncertain glance and shrugged her shoulders. "It's kind of a long story. I can explain. I just can't promise you'll believe."

"Explanations can happen another time," Keegan instructed with his take-control manner, the tic in his jaw bouncing. "Right now I need to get Marty home."

"Wait." Donald stopped them with a hand. "Let me at least briefly explain how this happened." A plea laced his tone. "Your mother, Marty . . . I—I loved her. I know what I did was wrong. I know the affair shouldn't have happened, but she was—well, she just *was,* and I couldn't stay away. She didn't know about Bobbie-Sue. She had no idea I was married. I know she wouldn't have become involved with me if she had."

Marty smiled in remembrance of her mother. Yeah, her mom had some pretty tough standards.

He shrugged his large shoulders. "I guess she found out. She never said so. Just broke it off and left, asking me to respect her wishes and leave her alone. And then I set about trying to salvage my marriage. Bobbie-Sue and I . . ." He shook his head. "We grew comfortable—it wasn't passionate, but we worked. The company grew, and I resigned myself to letting go of your mother. I swear, I had no idea you existed, or I would have found you long ago. But I *knew* the moment I saw you that night at the corporate meeting. You're Lucinda's exact replica." He smiled at that, a look of longing creeping over his face.

"Had I known Terrence was responsible for this, I'd have stopped it. Make no mistake, I could have prevented this. Terrence is spoiled, probably a result of my losing your mother. I threw all my effort into the company, rekindling my marriage and being a good parent." His words were adamant. Marty smelled his regret, the kind he literally threw from his aura in waves.

She gave a moment's thought to his words, and then she smiled with a calm certainty. "You know what? I believe you, but for now, I think I have a lot to think about. If you only knew what these past few weeks have been like, you'd understand." She sent Keegan a knowing look.

"So could I just have a little time to digest this? I don't want your money, Donald. I know that must be hard to believe because I was a die-hard Bobbie-Sue-er. I color-wheeled people to death, but I did that because I wanted to earn that money on my own. I wanted to be successful. Yet, somehow in all of this, I've found other more important things to focus on." Marty smiled in Keegan's direction once more. "Besides, I think it's pretty clear Terrence definitely doesn't want me to have your money." She snorted for effect. "But the most I can offer right now is, I promise to be in touch." It was all she had left to give at this point.

Donald nodded briskly, his eyes a medley of confusion and warmth. "Of course."

"And Terrence?" Keegan's granite expression grew glacial and fierce. "The word *dead* will have a whole new meaning if he ever attempts to harm Marty again. I think you know, after what you've seen, it can happen. Understand?"

Donald held a hand up in understanding. "I'll see to it. I promise you, Marty will be safe. You'll keep in touch?" His eyes sought hers again, and she returned his gaze, smiling.

"Promise," she answered. Though right now she just wanted to go back to Keegan's and moisturize. All that shifting couldn't be good for her complexion.

Keegan pulled her to him, kissing the top of her head. "C'mon, werewolf, let's go home."

Marty giggled, tucking closer to him as they climbed the steep set of stairs leading out of the basement. "Did you see me? I mean, holy fur and fury, huh? I tell ya, I felt like I could take on the world! It was incredible. I had almost total control, too. God, it made me so friggin' mad to be at someone's mercy. When he was waving that knife around—"

"Knife?" Keegan's roar of disbelief echoed in the stairwell. "He had a *knife*? I'll fucking kill him! I don't care if he is your family now."

Marty put a comforting hand on his arm. "Chill, Wolf-man. I got it covered. Oh, and look," she said with glowing pride, "no stumpy tail! Wait, I did have a *real* tail, didn't I? Like a nice long one? Not some pathetic—"

"Yes," he sighed, smiling and cutting her off. "You had a tail. It was quite a sight. You were really something, Color Guru. Now shut up," he ordered when they reached the top of the stairs, "and kiss me."

Marty happily allowed him to plant his lips on hers.

Well, alrighty then.

Hoorah, all things lycanthropic.

CHAPTER
16

"Do you think Donald will tell anyone about me—what he saw?" Marty asked, stepping over the threshold of the Flaherty household.

"Did you see the look on his face? For that matter, did you see Terrence? I have my doubts either of them will be able to form coherent sentences for a while. Besides, Donald won't risk the chance you'd tell the world who you are to him, because of Bobbie-Sue. Not yet anyway, and if you could have seen him ripping into Bobbie-Sue, I think you'd know that at least the part about him looking for you was genuine. Bobbie-Sue has a stake in this, too, honey. I hate to tell you, but she's about as thrilled as Terrence is over you. She had a hand in this, and she won't want it getting out."

Yeah. She had one humdinger of a secret. Just wait until she told Nina and Wanda . . . If she was going to use her leverage at all with this sudden windfall, it would be to ensure Wanda and Nina had a fair shake and that Linda

Fisher wasn't remotely a part of Wanda's Bobbie-Sue equation.

"Bobbie-Sue knew about me?"

Keegan's face softened, his eyes scanning hers. "Yeah, and she was willing to do whatever it took to protect Terrence. I'm sorry, honey."

"You know what the most ironic thing about this is?"

"What's that?"

"I loved Bobbie-Sue Cosmetics. I wanted to be successful just like her. I believed her family values crap and the Bobbie-Sue way of life she preached. In the end, she wasn't very Bobbie-Sue-like, was she?"

"I'm sorry, baby. You up to talking?" He pulled her to him again, running his hands over her back in slow, circular motions, lulling her.

Marty wrinkled her nose. "Not about Bobbie-Sue and not if you're going to yell at me for doing something so risky and stupid. I don't think I want to be yelled at today. It's really been a long night, and I need to moisturize. So if you're going to yell, save it until I can yell back." She gave him a mischievous grin. "I'm spent."

The rumble in his chest vibrated against hers. "That's not what I want to talk about, though I should have a piece of your hide for taking off like that on your own."

Marty rolled her eyes. Here it came.

"I want you, Marty." His dark chocolate eyes were serious, his tone a deep rumble. "I knew I wanted you from the moment I smelled you in that damned alleyway. You distracted me, and that's how Muff nailed me. I was caught off guard, but it doesn't change the fact that I want every last neurotic, impossible, stubborn, endless question-asking inch of you."

Had he said this a month and a half ago, she'd have never gotten the big picture, but now that she understood how important scent was to a werewolf, she got it in spades. She was a little unclear on the neurotic end of things though. Still, her heart fluttered. "Oh, reallllly? Would you call me neurotic? I prefer inquisitive," she whispered with a shaky chuckle.

He chuckled, gathering her against him in a tight hold. "Yeah, really. I want you to stay with us. I want you to consider me in your future. Me and *only* me." His tone was fierce, possessive.

Though her heart was clanging against her ribs, a frown furrowed her brow. Fear speared her gut. "But what about the council? You could be in big trouble, Keegan, and I can't let you give up your alpha status. It's not fair."

"I want you to listen to me carefully. I don't give a shit what the council says. You're here, you're mine, and nothing they say or do will change that. Period."

Her lips touched his, caressing the firm expanse of flesh, relishing the familiar ache he created with a simple touch. "Those are some pretty serious words there, Wolfman Jack." She hid her joy by burying her face in the warmth of his neck.

Voices, raised and growing louder, greeted their ears. Mara's, Sloan's, and another Marty couldn't place.

"Er, I think we have trouble." She stated the obvious, looking up at him with concern.

Taking her by the hand, Keegan led her into the family room, where Mara and Sloan were talking with an unfamiliar man who was casually dressed. Muffin yapped in delight, throwing herself at Marty's leg. Marty scooped her up, slinging the dog over her shoulder.

Mara flew across the room at Marty, hugging her. "Oh, thank God you're all right! Do you have any idea how worried we were?"

Marty was about to explain, but Keegan's voice, rough and low, stopped her. "If you're here to banish me from the pack, speak your piece."

Marty's eyes flew to the man, standing in the corner, his hands folded in front of him. The invisible council . . . He didn't look like the kind of guy who had a buttload of power. He looked like someone you'd see in the subway or at a coffee shop. His hair was cropped short and was dark and springy. He wore jeans and a T-shirt and sneakers, for God's sake.

He was a person who had all this power? Where was the long robe and white beard to match? Shouldn't spooky music be playing? Shouldn't he have an altar waiting? Candles lit? A sacrificial virgin? Hell. Where was the big cast of characters just waiting to hear her dramatic plea to have mercy on Keegan?

What kind of big kahuna dressed like some skateboarder to represent all this pomp and circumstance?

Well, no matter, she had a thing or two to say to him about all this toying with the newbie ex-human.

Cocky and bold, Marty handed Muffin to Keegan and strolled up to him, tightening the belt around Keegan's jacket, planting trembling hands on her hips. "You know, I realize I'm probably the last person on Earth whose opinion means squat to you, but do you have *any* idea the kind of mind fuck you've created with all your stupid rules and bullshit legacies? What is the matter with you people, anyway? How dare you threaten to take things away from people just because they won't do what you want them to do?" Her finger jutted under his stately nose with a shaky wave. "I am the product of an *accident,* and I'm here, like it or not. So quit with all the threats and crap, already. It's not terribly welcoming—"

"Marty," Keegan warned, surrounding her shoulders with his hands, kneading the tension there.

"No!" she yelled up at him. "I'm not going to sit back and just let them take everything from you. Look, do with me what you will, okay?" She held her hands out in front of her. "Lock me up, do whatever it is you want to, but I won't let you take Keegan from his family and a business you all profit from because you're feeling pissy that I was once a human."

Keegan circled her waist with an arm, hauling her against him. "Relax, Tiger."

For the first time the council member spoke, his voice light and easy and so not like the Darth Vader imitation she'd expected. "We have no qualm with you, Marty. Keegan could have eliminated us from this kidnapping equation by simply calling for a meeting of the council. While we understood his hesitation due to the situation with Alana, we would have heard him, and the answer would still be the same."

The frenzied fury she'd just whipped up fizzled, like air leaving a balloon. She had no response to that, nothing but a wide-eyed stare of disbelief. After all this it was just no big deal? How dare he tell her it was no big deal! It so fucking was a big deal.

"I won't tell you we're happy about this, Keegan. You know our rules. Rules that have been passed on for centuries. Yes, the council wanted you to mate with Alana. Pure offspring ensures the pack's longevity. However, the council isn't your problem when it comes to these attempts on Marty's life—a pack member of yours *is,*" he stated with the calm of the Dalai Lama, looking directly at Keegan.

Oh.

"It was Alana." Sloan finally spoke with compressed lips. "She sent the note threatening Marty, just like we'd suspected."

"The note?" Marty yelped.

Keegan gripped her shoulders again, which meant she should shut up. "So how is *she* responsible for the kidnappings?"

Sloan threw a cell phone at Keegan. He caught it and looked to Sloan to explain.

"Look at the number she dialed. It belongs to Terrence Bradford. After an interrogation by Mara and I, one I think you'd be proud of your little sister for, we discovered Alana was doing him. It was really a pretty fluky coincidence. They met a few weeks ago at some conference. Terrence got plastered and spilled the beans about Marty owning part of Bobbie-Sue. Of course, Alana recognized Marty's name. He and Alana had an alliance of sorts thereafter. She's the one who gave him the heads-up that Marty had left the house last night. Apparently, he's been watching her, waiting for her to be alone. He hired someone to nab her and bring her to him."

Keegan's hold on her tightened, his face distorting with rage. He directed his question to the council member. "Will there be punishment for this?"

He nodded passively. "You know our creed to live in peace with the outside world, Keegan. That remains in place. Alana will be punished. She'll lose her position at Pack. She's in council custody now. As to Marty joining the pack, we'll leave that up to your discretion." He smirked, then a placid look swiftly replaced it, and he looked at them stoically.

Poor, poor Barbie. Shackles and chains would be hella-fino on a manicure.

She wanted to feel sorry for Alana, but she couldn't summon up much more than pity that she'd so desperately tried to get her claws into a man who so obviously didn't want her. Money was definitely the root of Alana's evil.

Keegan took a deep breath, expelling it and bowing his head in respect. "Thank you."

"We do expect to hear from you, Keegan, and let this be a lesson to you and your pack. Had you come to us, we could have worked this out. Instead, your procrastination will lead your pack to believe we're all immovable when it comes to dire pack matters—especially when they're unin-tentional. It doesn't make us terribly approachable to them, does it?"

Duly chastised, Keegan lifted his eyes to the council member and nodded, his jaw clenching.

"Naturally, the council is concerned about a human en-tering the fold. We'll want to know your intentions where Marty is concerned. A close eye will be kept." His serious tone was lost on Marty.

She cut into the silent reverence in her excitement. "Does this mean I'm a *full* pack member now? Like, do I get the secret password? Or is it a handshake? Do we have a big ceremony or something? Like being inducted into the werewolf hall of fame? You know, drum beats, big bon-fires, all that ritualistic garbage—"

"Marty," Keegan interrupted, fighting a smirk.

"What?"

"Say thank you."

"Oh, right." How rude that she'd forget her manners at a time like this. "Thanks," she muttered, realizing her mouth was running away with her again.

"I'll leave you all to the business of the day. Oh, and Sloan?"

Sloan's face paled. "Sir?"

He cracked a smile for the first time since their conver-sation began. "You're next on our list of issues to deal with. I believe we've found someone appropriate for your mate. I'd highly recommend you clean up your act—soon." With those words of warning, he took his leave.

The heavy air, thick with ritual and legend, lightened immediately.

Squeals of delight erupted from Mara, as she hugged Marty, and Sloan made jokes about being tied down, while thumping Keegan on the back.

"I cannot believe Donald Bradford is your father!" Mara shook her head, smiling joyfully. "How do you feel about that? I mean, you loved Bobbie-Sue. This is huge, Marty."

Marty rubbed a hand over her weary eyes. "I think I feel really tired right now and really glad it's over. The Bobbie-Sue thing and having a father after all this time?" She shrugged her shoulders, making Keegan's coat crinkle. "I dunno. I'd like to think my mother would be pleased he found me, but she obviously had her reasons for keeping me away from him. She was pretty proud, and if what Don-ald said was true, that she found out he was married, I can see why she ran away. It explains a lot of things." She let loose a tired sigh.

"I think Marty needs some rest." Keegan put a protec-tive arm around her and kissed the top of her head, handing

Muffin to Mara. "But I gotta tell ya, you should have seen her take on Terrence. It was some shit."

Marty heard the pride in his voice.

Mara squealed. "You *shifted*?"

"Like I've always been doing it." Marty giggled, still proud of her coup. "I was so angry, everything just sorta clicked."

"Okay, enough, you guys. Marty needs to rest," Keegan said, directing her to the stairs.

"Yeah," Sloan cackled. "You guys go *rest*," Marty heard him say, while Keegan pulled her up the stairs, leading her to his room without protest from her.

"Go shower," he ordered, firmly closing the door behind him. "We'll talk after, if you're up to it."

"But don't we have like life things to discuss? I mean, you did just admit to really, really digging me. I think that deserves some wordage, bud."

"Huh. I did, didn't I?" His eyes crinkled, gifting her with one of those rare smiles, the deep grooves beside his yummy lips deepening.

"Yeah, you did, and if you want me to stay here with you, you have to quit being such a cranky pants. Always huffing and puffing about something, and you have to stop keeping stuff from me. Plus, do you really think you can mate with the neurotic likes of me?" She winked, pointing to her chest.

He rolled his tongue in his cheek and looked pensive. "I think it'll be a hardship, but I've always liked a good challenge."

"Are you going to get mad and yell if I ask more questions?"

"I promise to try not to yell."

"Can I have a job at Pack now that this lunacy has passed? It doesn't have to be a big job. I can start from the bottom, but it has to be something, because you don't want these hands idle, do you?" She peeked at him through the web of her fingers.

"I promise you can work in the mail room." Keegan flashed her a disarming grin.

"Do I get my own desk in the mail room?"

"Pushy, pushy."

"Oh, and endless sticky note pads, because you can never have enough of those."

"Any particular color?"

"Hellllooooooo—lavender, silly. I might not be a blonde anymore, but lavender is still a huge part of my color wheel."

"I'll see what I can do."

"Do you promise to help me pack up my apartment and get all my stuff? I have a lot of stuff. A *lot*. Shoes and purses and clothes and nail polish. I have way more purses than you brought and at least a gatrillion dresses. I can't live without them—"

"I promise to haul your shit around."

"Will you promise to love, honor, and cherish Muffin?"

He laughed with a hearty bark. "Are you kidding me? Princess and I are tight."

Turning, Marty placed a hand on his chest, forgetting how tired she was, how crazy the past few hours had been. She couldn't focus on anything but the yumminess of his tight jeans and the scent of him. "Okay, so—so what now? Do we have some sort of ritualistic mating ceremony? Do you knock me up when Mars and Venus align—"

His smile was complacent. "January through April, honey."

"Whenever. I still think it's archaic and crazy."

"Those are all negotiable points. How about we take the time to get to know each other without all the pressure of someone hurting you and the council breathing down our necks?"

"Do you mean it?"

"I swear on my color wheel."

Her nose twitched. "Well, okay then. Good. So can we do normal stuff? Like maybe go to a movie?"

His lips lifted upward, and his eyebrow rose. "As long as it's not some chick-flick."

Her giggle bubbled from her throat, but the twitch in her nose returned, distracting her. Keegan's scent wrapped around her senses with a powerful force.

"Can I ask you one more thing?"

"Shoot."

"Do you feel that?"

"What?"

"You know." She batted her eyelashes. "That, that."

"That?"

"You know what that I mean. I felt it the night of the full moon and right after the shift."

"Ah, *that*, that . . ."

"Yeah. *That*, that."

"It's very common to want to mate after a shift."

"So do you think we could do that now that imminent danger isn't breathing down out necks?"

"A shower," he reminded her. "You need a shower."

"You know," she said with a tilt of her head toward the bathroom, feeling bold. "I could always use a hand in there . . ."

He cocked an eyebrow at her before yanking his shirt over his head. "Oh, realllly?" Keegan shed his jeans and kicked them off his feet.

Marty let his coat fall to the floor in a pool of leather and sauntered to the bathroom with far more confidence than she'd ever displayed, bending to turn the taps on in the shower and adjusting the spray of the showerhead. "Yeah, really." She eyed him over her shoulder before stepping onto the cool, beige and burgundy tiled floor, reveling in the hard spray of the warm water.

Keegan came up behind her, closing the shower door and cupping her bare breasts, making her moan with each stroke over her rigid nipples.

She melted into his lean, rippled frame. The hairs on his belly matted to her back, wet with the water cascading over them. "So what do you suppose needs washing first?" he whispered against her wet hair. He grabbed the bar of soap and rubbed it between his palms.

Marty wriggled against him and sighed as his lathered hands floated over her ribs, just barely touching the undersides of her breasts. "Oh, I think right there," she whimpered when his thumb skated over her nipple, "is gooooood . . ."

Keegan chuckled, rounding her breasts with circular motions, skimming her tight nipples, letting his other hand drift with a silky glide to the wet place between her legs. He spread her flesh with deft fingers, sending hot flares of need to every inch of her nakedness. "Like that?" He teased the nub of her swollen clit with his forefinger.

Marty couldn't speak, but instead ran her hands down his thighs, kneading the knot of muscle and sinew, while the warm water cascaded between her fingers. Keegan's cock jutted between the cheeks of her ass, hot and hard, and she reached around to circle it with her fingers, making a slow pass along its length.

Keegan's grunt filled the tiled shower, and he turned her in his arms, wrapping them around her and covering her mouth with a kiss, sliding his tongue between her willing lips, sipping at her with humming approval.

Hands explored, tongues dueled, muttered words of approval were breathed on gasps growing harsh and heated.

When Keegan tore his lips from hers, trailing them over her collarbone, licking at each nipple with hot swipes before finding the soft skin of her inner thigh, Marty had to clench his shoulders to keep from falling against him.

His tongue, fire and silk, parted her, stabbing in and out with slow thrusts, rolling over her swollen flesh, the stubble of his chin adding to the building pleasure. His hands kneaded the globes of her ass, keeping her tight to his tongue.

Her eyes rolled to the back of her head, her hands gripped his slick hair, bringing him flush to the core of her need. When he began to take long, leisurely strokes, lapping at her needy center, Marty's hips bucked hard against his face, and she cried out, her toes clenching when the electric bolt of orgasm screamed through her. Her heightened senses experienced every delicious second of climax, leaving her shuddering.

His breathing was ragged when he slithered along her wet body and lifted her, placing her back hard against the tiled wall. Her gasps for air were soothed by his hands, roaming over her back and arms.

Marty wrapped a leg around his lean waist, drawing him closer, letting his cock slip between her throbbing lips. She watched when his head reared up at the contact, his teeth clenching, fighting for control, the bronzed length of his throat slick with water beading on the tightly pulled skin.

Hitching her hip higher, she invited him to enter her with a wanton thrust. No-holds-barred, she needed the hot length of him taking her, driving into her until she couldn't see straight.

Keegan lifted her other leg, hauling her upward high on his waist and plunging into her with a slick, hot drive of his cock.

Marty cried out again, reveling in the force of his thrusts, crashing her hips against his, and when he slowed, grinding himself against her, brushing against her clit with his abdomen, he stole her breath.

The rise of orgasm came without warning, clawing at her until she thought she might scream out from the sheer torture of the waiting. Her heart smacked against her ribs, her pulse crashed in her ears, and then Keegan tensed within her. In that moment, with him deeply embedded within her, Marty felt an unfamiliar shift, a possessive urge to never allow him to experience this with any other woman.

Ever.

Hot and rigid, he came, pulsing his seed from his cock with short jerks, pushing her to join him, his chest heaving against hers.

The sharp call of climax tore through her, driving into her gut, entangling her in its carnal web until she, too, tensed. Each muscle in her body grew rigid, inflexible, as that wave of now familiar heat assaulted her, ripping through her until there was nothing left but a small whimper of satisfaction. Boneless and weak, Marty sagged against the broad expanse of his chest, burying her face in his neck, a tear escaping her eye.

He let her slide down his water-slick body until her feet rested atop his. Curling his arms around her waist, he kissed her forehead and murmured, "You need sleep, honey."

She didn't protest when he turned the taps off and wrapped her in a big, fluffy towel, drying her with gentle hands. "Cupcake?"

Marty looked up at him with weary eyes. "Yeah?"

"Bedtime," he ordered, directing her to his big, plush bed.

"I thought we were going to talk." Her protest was feeble.

Scooping her up, he held her by the waist and walked her backward until the backs of her knees hit the edge of the bed. Marty plunked down on it, letting him drag the coverlet from the end of the bed over her. "We will. We have a whole lot of time to talk now." He smiled, kissing her lips with a tender mouth, brushing the hair from her face.

She held up a wobbly finger. "Pinky swear?"

Keegan's laughter came from deep in his chest. "Pinky swear," he agreed, latching his pinky with hers.

"Then it's a deal." Her mutter was weary, but she made a fist, her hand facing outward, snuggling into the sculpted width of his chest with a sigh filled with peace—fulfillment.

Keegan knocked his fist with hers, splaying out beside her. "Yeah, Monty. You got a deal. You got yourself a *lifetime* deal."

Six months later . . .

"I swear, Nina. I can't believe you'd rather go digging around in someone's mouth than sell Bobbie-Sue." Marty chuckled, leaning back into the warmth of Keegan's embrace.

Nina rolled her eyes. "Yeah. Color me all kinds of crazy

for not wanting to live my life creating color charts and stalking people so I can sell one whole lip gloss to some blind woman at Denny's."

Wanda ambled up to her, ducking beneath the multicolored balloons tied to her chair, and stuck her face in Nina's. "Crazy."

Nina threw her head back and laughed. "I really think I'm doing the right thing. I have a job lined up already, and it's a regular paycheck with benefits. Beats the shit out of those crazy color freaks."

Wanda clucked her tongue. "You just never believed, Nina."

Nina threw a hand in Wanda's face. "Are you saying they aren't whacked? Look at what Terrence tried to do to Marty, for Christ's sake."

Marty stepped between them wiggling a warning finger. "Quit. Both of you. We're here to celebrate Nina's graduation from dental hygienist school—not to talk about Terrence. And believe me when I tell you, you don't want He-Man here to get all excited on that subject. You get huffy, don't you, honey?"

Keegan grunted and popped a pretzel in his mouth, adhering to their agreement that he'd shut up about all things Terrence. If Alana was still considered family—even if she was in lockdown with the Lunar Council—then he'd just have to deal with Terrence. And really, Marty didn't fear him as much as she pitied him.

Both he and Bobbie-Sue. The woman Marty once considered an icon, who'd turned into a coconspirator in all of this, was now her stepmother. She tried to respect that when she dealt with Donald. She and Donald had taken slow steps toward a relationship. She'd grown quite fond of him. She'd even begun to understand what her mother must have seen in him so many years ago. He had some wonderful memories of Lucinda, and Marty found she'd come to treasure the time she spent with him.

"You should have killed the little freak," Nina said to Keegan.

He popped another pretzel in his mouth and crunched hard in response.

"Hookay, enough about killing people, huh?" Marty interjected. "It's not terribly friendly, and besides, I took care of Terrence. Trust me, he's still pretty freaked."

Wanda giggled. "I know. You should have seen him apologize to me after he took all of your accounts back from Linda Fisher and gave them to me. He could barely look at me."

Marty smiled, patting Wanda who'd just made the lavender tier, on her knee. "You should have seen Bobbie-Sue's face when I told her if she told anyone about what happened that night, I'd tell the world who I really am." Her promise to remain a silent heir only held water if the three of them kept their lips sealed. Bobbie-Sue, as vain as she was, had been plenty happy to agree.

"You know, Marty, I miss seeing you," Wanda said, smiling sadly. "I know Nina does, too—she's just incapable of expressing happy thoughts."

Nina grunted.

Ah, yeah. Good times. Good times. "I miss you guys, too, but pretty soon we'll have another reason to get together and celebrate."

"What now?" Nina squawked. "Do you like own Revlon and Max Factor, too?"

Keegan came to stand beside Marty. "Please, do not wish that on Revlon and Max Factor," he joked, grabbing Marty's hand when she playfully tweaked his abs.

"No. Keegan and I have something to tell you." She grinned at them both and rooted in the pocket of her jeans, pulling out her surprise. A key chain dangled from her index finger. A key chain made from a diamond ring attached to a set of keys.

Wanda cocked her head, her face confused.

"What now?" Nina quipped with a snort. "Were-man bought you a car dealership? Maybe a Ferrari? No wait, that's too typical. It's the keys to a Lamborghini, right? A whole fleet of 'em, I'll just bet."

"No, Nina. Keegan surprised me with a sky blue convertible and this." Marty brought the key ring closer for inspection.

A squeal erupted from Wanda's lips, as she hugged both Marty and Keegan. Nina rose from her chair and folded her slender arms over her chest, eyeing the chain. "You're getting *married*? So you bought into the whole life sentence thing?"

Marty flicked her arm with the finger that held the key chain. "Don't even start, Negative Nora, and it's life mate, not *life sentence*. And actually, this is a key ring that can be made into an engagement ring. Kind of a promise of things to come. When I'm ready, of course." She sent a warm smile Keegan's way. He returned it with a smug wink. Facing Nina again, she said, "So just shut up and tell me how happy you are for me."

Nina pointed to her face, circling it with a finger. "See? This is me happy as a whore in an all-male frat house. For both of you." She turned to Keegan, giving him a narrowed gaze. "You be nice to Marty. Don't go thinking because you're a werewolf I wouldn't poison your kibble if you hurt her."

Keegan chuckled, accepting the faint kiss she planted on his cheek. "I'll take good care of her. Promise."

Marty threw her arms around Nina and kissed her cheek soundly. "You soooo like me," she taunted.

Wriggling out of Marty's embrace, Nina made a face. "I don't anything you, you color ho. Not even a little." Her retort was sharp, but she fought to hide a grin.

Marty's heart did a flip in her chest again when Wanda grabbed her hand and admired the key chain Keegan had given her just two nights ago. Just seeing the diamond on her finger made her tear up, reliving the moment, under a full moon after they'd shifted, when he'd popped the question.

He'd offered her time to decide, telling her the key chain was his way of letting her know his intent to mate for life with her was serious. He'd said when she was ready, all she had to do was say the word.

She'd never been happier since she'd chosen to stay with Keegan and his family. Each day that passed since she'd agreed to become a part of the pack had been more fulfilling—each day with Keegan a new discovery, a deeper bond growing between them until she couldn't remember when he hadn't been in her life.

They'd shared many things in the six months since the incident with Terrence. Movies, dinners, long walks, kisses that lasted forever, those secretive smiles she thought only existed in cheesy Lifetime movies the morning after a particularly passionate encounter. Keegan had wooed her in his own way, and tonight she intended to say yes to his proposal.

Yes to a lifetime of rowdy pack mates who were finally warming to her. Christ, that had been like trying to coax a supermodel to eat a cheeseburger.

Yes to meals filled with raucous laughter and loud banter.

Yes to spending every night spooning against the warm shelter of Keegan's chest.

A hell yes to the kind of whoopee they'd come to perfect.

And yes to having children, making Pack Cosmetics bigger and better, and growing old together.

Nowadays, she couldn't much remember what she'd liked so much about her solitude. It just didn't measure up to having someone to count on. Many someones to count on.

Life was good. Like really good.

Filled with rich textures, brilliant colors, friends, family, and Keegan.

Always Keegan.

"Hey, color freak." Nina interrupted her musings.

"Yeah?"

"Let me make myself perfectly clear here. If you're determined to go through with this kissy-face shit, remember one thing."

Marty's face was puzzled. "Uh, what?"

"I will not wear a fucking yellow bridesmaid's dress. Got that? It's sooooo not in my color wheel."

Marty laughed, hugging Nina whether she liked it or not.

Yep, it was all good.

Somewhere Marty remembered reading a quote about creating a life so full you could hang your hat on it.

Okay, so maybe the hat rack she was metaphorically hanging her cap on howled at the moon, had more hair than a yeti, and looked like a German shepherd on occasion.

Yet, she had no doubt her hat was taking up residency.

Like the lifetime kind.

Turn the page for a preview of
Dakota Cassidy's next contemporary romance

WALTZ THIS WAY

Coming March 2012 from Berkley Sensation!

CHAPTER
1

"Cornflake?"

Melina Cherkasov smiled distractedly at the sound of her father's voice as she tucked her cell phone beneath her chin while trying her key in the lock of her small dance studio for the second time that morning. If one more thing had to be replaced, her husband, Stan, would blow a nut. "Hi, Daddy. How are you feeling?"

His grunt, gruff and short, made her smile. "I'm fine. Jake's fine. Still shits big, my Jake, the damn mutt. Everything's fine here in Jersey. I wanna know how *you're* feelin', spaghetti and meatballs?"

For as long as she could remember, whenever her father referred to her, his pride and joy, he always used endearments that involved food. It had become a game that made her giggle as a child, and still filled her heart with warmth as an adult. Joe Hodge was big, loud, and without censor, or as some might say, class, but he loved his little girl like no other.

Mel's stiff fingers jammed the key into the lock again

and twisted hard. "What do you mean how do I feel, Dad? I feel fine." She gave a perplexed glance at the door and fought a curse word, catching a glimpse of herself in her studio's glass window. She blew out a disgusted breath.

Her brown black chestnut hair pulled back so severely in a tight ponytail made her need for a touch up painfully evident in the early morning sunlight. And she noted her olive complexion was looking a little wan today sans makeup. Maybe that was because she hadn't heard from her husband in three solid days, and she'd spent half the night trying to reach him.

"Where's that sissy pants husband of yours?" her father barked.

Mel winced, giving up on the door to lean against the brick front of the old building with a huff. There was no love lost between her father and her husband, Stan. Stan was older than Mel by twenty-two years. Something her father had made no bones about disliking from the moment he'd been introduced to Stanislov Cherkasov when Mel was just nineteen. That he was an infamous Russian ballet choreographer slash ballroom aficionado, and now a national celebrity as a judge on *Dude, You Can Dance* meant squat to Joe.

Joe had often grumbled about paying for all those expensive ballroom lessons that had led Mel to three junior championships, two US titles, and the opportunity to pursue her dreams in the big city only for her to end up married to a man who was as unsightly as a wart on his ass.

A geriatric wart at that.

Joe called Stan twinkle toes or, while he twirled around with a finger over his head and cackled, the ballerina.

Often. Mostly directly in Stan's face over some holiday dinner until Stan had refused to even consider getting on a plane to the East Coast to endure, in her husband's words, "the stoopid American's free turkey dinner."

She chose to ignore the possibility that her father would go off on one of his tangents about men in tights and sought a cheery approach to her husband's whereabouts instead.

"Stan's in," she paused a moment. Where was Stan, and why couldn't she get into her dance studio? "Oh! He's in Wisconsin, Dad, auditioning contestants for the show."

There was a low growl, and then, "The hell he is."

"What?" Her question was vague while she dug through her purse to see if possibly she had the wrong set of keys.

"You watched the TV today?"

She chuckled indulgently. He always forgot the time difference between LA and Jersey. "No, Dad. It's only nine in the morning here. I just got to the studio. Besides, you know I don't do the news." Too much death. Too much sadness. Too much gossip. Gossip that, as of late, since the show's popularity had risen to stratospheric proportions, marked her handsome husband's every move.

There was a rustle and she supposed her father was repositioning himself in front of his TV. "Well, maybe you oughta find ya one. You got one in your studio, don't cha?"

"It's just an old black and white with crappy reception." There wasn't much in her studio that wasn't old.

"Bet Fred Astaire has a big flat screen the size of my ass in his office."

Mel sighed and closed her eyes, a slight throb beginning above her right eye. "It doesn't matter what Stan has, Dad. I have a dance studio where you're supposed to learn to dance—not watch TV."

"Don't matter, Mel—you need to go turn it on and watch what I'm watchin'. That *Hollywood Scoop*. You know, the twenty-four-hour access-to-the-stars show?"

"Daddy?"

"Sweet potato?"

"First, I can't get into my studio. The key won't work for some crazy reason. Second, since when have we watched TV together—long distance—"

"Since I can't get to where you are in La-la Land before you get the news. So I wanna be sure I'm at least nearby—even if it's only on the phone."

Still not giving her father her full attention, she paused again, lifting a hand to wave at a neighboring yogurt-store owner who gave her an odd look before quickly turning away and jamming his key into the door of his store.

At least someone's key still worked. "Third, Daddy. What have I told you about watching tabloid television?"

His sigh was long. She could picture him tipped back in his La-Z-Boy in his retirement village, his wide face wrinkling in impatience at being called to task. "You said half of it wasn't true and the other half was only mostly true," he offered, his tone that of a petulant child who'd been reminded for the hundredth time in a day to stop running in the house.

"Right. So why would I want to watch *Hollywood Scoop* with you? I love you, Dad, but I won't indulge those gossipmongers. They speculate far more than they ever hit the mark. Besides, I don't have cable here at the studio. A studio I can't get into right now anyway."

There was a pause on her father's end before he asked, "Don't twinkle toes own that rundown piece-of-crap building that just barely passes code you got your studio in?"

Once more, Mel hesitated. If she fed her father even a morsel of a reason to beat Stan down, he'd open wide and gnaw off her arm. Yes. Stan owned the building. Yes. It was rundown and badly maintained, and, yes, it was the lowest on her husband's list of priorities. Lower still because Stan didn't love that she allowed children who couldn't afford ballroom lessons to come to her classes whether he liked it or not. "Dad, that's not the point, and I really have to go. I have to call a locksmith."

"Honey, don't go. You need to listen to me."

His somber words caught her attention, but it was brief. She was too busy trying to figure out if the lock had rusted. Mel sank to the ground to eye the door's keyhole, accidentally tipping her purse on the pavement in the process.

She rolled her eyes at the scatter of makeup, antibacterial hand soap, and receipts galore. Tucking the phone under her chin, she began to sift through the mess, searching for her other set of keys.

"Melina Eunice Hodge!"

The use of her middle name was meant to bring her back into focus and force her to pay attention. All it really did, or had ever done, was make her cringe. God, she hated her middle name, even if it was because her mother's mother was a Eunice—and someone she'd really loved. It still sucked.

The use of her middle name also sent a shiver along her spine. Something wasn't right. "I'm sorry, Dad. I'm distracted. It's been a crazy week, and Stan's been gone a long time. So I've been a little cranky."

"Looks like he's gonna be gone a whole lot longer."

"Say again?"

"Girl, would you please sit still and just listen to me? Jesus, Joseph, and Mary, Mel! You were always a fidgeter. I need to talk to you. Now be still and quit fussin'."

Her fingers stopped moving upon command, her stomach jolted. "Stopping. Because now you have me worried. Are you sick, Dad?" Her worst fear since her mother had died five years ago was losing her father, too.

"Good, and no, I'm not sick. Not unless you count my God damn acid reflux and bursitis. Oh, and my knees. They drive me to drink."

"It isn't your knees that drive you to a Schlitz, Dad, and you know it." Mel smiled, pulling her own knees up to her chin. Well, almost up to her chin. If she could just lose these last fifteen pounds, she'd be closer to her fighting weight.

Okay. Maybe the real number for her fighting weight was twenty-five total pounds, but she was trying to remain realistic at forty. And twenty-five pounds wouldn't allow for the occasional Choco Bliss or ranch dressing on her salad instead of the fresh juice of a lemon.

"Listen, breadstick, you got trouble comin' your way."

Just as those words sank in, Mel heard someone yell, "It's her!"

Her head popped up at the thump of feet on the pavement coming from across the street. A throng of cameramen and smartly dressed reporters headed her way like a pack of salivating dogs.

The paparazzi. Here?

Huh.

She wrinkled her nose in total distaste. Shitty bastards. How had they found her? Stan kept her dance studio like some would a dirty little secret. She suspected he let her keep the studio open to keep her from complaining about his long stints away from home.

Stan had little tolerance for what he called her wish to save deprived children with a silly waltz. He'd declared the caliber of dancers she was drawing beneath him in almost as many words.

While Stan had been a well-respected, famous choreographer in the world of Russian ballet, he wasn't a household name until *Dude, You Can Dance*. Now everyone wanted a piece of him, and anyone who was directly related to him. They especially wanted a piece of the woman who was married to him because Mel fought so hard to stay out of the limelight. She was an enigma and a constant source of speculation.

Not that Stan was all that interested in having her share his limelight. He didn't want to do that with anyone. He especially didn't want to share it with Mel because he said lately she looked like she'd eaten too much borscht.

Which had hurt. But then, even if she wanted Stan to love her for who she was on the inside, Mel had to admit, the outside was a little like a can of freshly opened dinner rolls—sort of oozy in some places.

Lightbulbs were suddenly flashing and microphones were shoved in her face as she attempted to slide to an upright position in the midst of the chaos. "Melina! What do you have to say about Stan and Yelena?"

Her father's squawking fell on deaf ears as her phone slid from beneath her chin. She shoved it into the pocket of her ankle-length sweater.

"So what do you have to say about Yelena?" someone repeated.

Like the newest choreographer Yelena from *Dude, You Can Dance* who had a body so hard even a wrecking ball couldn't crack it?

Like the Yelena with no last name Yelena?

What could she possibly have to say about her, and what did she have to do with Stan? Other than the fact that he was her boss as executive producer and head judge of the show?

Mel's breath quickened when a male reporter she vaguely recognized from *Hollywood Scoop* turned to the crowd, froth but a bead of saliva away from forming in the corners of his mouth, and yelped, "Holy shit! She doesn't know! Back off, you bunch of piranhas, I got her first!"

Not to be outfrothed, a salivating blonde from another tabloid show with makeup too harsh for daylight hours gave the *Hollywood Scoop* guy an elbow to the ribs and jammed a microphone into Mel's face.

There was a flash of pity in her overly charcoal-lined eyes, and then she went all viper. "How does it feel to be left for a woman almost half your age? Have you seen this? It was taken by a fan of the show." She shoved a picture of Stan and Yelena in her face.

At some Wisconsin cheese festival. At least that was what the banner said. Holding hands while Stan swallowed Yelena's lips whole.

It was clear they'd been caught off guard. Stan's eyes were wide with surprise in the shot.

The ground beneath Mel wobbled and shifted, her vision becoming blurry and distorted. Thankfully, her tongue neither wobbled, nor blurred.

She forced her shoulders to lift in an indifferent shrug. Like it was no big deal Stan was sticking his tongue down Yelena's throat while experiencing the splendor of aged sharp cheddar. "How does it feel to spend a good portion of your paycheck from Satan on all that peroxide?"

The blonde's eyes narrowed for only a second before she regained her composure. Just as she was gearing up to lob another question at Mel, another reporter shoved the blonde to the side, while yet another crowded her up against the building until she almost couldn't breathe from their close proximity.

Fighting down a sob of rage, she stooped, hoping to gather her things and run as far away as she could, but they had her packed too tightly against the building.

Fuck her antibacterial soap. She grabbed at the important stuff, her wallet and her keys, her fingers scraping the concrete as she did. Mel rose, sucking in a harsh breath at the head rush that assaulted her, and in stoic silence, began to push against the cluster of hands holding microphones, her heart crashing out a painful rhythm in her ears.

Some of the neighboring store owners had begun to gather along the sidewalk; their obvious curiosity stung just as good as any sharp slap across her face. Their whispers made her sad. No one made a move to help her fight her way out of the throng of cutthroats.

And she'd once thought they were all sort of like neighbors. Like the kind that always had each other's back when vulture reporters were breathing down your neck? Nice neighbors, the lot of 'em.

Definitely not Mr. Rogers approved.

Biting her lip while making a conscious choice not to let the scourge of humanity get one single word from her, Mel went at them head first, bulldozer style.

Her yelp was warrior-ish and meant as a warning when she lunged into the crowd, caring little if she stepped on toes.

Then Tito Ortiz, twelve, and on his way to a brilliant Latin ballroom dancing career if his father would get over the "dancing is for girls" and let him, grabbed her hand. "Miss Mel! Hurry, follow me!" He gave her the last yank she needed to break free. Mel crashed into a cameraman, hissing when their shoulders made hard contact as Tito tugged her to freedom.

She clung to his sweaty hand, tripping on the edge of the sidewalk while trying to keep up. The distinct crunch of her toe, encased in canvas slip-ons, forced her to bite the inside of her mouth to keep from crying out.

"I know a shortcut, Miss Mel! Run faster, they're catching up!" he yelled, dodging and ducking until they reached an alleyway she was unfamiliar with. Tito stopped short at the end of it, gasping for breath in unison with Mel.

He took her forearms in his hands and squeezed them. His dark eyes, filled with concern, pierced hers. "You stay here, Miss Mel. I'll get Mama. She'll bring you home, okay?"

Mel nodded mutely, letting her head fall back on her shoulders while she fought to catch her breath. Her toe throbbed with a hot ache, but it didn't match the throb of humiliation or the sharp stabs of pain to her heart.

"Wait right here, Miss Mel. I'll make sure they don't find you." Tito's words, so sweet and reassuring, brought her reality into focus.

Stan was schtupping Yelena.

In Wisconsin.

During a cheese fest.

The bastard would pay.

Then a thought hit her. No. He wouldn't pay. Not in houses and diamonds anyway.

A tear slipped down her cheek. She swiped at it in an angry gesture when it fell to a patch of sunshine pushing its way through the two buildings.

It was such a nice day. Wow. It truly sucked to find out your husband was banging some hard-bodied choreographer on such a nice day.

News like that should only come on rainy days.

"DADDY?" Mel sobbed into her dying cell phone almost ten hours and a hair-raising escape with Tito's mother from the alleyway later. Hating how weak she sounded, she stiffened her spine and clenched her teeth.

"Ah, pork chop, I thought you'd never call back."

The gruffly gentle, sympathetic tone of her father's voice made a fresh batch of tears fight to seep from her eyes. "I think I need to come home now. Do you have room for me and Weezer?"

"I always have room for you, grape nuts. You come on

home and we'll make everything all right. Together. Just like we used to."

Like they used to. As if a banana split sundae could make this better. Well, maybe it could. If it had sprinkles. The chocolate ones. She shook her head at the memory. Her breath shuddered on its way out of her throat, her pride shattered. "I think I need to borrow money to . . . buy a ticket . . ."

There was a grunt on the other end, a familiar one of angry discontent. "That sonofabitch!"

Oh, if he only knew the half of the sonofabitch Stan was, Mel thought, taking one last look at her house in the Hills, her *locked* house in the Hills, before getting into her friend Jackie's SUV, giving Weezer, her Saint Bernard, a nudge into the backseat. "I . . ." she couldn't speak.

"You just get to LAX, Mel. I'll make sure a ticket's waiting for you and Weez. A ticket and a big hug from your old pop when you get here."

Mel choked on her gratitude. Jackie grabbed the phone from her. "Mr. Hodge? It's Jackie Bellows, Mel's friend here in LA. I'll make sure she gets to the airport, and I'll have what that asshole left her, which wasn't much, by the way, shipped to your house. Don't you worry about anything but catching her at the other end." Jackie nodded at the phone, then ended the call with a short good-bye.

Mel curled up in the passenger seat, pressing the side of her face to the window while she watched her house turn into a tiny dot among hundreds and simmered.

Jackie reached a hand over the console, squeezing her knee. "Stan's a fuckhead, a fuckwad."

Mel nodded. He certainly had the *fuck* part covered—in all contexts of the word.

Jackie shook her head of spiky, platinum blonde hair. "You need a good lawyer."

That got a reaction out of her. "For?"

"He locked you out of your house, Mel, and took the studio away. How can he do that shit? No warning. No nothin'? He just blindsided you. Not okay. Not legal by

California law, either. This is a community-property state. You need a lawyer to straighten this out."

Mel let her head sink to her hands. Where had this come from? Stan might not have been the most supportive, loving husband in the world, but he'd never been cruel. Jackie slapped her hand against the steering wheel. "But it is legal—if you signed a prenup, that is. You didn't . . ."

Oh, but she had. "I did. At the beginning of our marriage. I thought you knew that."

"Then we got trouble."

Mel's smile was watery and grim. "Right here in River City."

"You could always come stay with us, Mel. We have plenty of room." And they did. Jackie and Frank had eight thousand square feet, a guesthouse, four kids, two rabbits, a snake, five dogs, and a tarantula. All on three glorious acres.

Helpless rage sank to the pit of her stomach. "And do what? I have nothing, Jackie. No money. No job skills. I don't suppose you know of anyone hiring chubby one-time ballroom and Latin champions, do you?"

Jackie grunted at her. "You let that shit make you think you're fat. I've only told you a thousand times, Mel. You're not fat. But Stan is a fathead. Yes, that fucker is."

Yes. That fucker was.

"And you don't have to work, honey. It's not like we'd charge you rent. It's not like we're not filthy rich, you know. Why don't you just come to the house—let me baby you for a little while. I'll make pasta vodka," she cajoled, mentioning one of Mel's favorite dishes. "In the meantime, maybe Frank can talk to one of his lawyer buddies while they play the stupidest game on earth called golf, and we can figure out a way to squeeze something out of Stan's pocket. Nothing's ironclad anymore."

She used the corner of the collar on her sweater to wipe more tears from her eyes. "I think I just need to see my dad, Jackie. But I appreciate the offer." No way was she leeching off her rich friend while she hunted for a job at Target and planned Stan's homicide. The fewer people involved in the crime, the less she'd have to worry for their safety.

"I can't believe he put his shit out there on national TV like that. I didn't like Stan from the moment I met you two, and you know it, but I never thought he'd do something this craptacular."

That much was true. Jackie had never hit it off with Stan when they'd met at a function twelve years ago for a children's' cancer charity. She hadn't been afraid to share that they'd never do couple things together, but she and Jackie had been almost inseparable since.

"Do me a favor, would you?" Mel asked her friend.

"Just ask."

"You'll probably travel in the same circles as Stan, you know, being married to a big television producer? The next time you see Stan at some party or charity event, flip him the bird for me. In fact, use both hands when you do it."

As they pulled into LAX, Jackie growled, "You got it, BFF. Now you do me a favor?"

"Because I have so many to give."

"Don't rule out coming back to LA. Living with your dad in a retirement village is not the place for a forty-something, beautiful woman who has hips that should have been registered as lethal weapons back in the day. I'm just not a Jersey, the Situation, Snooki kind of girl. New York I can do—there's shopping. But I'm not sure I love you enough to fly to Jersey just so we can grab a hamburger and margaritas at some diner for BFF night." Jackie followed her joke with a warm grin.

She wanted to chuckle. She just couldn't. "I'd say I'm hurt, but I'm pretty sure there's nothing left on me to hurt." Mel popped open the door before Jackie could feel any sorrier for her, reaching back in to grab Weezer's leash and her wallet. The first step she took made her teeth clench.

Jackie was out and around the car in seconds, wrapping her slender arms around Mel's neck. The scent of her perfume made more tears sting Mel's eyes. "Make sure you ice that toe—it's broken. It's broken because of that fuckly-fucker," she snarled.

"It'll be fine. I've broken worse than a toe before."

"Yeah, but now you're old and fat. Takes longer to heal," Jackie joked.

Mel gave her one more squeeze, forcing back the bitter flow of tears threatening to fall. "Thanks, Jackie. I don't know what I would have done if you hadn't come to check on me."

Jackie leaned down and gave Weezer's big head a scratch. "You take care of Mommy, 'kay, pal?" Then she whipped around, her finger pointed. "And you," she yelled to a man, hovering in the departures area with a camera around his neck. "If you take that picture, you'll find out why yoga gives this woman a strong core." Turning back to Mel, she said, "Hurry up and get out of here before I have to embarrass Frank all over Tinsel Town."

Mel gave her a quick kiss. "I'll call you."

"You'd better."

She gave Weezer's leash a tug, hobbling behind him before turning one last time to wave good-bye to Jackie.

And every single thing in her life as she knew it.

Dakota Cassidy lives for a good laugh in life and in her writing. In fact, she almost loves a good giggle as much as she loves hair products and that's saying something.

Her goals in life are simple (like, really simple): banish the color yellow forever; create world peace via hot rollers and Aqua Net; and finally, nab every tiara in the land by competing in the Miss USA, Miss Universe, and Miss World pageants, then sweeping them in a stunning trifecta of much duct tape and Vaseline usage, all in just under a week's time. Oh, and write really fun books!

She loves people, loves to chat, and would love it if you'd come say hello to her on the Yahoo! group she shares with two other terrific authors at "The Truth About Big Hair, Books, and Babes." Join Dakota and friends in the chaos and send an email to TTABBB-subscribe@yahoogroups.com, or visit her website at www.dakotacassidy.com.

Dakota lives in Texas with her two sons, her mother, and more cats and dogs than the local animal shelter, and she has a boyfriend who puts the heroes in her books to shame. You can contact her at dakota@dakotacassidy.com. She'd love to hear from you!

Undead and Undermined

Vampire queen Betsy Taylor has awoken in a Chicago morgue, again, naked as a corpse. Her last memory is reconciling with her husband, Eric Sinclair, after a time-traveling field trip, including an indirect route to hell (literally), with her sister, Laura. Now she's Jane Doe #291, wrapped in plastic with a toe tag. Betsy can't help but wonder, what happened in hell?

Betsy heads back to her St. Paul mansion and discovers that she and Laura didn't time-travel alone. What followed them had a wicked agenda: to kill Betsy in a time when she was still young and vulnerable and end her future reign as queen.

But it's not just Betsy's future that has taken an unexpected detour. Everyone in her circle, alive or undead, is feeling the chill. Betsy can't let the unthinkable happen. It would be a cold day in hell if she did.

FROM *NEW YORK TIMES* BESTSELLING AUTHOR

Ilona Andrews

MAGIC SLAYS

⇒ **A KATE DANIELS NOVEL** ⇐

Kate Daniels may have quit the Order of Knights of Merciful Aid, but she's still knee-deep in paranormal problems. Or she would be if she could get someone to hire her. Starting her own business has been more challenging than she thought it would be—now that the Order is disparaging her good name. Plus, many potential clients are afraid of getting on the bad side of the Beast Lord, who just happens to be Kate's mate.

So when Atlanta's premier Master of the Dead calls to ask for help with a vampire on the loose, Kate leaps at the chance of some paying work. But it turns out that this is not an isolated incident, and Kate needs to get to the bottom of it—fast, or the city and everyone dear to her may pay the ultimate price.

AVAILABLE FROM ACE

penguin.com

M828T0111

SIXTH IN THE PEPPER MARTIN
MYSTERIES FROM

CASEY DANIELS

TOMB WITH A VIEW

**Cemeteries come alive for amateur sleuth
and reluctant medium Pepper Martin.**

Cleveland's Garden View Cemetery is hosting a James
A. Garfield commemoration. For Pepper Martin, this
means that she'll surely be hearing from the dead president himself. And when she's assigned to help plan the
event with know-it-all volunteer and Garfield fanatic
Marjorie Klinker, she'll wish Marjorie were dead . . .
too bad someone beats Pepper to it.

penguin.com